THE CHILD IN MY HOUSE

THE CHILD IN MY HOUSE

LUCY LAWRIE

Cover design by Emma Graves.

ISBN: 978-1-9989981-0-4

For Matt, Emily, Charlotte and Rebecca

1

JULIET

Laurel Bank, my childhood home. For a moment, standing there on the pavement, I forgot that it belonged to someone else now. It looked as if it had been waiting patiently all these years, through twenty-three summers and winters, its Edwardian red brick warmed by the sun and washed clean by the soft Suffolk rain. Waiting for me to return from school, or Brownies, or from my Saturday morning swimming lesson. And watching, with its windows that looked like eyes, set in a familiar face.

It looked smaller than I'd remembered, and a little neglected, with peeling windowsills and weeds poking through the paving on the front path. The lawn hadn't been mown in a while and the grass was thick and springy-looking, studded with daisies. Good for handstands. I remembered summer evenings in my gingham school dress, bare feet on cool grass. Throwing my legs up into the air, the tendons in my wrists stretching taut as I tried to balance on my hands. I never had the build for it.

Could I? Could I ring on the doorbell, and explain?

Maybe the people who lived here now would invite me to come in and have a look around.

No. And I couldn't linger here much longer – someone would notice. They'd think I was staking out the house. It was time to get on my way, to say a final goodbye.

But then came the noise of the front door opening; the click, creak and shush as it dragged over the heavy doormat.

It was the noise of visitors. Mum, Dad and I had always used the side door by the garage when leaving for school or work, bringing Gypsy in from a muddy walk, or carrying groceries in from the shops. But this was the noise of drinks on a summer evening, me waiting in my best dress in the kitchen – the one with the smocked embroidery across the chest – poised with little bowls of crisps and salted nuts.

A small figure was standing there, half hidden by the door.

Well, I was busted. I could either run away or I could walk up to the house as though I'd always been intending to do so.

Come on, Juliet, you're a grown-up.

'Hello!' I took a few steps forward, lifting my hand in a hesitant wave.

A little girl, clad in a faded *Hello Kitty* vest and sleep shorts, and a pair of red wellies, advanced onto the front step. She held a large mermaid doll against her chest, its plastic face moulded into a wide-eyed expression of delight that contrasted with the girl's own frown. She bit her lip, her jaw working as if she was deciding whether to say something or not.

She took a deep breath that lifted her chest and shoulders and jerked her chin up. Opened her mouth. Closed it. Tried again.

'Are you a police?'

'Me? Oh... no. I'm Juliet.'

Her eyes slid down.

'What's your name?'

She sat down on the step with a cracking, rattling noise and I noticed that she had a rucksack slung over one shoulder.

'That looks heavy,' I said.

She unzipped it and held it open so that I could see inside.

'Oh look! Beautiful stones and pebbles. Wow, you've collected lots, haven't you?'

The girl tipped her head to the side. She stuck her hand into the bag and rummaged through it.

'Are your parents in?'

Intent on her stones, she ignored me. The sun had slipped behind a bank of cloud and I saw the skin on her arms coarsen as the breeze shifted around us, ruffling the privet hedge and setting the lavender heads dancing beneath the bay window. My own skin prickled in sympathy, and a kind of unease. It wasn't right that she should be out here by herself, wearing next to nothing.

I scanned the empty street, the neat front gardens – Mrs Teddington's, the Davidsons', the Bramwells'. They'd probably moved away now, living near relatives or in old people's homes. There were no signs of life, other than the buzz of a distant lawnmower.

'Shall I call your mum down?' I stepped past the girl into the doorway. 'Hello? Anyone in?'

No response.

I hovered, shifting uncomfortably from one foot to the next. I felt like a would-be kidnapper. Someone from the stranger danger films that we'd watched at school, sitting cross-legged and craning up at the big telly that was wheeled into the classroom on its high stand for such occasions.

I should never have stopped to talk. But I could hardly just go now, could I, and leave her here in her vest and wellies? A little fairytale goblin with a bag of magic stones.

I sat down on the step. 'What's your *best* stone? Cos I'm interested. If you can, you know, cut me a deal?'

Her eyes narrowed. Maybe she suspected some kind of entrapment. I thought of the way she'd checked whether I was 'a police', before showing the contents of her rucksack.

She upturned it now and clunked the stones onto the paving, sorting through them until she found what she was looking for. Cocooned in her cupped hand she held out a smooth oval pebble – silvery gold flecks amongst the brown and grey.

'Iron pyrites,' I said softly. 'Fool's gold.' More childhood memories. Paddling in the river at Dedham Vale, sifting through the silt to find the shiniest pebbles while Mum unpacked the sandwiches and crisps from the cool bag, and unscrewed the Thermos that always smelt of curdled milk, however much it was washed.

'It's pretty,' I said. 'Why don't you show them all to me, one by one?'

Soon we'd made a little Hansel and Gretel trail, leading from the front step and spiralling onto the lawn, with the stones arranged in order of niceness.

I didn't even notice the police car until I heard the doors clunk shut. Two officers, a man and a woman, were walking up the path towards us. I sprang up guiltily.

'Afternoon,' said the male officer with a nod.

The little girl stood up beside me, eyes like saucers. Her nostrils flared, and she swallowed and bit down on her lip.

'A 999 call was made from this house, approximately fifteen minutes ago.' The officer glanced down at his watch. 'The caller didn't say anything.' He looked from me to the girl and back again. 'We've come to check that all's well.'

'I don't... I was just passing. This little girl was out in the garden. I'm not sure if her parents are around.'

Slowly, the little girl raised her mermaid doll up and held it aloft, showing it to the policeman.

But this was no time for games. The officer stepped past us. He rang the doorbell, rapping loudly on the open door. 'Anyone in? Come to the door, please. It's the police here.'

My pulse quickened. What if her parents were lying murdered in their beds? Or what if there'd been an accident? I imagined the crumpled shape of a mother, lying at the bottom of the stairs.

'I'll go in and have a look around,' said the officer, just as a voice sounded from inside.

'Just a second! I'm coming. Oh gosh, I'm sorry.'

A woman appeared, fastening the tie of her pink silk dressing gown, pushing a swathe of highlighted blonde hair behind her ear.

'What's happened? I was upstairs doing my meditation. I thought Kitty was in her room.'

The policeman cleared his throat. 'A 999 call was made from this house approximately fifteen minutes ago.'

'Oh, not again... Kitty! That's so, so naughty.'

Again?

'We found your Kitty here in the garden – this lady had stopped to keep an eye on her. She was concerned about her being out on her own.'

I gave the woman an awkward smile. 'I'm sorry. I never meant... I was just passing.'

The female officer checked her notepad. 'We understand that there have been thirteen 999 calls made from this house over the last twelve months. The caller was silent on each occasion.'

I could sense Kitty's agitation. There was a tiny squeak from the red wellies as she jiggled.

'She can't speak.' The mother laid a manicured hand on the top of Kitty's head. 'Selective mutism.' She half-spoke, half-mouthed the words, her face pulled into a wince that emphasized the wrinkles around her mouth. She was attractive though, with wide blue eyes, and a Marilyn Monroe mole on her left cheek.

The policeman frowned.

'But...' I looked down at Kitty, still as stone beneath her mother's hand.

You spoke to me. You asked if I was a police.

'It's the frustration of it all,' went on the mother. 'She finds it hard to deal with. She acts out sometimes. But oh, Kitty. These 999 calls – there's no excuse. I'm so sorry.'

The policeman crouched down to Kitty's level. 'How old are you then, eh, young lady?'

Kitty swallowed, and without looking at the policeman, she slowly unfurled all five fingers of her right hand, and the thumb of her left.

'Six, you say? Hmm.' He nodded slowly, regarding her. 'Thank you, Miss.' He rose up to his full height and drew the mother to one side, speaking to her in confidential tones. 'Six years of age is too young for a child to be left unsupervised. Especially a child with special needs. As luck would have it, this lady here stopped by.' He held out a hand to indicate me. 'But otherwise, there's no telling what might have happened. Your little 'un could have been off along the main road, half way to Colchester. Or worse.'

He paused for a moment, allowing the mother to contemplate places that might be worse than Colchester. She put a hand over her mouth and shook her head.

'In cases where we feel a child may have been put at risk, we need to consider making a referral to social services.'

Woah... that seemed a bit heavy-handed. She'd only been playing in her own front garden.

The mother shot me a pleading look.

I looked down at Kitty. Her gaze skittered off to the left.

Kitty... Hello Kitty. The faded old vest wasn't just a vest. It was how she told people her name.

Suddenly, I found that I couldn't speak either. The world seemed to shrink to just Kitty and me, standing on that green summer lawn, as if we had always been there and always would be.

'S-she wasn't out here for long,' I stammered, eventually.

Both the officers turned to face me.

'How long, exactly?' said the female officer.

'A minute perhaps,' I lied. 'Certainly less than two. But more like one. Yes... one.'

The policewoman sighed and closed her notebook.

The mother flashed her eyebrows at me and arranged her lips into a silent *thank you*.

As she walked the police officers down the drive, I heard her warning them to watch out for the pothole just before the turning on to the main road – she'd scraped one of her alloys on it last week. Then she stood on the pavement in her pink robe, waving them away as if they were friends who'd just been over for lunch.

It was then that I turned to Kitty and noticed the droop of

her shoulders, the expression on her face as she watched the police car disappear down the street and out of sight.

It was exhaustion. It was... resignation. It was an expression that was far too old for that little face.

My throat felt tight, suddenly. What had I done?

I would never find out. In a moment I'd have to walk away and leave her.

When the mother came back along the path, I winced and shifted from one foot to the other and back again.

'I'm so sorry to ask... but I don't suppose I could be a terrible nuisance and ask to use your loo?'

2

JULIET

W hat was it that made a house smell the same, after twenty-three years? The faint gluey tang of the varnish on the banisters, maybe, or the warm, dusty scent of the bricks themselves, beneath the magnolia smoothness of the walls.

Kitty's mother, who'd introduced herself as Beth, showed me where to take my shoes off. Then she directed me towards the downstairs loo – the 'cloakroom', as my parents had always called it – and said she'd put some coffee on.

I could scarcely believe it, but the room was virtually unchanged, with the same Victorian porcelain bathroom fittings and bluebell-patterned tiles behind the sink. And the faint mineral, soapy smell from the water softening unit was so familiar it made my heart clench. I could almost imagine that my mother was somewhere in the house, folding towels or listening to Radio 4, and that Dad was pottering in the garden, or dozing with a newspaper on the sofa.

But it was Kitty who was there, waiting in the hall for me when I came out. She stretched out a hand, soft fingers splayed out in a star. I smiled and reached out my own, but she scampered away.

I followed her into the kitchen, stepping over a large butterfly jigsaw that had been half-assembled in the doorway. 'Ooh, is that a Red Admiral?' I asked, but Kitty had slipped under the kitchen table.

Beth was clattering around with the components of a large chrome coffee machine. 'Thank you *so* much again – what did you say your name was? You'll stay for a coffee, won't you? Sit down, sit down.' She waved an impatient hand.

'It's Juliet. A coffee would be lovely, thank you.' I peeped under the table as I carefully drew back a chair. Kitty was emptying out another jigsaw from its box – a family of monkeys swinging through the jungle.

'So do you live locally?'

'I've been living in Edinburgh the past few years.'

'Oh, lovely!' Her face brightened. I noticed that her two front teeth were crowded together, slightly overlapping. It gave her a bunny-ish look that softened her otherwise perfect appearance.

Maybe there was no reason to worry, no reason for the nerves crawling in the pit of my stomach. Beth seemed nice enough, and Kitty seemed happier now, playing contentedly under the table.

It was fine for me to walk away. Really.

'So what brings you all the way down here to the depths of Suffolk?' Beth went on.

There it was – a tiny space in time when I should have told her that this was my childhood home, and that I'd grown up in Boxley Wood. In the time between heartbeats, it was there and gone.

I gave a nervous laugh. 'I was a bit lost, actually. I was

looking for the B&B I'm staying in tonight.' I *was* staying in a B&B, but I knew exactly where it was – just up the road by the golf course. 'I've just had a job interview. Near here.'

Well, sort of. The interview had been in Chelmsford, some fifty miles away.

'Oh?' said Beth. 'What do you do?'

'I'm a nanny.'

Beth raised an eyebrow. 'And why did you decide to come all the way down here?' There was a skull-rattling clang, as one of the bits from the coffee machine rolled off the worktop and onto the floor.

I felt a poking sensation on my foot. Kitty was nudging it to one side – the jigsaw needed to extend out. There was a small flipping noise as she moved a piece into place.

Beth was looking at me, still waiting for me to answer her question.

'To tell you the truth, I wanted to get away from Edinburgh for a bit. My husband and I, well, my ex, my ex-husb... we broke up recently. And my... my –'

No. I didn't want to remember it. Lying in my mother's bed with the curtains closed while minutes ticked into hours, and one day blurred into the next. The damp cardboard smell from the packing boxes piled up by the fireplace.

I drew in a breath, but it didn't seem to reach my lungs.

I remembered my friend Cassie's advice about talking to myself in a 'calming, compassionate voice' – a technique she'd learned during her counselling training.

It's okay, Juliet. You're perfectly safe.

It was fine. This feeling was caused by being here at Laurel Bank again, that was all. The memories it held were too heavy. Kitty and her mother were fine. I'd drink my coffee and get on my way.

But then I remembered Kitty's face when the police had driven off. And they'd driven off because of *me*.

A mad idea came into my head. I steadied myself and chose my words carefully. 'This family... the one I had the interview with? Well, they're looking for a specialist nanny to live in. They need that extra level of support. And it seemed like a time in my life when I could do that, you know? Just throw myself into it.'

The Chelmsford family had two pre-teen boys on the autistic spectrum and a toddler with behaviour issues (and an unfortunate resemblance to Damien from *The Omen*). The parents had been desperate – when I'd got up to leave, the mother had actually come towards me with her arms extended out like a zombie.

'I can't say too much – confidentiality and all that. But they'd heard about me from a family I worked for in Edinburgh. I was nanny to their little boy, Harry. He's autistic. Lots of issues at school. He was pretty much non-verbal, so there were a lot of challenges.'

'Kitty's not... *autistic*,' said Beth in a whispery voice, placing my coffee on the table in front of me. 'In case you were wondering. Selective mutism is completely different.'

'It's a type of anxiety disorder, isn't it?'

Beth nodded. 'In Kitty's case it's very severe. In fact, the doctors are saying it has now become *progressive* mutism. It used to be that she wouldn't talk outside the home – to children at nursery, or the staff. Or in unfamiliar situations. That sort of thing. But since she started school a year ago it's got worse. Now she doesn't even talk to Frank or me.' She raised her hands in a gesture of hopelessness. 'The truth is, she doesn't talk at all.'

Except to me. She had talked to me. She'd asked if I was a police.

I wiggled my toes towards the edge of the jigsaw, and felt gentle fingers trying to lift my socked foot. I let my toes go still for a few moments, and then wiggled them suddenly. A squeal came from under the table.

'Lovely coffee,' I said. 'Thank you.' I took my time stirring in some milk, clinking the teaspoon gently against the side of the cup before laying it down on the side of the saucer. It was part of the whole Mary Poppins, tea-in-the-nursery thing I'd developed over the years to mask my shyness. Parents loved it. It calmed them.

'I was with Harry and his family for three years,' I said eventually. 'We worked on lots of different techniques. There were no quick fixes, but after a lot of careful research, we got him a special needs dog. Her name was Cocoa.' I sat quiet for a minute. Kitty peeked out from under the table.

'Yes – Cocoa,' I said to her. 'Isn't that a nice name? She had a lovely brown coat.'

I smiled sadly. I missed Harry. And I worried for him if anything should happen to Cocoa. She was eight years old when they got her, and she already had the beginnings of arthritis in her hips. 'By the time I left he was able to say a few words to Cocoa. But the main thing was that he was much happier.'

Beth put her head in her hands. 'I'm just... Oh, I'm sorry. I find this all very hard to cope with. This just wasn't how I expected things would be. Frank is away a lot. He's involved in several charities, some of them abroad. And I'm finding it hard to get out – Kitty can be very difficult.'

She was also right there, under the table.

'I've recently started up my own business. I've opened a

coffee shop – The Old Coach House, it's called – just down the road. And I'm doing wedding cakes.' A tear slid down the side of her face, coming to rest just next to her mole. 'I have zero time to myself. I mean, I take *two minutes* to do a bit of mindfulness to try and keep myself *sane*, and next thing I have the *police* at my door...'

'Hmm.' It came out sounding growly and I realised my jaw was clenched tight shut. 'Oh *dear*,' I added. I took a sip of my tea, and placed the cup back on the saucer. 'I'm sure that with the right support, things could improve with Kitty's speech.'

'Hopefully,' Beth sighed. 'And what about you? Will you take the job with this family?'

'To be honest, I'm not sure. I didn't get quite the right vibe from the family. So important if you're going to live in.'

I imagined the zombie arms flailing towards me, the Damien child riding manically around the hall on his tricycle.

Beth leant forward. 'It's the Baxters, isn't it – the family? On Crackthorn Lane? No, no, you don't have to tell me. But, let me just say... *issues.*' She raised an eyebrow and gave a meaningful nod.

There was no need to say anything. I just dropped my gaze, and brushed a pretend piece of fluff from my skirt, thinking of the folder of documents in the boot of my car – my professional but warmly worded CV, the glowing references from Harry's parents and the family I'd worked for before that, and my up-to-date police disclosure certificate proving my squeaky clean record.

'I think I'll keep looking. I want to be in a family where I can make a difference.'

Beneath the table, the flipping noise had stopped. Kitty had stopped moving.

'Have you finished your puzzle, Kitty?' I asked.

The edge of the jigsaw slid slowly into view.

'Oh, that's lovely!' I said. 'I've always liked monkeys. Do you know my second name is a bit like a monkey's name? It's Monklands.' It was important to say it clearly, so Beth remembered. 'Yes... Juliet Monklands.'

3

LYNNE

Dearest Juliet,

Would you believe it – it snowed this morning!? Well, hailed anyway. I was sitting doing my crossword and suddenly there it was, bouncing off the windows. Making a right old racket. I hope my wildflower boxes are going to be all right. I'm sure they didn't expect it to snow at this time of year. Poor little things.

Oh darling, I must tell you. Mrs Biggs came round yesterday with some of her organic spinach soup. She stayed for a cup of tea – we used those nice cups that you got me for my birthday, with the bluebells on them. And then she left around three because she had to go and collect the raffle prizes for Friday's do. I got up to make myself another cup of tea and I know it was naughty of me, but I poured the spinach soup down the kitchen sink.

Now, I know there are millions of starving people who would really have appreciated that soup. But what would be the point of dutifully putting it in the fridge, only to leave it to moulder and feel guilty every time I opened the fridge door? So down the sink it went.

But then, what do you think happened? The kitchen door swung open and there she was – Mrs Biggs! She'd forgotten her umbrella! She took one look at the empty Tupperware, and oh, the look on her face! Do you remember that photo of you on your fourth birthday when Charlie blew out the candles on your birthday cake? The scowl, and thunderous eyebrows? Well, picture that, but a hundred times worse. Oh darling, I was mortified. I was racking my brains for some sort of excuse. I even thought of blaming my medication – forgetfulness or something! But then you came into my mind and I thought of how you would have laughed. I felt the most enormous giggle bubbling up inside me and I just couldn't stop it! It came right out! I clapped my hand over my mouth, but it was too late.

Well – honesty is the best policy and all that. So I said, 'I'm so sorry. You've caught me out. That was unforgiveable. It's just that I've never liked spinach.'

'Spinach is very good for you,' she huffed, and then off she went, forgetting her umbrella again. Oh dear. I suppose that means I shall have to telephone her and offer to take it over or something.

Anyway, I thought that might make you laugh, darling. And I thought you might like the enclosed – *Little Miss Giggles*. She loses her giggle, remember? I found it when I was clearing out the hall cupboard. The book, I mean, not the giggle!

Sending you the biggest hugs ever.

Mum xxxx

4

JULIET

I folded away Mum's letter and lay back on the stiff patterned bedspread in my B&B room, wondering what to do next. There was a small television fixed to a wall bracket on the other side of the room. Or I could make myself a hot drink – there was a basket of sachets and thimble-sized portions of UHT milk next to the mini-kettle on the varnished pine sideboard. Was seven o'clock too early to go to sleep? It was so *hot*... the window wouldn't open.

As I lay there in the stifling quiet of the room, my thoughts began to circle back to that horrible day in June. It had been a Tuesday. My jeans had split at the crotch, just at the base of the zip, so I'd gone into Next on the way home from the hospital.

There really was no point in going over it all again. I picked up the remote and scrolled through the TV guide. I found a three-hour programme about the nation's favourite '80s love songs. A fly-on-the-wall documentary about an STD clinic. Or in twenty-two minutes there'd be a programme about a biscuit factory – maybe it was worth holding out for that.

As I recalled, the light in the changing rooms had been particularly unflattering that day. The mirrors surely weren't right. The flesh that spilled over my waistband like over-proved dough – that hadn't been there before. Nor had the bulges around the back of my bra. Those hormone injections certainly had a lot to answer for. Or maybe they were making the sizes smaller these days. But it was okay... I was pregnant, wasn't I? Nearly. Very nearly. We would be getting a call from the hospital soon, to say how many of the embryos were viable, and then it would be full steam ahead. What a relief it would be to visit the maternity section of the shop with its soft stretchy waistbands and generous floaty tops.

I thrust armfuls of badly fitting jeans at the changing room assistant and made my escape with a vague 'sorry'. And on the way to the car I gave into temptation – I popped into WH Smith and bought *Pregnancy and You*!

Eddie wouldn't be back from work until six. I'd have time to get home, make a pot of peppermint tea, and curl up on the sofa with my magazine. For an hour or so I would banish all negative thoughts, and immerse myself in a cosy, rose-tinted world where everything was going to work out.

As soon as I turned the key in the lock, I could tell someone was in the house. The air felt charged, like someone was holding their breath.

He was standing in the living room, a dark shape silhouetted against the bay window.

'Eddie! What are you doing home?'

'I can't do this, Juliet.'

'Can't do what?'

He looked at the floor, and ran a hand through his floppy

hair. 'I can't go through this with you. Your mum and all that shit... and the IVF. It isn't right to have a kid with you. Not when things aren't right between us.'

My first thought was for my babies. My babies in the little Petri dishes. The ones that the doctors were trying to coax into life.

He came forward and touched my arm. I caught the faint whiff of eggs from his breath. 'I should be prepared to do anything for you. To walk through fire with you. But I can't. I can't *breathe* when I'm with you.'

'But we... we could just wait and...'

'It would be cruel of me to stay with you now, when all I can think about is how soon I can leave.'

I looked down at what I was holding – *Pregnancy and You*! And I was embarrassed. This world – of white blankets with satin edging and choosing which baby car seat to buy – was never going to be mine.

From somewhere in my bag, my phone rang.

'Do you mind if I answer it?' I said, politely. Was it the done thing to take a call, when you were being dumped by your husband?

He gestured at me to go ahead.

'Juliet? It's Carmelita here.'

Carmelita. Such a strange name for a nurse. Like she should be wearing a Spanish dancing dress rather than her white uniform with the navy bands on the sleeves, and shoes that squeaked when she walked. But there was something about the tone of her voice. My legs turned to concrete, useless heavy blocks unable to hold me. I toppled back on to the sofa, registering a tiny ripping round as the split in my jeans gave a little more, and the pouff of the leather sofa as it absorbed my weight.

'Oh, Juliet. I'm so sorry.'

THE PING of a new message brought me back to the present. I grabbed for my phone, nearly sliding off the shiny bedspread.

It was Beth. She'd found my nannying page on Facebook. She asked if I would come and see her and Kitty again the next morning. My eyes prickled with relief as I lay back on the pillow, phone held against my heart, counting down a careful ten minutes before responding.

Laurel Bank looked even lovelier in the morning, with sunlight slanting between the leylandii onto the cool green of the grass. Beth opened the door dressed in yoga gear with a long cardigan over the top. We had coffee in the living room this time, and I was only a few sips into my first cup when she offered me the job – on a trial basis, and subject to checking references, of course. But would I be happy to start straight away?

'I'm happy to give it a go,' I said, feigning surprise. I wasn't sure if I was *happy* about it or not – the fact that Beth was so desperate to get Kitty off her hands that she would employ a stranger who'd literally walked in off the street.

I had to pretend that the house was new to me. That I didn't know that the fourth stair up always creaked, or that the stained glass panel above the front door shuddered when lorries went past. Beth took me up to show my room – the Forget-Me-Not Room, the one on the attic level of the house with the sloping ceilings.

I did a double take as I walked in. The old mahogany bed, wardrobe and matching dressing table were still there, still just the same, even down to the antique porcelain mirror and hairbrush set laid out on the glass top of the dressing table. It was as if Mum had just walked out and left it.

The only thing missing was Mum's Laura Ashley bedding and matching frilled valance – blue forget-me-nots, hence the name of the room. The bed was stripped bare, with a pile of white cotton bedding waiting to be put on. Maybe Beth expected me to do that myself?

Trying to hide my confusion, I went to the window and murmured my appreciation at the view – the church spire in amongst the red and grey roofs of Boxley Wood, the corn-fields stretching away to the west. The Common and the golf course to the east, and the apple orchards beyond that. I wondered whether the house martens still made their nests under the eaves in summer, little dark shapes flashing past the window.

'You've got your own bathroom next door,' Beth pointed out. 'And there's a small box room on the other side that we could set up with a fridge and a microwave and whatnot. It'll give you some privacy.'

Kitty pointed to another narrow door, between the bedroom and the bathroom.

'Oh yes, the airing cupboard,' said Beth. 'I'll clear that out, if you like, and you can use it for extra storage.'

But Kitty looked unsure. She pulled open the airing cupboard door and crouched down to show me a family of tiny elephants. They'd set up home on a pile of towels folded on the lowest shelf.

'Oh, look,' I said, kneeling down beside her. 'Is this the mummy ellie?' I picked it up and jiggled it. 'I like her dress. And is this the baby?'

I turned my head to smile at Beth, who was standing in

the doorway of the Forget-Me-Not Room, silhouetted against the morning light that flooded through the south-facing window.

It's hard to explain what happened next. I can only describe it as overwhelming sadness. As if sadness took a physical form and clung to me, hanging its arms around my neck.

It made me think of terrible things... the sound of quiet sobbing in a hospital bathroom. Shattered glass on wet tarmac on a black night, the tick of a cooling engine.

Kitty picked up an elephant and pressed it into my hands.

'Someone walked over your grave?' said Beth.

'I'm fine. I think I climbed those stairs too quickly. Phew!' I sucked in a breath and blew it out slowly.

She smiled, trailing a casual hand over her tiny, toned midriff.

'Maybe Kitty can show you the rest of her toys later.'

'Good idea,' I said. 'How about Kitty helps me to get my things in from the car? I'm sure you have loads you need to get on with.'

'Well,' said Beth. 'There *is* actually a yoga class at twelve... if you're sure?' She drew her long cardigan around the yoga gear she was already wearing. 'It's just at Seekings, five minutes away. I can be there and back in an hour.'

'Seekings Country Club? Is that –' I stopped myself. I'd almost asked if it was still going, after all this time. My parents had been members, back in the day. We'd gone there for lunch sometimes on Saturdays, after Dad's round of golf. Scampi that came in a basket with chips. Lemonade in a spotty glass tumbler.

A wave of emotion came again. It took every ounce of my strength to summon a bright smile.

'Absolutely. Kitty and I can get to know each other.'

Now, two days later, we were the picture of blissful domestic-
ity. Beth was icing a cake, I was sewing name tapes onto
Kitty's uniform, ready for the school term starting tomorrow,
and Kitty herself was under the kitchen table.

'It's a bit of an art, getting the right shade of pink,' Beth
said with a frown, her thumb and third finger poised around
the bulb of a dropper of red food colouring. 'We don't want it
Barbie pink. Nothing too tacky.' Lips twisted, she let a single
drop splash into the bowl of glossy white icing. 'Just a pale...
pearly... shell pink.' She let another two drops fall. 'There we
go. We'll give that a try.'

I thought of the opening scene of *Snow White*, the drops
of blood falling onto the white sweep of the queen's
embroidery.

Beth tucked the mixing bowl into the crook of her elbow,
took up a wooden spoon and began to beat the red into the
white.

I remembered the picture in my old Ladybird version of
the book – the look on the queen's face as she pricked her
finger, her mouth fallen open and her thin eyebrows V-
shaped in shock. Had that been the good queen – Snow
White's real mother – or the wicked stepmother?

Lips as red as blood. Cheeks as white as snow.

Beth looked over to meet my gaze with an open, questioning expression.

I cast my eyes back down to my sewing. The first name
tape had taken me twenty minutes and it looked like Kitty

might have done it herself – and I still had another fifteen items to go.

Beneath the table, I felt a Sylvanian badger land on my little toe and hop across the top of my foot in five jumps. The badger family had been yanked out of their turreted manor house in Kitty's bedroom, and had been driven all the way down the stairs in their car (all the family members being thrown from their seats in the process). Now, a tiny tartan picnic rug had been set up by my foot. I wiggled it in friendly acknowledgement of Kitty's game, and felt the flat of her hand pressing it gently back down.

'I need some more bits of thread cut,' I announced. There was a shuffling sound and her head and shoulders emerged from under the table. I held out the scissors, just far enough that she had to crawl out and stand up to take them. I measured out a length of white cotton, holding it taut in front of me.

'And it looks like Mum could do with some help with that mixing,' I said, after we'd cut four more pieces of thread.

'Oh yes! Kitty loves helping with the baking,' said Beth, casting a winning smile in my direction.

Suddenly, I seemed to see my mother, standing just where Beth was standing now, spooning billows of airy sponge mixture into round tins while I stood by waiting, jiggling from one foot to the other.

Can I lick the bowl, mama?

Kitty skirted round the table and took the wooden spoon from Beth, dragging it once or twice through the mixture with an ineffectual, limp-wristed action, before darting out of sight again.

Beth shrugged, and took a sip from her wine glass. It was

quiet in the kitchen, with just the low rumble of the dishwasher in the utility room next door. I'd half-fancied that there was a faint doggy smell, in the corner where we'd kept the dog's food and water bowls, and his leads and toys. If Gypsy had been here, I wondered if he'd have been able to pick up our old scents too – mine and Mum's and Dad's. I imagined him haring around the house, claws skittering and tail wagging at the prospect of seeing us again after two decades dead in the ground.

I shuddered. Where did that come from?

'Oh gosh, is that the time? I'll need to get going soon,' said Beth. 'I've got Pilates.'

I peeped under the table. 'Is that bath time for little kitties?'

But Kitty was gone. Far away, upstairs, came the sound of water rumbling through the pipes and cascading into the bathtub.

'I'll get her ready for bed,' I offered. 'Unless you'd prefer to?'

'Oh *would* you? Thank you so much, Juliet.'

Up in her room, Kitty had shed her clothes and was crouching naked over her schoolbag, feeding crumpled bits of paper into it. I handed her a towel, and she stood up and drew it around herself like a cloak.

'We could put some bubbles in that bath,' I suggested.

She nodded briefly, eyes fixed on the floor.

It turned out there was no bubble bath, so I had to make do with my own shower gel, which I swished under the tap until it frothed up. Once in the water, Kitty appeared absorbed in a private game, humming and moving two shampoo bottles around in a dance.

Was this the right moment?

'Kitty... I've been meaning to ask you.' I kept my voice low. 'I've been wondering why you called 999 all those times.'

It sounded wrong as soon as it was out of my mouth – like I was going behind Beth's back. Imagine if she'd walked past the bathroom and heard me whispering, snooping into matters that weren't my business?

Kitty didn't look up. Had she even heard me? She grabbed the bath handrails and began to swish back and forward. Slow at first, and then faster, creating momentum.

'You're making a tidal wave, are you?'

Bubbly water slopped onto the floor. With my foot, I shoved the fluffy bathmat closer to the edge of the bath.

'Oh I *see*... you phoned 999 because there was going to be a flood?'

She sucked her lower lip into her mouth.

'A *tsunami*?'

She nodded quickly, keen to show she knew the word.

'Did too many hippopotamuses go swimming at once? Was there a hippopotamus swimming party? Where was that? At Mummy's swimming pool at Seekings?'

She threw back her head and laughed in pure delight, revealing a mouthful of small white teeth with Halloween lantern gaps.

Perfect. She was perfect. For a moment I couldn't find my breath.

'I went to an aqua-aerobics class once that was a bit like that,' I said, taking her towel off the radiator and holding the warmth to my face for a second.

She began flinging her arms around, rolling her hands in front of her. I copied and we had a silent disco for a minute or two. Then I picked up the two shampoo bottles and they joined in too, until one of them somersaulted and splatted down on the tiles.

'Well, you can tell me about why you phoned 999 if you ever want to. Hippopotamuses or no hippopotamuses.'

Was I imagining it, or did her face seem to close over, the blank expression coming on too quickly? She glanced at her mermaid doll, who was propped up on the vanity unit, watching proceedings.

I picked up the doll. 'What do you think, Mermaid?' I jiggled it to activate its voice and one of its recorded phrases.

'I *love* to swim!' it said, in a tinny American voice.

'Hmm.' I put it down and reached for Kitty's fluffy towel. 'Come along then, Kitten.'

5

BETH

Villa Saint-Pardoux stood high above the town of Vevey, overlooking Lake Geneva and the hills beyond in their blue haze. It reminded Beth of the houses in her old *Babar the Elephant* books, tall and narrow, with slatted shutters on the windows. In the summer it was too hot to go out in the middle of the day.

Beth lay down carefully on the bed, propping herself up on a pile of oversized velvet cushions. She didn't want to wake Kitty, who had finally gone down for her nap after her lunchtime bottle, and who now lay spread-eagled in the middle of the bed, wearing only her nappy. The help, Rosa, had called in sick, Beth barely understanding the woman with her guddle of French words over the phone.

It was a relief, in a way, to just be herself. Not to have to pretend to be the perfect wife and mother.

Which was ironic. Because what could be more perfect than this luxurious villa, this languorous lifestyle? She had fresh pastries and melon each morning for breakfast. Then she was free to do whatever she pleased while Rosa kept an eye on Kitty – who would lie quite happily on her playmat, kicking her legs as Nickelodeon cartoons blared from the television, and Rosa dusted already-spotless surfaces and mopped the cool tiled floors. Then there'd be Martinis on the verandah in the evening once Frank was home – one of the advantages of not breastfeeding.

It was quiet, though. Too quiet. Occasionally she would summon the energy to strap Kitty into a baby sling and they would take the funicular railway down into the town centre of Vevey. She would order a citron pressé in a little café near the lakeside promenade, or pass the time going around the tourist shops that sold fridge magnets and giant Toblerone bars.

There was no excuse for this heaviness, this boredom, because she had Kitty now, with her plump limbs, her fat little hands clenched even now as she slept.

Yet Beth couldn't get rid of this unsettled feeling, this longing to be home... wherever that was. She'd mentioned it to Frank once or twice and he'd dismissed it with a kiss on her forehead, or an offer to pay for a spa visit. She'd had more spa treatments than she could count, in the five months they'd been here. Although she would never had said so to Frank, she disliked going to the Grand Hotel, sitting in the spa waiting area sipping cucumber-scented water alongside the wives of Russian millionaires whose faces were stretched tight and shiny, but whose necks were as leathery as their designer handbags.

She wasn't one of them. She longed for the fresh air of England – the pale sunshine and the Yorkshire rain on her face. Once, after several Martinis, she'd told Frank about her childhood dream of opening a coffee shop near the shore in Scarborough, or down the coast in Bridlington. With vintage teacups and home-made scones. He'd taken a long drag from his cigarette, and asked if she had any idea how much pressure he was under, trying to get his new business off the ground?

But recently she'd been thinking more and more about her childhood – about this 'home' she seemed to miss but had never really had. Careful not to disturb the baby, she slid herself off the bed and padded over to her dressing room. From beneath one of the shoe racks, she drew out an old biscuit tin. She used to call it her 'treasure box' – once she'd even told her foster sister that it contained rubies, what with her being the secret daughter of a foreign princess. She took it over to the bed and tipped out the contents beside Kitty.

Here was the rosette she'd received at a summer fete in 1987 for a lopsided sponge cake. A programme for the ballet in London – she'd won a trip by filling in the back of a Cornflakes packet, aged just seven.

She had one photograph of her mother, from around that time, when she was still pretty, and had dimples and sparkly eyes. Before things had gone so badly wrong after Dad had gone off to work on the cruise ships, leaving the house to fill up with cold, stale air, as if nobody lived there. Like Mrs Spink's house when she went into hospital and Beth had to go in and feed her cats.

The first foster home had been a temporary one, to give Mum 'a chance to get herself back on track'. She'd spent most of the time looking out of the window, her Snoopy suitcase packed on the bed beside her, waiting for the social worker, Ange, with her orange Bonnie Langford perm, to ring the doorbell and say that she could go home. Then there'd been that brief, confusing spell back home, where she'd had to make her own Primula cheese sandwiches each morning for her packed lunch, and where she'd had cereal for dinner most days. It had ended with that awful day when she'd returned home from school to find Mum unconscious on the sofa, a trail of pink sick glistening from the corner of her mouth. And two empty bottles and a packet of pills on the carpet.

It had been raining heavily when she was bundled into the back seat of Ange's Austin Maxi in her puffy brown anorak, clutching her Snoopy suitcase. They'd been on the road for half an hour or so before she remembered she'd forgotten Blue Bear. She'd left him on Mummy's bedside table that morning, patting him and telling him to keep an eye on her while she slept.

'We need to go back!' she'd wailed. The social worker had smiled a tight smile, glancing at Beth in the rearview mirror, and said they'd send for Blue Bear later. She'd personally make sure of it. It was only the other side of Doncaster, not the other side of the planet.

Viv, her new foster mum, had been waiting at the door of her 1960s semi to welcome her inside. The brightly lit hallway smelt of frying and the damp, blue scent of washing drying on the radiators. While Beth sat at the kitchen table, sitting on her hands to stop them shaking, Viv cooked chips in a pan of oil, lifting the dripping wire basket from time to time to check if they were golden, and she served them up with thick gammon steaks and a fried egg each. When Beth cried for Blue Bear that night, Viv tucked the duvet around her, and said firmly that things would come right, and she wasn't to fret. It felt too strange – too final – to cry for her mother, strapped onto the ambulance stretcher like an Egyptian mummy. All she knew was that she was 'receiving treatment' somewhere unknown and unknowable. And it was strange, but when Ange had rocked up in the Austin Maxi a few months later to tell her the 'sad news' that her mother had died, she'd felt nothing at all. No words would come, except to ask Ange what had happened to Blue Bear. Ange had frowned, and taken a careful bite from her Mr Kipling French Fancy, but she had never answered the question.

Here was another photo – a Polaroid snap of herself and Viv, sitting together on a striped blanket laid out on a scorched summer lawn. Ten-year-old Beth looked uncertain in her new Speedo swimsuit, her pale legs straight as pins out in front of her, her thin shoulders encircled by Viv's arm. The brown curly frizz of her hair was tied back in a half-ponytail and her face was tilted away in shyness as she half-smiled at the camera. It was just a tiny smile, but her expression betrayed a soft naked hopefulness that embarrassed the present-day Beth, made her want to cover the photo up, as though it had been physical nakedness captured there in the blink of the shutter.

And there was Viv, with her corned-beef mottled skin, and her hair set stiffly in the style of Princess Di, looking so kind and so capable. None of it had been her fault – none of it. She wasn't to know the cough she'd developed the previous Easter, the annoying one that wouldn't go away, even after a holiday in Majorca, was caused by a tumour lodged deep inside her left lung. Or that her gruff, kindly bear of a husband, Steve, would decide, just the day after Viv's funeral, that he couldn't keep Beth any longer, that he wasn't up to it on his own. She wasn't to know that Ange would drive up in her Austin Maxi again, her face long and apologetic, her perm droopy like a spaniel's ears.

Looking at it now, Beth thought that Viv and Steve's semi,

with its neat white window frames and its front door with the
frosted glass panels, looked like a Lego house. A house that
was only ever part of a game, and could be crushed at any
moment by a careless foot or swept away in a tidy-up.

By the time Beth had arrived at family number four, aged
fifteen, her eyes had lost that optimistic, wanting-to-belong
look. She'd wrapped up her soft insides within a hard exte-
rior, like the shiny shell of a cockroach. She'd bleached her
hair and gelled it up in spikes, pierced her bottom lip and the
tender flesh of her belly button – oh, how it had hurt when
the spike went in. On the whole she thought it would be
easier if they could know, as soon as they looked at her, that
they wouldn't want her, rather than going through the
motions for a few painful weeks and months.

It wasn't surprising, perhaps, that she'd flung herself into
a bad relationship, getting together with Rick, who owned
the blood-red, sticky-carpeted saloon bar where she and her
school friends had gone to drink Snakebites on Saturday
nights. She'd moved in with him a few months after her
sixteenth birthday – the scandal of the town, not that
anybody really cared. The years that followed were a blur...
drinking in the bar most nights, crying, at first, when the
occasional slap came her way from Rick after he'd had a few.
Then crying upstairs in bed when Rick was down in the bar
with his other girlfriend, Tracey from the brewery. Then
having no tears left at all when he'd hit her in the face with
the iron, that night when she'd first threatened to leave him.

It was pure luck, really, that Frank had been on duty at
the homeless shelter, when she'd walked in there on that
freezing December night just before Christmas. He'd been
elbow-deep in a sinkful of dirty dishes, but he turned to face
her and just stood there, sudsy water dripping from his

yellow rubber gloves onto the lino. From that moment on – he described it as an 'epiphany' – his eyes had burned with love, the age difference never mattering one jot.

Old enough to be her father, someone had said once. But Frank was nothing like her father. She pulled out the final photo from the bottom of the box – Daddy in his dinner suit and bow tie, on the curving stairs down to the ballroom in the *Ocean Glory*. A row of white teeth and hair slicked back like a film star. She had spent years wondering what on earth she must have done to make him leave her the way he did.

Frank had said they'd stay here in Vevey for five years or so. Better to let some time pass – no sense in rushing back. And there was no need for her to work, he said. She should just relax and enjoy being a mother. Wasn't that what she'd wanted, after all?

Frank could never have understood it, but it seemed to Beth that her mother-feelings were all back-to-front, as though she were the child, sometimes, and not the mother at all. So she stayed up with Kitty when she cried, practising her mothering in secret in the dark of the night, and she slept her mornings away, a princess in her canopy bed, with the gauzy veils that shifted in the breeze from the open window. And then dozing on her sun-lounger as the afternoon stretched into early evening, her body kissed by the glimmering light that danced off the pool, her hair shining palest gold where it had been touched by the sun.

Kitty would be awake soon. Beth put the biscuit box back, and went down to the kitchen to prepare another bottle, measuring out the spoonfuls of formula and tapping them into the cooled boiled water. But the box seemed to glow from the bottom of her wardrobe, like something radioactive. Something she couldn't ignore.

6

JULIET

The walk to Boxley Wood Primary seemed familiar to my very bones. I'd walked this way each morning as a little girl, starting from Laurel Bank and turning on to the main road, then the seemingly endless trudge along the edge of the Common, feet scuffing the dust of the rough footpath, cutting off again at the Post Office, which was in a squat, thick-walled cottage, painted Suffolk pink. The Spar at the end of Church Lane, with its shiny plate glass windows and its and three-for-two offers, was new.

One of the books I'd read about infertility had extolled the benefits of visualization. It had started with imagining a plump, rosy egg nestling into the velvet darkness of my womb, effortlessly dividing into two, and then four cells. Then, my tummy growing rounder week by week until it was tight as a drum. Holding a newborn in my arms, her skin waxy and blood-streaked, the rigidity of her body when she cried. And my visualisations had shot ahead impatiently, through the years that would surely follow. I'd imagined – countless times on restless nights when I couldn't sleep –

walking my daughter to school on her first day, the smallness of her frame within the stiff tailoring of her new blazer, hands disappearing into the too-long sleeves. Her freshly washed, nut-brown hair gleaming in the dappled light of the late-summer morning, and corn marigolds blazing in the ditch by the side of the road.

Kitty, in her perpetual silence, seemed to collude in this piece of fiction. She was making herself into anything that anyone wanted her to be.

The process of getting ready for school, always so hectic in other households where I'd worked, had felt calm this morning – almost unnervingly so. It had occurred to me, when I was downstairs in the kitchen making Kitty's toast, that Laurel Bank just didn't feel like a house where a child lived. It wasn't just that Kitty didn't speak, but she rarely made any other noise either. She moved silently around the house. I'd leave her upstairs playing in her room, only to find her propelling herself round on the office chair in the study a minute later, or perched on the low windowsill in the living room, a shadow between the glass and the voile curtain.

There were no bubble baths or princess toothbrushes in the bathroom, no children's yoghurts or chocolate milk in the fridge. No crumpled artwork or swimming certificates tacked to the walls. Her toys were neatly tidied away in her room with only one thing out at a time. Except the jigsaws. She left them lying wherever she completed them, like little windows into other worlds beneath the floor. New England in the fall. A mediaeval jousting match. Jeremy Fisher in his boat on Esthwaite Water.

Beth left early in the mornings to go to the Old Coach House, and arrived home late, usually after attending some form of exercise class at Seekings Country Club. When she was in, she seemed to spend most of her time in the kitchen, baking or poring over recipe books, and humming along to Classic FM. She'd told me that she'd be out two or three evenings a week, if that was okay with me. Her husband, Frank, was away 'in the field', with one of his charities, so it would 'just be us girls' for the next few weeks anyway.

We were getting on quite well, I thought. At the weekend I had seen a ceramic chicken egg holder in a little homeware shop in Sudbury – just like the one my mother used to have – and I'd bought it for Beth as a present, my cheeks reddening as I'd handed it over.

She'd accepted it with a gracious smile. Kitty, her face alight, had scampered to the fridge and transferred the eggs across, one by one, before replacing the top half of the chicken with a soft clunk.

'Who's your teacher this year, Kitty?' I asked now.

She pressed her lips together, like she was trying to keep all her words safe inside her mouth. As though they might tumble out like broken teeth.

'I think Mummy said it was Mrs Robson?'

A small nod.

'Is she nice, do you think?'

One of the stiff shoulders of the blazer shifted slightly in a shrug.

'Hmm...' I said doubtfully. Kitty glanced up, but looked away before I could catch her eye.

'Mummy told me a list of things about school, but I'm not sure if I've remembered them all.'

We kept walking for ten more steps.

'I was thinking... if I try and remember them, can you nod if I get them right?'

Kitty nodded.

'So, Mummy said that sometimes you like to play with the other children in the playground, and that your favourite game is playing horses? But if someone does something that you don't like, you hold up your hands and they have to stop. That's the rules. Otherwise you let the teacher know.'

She nodded again.

'And for things like that, you have a special notebook in your schoolbag.'

We'd packed it that morning – a pink notebook with a unicorn on the front, and a pencil attached to it with a silky ribbon.

'You can also write messages if you need to say something about your work. So, for example, you could write, "Oh dear, I've forgotten how to add two plus two?"'

Nothing.

'Or, "This Biff and Chip book is so boring that I'm falling asleep?"'

A smile played around the edges of her mouth, but she extinguished it quickly, pulling her lower lip back inside.

'Right. And Mummy said that if you need to go to the toilet, you... let me see... you stand up on your chair and wave your arms around? No? Oh I know, you do a handstand and wave your *legs* around!'

A little chuckle this time, and she skipped a step.

'What do you do then? You show me.'

I stopped and turned to face her. She still wouldn't look at me, but she put her hand in the air.

'Oh, you put your *hand* up. I see. That makes a lot of sense. Thank you, Kitty.'

We turned in to a cul-de-sac to see the low red brick building of Boxley Wood Primary, set back in its playground, with the monkey bars and faded hopscotch numbers on the asphalt.

I wondered if any of the staff might still be there, might recognise me. But it seemed unlikely, especially since I'd changed my name when I'd married. And after all I was a nanny, invisible and interchangeable. Nobody needed to know where nannies came from.

The gate into the playground squeaked in exactly the same way as it had always done, but now there was a silver keypad on the door.

'What's the number?' I asked Kitty. She reached up to key in the numbers – 7, 8 and 9 – but she couldn't quite reach the 3 on the top row. Raising my eyebrows in a question, I held out my hands towards her waist, and she nodded. I lifted her gently so she could complete the sequence, her shiny school shoes suspended for a moment in the air. A low buzz came from the door as the code was accepted. Kitty's feet skittered down and she rushed with both hands for the panel which said 'push'.

It was like stepping into a disinfectant-scented, Alice-in-Wonderland world where everything was too small. I peeked into doorways, seeing tiny sinks and toilets, mini-sized tables and chairs, a long table set out with xylophones. The coat pegs lining the corridor were at hip-height, and the little benches that ran underneath were just inches from the floor.

The parents seemed like giants, talking in loud, excitable voices and wielding schoolbags, gym bags, spare welly boots, violins... somebody was even waving around a pair of children's crutches. Some stood chatting in the middle of the corridor, forming islands that everyone else had to squeeze around, while others were focused on finding the right peg and the right classroom. Kitty advanced with her head down and her hands over her ears until we found Miss Robson's room, with a rainbow painted over the door.

She made straight for her tray, a yellow one amongst blues and reds stacked in a low wooden cabinet, and busied herself with arranging her stationery.

'Remember your snack for breaktime.' I handed her the shiny red apple that Beth had popped into the front pocket of her school bag. She'd come down to the kitchen just as we were getting ready to leave, and thrown her arms around her daughter, trailing the sleeve of her dressing gown into a beaker of orange juice.

Kitty was spending too long on her tray. Her chin was dipped low so that her hair fell down the sides of her face, like blinkers.

'Where's *your* desk, Kitten?'

At the nearest table stood a thin little blonde boy, his mum behind him, and the dad crouching down in front of him with an arm around his shoulders. The boy nodded as his dad spoke, but his eyes were cast down and I could detect the beginnings of a wobble in his chin.

The mum shot a glance at the dad that seemed to contain a silent instruction. Slowly, he unfurled himself into a standing position. Maybe he could feel my gaze on him, because he turned to face me.

Charlie.

In a way it seemed right to see him here. It seemed like I'd always known. I'd always known that one day he was going to stand up in just that way, and turn, and look at me again, his forehead pinched into a frown and his eyes full of light and confusion. The way you might look if the sun came up in the middle of the night.

Charlie.

Through all the days and months and years since I last saw him, I'd lived inside the stories in my head. A life of what ifs and maybes. It was how I'd survived.

I'd kept a space in my mind where I still had a happy family, with Dad in his armchair reading the newspaper, and Mum busy in the kitchen, cheeks flushed and wiping her hands on her apron. Then there'd been the jobs, where I'd gone away to hide in other families, as practically perfect as Mary Poppins herself. The relationships with men who had never quite managed to be Charlie. And the fertility treatments, the fragile eggs and the unviable embryos. Each twist of DNA had been a tangled love story, held tight in the bud, never to be unravelled. A world of possibility, falling away each time.

What if, what if, what if...

And now, standing there looking at him... now I had an overwhelming sense that I could just let it all go. I could let it all go because I was home.

'Juliet.'

He'd always said my name differently from everyone else, with the stress on the last syllable. Now it came out as a sharp exhalation, as though he'd been punched on the back as he'd tried to speak.

I became aware of Kitty's hand, pulling at mine.

'Kitty, this is Charlie. We were at school together, when we were little!'

Charlie's teeth were dug into his lower lip, as though he couldn't allow himself to say whatever it was that he might have said.

The woman stepped forward. 'I'm Tasha. Hello.'

'I'm Kitty's nanny. My name's Juliet.'

Charlie blinked and cleared his throat. Once, twice.

'Sorry, yes, this is Juliet. We knew each other at school. And this is Tasha, my wife.'

Wife. It seemed such an old-fashioned, proprietorial word for this woman who stood in front of me, completely self-assured with one hand on her hip and her feet planted apart on the carpet tiles. She wore summer sandals, chipped polish on her nails. Her blonde hair was twisted into a long rope of a plait that she'd pulled forward over her right shoulder, its tapered end resting on the curve of her breast.

Wife.

I had a flashback to Eddie's wedding speech, the way he'd worked in the words, 'My wife and I' with an arch lift of his eyebrow, the cheers and hoots from the audience filling the pause that followed.

Had Charlie stood in a marquee, or in the function room of a country house hotel somewhere, and said those words in front of all his loved ones? What had I been doing at that exact moment? Had I felt the world tilt?

I pulled my gaze away from them and turned to the little boy. 'Hello. What's your name?'

Oh God, he was beautiful. But beautiful in a way that I already knew. With Charlie's eyes, and the shape of his chin.

I tried not to think it. I tried with all my strength, but it was impossible. This was the child I should have borne. I should have carried him in my body, Charlie's genes laced tight with mine to form this translucent skin, these eyes with their dark sweep of lashes, these fingers that still had dimples at the knuckles.

He opened his mouth, hesitated and then spoke. 'I'm Cameron-on-a-Thursday.'

'Hello, Cameron-on-a-Thursday,' I said, trying to keep the shake out of my voice. 'It's really good to meet you.'

'Thursday's my violin lesson,' he said.

I nodded, pretending to understand.

'So you're back in Boxley Wood?' said Charlie. 'We just moved back last year.'

Tasha cut in. 'Charlie's a GP at the local practice and I'm, well I'm a mummy most of the time but I'm also working at a coffee shop – the Old Coach House.'

This was too weird – that was Beth's coffee shop.

'Oh! Actually, I'm nannying for the Seiglers. The Old Coach House – that belongs to Beth, Kitty's mum.' I smiled weakly, pretending to be delighted at the coincidence.

Tasha made the appropriate noises, saying what a small world it was.

Kitty's hand tugged again.

'Sorry, Kitty. Are you wanting to get set up? Okay then. Well, it was nice to see you again, Charlie. And to meet you, Tasha and Cameron.'

Tasha stepped forward as I began to turn away, laying her hand on my arm.

'We're having a garden party on Saturday afternoon – a welcome thing for all the parents,' she said. 'Beth hasn't replied so I'm assuming she's busy. But you'd be very welcome to bring Kitty along if you're free. Two o'clock.'

That was kind of her. Mostly the yummy mummies ignored the nannies – didn't see them as part of their social set.

But Charlie wouldn't have married someone who wasn't kind.

'I'll check with Beth,' I said. 'That sounds lovely, though. Thank you so much for inviting us.'

It was only when I'd got Kitty settled, and was walking back down the miniature corridor, that I realised.

I'd told Tasha that Charlie and I had gone to school together... which meant Tasha might mention it to Beth.

Had we mentioned Boxley Wood Primary, or had we just said 'school'? Maybe she'd assume we meant secondary school.

Breathe, Juliet.

But hadn't I talked about us being 'little'? I scanned back through the conversation, trying to remember. It was full of maddening blanks and blurs. I couldn't remember anything except the look on Charlie's face.

And anyway, either way, I wasn't safe. Charlie might have filled Tasha in afterwards, as they walked back to the car, or wherever they were heading next – him to the GP surgery, probably, and her to the Old Coach House. Tasha had probably been... well, curious. About me. About what had happened to Charlie, and his ability to speak, back there in the classroom.

'Yeah, we were at Boxley Wood Primary together. Juliet's family lived just a few streets away from mine, on St Mary's Lane... a lovely old house called Laurel Bank. Come to think of it, don't the Seiglers live on St Mary's Lane? What a coincidence.'

'Oh, well I wonder if that's how Beth knew Juliet in the first place... through the neighbours or something... so difficult to get nannies you can trust. Ooh, I'm curious now. I'll have to ask Beth when she comes in.'

I sank down on to a bench in the playground, feeling quite dizzy. I pictured Beth, when she got back tonight, telling me to pack my bags and leave. I thought of Kitty's face, clouding over as she realised what was happening. Then I thought of never seeing that face again. Not even one more time. The blank space of my life, going on afterwards.

BETH'S OLD COACH HOUSE – her coffee shop – was picture perfect. The archway that had once been the entrance for coaches was now a huge window, with pink flowers cascading from hanging baskets on either side. A chalk board was positioned on the cobbles at the side of the door, advertising the day's specials. Rhubarb and polenta cake. Apple and cinnamon scones.

It was busy, too. A group of yummy mummies had gathered there to catch up after the first drop-off of the new term. I recognised the woman who'd been waving around the crutches in the school corridor. She was regaling everyone with the story of a helicopter trip over the Niagara Falls, how she'd thought it would have to be cancelled when Marcus broke his leg falling off his cousin's climbing wall.

I felt a momentary jolt of shame, as if they'd all arranged to meet there and purposely omitted to tell me. Ridiculous, since I'd never even met any of them before. I wasn't fifteen anymore, backs turning on me like dominoes as I looked for a group to stand with in the school yard.

Tasha was behind the counter, slicing a chocolate tray bake into thick chunks. 'Hello! Juliet! Coming to join the madhouse? Shall I introduce you to people?' Her face was open and kind, and I tried to work out if it was beautiful. She had a bit of a strong jaw, I decided. And her teeth were too white and sharp-looking.

Oh, hell. She was beautiful – of course she was.

'Actually, it was you I wanted to see.'

'Oh?'

'I need your help. I've really messed up.'

'What is it?' A frown creased her forehead, a slight smile

playing around her lips. Her idea of 'messing up' was probably forgetting to put the baking powder into a batch of scones.

I swallowed hard. All I could do was throw myself on her mercy.

'So... you know I'm nannying for Beth Seigler. But I haven't told her that I went to school at Boxley Wood Primary.'

'Okaaay...'

'And it's worse than that. I used to *live* at Laurel Bank, their house. I grew up there. It was my house.'

It sounded so silly. For a mad moment I felt a giggle rising in my throat and I brought my hands up to cover my mouth.

Tasha watched me closely for a moment. Then she put her hand on my arm. 'Are you all right?'

'I should have mentioned it to Beth. I don't know why I didn't, there was no reason not to. It's not as if...'

Oh God – my chin was wobbling, my words wavering.

Suddenly she was beside me, her arm around my shoulders, sheltering me from the view of the mummies at the nearest table.

'It's okay, it's okay. My goodness.'

'It was just one of those – those stupid things.'

She was handing me a napkin.

'I think I know what you mean. When it's too late to say something?'

I nodded, blinking furiously.

'Well,' she said. 'I don't know my nephew's birthday. I know it's some time in the middle of June, but I don't know the exact day. There came a point when it just became too late to ask.' She widened her eyes in a naughty, child-like expression that made me smile. 'And I've got an old school

friend who still doesn't know I'm married. I was her brides-
maid, and it would have been too awful to tell her I didn't
want her to be mine. She wanted to come and visit last year
and I had to pretend we were on holiday, because I didn't
want to have to take down all the wedding photos.'

'I would understand if you felt you had to tell Beth –'

'Ouff...' She waved a dismissive hand. 'It's none of *my*
business. Oh crikey. Come on, you. Sit down and I'll make
you a coffee.'

The look on her face... she was trying to *mother* me. Tears
pooled and began to spill down my cheeks.

'Oh you poor thing, you are in a state, aren't you?'

'I just want to stay with Kitty. I think I can help her.'

It was true, but it wasn't why I was crying. I was crying for
the deep, dragging feeling inside me.

Because I'd held Charlie in my heart, all these years, and
he hadn't been holding me. Not only had he found someone
else, but he'd found someone so much better than me.

I felt like a walk-on part in my own life story.

Just for one moment, I laid my aching head against her
shoulder, as though she could somehow make it better.

Then I pulled myself together. 'I'd better go,' I said.
'Thank you, Tasha.'

'Hold on.' She wrapped a piece of chocolate tiffin in a
napkin and thrust it into my hand, folding my fingers over it.
'Cup of tea. Feet up. Chocolate tiffin. The world will seem like
a different place. Trust me.'

7

JULIET

We were going to be late. It was half past two and Kitty wasn't even dressed. Over the last hour, she'd ignored my gentle reminders that it was time to stop doing her jigsaw and get her party clothes on, and then she'd rejected outfit after outfit, tossing them towards the corner of the room where they now lay in a heap. She was lying face down on her bed, wearing only her pants. Not screaming, not shouting, just silent.

'Oh, ignore her,' Beth said now, trailing past the door on her way to her own room. 'She's got the hump about something.'

I sat down on the bed, dropping the dress-and-leggings set that I was holding. 'It's a funny expression, isn't it?' I said to Kitty's back. '"Got the hump about something"? When I was little I thought – well.'

I'd thought it was something to do with Dad. The way he sometimes stayed in bed when he was having a 'bad day', not getting up for breakfast, or lunch, or even sometimes tea. If I ever peeked into the bedroom he'd be lying in the same position, facing away from the door, with only the top of his grey, thinning hair visible, his back and shoulders forming a large hump under the floral counterpane. Sometimes Mum sent me up with a cup of tea, or a plate of toast or a boiled egg, but I always left the tray on the bedside table and ran off without looking at him. I was afraid that his face would be different, and that my own real daddy who loved me had been replaced by this silent, blank-eyed daddy with the hump.

'Oh, Kitty. It makes me think about my Daddy. I miss him sometimes.'

Slowly, she twisted round and sat up. She didn't look at me, but she pushed her bottom lip out into a babyish pout and gave a tiny nod.

Beth passed by the door again, on her way back downstairs. 'Clothes on! Now!'

Kitty tensed again, curling in on herself.

'How about this one?' I suggested, picking up an outfit from the pile at random. But she opened one of her drawers and pulled out a calf-length Disney *Frozen* nightdress.

I put my head to the side. 'Hmm.'

What the hell. Beth wouldn't even notice. 'Don't forget this.' I rummaged in the drawer and found the long silky cape that attached to the shoulders of the nightdress with Velcro pads.

She nodded.

'And you could dress it up with your Lelli Kelly's and the sparkly bag?'

Kitty pulled the nightdress on and turned away from me to let me fasten the cape.

'And teeth, young lady,' I added in a whisper, remembering that she hadn't done them this morning.

I sat on the lid of the toilet while I supervised her tooth-brushing, setting a timer on my phone for two minutes. She grimaced as she worked her way around her mouth, holding the brush at awkward angles as she tried to avoid a wobbly incisor.

'Ready to spit out?' I asked, reaching to turn the tap on for her.

But when I looked down there was blood in the sink, a swirl of crimson against the white porcelain.

I gasped. 'Kitty? Are you okay?'

She frowned and spat again, and I saw that it was just toothpaste foam. It was white, not red.

'Let me see your teeth?'

Obediently, she opened her mouth. 'Okay,' I whispered, and stroked the back of her head.

I blinked a few times and looked in the mirror – was this a migraine starting or something? In the mirror I was bone-pale with dark-smudged eyes, my lips curved into an odd little smile. For a moment I saw myself holding a pair of silver nail scissors, drawing the blade across my wrist.

Calm down, Juliet. This isn't real.

Notice three things you can see.

The top of Kitty's head, her hair shining under the ceiling spotlights.

The droplets of water on her toothbrush.

The mermaid doll, its red smile scored into the beige plastic.

And three things you can hear.

A blackbird far away in the garden, its song breaking my heart.

Kitty picked up the doll and left the room.

I closed the door, sank down onto the floor and put my head in my hands.

CHARLIE AND TASHA lived in an old Victorian house on the outskirts of Boxley Wood, on a winding lane with crumbling tarmac that bordered the apple orchards of a neighbouring farm.

'Ready?' I asked Kitty as we walked up the steps. She gave no sign of having heard me. Her cape lifted in the breeze and fluttered back down again.

Tasha opened the door, looking perfect in a yellow sundress printed with daisies. Once again, her hair was twisted into a long braid that hung over her left shoulder and down her front.

I had a sudden urge to pull on it and then run away.

But I unclenched my fingers from the Tupperware box containing Beth's pavlova, and offered it to Tasha.

'Wow! Thanks, you two! Good to see you.' She stepped aside and ushered us in.

So this was their house – burnt orange walls and polished wooden floor boards, rugs in warm colours. And pictures. So many of them, pulling my gaze this way and that like a dizzying hall of mirrors.

To my right was a staged family shot against a bright white background, the grown-up faces lit with open-mouthed smiles (one of those jokey photographers no doubt) while Cameron frowned.

Then Cameron as a newborn, his tiny head cradled on a strong male hand, his eyelids sealed shut and his forehead wrinkled.

Above the hall table was one of Charlie and Tasha on their wedding day, him in a dark suit, her in an ivory dress with the long train arranged to flow down the stone steps of some stately home entrance.

Then one of the two of them at some outdoor restaurant, amid lemon trees and lanterns, Charlie awkwardly down on one knee, Tasha smiling straight into the camera with her face flushed and her shoulders sunburnt, holding up her hand to show the ring on her fourth finger.

And here they were graduating, gripping their scrolls, Tasha's gown flapping around her bare, slender arms on what must have been a windy day... Oh God. So he'd met her at university, just a few short, raw years after... well, after me.

Kitty pulled on my hand, bringing me back to the present. We continued through the large kitchen-diner and into the back garden. Tasha had suggested that each family should bring a picnic rug, and the colourful squares lay dotted around between the flower beds and in the shade of the trees along the back wall.

On the patio stood a long trestle table which had been draped in a snowy white tablecloth and then laden with sausage rolls, smoked salmon and cream cheese bagels, and half a dozen different kinds of sandwiches. Tasha set down Beth's pavlova beside two summer puddings, a cake stand piled with strawberry scones and little squares of carrot cake decorated with sugar bunnies. It looked like a photo-shoot for a food magazine.

Together, Kitty and I unrolled the striped picnic rug that we'd brought with us, and I fetched a glass of lemonade for each of us. I was looking around the garden, wondering if any of the other families looked friendly enough to talk to, when I heard the rug rustle behind me and I turned to see Kitty curled up on her side, her thumb lodged in her mouth.

'Are you okay?' I stroked a wisp of hair back from her

forehead. She seemed even quieter than usual, if that were possible. The skin under her eyes had a bruised, purplish tinge.

'Did you not sleep well again?'

I'd heard her moving around in her room, the last couple of nights. Whenever I went and looked in on her, she'd be lying curled up in bed, eyes shut, just as I'd left her – but with the ceiling light switched on. I'd made a mental note to look for a different nightlight for her bedside table. My mother had bought me a lovely fairy toadstool one as a child, with little windows for the yellow light to shine through.

'Are you not feeling well? Does something hurt?'

No response.

'Shall I get your notebook and you can write down if something is wrong?'

No response again. I didn't hold out much hope for the notebook. It was empty except for the words 'I don't like keesh' on the first page. She didn't seem keen on using it.

Cameron appeared from the back door, racing down the steps with a picnic rug. Tasha, close behind, took the rug from him, undid the Velcro fastenings and unrolled it on the grass. As she leaned over, I could see varicose veins standing out on the backs of her calves. Bubbles of blue under tanned skin.

Did she hide her legs, I wondered, when she and Charlie made love? Or did she move calmly and freely, comfortable in her skin and in Charlie's total acceptance of her? The woman he'd chosen for his life. The woman who'd borne his child, had grown part of him inside her body.

The afternoon inched on. The sun shone hotter and the noise of chatter rose higher as the parents moved between rugs to mingle and their children played. In an attempt to include Kitty, I got a game of hide and seek going amongst some of the children, but one of the mums put a stop to it after her son tried to hide behind a clump of nettles.

I was in the kitchen getting water – Kitty hadn't drunk any of the lemonade and I wasn't sure if she liked it or not – when I heard someone come up behind me.

'How're you doing, lovely?'

'Tasha. What a great day. Thank you so much for inviting us.'

'You're welcome.' She reached up to a shelf on the kitchen dresser – a shelf of beautiful, mismatched items – and brought down a large glazed earthenware jug, in a blue-grey colour that made me think of the sea.

'What a gorgeous home you have.'

'Thank you.' She turned to the sink and gushed cold water into the jug. 'We were very lucky. We snapped it up before it even went on the market. It used to belong to friends of Charlie's grandparents. In fact, perhaps you've been here before?'

'No, no,' I said quickly.

'Charlie was saying that your families knew each other quite well.'

'Well, yes. We kind of grew up round at each other's houses.'

It had been an eleven minute walk to Charlie's old house if you went the proper way, along the road. But only four minutes if you went through the gate in our garden fence and cut through the bluebell woods, skirting the high stone wall around the church yard. I closed my eyes for a second, remembering the smell of creosote and damp earth, the snap of twigs underfoot.

'Our mums were friends. They both volunteered at the

church playgroup. But then they moved away when Charlie's mum got ill – to be near her parents, I think. But we met again later at Colle –'

I stopped abruptly.

'Collecott Hall?' said Tasha.

The words sounded ugly, like swear words. Out of place in this beautiful kitchen.

'The boarding school?' she went on.

My legs felt weak suddenly. I leaned against the kitchen counter.

What happened at Collecott Hall couldn't come out. It couldn't.

'Umm...'

What if Charlie had already told her about it? The room seemed to sway.

'I need to –'

But suddenly Charlie was there, coming in from the garden with a pile of empty plates.

Tasha smiled. 'I'll leave you two to reminisce.' And she walked into the garden with the jug.

Charlie watched her leave and then turned to me, giving me his full attention in that way he had, that made you feel you were the only person in the world. 'How are you doing?'

'I'm fine.'

Notice five things you can see.

His face. Oh God, his face.

'This is weird, isn't it?'

'Yes,' I managed.

'And you're living at Laurel Bank now!' He smiled, as if it was one of those funny coincidences. I imagined Tasha going home to tell him about me, blubbering in front of her at the Old Coach House: 'Hun, you'll never *guess* what happened...'

I looked around me, out of the open door.

'Don't worry,' he said quickly. 'I won't say anything. Tash explained it was, well, delicate.'

'Okay. Thanks.'

'I tried to call you. Back in June. After I'd heard. I called your number in Edinburgh.' His eyes were full of concern.

He'd called me? How had he even got my number?

'Someone answered and he said he'd give you a message.'

'Ah – Eddie. He's my... he was my husband. And no, he didn't pass on any message.'

Here it came... his lips worked as he tried to find the words. 'Juliet, I'm so sorry –'

I raised a hand to cut him off. 'Charlie...'

His sympathy was pulling me back there again, to that timeless time in my mother's flat, caught between the past – too painful to think of – and the future, as blank and hard as a concrete wall. The only relief had been the darkness, the feel of my mother's soft cotton pillowcase under my cheek, and sometimes, just barely, the sense of her still in the room in the moments when I hovered on the edge of sleep and waking.

Cassie had suggested that I come to stay with her for a while, that she could easily clear out the playroom and put a bed in there. But no – forcing myself back to work had been the right decision. My job now was to look after Kitty and that was enough to get me from one day to the next.

'It's okay,' I said now to Charlie. 'Thank you. But I'm fine. Look, I need to take this to Kitty.'

I could see, when I reached the steps from the kitchen door down to the garden, that Kitty wasn't on the picnic rug any more. I scanned the garden – was she playing hide and seek after all? Was she waiting patiently to be found, even though the other kids had moved on to playing croquet, bashing each other over the head with plastic mallets?

'Can you see her?' I asked Charlie.

'Maybe she's gone to the toilet. I'll go check.'

'Have you seen Kitty?' I walked down the lawn and up again, asking people. They all looked at me blankly. They didn't seem to know who Kitty was, let alone where she was.

Charlie reappeared behind me. 'She's not in the bathroom. But don't worry. She won't have gone far.'

'She's not out here,' I said. 'Nobody's seen her.'

'Maybe she came into the house to look for you. Cammie? Have you seen Kitty? Is she still playing hide and seek?'

He shook his head. 'I fink she's not feeling well.'

'Why, Cammie?'

He shrugged.

'Let's check inside,' said Charlie. We went through the house, flinging open doors, checking behind sofas and under beds.

Calm down, I told myself. This wasn't like me. As a nanny, I was used to the fact that children wandered off – it had inevitably happened on my watch from time to time, and they'd never gone far. I'd always prided myself on being unflappable in these situations.

Nevertheless. Alarming scenarios began to run through my head. Kitty wandering over the fields to the river, or to explore the lily pond in the woods... Kitty standing by the side of the road in her *Frozen* nightdress, unable to ask anyone for help... A car door opening to let her in...

I checked my watch. We'd already been searching for fifteen minutes. Tasha wandered in with a stack of empty plates. 'Are you still looking for Kitty?'

'I'll check the maid's rooms,' said Charlie.

The maid's rooms? Did Charlie and Tasha have *staff*?

Tasha frowned, then shrugged and turned to the sink. I followed Charlie through the utility room, beyond which was short passage leading to a narrow staircase. The air was cooler than in the main part of the house, thick with the damp stone smell of old houses. I followed Charlie up the stairs, where there was a small landing that gave onto three rooms. There was a bedroom piled with boxes, a small empty room with a swirly orange carpet and an electric fire, and a cold bathroom containing a long Victorian bath and a wooden-seated toilet with a pull-chain.

'Kitty?' called Charlie.

Where could she have gone?

I thought of Kitty when I'd last seen her in the garden, the noise of children shouting, the bright sunlight slanting onto the coloured rugs and the grass.

'Somewhere quiet and dark,' I said.

'The linen cupboard,' said Charlie. He went back into the bedroom and moved some of the boxes aside to reveal a small, half-height door in the wall.

And there she was, curled up on her side, on a pile of towels. I exhaled loudly and rolled my eyes at Charlie.

'Hello, trouble!' I put a gentle hand on her back. 'We've been looking *everywhere*.'

No response. She didn't even seem to notice I'd touched her.

'Kitty.' I pulled at her shoulder, more insistently this time. Had she fallen asleep?

'Can I...?' said Charlie. He moved past me and leaned into the cupboard.

'Kitty, can you hear me?' He felt her forehead. 'She's boiling. Kitty! Can you hear me?' He patted the side of her cheek, lightly at first and then briskly. 'Let's get her out of there.'

Together, we lifted her out of the cupboard and laid her on the carpet.

Oh no. This wasn't right. This wasn't right at all.

Charlie held her wrist between the thumb and fingers of his right hand and sat silent for a few moments, looking at his watch and frowning in concentration.

Her wrist looked so tiny in his hand. I thought of all the people he'd helped with those hands, who came to him with their hurts and their worries, the people he'd touched and treated and reassured.

Help her. Please help her.

'Has she got too hot?' I said. 'Was it too hot in the cupboard?'

'Her pulse is racing. And see how her hands are quite pale and the skin is mottled and blotchy? Something's going on, but I'm not sure what. I think she might be dehydrated. I think we should get her to the hospital, just to be on the safe side.'

'The hospital?'

'Just as a precaution. I expect she's come down with a virus but it's best to get her checked out.'

'Kitty,' I said, stroking her hair back from her clammy forehead. 'It's okay, my love. You're a little bit poorly, that's all, and we're going to take you to see the doctor.'

Her eyelids flickered.

'That's good, Kitten, that's very good. You just keep listening to me. You're okay, I promise.'

Charlie drew his phone out of his pocket. He was phoning ahead to the hospital. 'Six-year-old... Drowsy and confused... High temperature... Want to rule out sepsis.'

I wondered for a moment if they would send an ambulance. I thought of Kitty, dialling 999 all those times, for reasons only she knew.

'I need to phone Beth.'

'Car first.'

Kitty gave a little moan when he lifted her, but she didn't resist. She just hung in his arms like a rag doll.

I went ahead and opened the door, guided him down the steps. 'Keys are in my pocket,' he said, tilting his head to indicate that I should get them out.

I hesitated, then slid my fingers into the warmth of his pocket and drew out the keys.

'What's going on?' barked Tasha from behind us.

'We're taking Kitty to the hospital,' said Charlie, laying Kitty onto the back seat now. 'She needs to be checked over. Just to be on the safe side.'

Tasha frowned. 'What's wrong with her?'

Charlie's voice was tight. 'High temperature.'

'Shouldn't you phone the NHS helpline? Let them make the call?'

He gave a pointed sigh in her direction, then turned to me. 'Can we try and get the seatbelt around her somehow?'

Tasha sighed in return and lifted her hands in a 'whatever' gesture, as though she'd decided to let us go on with our game.

'I'm sorry about this,' I said, to nobody in particular.

I got in beside Kitty, and pulled her up so I could hold her snug against my side. Charlie leaned in and stretched the seatbelt over her and clicked it into place. The back of his neck was inches from my face. I could see short, greying hairs straying from his hairline, where it hadn't been cut in a while.

I tried not to breathe him in. The scent of him. It was nothing to do with me.

But the thought came into my head, nonetheless – it felt as though we were a family, and Kitty was our child.

I sighed and pulled Kitty closer. I was used to this kind of thing, from the hormones and the rollercoaster of expectation and disappointment. My imagination had become way too active. One time, after a particularly heavy week of hormone injections, I'd married the sweet, brown-eyed man behind the counter in the newsagents, had four sweet, brown-eyed children with him, moved into an old vicarage and begun converting the attic into a nursery for number five. All in the space of thirty seconds while I'd watched him changing the till-roll.

'Did you get hold of Beth?' asked Charlie, as he pulled deftly into a parking space in the hospital car park.

'I've left her a voicemail and a text,' I said. 'She had to take that cake to Belton Hall for that wedding. She's probably not back yet.'

'Come on, young lady,' said Charlie, opening the passenger door and making an 'umphh' noise as he gathered Kitty into his arms.

His voice was calm. But I could see beads of sweat, prickling the skin on his brow as he strode past me and straight up to the triage desk.

8

JULIET

Collecott Hall

I had so wanted to love Collecott Hall. I'd wanted to go there for as long as I could remember. It had assumed a storybook significance, like Malory Towers, or the Chalet School, except that this was *my* story, just waiting for me to walk into it.

Mum always used to point out the school from the train window, a highlight on the long journey up the East Coast line to Edinburgh, where my grandmother lived.

She'd place her hand on my arm, priming me for the few seconds when the school became visible from the window, a Georgian manor house in grey stone, high on a wooded hillside that stretched up from the tracks.

'That's where Daddy and I met,' she would say. 'That was our school.' Then she'd reach her other hand across the table to Daddy, and he'd look up from his newspaper, peering over the top of his glasses, and smile at her.

And I used to whisper it under my breath, in time with

the sound of the train running along the tracks... Colle-cott-Hall, Colle-cott-Hall, Colle-cott-Hall...

Now, as I sat alone by the window in the wood-panelled school dining room, staring out at the rain, it occurred to me that I was at looking at the same view from the opposite perspective. The same fields, sodden from the squally October rain that had lasted for a week now. The same trees, tired and blown about, their leaves almost gone. Wishing I was anywhere but here.

The dining room was filling up now, the noise level rising as the lacrosse team came in, and then the chamber choir after their lunchtime rehearsal, two of the girls still practising arpeggios. Cutlery and crockery clattered, and a table near the door had to be vacated when someone dropped their plate of kedgeree (to loud cheers from the rugby crowd). But still nobody came to sit at my table.

Then I saw with relief that Susi had come in and was sitting with Miranda Jones on another small window table that had a space free. Susi, with her Minnie Mouse face and round eyes, was the best friend I had here. And Miranda Jones... well, she tolerated me.

I scuttled over, spilling my water a bit as I put down my plate of carrot and cucumber sticks.

Susi passed a napkin to me, her lips twisted. Then she shot a meaningful look at Miranda, who nodded decisively and turned to me.

'We need to speak to you. We've been meaning to do it for a while. But basically, this can't go on. It's just not fair on us.'

'What isn't?'

'You, following us around everywhere? We know you don't mean to, it's just. It's just... holding us back.' She made a dramatic 'holding us back' gesture.

'Yeah. It's holding us back.' Susi nodded, wide-eyed. She actually looked like she might cry, at her own plight. 'They're starting to slag us too. If we let it go on like this we'll be...'

'Finished, basically speaking.' Miranda's eyes were as cold as a dead fish.

'And we've got, well, exams and stuff. Both our parents said it was really important not to let anything distract us because it's an exam year. We should just, you know, keep our heads down.'

I nodded. Nodded harder and harder, and looked out the window, pretending to be interested in something out there. For some reason it seemed vital to show I wasn't upset. At the bottom of the valley a train sped past, heading south, a blur of yellow-lit windows in the rainy afternoon.

'Yes. I see. Yup. It's cool, honestly. I mean, I'm busy anyway with my...' I looked down at my plate. 'My healthy eating plan.'

'Yeah,' said Susi, getting up. Her hand hovered near my arm for a moment, like she was thinking about touching me but decided against it. Her fingernails had white strips on the ends where she'd tried to French polish them but the white stuff had gone thick and gluey, like Tippex. 'Really good luck with that, yeah? I'm sure you'll slim down in no time. Just concentrate on that, and your exams. We don't have anything against you, pacifically.'

'Specifically,' I murmured.

'We'll still, like, *talk* to you and stuff.'

I nodded. 'That would be good. When nobody's around, in the dorm maybe?'

Unsure, Susi looked to Miranda.

'Yeah... yeah.'

As they walked off with their trays, to sit at another table,

I realised that I hadn't so much *liked* Susi as clung to her, like a drowning person to a perky piece of driftwood.

But now the worst had happened. I was alone, completely alone. I felt a tear trickle down my cheek, leaving a cold trail. And then another, and another. Just slowly finding their way down, like the rain on the windows.

And then I felt a hand on my shoulder, and deep voice spoke: 'Joolz. Can we have a word?'

MR REDWOOD, Head of Pastoral Care, looked like a 1970s version of Jesus with his longish hair, his brown beard and his piercing eyes. Once he'd even played guitar in assembly.

Kumbaya, m'lord, kumbaya.

Excruciatingly, he was also an alumnus of Collecott Hall and an old friend of my parents. I'd almost died earlier in the term when he sat in on one of our sex ed lessons, when a grim-faced 'guest speaker' came in to talk to us from the Family Planning Clinic in Durham. Mr Redwood had assisted by handing round bananas from a Sainsbury's cardboard box so that we could practise putting on condoms. Ughhhh.

Sitting there in front of him now in his office, on the other side of his mahogany desk, I could feel a flush rising up my neck, a crawling sensation across my skin.

Don't think about it. Don't think about it.

'Okay, Joolz,' he said, placing both his hands flat on the top of his desk. 'Tell me what's been happening.'

I wanted to tell him that my name was Juliet, not *Joolz* – nobody else called me that. And I wanted to tell him that I'd settled in well and everything was going fine, thank you very much. But I was too tired. When I opened my mouth, only the dismal truth came out.

'I don't have any friends. Nobody will talk to me.'

'Yes.' He nodded slowly. 'I've noticed that.'

Great. *Everybody* knew.

He tilted his head to one side. 'Have you heard of group dynamics? The group will look for a black sheep – for someone they can gang up against. It makes the other members of the group feel stronger, more cohesive as a group. At the moment the black sheep – the victim, if you like – is you.' He left a meaningful pause. 'You need to think about *why* it's you.'

Because I'm fat? Because I'm useless? Because since I got to this school I've felt so awkward I can barely string a sentence together?

'It's good to join in with things, get involved. What have you signed up for, so far? The hockey team? Lacrosse? The drama production? Or remember you're allowed to go into town on Saturday afternoons.'

Yes, but only in groups of four or more. I'd spent last Saturday afternoon re-watching *Brief Encounter* in the dark windowless TV room that smelled of old trainers, and the yellow crumbs of foam that had been picked out from the splits in the seats. I'd been alone in the dark, crying for Laura as Rachmaninov surged in the background. Crying for her misery that surely, surely couldn't last.

'Think about what behaviours you might display that may cause the other members in the group to form beliefs about you, even on an unconscious level. It's fascinating what signals we can be giving off without even realising it.'

I nodded. He should know this stuff – he'd done some kind of course in psychology. We'd had to go to his special graduation ceremony last year. Mum had worn her string of pearls and she'd twisted them so much that they had broken and spilled all over the floor of the hall. Dad had got down on his hands and knees and found them – every single one. I remembered him crawling around between people's legs with whispered 'Excuse me's, his bald spot on display for all to see. My face had grown hot with embarrassment.

'What kind of signals?'

He leaned forward in his seat. 'You probably won't know this – unless your parents have mentioned it – but after leaving university I toured with a circus in Turkey for a year.'

I nodded again, raising my eyebrows politely. An image came into my mind of him on a trapeze, juggling bananas.

'My job was setting up the ring each night, moving the staging and so on. But I loved the lions, and Vasile, the lion tamer, sometimes used to let me get in the ring with them. He'd lost two fingers off his left hand to one of the lions, but I'll never forget what he taught me – you have to look them straight in the eye, and show them you're not afraid.'

I pictured the girls in my dorm as lions, and me as a curly-horned wildebeest, trying to stare them out instead of thundering away across the plains. 'Okay,' I said. 'I'll try.'

His face widened slowly into a wolfish smile. Then he threw back his head and laughed. 'Ah, Juliet if only that were true. I would have loved to work in a circus! After university I did my teaching qualification and went to teach in a girls' school near Bognor.'

The flush had risen up, flooding my entire face. I could imagine it, glowing like a beacon.

'But the lesson rings true, doesn't it? Hmm? Remember those lions, Joolz. Straight in the eye.'

9

JULIET

We were seen straight away. A young doctor with blonde hair and blue scrubs rattled the curtain around our cubicle and examined Kitty, frowning in concentration.

'When did her symptoms begin?' she asked me, as she poked an ear thermometer into Kitty's ear. 'What was she doing at the time?'

'We've been at a garden party. I thought she looked a bit pale earlier, but because she doesn't speak, it's often difficult to know what's wrong. She has selective mutism.'

The doctor frowned again. 'Temperature's up at forty point one. Has she had anything to drink in the last few hours?'

'I gave her some lemonade, but... to be honest I couldn't be sure whether she drank it or not.'

God. What kind of nanny was I?

'Has she complained of any pain?' The doctor was pressing around Kitty's lower tummy, watching her face intently.

I shook my head. 'I asked her if anything hurt but...'

'That's a bit tender down here, I think. Sorry, Kitty, my love. Can you tell me if that hurts if I press here?'

Kitty moaned and drew up her legs.

'Has she been urinating?'

I shrugged helplessly as the questions went on.

'Okay,' said the doctor finally, sitting down on one of the plastic chairs and clasping her hands. 'I think she's got some kind of infection, and I think it's most likely a urinary tract infection. Her temperature's high and she seems quite dehydrated, which will be why she's feeling so poorly. We'll take some bloods to try and get a better idea of what's going on, and we'll get some fluids and some antibiotics into her. Okay?'

When the doctor left the cubicle, Charlie turned to me.

'I know what you're thinking,' he said. 'But this is *not* your fault.'

'I should have known. She wanted to wear her nightdress to the barbecue.' She'd been trying to tell me she was unwell, that she just wanted to go to bed. She hadn't want tight waistbands around her sore tummy, or clothes that would take time to get off if she needed the toilet in a hurry.

I turned to her now, so small on the bed, and stroked her back gently. 'Shhh, Kitty, shhh. You rest now. The doctors are going to give you some medicine to make you better.'

'They'll sort you out in no time,' said Charlie.

'I shouldn't have brought her to the party when she was looking so pale this morning. And I should have kept an eye on what she was eating and drinking.'

My eyes stung with unshed tears. I stayed very still, willing them not to fall, but then I felt his hand on my back.

'Juliet,' he said.

All the feelings from the last few months swelled up inside, ready to crack out of my chest like red hot lava. I put my hands over my face, held my breath like a child.

Charlie stroked my back very gently, his hand moving down just over my shoulder blade, then up to the top and down again. I began to breathe... in... out... falling in with the rhythm of the strokes, as though, in that moment, it was the only safe way to breathe.

~

BETH SWEPT in a couple of hours later, trailing her Jo Malone scent – grapefruit, lime and basil, or whatever it was.

'Kitty! Oh, darling.'

'Careful,' said Charlie. 'She's got an IV in.'

Kitty opened her eyes, blinked when she saw her mother, and then closed them again.

'What happened?' Beth turned to me, her face unguarded and curled with dislike.

'She has a urinary tract infection,' said Charlie.

'How did she get that?'

'The paediatrician said they're quite common in children with selective mutism. Sometimes they hang on, instead of going to the toilet when they need to.'

'Because they can't ask, when they need to go,' I added.

Beth frowned again. 'Kitty knows how to ask to go to the toilet.'

I saw that Kitty's eyes were open. She was listening intently.

'Kitty,' I said. 'Does Mrs Robson let you go the toilet when you put up your hand?'

Kitty bit her lip, which meant she didn't want to commit to a nod or a shake of the head.

'Does she just let you go, when you put your hand up, or does she ask what you want?'

She lowered her eyes and fingered the edge of the hospital blanket.

'Does she try and make you say it?'

Her eyes filled with tears. She lifted her hand to hide her face, and I gently reached for it and lowered it to the bed.

'You need to try and be careful of that tube,' said Charlie. 'It's got your medicine in it.'

'Beth,' I said. 'You said you'd had a meeting with Mrs Robson about Kitty's needs?'

'I set up a meeting, yes. But Mrs Robson cancelled at the last minute, so it didn't happen. Naturally, I assumed that the school would brief her. Miss Potts, her teacher last year, knew all about it.'

I thought of Kitty, raising her hand again and again, the teacher asking her, in front of the whole class, what she wanted. The other twenty-eight children waiting expectantly for her to answer. Then I remembered that Kitty had come home with a pair of pants in a plastic bag on Tuesday, with a scribbled note from the school nurse – 'Accident (bring in spare pants please)'.

I'd asked Kitty about it but she'd just turned away and pretended she hadn't heard me.

'Have you been drinking less and less water, because you were worried about needing to go to the toilet?'

She nodded, and gulped in a breath. A tear escaped, darting down her face.

God, this physically hurt. I felt weak and sick, as though it was *my* body that was reeling with infection and dehydration.

I wanted to scoop her into my arms and tell her it would be all right. But I couldn't, because she wasn't mine. She was Beth's, and Beth was standing right there, looking like she'd just chewed on a wasp.

I tried to keep my voice calm, but it came out with a shake in it. 'If you had told me that the meeting hadn't taken place, I would have gone and spoken to Mrs Robson myself.'

Beth drew herself up very straight. 'Thank you for staying with Kitty. I do appreciate it. I've got things covered from here, though. I've blocked out my diary for the rest of the day, so there's no need to hang around.'

'They didn't say how long she'd need to stay in for,' said Charlie. 'Do you want us to stay around the hospital, so that we can give you a break if necessary? We could go and get a coffee and come back.'

'No, thank you,' said Beth. 'That won't be necessary.'

I couldn't leave. I couldn't walk out of there with Kitty in tears. I looked at Charlie for help. He inclined his head towards the door and gave a reassuring nod. He was trying to tell me it was okay to go.

'Kitty... me and Charlie are going to go now, okay? But Mummy's here. And the doctors. They'll look after you now.'

She seemed confused, looking from me to Beth and back again.

I wanted to tell her that I'd be waiting for her when she came home. That we'd sort things out at school. That I'd make sure her tummy didn't get sore like that again.

'Oh, and Juliet?' Beth's voice was light, casual. 'When Kitty comes home, I think we'll have some special mummy-daughter time, so...' She gave a tight smile.

Quiet on the bed, Kitty closed her eyes, shutting us all out.

Beth's meaning was clear – she didn't want me hanging around the house. What was I supposed to do? Wander the streets? Hide in my room?

Except that it wasn't 'my' room. It wasn't my home at all. Beth didn't ever have to let me in that house again, if she didn't want to.

With every ounce of my strength, I summoned Mary Poppins.

'Of course,' I said. 'I've got a few things to pick up in Sudbury so I'll pop off and do that, and I shall see you when I see you. There's a cottage pie in the fridge if you fancy something to eat later. And just ring me if you need anything. I won't be far away.'

10

JULIET

Eight o'clock on Monday evening and the first page in Kitty's 'Weekend News' jotter was completely blank.

Beth had shot me a raised eyebrow as she'd swept out of the door to go to her Pilates class at Seekings. 'Good luck with the homework.'

She'd been all sweetness and light when I'd returned late the previous night, exhausted with the effort of 'making myself scarce' for over twenty-four hours. After leaving the hospital I'd spent a couple of hours in Pizza Express, picking at some dough balls and a Caesar salad. Then I'd spent Sunday walking for miles along the River Stour, before watching two films back to back at the cinema.

'Kitty's feeling *so* much better,' she'd said when I got in. 'And thank you so much for everything, Juliet. I'm so glad you were there to look after Kitty when I couldn't.'

And now Beth had decreed that Kitty was well enough to go to school the next day. Which meant homework.

'You need to write a little story about your weekend, Kitty.'

She sat, mutinous, on the floor of her bedroom, her arms crossed in front of her. She was already grumpy from having to take her antibiotics after tea – horrible yellow gloop in a dosing syringe.

But then she rolled onto her back, rather dramatically, and put her hands on her head.

'Does it hurt? Have you got a sore head?'

She nodded.

'You look a bit hot.' Her forehead felt clammy. Was her body still trying to fight the infection? I decided that I'd suggest to Beth that I take her back to the doctor in the morning if she was no better. 'Would you like me to give you some Calpol?'

Another nod. The bottle that Kitty had been given at the hospital was nearly finished, so I went into the bathroom to look in the cabinet. There didn't seem to be any Calpol in there – in fact there were no children's medicines at all, other than a box of tablets with a prescription label for Kitty, over a year old. Promethazine – what was that for? It had been prescribed on the seventh of July last year.

Oh God, the seventh of July. It had been my due date. The due date that was never meant to be. In the end I'd spent that day with Cassie, going for a long walk in the Pentland Hills. We'd talked about her counselling diploma, and laughed about the strange people on her course. On the last stretch back to the car park I confided in her that Eddie and I had saved up for some more IVF and she squeezed my arm and said we should have another Twix to celebrate.

But this was no time to get caught up in the past. I rummaged some more, amongst the plasters and cotton buds, and a dark plastic bottle fell out of the cabinet, rattling into the sink. I picked it up and saw a prescription label in French, marked for Beth Seigler. For something beginning with 'z'.

I wondered about it as I walked back to Kitty's room. Did Beth have some kind of condition? Perhaps I could Google the name of the tablets...

None of your business, young lady.

I smiled. It was Mum's voice. Nobody else would call me a 'young lady' at forty.

Maybe there was Calpol in the kitchen cupboard? Yes – I was sure I'd seen some.

I hesitated at the top of the stairs, seeing that the hallway downstairs was dark, lit only by the lamp on the hall table, its tassled shade casting thin shadows on the wall.

Come on, Juliet. One foot in front of the other.

There were five picture frames positioned on the wall of the staircase, each in the shape of a little wooden little house and divided into 'windows'. Kitty's shy face peeped out of some of the windows, and Beth grinned delightedly out of others. In one of them was the blur of a man behind Kitty, as if he'd moved just as the shutter clicked. As I continued on down the stairs, the skin on my arms crawled.

The faces in the pictures were watching me.

I swung a hand out and caught the banister, startling myself with the noise of my hand hitting the wood. I took a few deep breaths in and out but my heart was racing.

I should run. I should run and hide in the airing cupboard, and bury my head under the towels. I wouldn't be able to hear anything or see anything there.

What? Where had that come from?

'I'll be back up in a sec,' I called out in a faint, falsely bright voice.

No response. The only sound was the ticking from the old mahogany clock in the hallway below.

There was no Calpol in any of the kitchen cupboards. I realised with a jolt that I had been thinking of the Calpol *my* mother had kept in her kitchen cupboard all those years ago.

Enough. Enough of this.

Back upstairs in Kitty's room, I poured the last trickle of pink sticky liquid from the hospital bottle onto a white plastic spoon, and popped it into her mouth.

'There we go,' I said softly.

She swallowed and sighed heavily.

'So,' I said. 'What kind of thing do you normally write for Weekend News? Does it have to be sentences, or could it be a picture?'

Kitty took up the pencil and curled herself over the page. She wrote two words in immaculate, tiny writing: 'No news.'

'I don't think that'll be enough, Kitten.'

She sighed and slid off her chair onto the carpet.

'Come on Kitty. Let's get this done and then I can read you a story if you like?'

She shook her head.

'Or how about... a bubble bath? *This* deep.' I gestured with my hands. It was really getting too late to be starting bubble baths, but I was getting desperate.

Kitty put her head to the side and considered.

She came and sat at her desk again, and rubbed out 'No news' laboriously, crumpling the paper. I straightened it out for her, brushing the rubbings away so the page was clear. Kitty took the pencil and held it in an iron grip.

'We went to a garden party. Frens from schole came. It

was sunny. Her made pavlover. At leest Her can cook nise caks. Then I went to hospitil after. I had a nise weekend.'

She slid off her chair again onto the ground, as though every ounce of her energy had been exhausted.

'Brilliant work! Well done, missy.'

I decided not to point out the spelling mistakes. Most teachers didn't take a strict line on spelling when children this age were doing creative writing. I'd check that with Mrs Robson next time I saw her.

'Just one teeny thing though. I think when you've written 'Her', that should be 'She'. So, "*She* made pavlova"... "*She* can cook"... Shall we change that so that it reads nicely? And then we'll be done and we can do your bath.'

There was an ominous silence. Then a noise that sounded like a groan but turned into a growl... it rose in pitch, second by second, to a full-blown scream of frustration. Kitty pounded her fists onto the carpet.

God, what had I done?

I crouched down beside her and placed my hand on her back. I held it there as she pounded, just to let her know that I was there.

The fist-banging increased in intensity. She picked up her mermaid doll and threw it against the wall with an ear-splitting shriek. Her face had flushed to deep pink, blotches standing out on her forehead, her features hard and distorted like a Halloween mask.

Then she pitched her body forward and began banging her own head against the carpet. As though she were trying to bang something right out of her head.

Without a word I pulled her in towards me so her head was banging against my thighs, hard skull against soft flesh.

Then screams gave way to sobbing – great rending sobs that sounded like her heart would split in two.

'I've got you,' I whispered. 'You're safe.'

In all my years, I'd never heard a child cry like that.

Slowly, slowly, the sobs subsided into sharp intakes of breath, the whole of her upper body shuddering with each one.

I stroked her damp hair back from her forehead, each stroke in time with the rise and fall of my breath until her breathing slowed. Her body softened and relaxed into me. I kept stroking, watching her shoulders rise and fall.

Rise and fall.

Rise and fall.

I've got you. I've got you.

Collecott Hall

I skipped dinner that night so that I could get ahead of the queue for the payphone, in its dingy cubicle next to the first floor toilets. I dialled home, nervously twisting the curly phone cord around my fingers. I only had thirty pence so it would have to be quick.

'Juliet! How are you, love?'

I closed my eyes so I could picture her face, lit up and smiling, creases softening the pearly skin around her eyes.

'Hello, Mum. Have I caught you in the middle of baking?' She always hosted the church sewing group on a Thursday morning.

'All done. I did a gingerbread and a lemon drizzle this time. And an extra gingerbread for you – I added an extra spoonful of golden syrup to make it squishy how you like it. I'll wrap it up and post it tomorrow.'

Something tight started to unwind, deep inside me. I pictured myself unwrapping the brown paper package with

Mum's neat square handwriting on the front, and the smell of ginger filling the air and making the dorm seem – just for a moment – as safe and warm as my own kitchen at home.

She began telling me about the curtains she was planning to sew for my room in time for me coming back for the holidays, and the material she'd ordered from Laura Ashley in Colchester – white with a pattern of tiny green flowers. Then without pausing for breath she launched into the latest about Dolly Landry, who helped with the church flowers but was 'really quite opinionated, darling, and not very easy to manage.'

Last time I'd been home for the weekend, Dolly had bought flowers from the market as usual, and made the displays for around the church, but then she'd cut all the heads off the flowers. She'd said it was to remember the children who'd died from AIDS in Africa. Mum had rescued the cut-off heads from the compost bin and floated them in bowls of water, placing them around the altar with candles. 'To remember the beauty of their short lives,' she'd said brightly, squeezing Dolly's shoulder to show that she cared about AIDS victims too. She *understood*. And the thing was – she did. I'd seen her wiping away a tear with the corner of her apron.

'How's school anyway?' she asked.

'Fine.' I paused for a moment, thinking of all the things I wished I could tell her.

But instead: 'I've started a healthy eating thing.'

'Ooh, not too healthy I hope. Can you still have gingerbread?'

My heart sank. They'd all smirk and swap secret glances if they saw me eating cake. I'd have to hide it at the back of a drawer and tear off pieces to eat under cover of darkness, munching it silently beneath my duvet.

I cleared my throat and adopted a jolly voice. 'Oh, it'll be fine. Gingerbread's practically a health food.'

'I couldn't agree more,' said Mum.

I sighed. 'I really miss...'

I really miss you. I'm so homesick.

'I miss Gypsy.'

'Oh, love. We miss him too. Did I tell you, they're expecting a litter of Labrador pups on the Maddon farm? I've been trying to convince Dad.'

'Oh!'

'Now just wait there a moment because your father's just here. He wants to say hello.'

And then I heard her calling over her shoulder: 'Graeme! Graeme! It's Piglet on the phone, come and say hello... yes... it's PIGLET!'

But then came the beeps – I'd run out of money.

'Mum... Mum!' But the line went dead.

The cosiness of home vanished. I sat in the darkness of the phone cubicle and put my head in my hands, wishing for a moment that I could press that same switch on myself and just... stop.

I opened the door, tears running down my face, and walked straight into Charlie McGrath, who'd been waiting outside to use the phone.

'Oh! Do you want to borrow some more change?'

I shook my head and wiped my nose with my sleeve. I didn't want to talk to Mum while I was crying.

'What's up?' he asked.

Charlie was in the year above, and I'd never really spoken to him. Well, not since he was eight, that serious little boy with neatly cut blonde hair, who I'd chased around my house in games of hide and seek. I remembered hiding in awkward places – under the hedge at the back of the garden – in Dad's greenhouse with its hairy hanging vines of tomato plants – to see how dishevelled I could make him.

And now he was... well, almost a man really. His hair had darkened to light brown and his body had widened out. I'd seen him wandering around the boarders' kitchen in the evenings making toast, wearing just a t-shirt, army camou-flage shorts, and bare feet, had noticed the sweep of the muscles that formed the shape of him beneath his skin. But there was a little-boy sweetness around his mouth and chin, and sometimes, when he looked worried or excited, his features were those of the eight-year-old Charlie I remembered.

'Oh, nothing. The phone's free.' I gestured behind me. 'You should probably get in before the queue starts.'

'I saw you coming out of Redwood's office earlier.' He had deep voice now, too – almost unrecognizable from the thin, high, 'Juliet, *please*...' when I had tried to get him to slide down the stairs headfirst or steal biscuits from the Sunday School box. 'Has he been giving you a hard time?'

'Oh,' I sighed. 'He was trying to help. He says I should try not to be such a victim. I have to stare everybody down like a brave wildebeest, or something.'

Charlie shook his head slowly. 'He's full of it, that one. Thinks the sun shines out of his own backside.'

I laughed, and then fell quiet, as a memory bubbled to the surface. 'You know, when I was really little and they talked about "the Lord" in church, I thought they meant him. I thought they meant Mr Redwood. I thought that "the coming of the Lord" meant that he was going to come and stay for one of his visits at Laurel Bank.'

'Mine eyes have seen the glory of the coming of the Lord,' said Charlie. 'Glory glory halleluuuuuuujah...'

'Teacher hit me with a ruler.'

'He's a dick,' said Charlie. Then he paused, and added, 'Do you want to see something?'

I followed him up the stairs that went up behind the dining hall, and along the science corridor, which was supposed to be out of bounds after lessons had finished for the day. We reached the fire escape door, and with a swift look over his shoulder, he pushed down the metal bar and kicked the door open.

I gasped. 'The alarm will go off!'

'It doesn't actually work,' he said.

It was cool in the stairwell, with an echoey, unused feel and the smell of plastic floors. He led the way up two flights until we came to a small door at the top.

'Are you coming in?'

'What's in there?'

'It's a storeroom.'

It was musty inside, and dark except for the light coming in the door behind us, and glints of light from the air vents along one wall.

There were a few boxes of stuff with names scrawled across them... 'Orpheus costumes', 'Alumni, 1965–1968', 'Alumni, 1969–1972'.

For a moment I imagined Mrs McCredie, the head-mistress, had shrunk them all down, all the former pupils, and put their wizened leathery bodies into these boxes. Perhaps these were the unfortunate ones who didn't make it into top universities.

At the far end, up against the wall was a bunch of old gym mats, half disintegrated, with foamy, crumbly stuff spilling out of the splits.

'This is sooooo cool,' I said, sitting down on one of the gym mats and letting myself fall back onto it with a smack.

Charlie settled down next to me, propping himself up on one elbow. His pushed-up shirt sleeve had untucked itself and the cuff was hanging loose about his forearm.

'Look through there,' he said, pointing to an air vent positioned low on the wall to the left of us.

I peered through, and made out a room lined with bookcases, with a large mahogany desk and a green velvet sofa. 'Is that Mr Redwood's office?' My voice rose incredulously.

'Yup,' said Charlie. 'The enemy's camp.'

'This... this is *risky*,' I said, impressed.

He shrugged.

'You're different,' I observed. 'From when you were eight.'

'Yeah, I guess. A lot of stuff happened after we moved away from Boxley Wood.'

'Your mum, you mean?' I blurted it out without thinking. I remembered Mum coming into the kitchen to say that Audrey had 'lost her battle', one day just before my eleventh birthday. 'What battle?' I'd said, not looking up from my history project. I thought she'd been ill in hospital with (put on a sad, low voice) bowel cancer. Not charging around battlefields like Joan of Arc. And I remembered Mum packing up a freezer box full of stews and pies and soups, making grim-faced Dad drive it all the way up the motorway to Yorkshire. And Dad returning, his grey hair sticking up at the side, his eyes red-rimmed from the long drive. Mum had pressed her mouth into a sympathetic line and patted him on the shoulder – two brisk, bouncy, 'let's get on with it' pats –

and gone to put on the kettle. He hadn't wanted tea, though, or the cottage pie she'd kept warm. I wanted to ask if I could have it, but it didn't seem respectful, somehow.

'Yeah,' said Charlie, pulling the sleeves of his shirt up over one forearm, and then the other, then clasping his hands so that they formed a V across his open knees. His right arm was just a few inches from mine – I could almost feel the heat coming off it. And I found that I wanted to run my fingers over it, over the sweep of fine brown hairs and down to the metal links of his watch strap. I wanted to drive my fingers underneath and feel the press of his skin, the pulse jumping in the underside of his wrist.

'What are you thinking?' he said.

I paused. 'You're very... dishevelled.'

'You have a dishevelling effect.' There was just a little bit of edge to his voice. And after a small silence he said gently, but with obvious curiosity: 'So you've been having a bit of a crap time recently?'

I sighed and curled myself upwards into a sitting position. Comfy as it was, I couldn't lie there like a piglet on a spit.

'Oh,' I sighed. 'I'm just not fitting in here. I'm trying to work out what's wrong with me.'

'There's nothing wrong with you,' he cut in. 'Nothing at all.'

I shook my head. 'I hate this place.'

It wasn't quite true. I *almost* loved this place. I loved the dark swathe of woods on the crest of the hill that you could see in the distance from my dorm window – I'd decided I'd go there if I ever committed a murder and had to bury the body. I loved the way the English oaks and the hedgerows bobbled the hills with green, like the pictures in a Mr Men book, and the fields stretching down to the railway line.

And I loved the trains. I loved them in summer, the way they shook the heavy air that hung over the yellow rapeseed, sending the crows wheeling up. I loved them in winter, the blur of yellow lit windows.

I loved the whump and rattle of the non-stop train, which didn't slow down for Durham station but hurtled all the way up the line to Newcastle, Berwick on Tweed, and on to Edinburgh Waverley. Which always made me think of Granny in her draughty tenement flat in Morningside, making scones and watering her window boxes.

And then there were the trains that went south. Towards home. Where the wood pigeons cooed in the green shade of the garden, and the air was so still that you could hear a dog barking half a mile away. Where the wide Suffolk skies were streaked with pink on summer evenings, and where bats played in the garden at dusk, swooping and disappearing under the eaves.

'I don't know who I am when I'm here.'

'You're Juliet.'

I sighed, scratching my arm under the itchy school shirt, and sat up, clasping my hands in front of me in a mirror image of his body position. A trickle of blood ran down the inner side of my left forearm. My right hand shot across to hide it, but Charlie's hand was on my arm, stopping me.

'What happened?'

I shook my head, pressed my lips together.

'So...' I racked my brains. 'Have you been doing a lot of rugby practice?'

He reached over, pulled gently on my hand until my arm was straight, and slowly pushed up the sleeve of my shirt, just an inch or so.

'It was in history... we were making, er, catapults.'

He just looked at my arm, at the ugly red line I'd scored into myself with the point of my compass that morning. I'd stood calmly before the grey-spotted mirror in the dorm bathroom, my pig skin coarsening in the chill that bounced off the white tiled walls, and I'd pushed the point deeper as first Susi, and then Pamela, had thumped on the door, telling me to hurry up.

He held my arm still, his face full of puzzlement.

'How long have you been doing this to yourself?'

I snatched my arm away, pulled a crumpled tissue out of my cardigan pocket and blotted away the blood.

'Juliet?' He closed his jaw tight and I could see the muscles flex in his cheek. I used to call it his 'Skeletor face' when we were little – it would appear when the bad boys stole my lunch money, or the teacher kept me in at break to write lines.

Wrenching down both sleeves, I turned away.

'Why did you do that?'

I could feel my lips tightening. Knitting into a firm line. All the words gluing together. I couldn't tell him about the rush of warmth I felt when the blood started to flow, the comforting familiarity of a pain that I understood and knew the shape of. Or the strange calm of sorting myself out with antiseptic and plasters afterwards.

'Juliet?'

I shrugged; a 'whatever' gesture, pushing him away.

'Do you want a crisp?' He pulled a scrumpled-up bag of Golden Wonder out of his blazer pocket.

Then I could speak again, and my voice came out in an urgent rush. 'I don't like salt and vinegar.'

'Okay, okay.' He raised his hands. 'I'll get cheese and onion next time then.'

Next time.

'Don't like cheese and onion either.' I turned to look at him and I breathed, once, twice, adjusting to the feeling. We might only be talking about crisp flavours, but I could look him long and straight in the eye and in that moment I wasn't some kind of wildebeest outcast. I wasn't even Piglet.

I was Juliet. Just... Juliet.

There was a shifting sensation, all through my body.

'Tell you what.' He clapped his hands together, and clasped them between his knees again. 'Meet me outside the sports hall, tomorrow at four.'

JULIET

The air inside the Old Coach House was thick with the fug of ground coffee. A group of women sat around two wooden tables pulled together, their chatter rising above the noise of the coffee machine – mums from the school gate. And Tasha was there, propped against the counter.

A couple of the mums looked up as I came in the door... Annabel, with her Barbour jacket and strident voice. And Mimi, a waif-like creature who wore a long drooping cardigan over her gym clothes and was mother of twins Robin and Tyler, the worst behaved boys in the class. I saw a fleeting recognition in their eyes before they returned their attention to the chat. But Tasha pulled out the chair nearest to her, moved a pile of jackets from it, and gestured to me to sit down.

'Hello,' I said. 'How are you? I was looking for Beth.'

'She's just out the back, I think. Sit down and I'll grab you a coffee.'

Obediently, I sat. I felt awkward – bulky and masculine in

my Scottish Rugby fleece, when the other yummy mummies were like an advert for Boden or some fancy brand of 'active wear'.

'Oh, thanks. Can I have a peppermint tea, please?'

She lingered for a moment, both hands holding the back of my chair as though she was settling me in. 'Coming right up, lovely.'

Mimi was saying, 'Oh, I'm just exhausted with it all. I was awake half the night, with it just going round and round in my head.'

I wondered what had happened... a health scare perhaps? I rearranged my face sympathetically, on the off chance that any of them should throw a glance my way.

'So what happened when you went back yesterday?' asked Annabel.

'I just thought that I needed to see it again – to touch it, you know, put my *hands* on it? To see if I got the feeling?' She shook her head sadly. 'But I just felt... nothing. I just didn't love it enough.'

Annabel nodded furiously.

I wondered what they were talking about... horses, perhaps? Or puppies? Annabel had two enormous Labradors – I'd seen them tied up outside next to a big bowl of water.

'It's so important to get one that you really like,' she was saying. 'I mean, you might have to live with it for decades. You'd have to look at it every day across the breakfast table. It'll just be a constant source of irritation if you choose the wrong one.'

Surely they weren't talking about... *husbands*?

'Oh, I know it's silly,' sighed Mimi. 'It's just a range cooker, but...'

There was a chorus of 'No, no, you're not silly'.

'It is a bit silly,' said one of the others – a small, pretty woman called Shami. She didn't have children at the school, but she ran an after-school yoga class which some of the children in Kitty's year attended.

Silence fell on the group. Annabel's left eyebrow shot up beneath the line of her fringe. Mimi's cheeks reddened and she pressed her mouth into a thin line.

Tasha swooped in with my tea, and then moved quickly to place a hand on Shami's shoulder – in warning, or solidarity, I wasn't sure which.

'First world problems, eh?' she said with a winning smile. 'I spent three hours online last night looking at cushions to match our new rug!'

And everything was okay again. The mums laughed and rolled their eyes.

'What are we like,' murmured Mimi.

Beth appeared behind me. 'Juliet. Were you looking for me?'

I stood up. 'Could we have a word? It's about Kitty.'

'Of course. Come through the back.'

I followed her through.

'I'm just trying to sort out some invoices. The bloody computer is ancient, keeps grinding to a halt. This is the fourth time today I've had to reboot.' She pulled out a sheet of passwords from an overflowing desk drawer and typed one in. 'Finally.'

'This is quite some place you have. It's beautiful.'

She sat back and smiled, sliding her blonde hair into a ponytail shape and then letting it go. She'd had her highlights redone, I noticed. 'Thank you. It's always been my dream to open a place like this.'

'I'm sorry to bother you at work. It's just that I wanted to have a word when Kitty wasn't around. The thing is, she got extremely upset last night, when you were out.'

'Oh?

I studied her face, her cobalt blue eyes – surely they were coloured contact lenses? – and her Marilyn Monroe mole. And her overlapping front teeth, pushing her upper lip out just slightly. I wondered why she hadn't had them straightened, when she was so perfectly groomed in all other ways.

'It started when I pointed out a mistake in her Weekend News. But she was so upset, trying to bash her head against the floor. It was like she was trying to hurt herself. I wanted to ask you how you normally deal with tantrums, so we can make sure we're on the same page. Because it's really important to have a consistent approach.'

Beth frowned. 'Kitty doesn't do tantrums. She can be stubborn, of course. She'll pretend she hasn't heard you. But tantrums – no. That's not her style.'

A six-year-old who'd never had a tantrum?

'What, never? Even when she was a toddler?'

Beth shrugged the question away. 'Maybe she was acting up because she's still feeling unwell from her infection.'

'Maybe. Listen, Beth, I was wondering if you'd ever thought of trying sign language with Kitty?'

A blank look.

'It just occurred to me that the tantrum might have been due to frustration, you know, because she can't express herself.'

'She's got her notebook.'

'Yes, but for some reason she's not keen on the notebook. I wondered if it's because it's not spontaneous. It slows her down. I just wondered if she had a few basic signs, then she could have conversations – and contribute to them – in real time.'

'It's *so* good of you to think about all this, Juliet,' said Beth, plastering a smile on her face. 'You've no idea how much I appreciate it. But Frank and I have discussed this before. It wouldn't be practical for her to use sign language when nobody else at the school would understand it. And we don't use it at home, obviously.'

I cleared my throat. 'Have you talked to the school about it, though? Because some of the teachers may have a basic level of sign language. And I know a little bit myself... Harry used to find –'

'Using sign language would only mark her out as different from the other children. And our goal for Kitty is *integration*. For her to be the same as everyone else.'

Kitty would never be the same as everyone else. Never.

'And also, if people start communicating with her in sign language, she won't be motivated to use her voice, will she?' Beth smiled, as though I were a child who'd said something silly. 'A positive attitude, Juliet – that's what's needed here. In my book, if you believe in something strongly enough, it will happen. We need to encourage that attitude in Kitty, too. It's all too easy to become stuck in self-limiting behaviour.'

Irritation flared. 'Positive thinking' had been one of Eddie's mantras. He'd found me once, crying in the bathroom after a negative pregnancy test. 'You'll never get pregnant if you wallow in negativity,' he'd said, pulling me up off the floor. 'Believe it will happen, and it will.'

Screw that.

'Look, I was speaking to Charlie McGrath when we were at the hospital. He said that if you bring Kitty in to the surgery, he can check what's going on with the referral to speech therapy.'

Beth inhaled slowly. Her nostrils flared and contracted again.

'How kind of him. Yes, that's a good idea. I'll check my diary later today and I'll make an appointment. It's usually Doctor Atkinson we see, so I'll probably stick with her.' She gave a tight-lipped smile. 'If that's okay with you, Juliet.'

I walked out of the Old Coach House, waving to the yummy mummies, although none of them noticed me except Tasha, who waved, and then pointed to the sole of her shoe and then at me.

I smiled vaguely, only realising when I got to the car that there was something stuck to the bottom of my shoe. My heart sank. Had I been trailing toilet roll around with me all morning?

But it was a Post-it note. It said:

BEK1971xmpw

Was it a password for something? I peeled it off and opened the car door again, to go and give it back to Beth. But something made me change my mind – maybe I didn't want to walk past the yummy mummies again, or maybe it was some other instinct, flashing across my mind like a shadow, there and gone before I could catch what it was. I don't know. But I stuck the Post-it in the pocket of my fleece.

Collecott Hall

I had thought Charlie wanted to meet me by the sports hall so that he could suggest some kind of exercise routine to get me in shape. So that I could shed my Piglet skin and I wouldn't have to hurt myself anymore. But he led me along a path and down some steps through the woods until we came out near a big house, set back against the trees. It had its own garden, surrounded by a wooden fence painted in rainbow colours.

'The nursery?'

'Yep,' said Charlie. 'I did some volunteering here for my Duke of Edinburgh last year. They're always looking for helpers.'

A plump woman in an apron came bustling up the path, holding a little boy by the hand. With her rosy cheeks and her light brown hair pushed back in an Alice band, she reminded me of Mum. 'Well come in, if you're coming,' she scolded. 'Don't just *hover*.'

She held the door open and ushered us into a different world, a world filled with the smell of cakes baking, and the sticky smell of plasticine, and hands washed in soft baby soap.

'Are you wanting to volunteer?' asked the woman. 'Best go and speak to Nanny Parker then.'

'Nanny Parker?' I whispered to Charlie, trying not to laugh.

'All the staff are called Nanny,' he said. 'You'll be Nanny Hazelwood if you work here.' He raised an eyebrow, his mouth pressed into a smile that was trying not to be a smile.

'Look!' I whispered, as we passed an open door which had coloured lettering on it: 'The Rainbow Room'. It was a large, sunlit room with a faded red Persian rug covering most of the floor. Near the window, six children were sitting cross-legged around a cherrywood upright piano, faces bright with expectation. A member of staff was settling her amble behind onto the piano stool, arranging music on the stand.

'That's Nanny Pratt,' whispered Charlie.

A laugh began to erupt in my throat but then Charlie poked me in the arm – a tall woman was coming towards us.

'Marjorie Parker,' she said. 'Charlie, are you going to introduce me to your friend? And then unless I'm much mistaken, we'll need some helpers for music time.'

'Moothic time?' cried one of the little girls, looking over at me and waving both hands.

I went over and crouched down beside her. 'Which of the instruments do you like best?' I asked it as though it was a burning question, one I'd always wanted to know the answer to. And in that moment, it was – nothing seemed more important. 'The tambourine? The bells? The shakers?'

She jiggled up and down. 'Thakers.'

'Can you show me what to do?'

She reached out a hand, a soft little star of a hand, and I took it in mine.

I looked round at Charlie to see if he knew it, that he'd given me the best present in the world. He just smiled and looked away.

We dawdled on the way back to school – I was in no hurry to return. I pointed out a rough little path that led through the woods to the north of the main drive.

'I've always wanted to go down there,' I said. 'I think it must lead down to that pond or lake or whatever it is. I can see it sometimes from my dorm window, if I lean really far out.' I loved the way the water glinted on sunny days.

'We can get down, but it's very overgrown. You do know it's strictly out of bounds, the lake?' He frowned, and he was eight-year-old Charlie again.

I shrugged. Apparently a boy had drowned there in the 1970s. He'd been trying to run away from school in the middle of the night and he'd missed his footing in the dark. We weren't supposed to talk about it. But Charlie and I seemed to be making our way through the woods anyway. He led the way, holding the branches to stop them pinging back on me, parting bracken and nettles with a stout stick where the path grew so narrow as to almost disappear, until, just when I was beginning to think we were completely lost, we emerged from the trees to see the lake some fifty feet below us. We half-walked, half-slid down the path, causing a bit of a landslide down the sandy bank.

'Here it is,' said Charlie, carefully casual but proud, like it was his own private lake.

On the other side of the water was a thin coppice of trees

and a low stone wall, and beyond that, a single track road, cut into the deepest part of the valley.

'Where did the boy fall in?' I asked.

'Not sure,' said Charlie. 'Maybe he fell from that bank over by the trees – see that steep bit where the tree roots are sticking out? The water's really deep over there – see how dark it is? Do you want to go and throw some stones in?'

'Maybe later,' I said. 'Let's sit down here for a bit. It's almost like a beach.'

We spread our blazers on the sandy gravel and lay down on them.

'We could escape,' he said. 'Just leave this place and never come back.'

It was funny, because I wasn't sure I *wanted* to escape, now that I had found the nursery... and this. This deep, settling sensation that came over me when I was with Charlie. 'Where would you go, if you could go anywhere?'

He lay there, staring up at the sky, thinking. 'I'd like to see the Amazon rainforest before it's all gone. Or Spitzbergen – to see the polar bears and the northern lights. Or a scientific expedition to Antarctica. I'd like to go right to the end of the world. What about you?'

'I'd probably just go home.'

He nodded. He seemed to understand.

'I miss my mum so much,' I whispered. 'Oh – I'm sorry. I'm really sorry.'

'It's okay,' he said.

'It's not okay,' I wailed, sitting up and waving my hands around. 'How can I complain about missing my mum when you'll never see yours again?'

'I *do* see her,' he said with a slow blink.

'What do you mean?'

He lay still for a while, his chest rising and falling with his breath.

'There was this day,' he said eventually. 'This perfect day. It was just before she got ill. We went to Dedham Vale to see the heavy horse centre. They were cutting the corn and the sun made the fields all golden. She was so happy because they had Battenberg cake in the café. She ordered some to have with her tea, and ten pieces to take away, and the lady behind the counter made this cross face. Mum started to giggle and couldn't stop – she said the lady looked like one of the horses. When I miss her at night, I go back there. I sit in the café with her and watch her laughing.'

His face had gone red.

'I remember going to that horse centre with school,' I said. 'And I remember Mum making Battenberg cake and sending it up to Yorkshire. When your mum was... when she was poorly.'

He nodded. 'It used to cheer her up.'

'She was really cool, your mum,' I said, because weren't you supposed to say nice things about people who'd died? 'I really liked her drawings. She made science seem really interesting.'

She'd been an illustrator of science textbooks – pictures showing the water cycle, the circulatory system, or the forces in an atom. Some of her illustrations had been framed by Charlie's father, and hung on the walls of their house. My mother had once said, 'I never knew a man so much in love with his wife.'

'I don't think my mum's happy,' I blurted out.

'Why?' he said, frowning.

'Oh, nothing.'

'What?'

I sighed. 'Well, one day in the summer holidays, she'd been doing the church flowers, and I had to come and find her, because Daddy didn't know the oven temperature for the roast beef. I ran through the bluebell woods and went in the back door of the church – you know, the one by the little porch where the sink is, where they keep all the green foamy stuff for the flower arrangements.'

'Oasis,' he said, nodding.

'So she didn't hear me come in. But she was in there all alone, sitting in one of the pews near the front, with a bucket of flowers on the floor next to her. She was praying. Or, I think she was. But she had her face in her hands. And her shoulders were shaking.'

I looked at him, to check whether he seemed shocked, but he didn't.

'And I just got this terrible feeling. Like something was wrong. Badly wrong. You don't think she's ill, do you?' I remembered Charlie's mum, with her face gone all thin, and her headscarf, and my heart squeezed.

'Have you asked her?'

I shook my head. It wasn't that simple with Mum.

'We don't really talk about sad things.'

'Well I'm sure she's not ill. Maybe she was sad about something else.'

'Maybe. She's been really sad since Gypsy died.'

Charlie's face fell. 'Oh no – Gypsy died?'

'Yeah. He died at Easter. Dad was... God, Charlie, Dad was devastated. He wouldn't come out of his room. Mr Redwood had to bury him in the garden.'

'Huh?' Charlie propped himself up on an elbow.

'I mean, Mr Redwood had to bury Gypsy,' I explained quickly. 'Not that Mr Redwood had to bury Dad.'

Charlie snorted.

'He was staying with us...' I started giggling. 'For one of the charity meetings.'

I poked Charlie, whose face had gone red again with the effort of trying not to laugh out loud.

'Mine eyes have seen the glory of the coming of the Lord,' I whispered.

He gave a shout of laughter.

I lay back, pleased with myself.

'You should phone your mum tonight, and tell her about the nursery,' said Charlie. 'That'll cheer her up.'

He got it – he got that I'd found my 'thing'.

We lay back down on our blazers and stared up at the sky, our arms flung out to the sides and our hands almost touching, like snow angels in the weak October sun.

14

LYNNE

Dearest Juliet,

I hope so much that you are well, darling. I must say I think about you all the time, these days. I hope you are enjoying the autumn colours and are getting out for some good walks. Walking does one so much good, I find.

I thought that you might like the gloves I've enclosed. I got out my knitting bag the other night and decided I would try and knit some for you, now that I've got all this time on my hands. But I'd forgotten how fiddly it is with that fine wool, and my fingers weren't up the job I'm afraid. But today I was going past that little gift shop in Morningside, and what do you think – these gloves were right there in the window display! They're just like those pink and white striped ones you used to love when you were little. You used to wear them with that nice sweatshirt with the pink and white stripes. That was from Tammy Girl – we got it in the sales. Do you remember – that was the time Daddy came round the shops with us, carrying our bags, because I'd sprained my wrist? He took us for tea and cake afterwards, to that tearoom next to the art gallery. You cried because you accidentally ordered a cheese scone instead of a plain one, and then I spilled my tea all over my new coat. Anyway, the gloves. I suppose they'll get grubby quickly but you can always wash them. You could stick them in the machine with some Woolite, darling.

Lots of love,

Mum xxxx

15

JULIET

I held the soft gloves up to my cheek and closed my eyes. Mum's letter had arrived over a week late. Her solicitor – full of apologies – admitted she'd forgotten to make a note on the file about my change of address. Luckily, Eddie had sent it on with some paperwork about the divorce. He wanted me to agree that his flat shouldn't be included in the list of assets to be split between us, as he'd paid for it with an inheritance from his gran. I was also supposed to make a list of my own assets. Well, that would take all of about thirty seconds. The divorce should be a straightforward process, his lawyer had said, since there were no children of the marriage.

No children, apart from the nameless baby whose heart-beat I had seen, just once, a flicker on a grainy scan. Who should have been a summer baby, but who had arrived in the world – and left – in a rush of bloody fluid on New Year's Day.

But there was a basketful of Kitty's clothes that needed ironing – including her new much-loved, pink-checked pyjamas. I could put on Radio 4 in the background and banish all thoughts of solicitors, concentrating only on the gentle hiss of the iron and the smell of warm cotton filling the kitchen.

When I got up to fetch the basket from the utility room, I saw Kitty's lunchbox sitting on the worktop by the fridge. Earlier that morning, she'd ignored my requests for her to get her school uniform on, and to brush her teeth, and in the rush to get out the door the lunchbox had been forgotten. It was surprisingly hard to reason with a child who wouldn't – couldn't – answer back. And I couldn't forcibly pull off her pyjamas, or shove protesting feet into shoes like an impatient mother might have done.

By the time I arrived at the school it was morning break, and I could hear the children shouting and playing from two streets away. But Kitty – I scanned around for her as soon as I came within sight of the playground – was sitting on her own on a bench set back against the wall, looking down at her hands, her shoulders hunched in like she was trying to make herself disappear.

I keyed the code into the gate and was met by the teacher on playground duty – Miss Green, according to her lanyard.

'Kitty's lunchbox. Thank you. I shall make sure she gets it.' She stood with her hand on the gate, indicating with her fixed smile that I was supposed to leave now.

'What's wrong with Kitty? She's over there. I think she's upset.'

'Is she?' said Miss Green, glancing over. 'She was fine a minute ago.'

'I'll just go over and say hello,' I said, walking off before the teacher could stop me.

I waved to Kitty, who glanced up briefly before casting her eyes down to study her shoes. As I got closer I saw a laminated sheet of A4 stuck to the brick wall behind the bench.

The words 'Friendship Bench' were emblazoned on it in glittery pen, and instructions were written below.

IF YOU NEED SOMEONE TO PLAY WITH, DON'T WORRY, JUST COME TO THE FRIENDSHIP BENCH!!

IF YOU SEE SOMEONE WAITING AT THE FRIENDSHIP BENCH, INVITE THEM TO JOIN YOUR GAME!!

I turned and walked back to Miss Green.

'How does the friendship bench work?' I demanded.

'Oh. That sign's been there for ages,' she said.

'And...?'

'Well, it was an idea the children came up at their little social committee. They used it a bit to begin with, but nobody really uses it now.'

'Kitty is using it.'

'Is she?' Miss Green looked disinterested.

'Can't you suggest to some of the other children that they go and play with her?'

'We try not to micro-manage playground politics. Not unless there's actual violence,' she added as an afterthought. 'And maybe it'll encourage Kitty to speak, eh? She might ask the other children to play, if she wants to badly enough.'

'I know Kitty's condition can be a tricky thing to understand,' I said, trying to keep my voice neutral, because perhaps it wasn't this woman's fault that she was ignorant. 'But it's not that she doesn't want to speak. She simply can't. She can't make her mouth form the words. It's the condition, you see – the sympathetic nervous system takes over when they're expected to speak, and it causes a 'freeze' response that they have no control over.'

I'd been reading about selective and progressive mutism, poring over articles late into the night as I lay in my bed under the eaves in the Forget-Me-Not Room.

The teacher pushed her lips into a pout. 'She has her notebook, though? She could approach the other children that way.'

I pictured Kitty, notebook held in a wavering hand, trying to edge her way into one group of noisy kids after another.

'Are you saying she sits on that bench every playtime?'

'Sometimes Anya and Libby play with her, but they're over on the monkey bars today. And Cameron McGrath – I've seen him sitting with her a couple of times. He's not got a lot to say for himself either, though. We'll be going in soon anyway. They've got music after break.'

I went over to Kitty and crouched down in front of her.

'I brought in your lunchbox, Kitten. I've given it to Miss Green.'

She swung her feet, shoes scuffing against the asphalt.

'Are you feeling okay today?'

She gave a tight little nod.

'Well, I've got to go now. You've got music in a minute.' My voice was falsely bright and suddenly I hated it.

'But listen, Kitty. We'll sort this, okay? You and me, we'll sort this.'

She didn't even look up. She didn't think anybody could sort this.

I made myself walk away. With every step further away from her, there was a an aching pull in my chest as though there was an invisible string between us, and I was stretching it tighter and tighter.

You're only ever as happy as your unhappiest child.

I shook my head to dislodge the thought. It wasn't supposed to apply to me.

It wasn't supposed to apply to me, because Kitty wasn't my child.

LATER THAT EVENING, after tea, Kitty did one of her disappearing acts. One minute she was helping me to clear the table, and the next she'd gone. I switched off the radio and went to look for her.

'Kitty?' I stopped in the hallway. The tick of the clock on the hall sideboard sounded too loud. It seemed to go right through my head.

I checked the living room... the study... her bedroom. At first I thought she wasn't in there, but then I saw that she was sitting on the floor in the space between her doll's house and her wardrobe. She was sitting there in her pink-checked pyjamas, legs crossed, staring at a blank stretch of wall. The mermaid doll lay on its back beside her, its sequinned fishtail glinting in the light.

'Oh, there you are! Are you playing with your doll's house?' My voice sounded bright and false. She clearly wasn't playing. I had the uncanny notion that she wasn't actually there at all, that her still little body was quite empty. That it was just me and the mermaid in the room.

'Kitten? Are you okay?'

I sat down on the floor. I noticed that her fists were clenched and I took one of her hands and held it gently. She swallowed, blinked... She was back.

'I had a chat with Mrs Robson today at home time,' I said. 'I thought that if nobody really uses the Friendship Bench these days, we could make it into another kind of bench. I thought we could think of some ideas, and you could take them to the pupil social committee on Friday.'

Kitty didn't react.

'I've been on committees before,' I lied. 'What people often do is write a briefing paper and hand it out at the meeting so the committee can decide on something.'

She twisted her lip between her teeth.

'And I've got some ideas. Shall we brainstorm?'

I got a piece of paper and a pencil from Kitty's desk and I wrote down: 'Reading bench'.

'So here's my idea. Somebody could be the Reading Bench Rep – or people could take it in turns – and each day they could bring some books out from the library, and if anyone was a bit tired, or just wanted to have some quiet time, they could read.'

Kitty shuffled round and knelt over the paper, reading what I'd written down.

'Weather could be a bit of an issue. But they could always move the bench to under the covered area. You know, the bit where you play where it rains?'

She nodded.

'So do you have any other ideas?'

She took the pencil and wrote.

JIGSAW BENCH

'Wow!' I said. 'That's even better. I know – people could bring in jigsaws from home that they don't use any more, and you could make a whole box of them. You could have a Jigsaw Rep who could bring the box out each day.'

Kitty's face broke into a shy smile.

'Right. Let's get this proposal written, missy. We've got half an hour till bath time. That should do it. Where are your felt pens? We can do some pictures to show what we mean.'

IT WAS ONLY a small detour to walk home from the shops past the school. It was a sunny day, and kids were running about wild. But under the shade of the covered area, half a dozen kids were sitting on the ground on squares of carpet, poring over jigsaws. Kitty and Cameron had pulled two carpet squares together and they were kneeling forward side by side, resting on their elbows, their bottoms sticking up in the air. A pile of small jigsaw pieces lay there in front of them. Cameron was holding the lid of the box, a quizzical expression on his face, and Kitty was pointing to some detail in the top left-hand corner.

I hurried on before Kitty could see me. She didn't need me there.

As I walked home, I looked out over the quiet village scene that was the same as ever... the same as this morning when I'd dropped Kitty off. The same – very nearly – as it had been when I'd walked this way to school myself. The sun still shone, a white disc behind a pearly bank of cloud. The leaves still skittered along the pavement. And yet everything was different now – a mirror image world where nothing was quite the same.

I wasn't supposed to love Kitty like this. She wasn't mine.

And yet, it had happened. I might as well have pulled my own heart out of my chest and torn it in two.

Because somewhere in the future, there was a day when I would have to say goodbye to Kitty. When Beth no longer needed me, or had found out that I'd lied about Laurel Bank.

That day might be years away, or it might be next week. There might be promises to keep in touch, if it ended well. I might receive Christmas cards for a few years, with Kitty's signature scrawled in by Beth. Or if I was lucky they might ask me to babysit or come for coffee occasionally. Would I stay in Boxley Wood, live here just to wait for an invitation that might never come?

The only way to do this was to forget about me. I could forget about me, and concentrate on building her up, bit by bit, every day, trying to get her to a place where she could talk and laugh, where she could make friends and feel happy in her own skin. To a place where she wouldn't need me any more.

16

BETH

Kitty had gone down for her nap without a fuss after lunch, and Beth hadn't even needed to swallow one of her pills to take the edge off the afternoon. Standing at the window of the nursery, shutters flung wide, she looked out over the rooftops to the shore of the lake far below and reflected that Vevey was, by any standards, a beautiful place to live.

But Beth had always thought the town had a strange, restless feel to it. Like it was a stop on a trainline, a place that you passed by on the way to somewhere else. Not somewhere to settle. Sometimes she wondered if it had really been necessary to run away quite so far, or for such a long time. It was true that her ex, Rick, had found out where they lived in Colchester, and had come banging on the door one night, just before Kitty was due to arrive. Beth had hidden upstairs, in the built-in wardrobe in the bedroom, holding her face in her two shaking hands, remembering their last encounter and a mouthful of broken teeth, spitting them out into the sink afterwards. Frank had dealt with him 'accordingly', he'd said – no point calling the police, not for that sort of scum. You had to speak in a language they would understand.

He was her knight in shining armour, she supposed. But he'd sneered at her afterwards, when she wouldn't come out of the wardrobe. She couldn't tell him that she'd wet herself, that it had gone all over the Mulberry handbag he'd bought her for Christmas.

He'd apologized, afterwards, and brought her flowers. And he'd said all this was for her – the running away. He was going to make a new life for Beth and her little 'whoops baby', as he liked to refer to Kitty (as if the 'whoops' had all been down to Beth and had nothing to do with him). He was going to keep them safe. And he'd sorted everything in a matter of days. His brother had said they could stay in his summer house in Vevey, while he was away working for the UN in New York. And Frank could work anywhere, now that he'd set up his life coaching business and was writing his Dr Seigler articles. But there'd been whispers about problems with that charity he was involved in. She knew something had gone wrong. Sometimes she got the sense that it suited *him* to get away.

Frank said they couldn't tell anyone where they'd gone, or there was no point in doing it at all. Not that she had anybody to tell. Frank kept 'popping back' to the UK to see his life coaching clients – the ones who paid extra for face-to-face sessions. His trips had got more frequent, in the two years since they'd been here. Sometimes Beth wondered if he was seeing *her*. She wasn't sure why, just a certain look in his eye when he got back, a tightness in his movements. It should have broken her heart, to think of it, but these days it was difficult to feel anything much at all.

Even her walks with Kitty, down on the lake shore,

seemed tiring and tedious these days. 'Look for stones, Mama,' Kitty would say, and Beth would plaster on her 'nice Mummy' face and say, 'How about this one?' When all she really wanted to do was to lie down on the pebbly beach, close her eyes, and let the glass-green water lap over her, right over her mouth and her nose and her eyes, until it washed all of her thoughts out of her head.

In fact, one night last week – she could *never* tell anybody this, *never* – she'd stood over Kitty's cot-bed as she slept, holding a kitchen knife, imagining slicing it across her throat, where her pulse jumped under the soft white skin. She'd wanted to see if the thought of it would shock her cold lump of a heart into warm-blooded life.

Frank would be royally pissed off if he knew she was thinking of contacting the social work, back in Doncaster, to ask if they had any information about her father. And she wasn't about to tell him, she wasn't stupid. But she'd imagined herself justifying it to him – explaining how it felt to have been torn away from England, from her past, like a plant from its roots. How there was nothing to anchor her now – no family, no friends, nobody to see except Kitty, who only spoke a few words, and Rosa, who didn't even speak English. It made total sense that she'd want to find her dad.

She wasn't sure whether she loved him or hated him. She only knew that when she thought about him, she felt a flicker inside of *something*. And something, she thought, was better than nothing.

Ange, the mournful social worker from back then, had always said that 'they'd looked at all the options', but it 'wasn't possible' for her father to look after her after her mum got ill and then died. She probably didn't know where he was either.

He'd come back home, after his first season on *Ocean Glory*, and had stayed for the afternoon. He'd looked the same but also different, with a tan that was too bright for Doncaster in October, and a smile that creased the skin around his eyes, but didn't quite make them sparkle. He'd put on a Chuck Berry tape, clicking it into the cassette player and whirring it back to the start, and he'd held out his hand and asked her in a posh voice if she would give him the honour of a dance. They'd jived around the living room, him in his white chinos and a Hawaiian shirt, and Beth in her school uniform with her socks fallen down around the ankles. Feet flying everywhere, she'd knocked the sailor jug off the fire-surround with an ominous clunk. It hadn't broken, though – Daddy had winked and put it back on there, holding his finger up to his lips.

She'd asked if he was coming back soon, and he'd said he was off to the West Indies for the winter season – the lonely old ladies needed him to dance with them in the evenings and keep them company. He would send her a postcard, though.

At first the postcards had come every few weeks, then there was a gap of a few months, and then they stopped alto-gether. It had worried her greatly, when she went to live with Viv, that Dad wouldn't know where to send his postcards.

She'd always been too embarrassed to ask Ange, outright, why they couldn't just find out which ship Daddy was on and make him come home and look after her. Surely they could just try a bit harder to find him? She imagined Ange, rowing around the Bahamas in a little boat, pulling on the oars with all her might, a grim expression on her face as she tried to catch up with Daddy's ship. The world wasn't that big, there couldn't be so many cruise ships. And only a handful of gentleman dance hosts on each one, surely? There couldn't be that many lonely old ladies that needed dancing with. And she was lonely now too.

Someone shouted out, in the street below, and a horn blared. Kitty made a little fussing noise and kicked her legs, but she didn't wake, thank goodness. Beth drew the shutters closed and tiptoed out of the room. It wasn't that she didn't want to spend time with her daughter, it was just that she was tired. So tired.

As she sank down onto her own bed for a rest, it occurred to her that it had been easier for her, as a child, to assume that they couldn't find Daddy than to face the alternative. Because what if they'd managed to find him and he hadn't wanted her? What then?

17

JULIET

This time the tantrum kicked off after school, while I was making Kitty her fishfingers and trying to help with her homework at the same time.

I hadn't had much time to get things sorted while Kitty was at school. Before leaving for the Old Coach House this morning, Beth had asked me to phone her broadband provider about a fault on the line – which had resulted in three half-hour-long phone calls – as well as taking her dry cleaning to a specialist place on the other side of Sudbury. Not to mention changing and laundering all the bed linen in the house and 'giving the surfaces a quick going over' as she thought the house 'smelled icky'.

She was taking the piss. That was what I'd muttered to myself anyway, as I'd pummelled her pillows into fresh pillowcases and chucked them back onto her super-king-sized bed. But this fitted in with my strategy – to make myself indispensible. I had even, grudgingly, spritzed her bed linen with the 'Sleepy Heads' lavender and chamomile spray that I'd bought for Kitty.

So I hadn't had time to make the lasagne that I'd promised Kitty, and her face had darkened when I'd mentioned fishfingers. A strange thought entered my mind – that she didn't look *cross* exactly... but scared. But I dismissed it. How could anybody be scared of a fishfinger?

'I'll make lasagne tomorrow,' I promised. 'Now let's see what you've got for homework.'

With a sigh, she dragged a paper booklet from her schoolbag.

'All About Me.'

'Oh, this is fun,' I said. 'You have to make a timeline about yourself, starting with when you were born. You need to write something about each year of your life so far. And the first thing to do is to find a photo of yourself when you were a baby.'

Kitty looked unimpressed.

'Where do you keep all the family photos?' I persisted. 'Can you show me?'

Kitty shrugged.

The oven was up to temperature. I clattered some fishfingers onto the grill pan and slid them in to heat.

'Beans too? Or just ketchup and peas?'

Silence.

'Aren't there some photos of you in the living room? Let's go and see those.' I held out my hand and she came through to the living room with me.

'Yes, you see. Look at these.' I waved my hand towards the triptych of arty, black and white photographs above the fireplace, all of Beth with a newborn Kitty held up close against her face.

'I can take a picture of one of these on my phone and we can print it off.'

Silence from Kitty.

'Oh, and look, here are some more of when you are a bit bigger. We can use these for the later bits of the timeline.'

On the coffee table stood a silver-framed photo of Kitty frowning in her school uniform against the front hedge, and one of her standing alongside a snowman with Beth, who was smiling and glossy-lipped beneath her oversized pom-pom hat.

I held my phone up close to one of the photos in the triptych.

'Oh... that's funny. This one's scratched.' I moved to the side, so that the glass caught the light in a different way. 'Hmm.'

It looked as though someone had taken something sharp – scissors, perhaps, or even the point of a compass – and scored a cross over the baby's face, in each of the three pictures, and then gone over it again and again.

Who had done this? With a creeping feeling, I wondered if it had been Kitty herself. Maybe it wasn't enough for her to be silent. Maybe she wanted to erase her image too – going right back to her baby self.

Hadn't I wanted to do the same thing to myself, standing in front of the mirror in the school bathroom?

'Kitty?'

I turned and she was lying on the floor, face down. Quiet.

Slowly, I knelt down beside her and placed a hand on her back. She writhed away from my touch with a strangled cry.

She knelt up suddenly and lunged for the photo of herself in her school uniform, which I snatched away just in time. She seized the other photo and threw it towards the marble fireplace, but it just landed with a dull chink on the white hearth rug.

She hurtled towards me with an ear-splitting scream, her fists beating down on my arms as I held them across my chest to defend myself.

'Kitty!'

She clawed at her own skin, gouging three red scratches onto the inside of her forearm. I took hold of her wrists and told her I couldn't let her do that. She bared her teeth like she wanted to bite. As she kicked and struggled, I managed to pull her body close against mine. I remembered the last tantrum in her bedroom and I held her tight.

'I won't let you go,' I said. 'I've got you and I'm not letting go.'

She sobbed in my arms, her wails rising up higher in pitch, and I wondered what she would be shouting at me if she only had the words.

The clock on the wall ticked onwards... four minutes... five. Surely she'd tire herself out soon.

Then she twisted her head and shoulders round and she looked at me.

Eye contact. For the very first time. It blazed between us for a single second before she turned and buried her face in my lap.

That's when I realised. Her tantrum had been an act of trust.

I stroked the back of her head, feeling the shape of her skull beneath my fingers. I closed my eyes and visualised calming neurochemicals flooding through her brain, soothing angry red neurons. The crying softened to a whimper and then stopped. I sat there stroking, stroking, until I smelt something... was that burning? Oh God, the fishfingers. A second later came the shriek of the smoke alarm. I jumped up and ran to the kitchen.

THAT NIGHT I dreamed about babies – rows of them, eerily silent in identical cots, in some kind of institution. One of them was mine, but I couldn't remember which. I unwrapped them from their blankets one by one, but the blankets turned into bandages, soiled and blood-stained, unravelling and unravelling to reveal... nothing. Empty cots. But there was crying coming from somewhere.

I'm coming. I'm coming...

I woke with my heart bursting in my chest, my jaw clenched tight, sweat soaking the sheets. I lay still, staring into the dark, waiting for my heart to slow, for my breathing to become regular again.

But *was* that crying? I heard it again – a high pitched sound like a little mew.

Kitty.

I was out of bed in an instant.

A slant of light fell across the hall carpet from her bedroom door, which was open just an inch or so. She was fast asleep, her cheek flushed against the pillow. I noted with satisfaction that she hadn't turned on the ceiling light – she seemed to like the soft light from the toadstool fairy-house lamp that I'd ordered for her online. It was even better than the one I'd had when I was little, and it played a twinkly lullaby if you pressed a button.

Was the crying sound coming from downstairs?

I found Beth in the kitchen, sitting at the table in her dressing gown. She held a crumpled tissue in one hand and a glass tumbler in the other, half-filled with amber liquid. Her dressing gown had a white mark on the front, like dried toothpaste.

I shrank back into the doorway. 'Oh! I'm sorry. I didn't mean to disturb you. I heard someone and I thought it might be Kitty.'

She lifted the glass off the table. 'Want one?'

'No thanks.'

She looked at me grumpily. 'Suit yourself.'

I hadn't seen Beth like this before, with her 'perfect' mask off.

'Can't sleep?' I edged forward and perched on the edge of a kitchen chair. I wondered if Beth had noticed that the kitchen still smelt of burnt fish, despite my best efforts to get rid of the smell before she got home.

She shook her head. She looked like a much older woman without her make-up, her eyes rheumy, the lashes sparse and colourless.

So much for the 'Sleepy Head' spray – I wouldn't waste it on her next time.

'I heard Kitty's meltdown earlier,' she said.

'Oh! I thought you were out?' I was confused. Beth hadn't arrived home until after nine.

'I came home, heard all hell breaking loose, and went straight back out. I went to Seekings and did a body balance class.'

'Oh. Well, she calmed down pretty quickly.'

'The other day, when you asked me how I deal with her tantrums, I told you she'd never had one with me. But I have heard her having them. Upstairs in her room.' She gave a little shudder. 'I don't go up.'

Bitch.

'Tantrums can be upsetting for everyone,' I said. 'But I try to think of them as being... like weather. Storms. They build up, they break and then they're over. They're a positive thing.

Think about when you have a good cry. You always feel better afterwards.'

'You'll think I'm crazy,' she said softly. 'But sometimes I'm scared to be around Kitty.'

'Why?'

Beth shrugged. 'She makes me think bad thoughts.'

Cold snaked down my back. 'What do you mean?'

'Terrible thoughts,' she said. 'They just come into my head. When she's around.'

She sniffed slowly and I realised she was on the verge of being drunk. How much whisky had she had?

'Haven't you noticed it?' She gave a watery smile.

I remembered the time in the hall outside the Forget-Me-Not Room when I'd been overwhelmed with sadness. The moment of terror in the bathroom where I thought I'd seen blood in the sink.

Beth looked at me. 'Sometimes I think that there's something... *not right* with her.'

I pulled the sleeves of my pyjamas down over my hands, curling my fingers into the stretchy cotton. I should have put on my fleece before coming downstairs.

'Sometimes,' she muttered, 'I look at her and it's like she's... not even there.'

Dissociation disorder. Sometimes seen in children with selective mutism. I'd been reading up about it. Wondering if Kitty had it.

But I spoke in my 'tea in the nursery' voice: 'She goes into her own wee world, bless her.'

'I was looking forward to being a mum, to having a real family. I thought it was going to be... well, not like this.' She shook her head.

I thought of the way Beth was away from the house at

every opportunity, the way she'd practically begged me to come and work as a nanny, and I wondered if she had experienced post-natal depression. Perhaps something had interrupted her bonding with Kitty.

'Parenting is no picnic,' I said. 'It's hard at the best of times. Everybody needs support, and it can't be easy with your husband away.'

'He's not exactly a hands-on dad. Sometimes I think that he never really wanted Kitty in the first place, and that's why – oh God, that's a terrible thing to say. Please forget I said that.'

'I'm not here to judge,' I said, my insides curling with a sudden hatred for Frank. 'But you must feel like you're dealing with it all on your own. Haven't you got any family nearby? Sometimes grandparents can –'

Her shoulders inched up a fraction. Had I crossed a line? 'I grew up in foster care,' she said, her voice wooden. 'I've got nobody.'

I sat for a moment, wondering if this altered my opinion of Beth. Did this explain her indifference to Kitty? Had motherhood brought up feelings about the past that she couldn't come to terms with? And did 'nobody' include Frank, her husband?

For a moment I had a wild daydream that she would come to me one day, saying she couldn't cope any more – would I mind adopting Kitty and looking after her permanently? I imagined her packing her things up in boxes while Kitty looked on, bewildered.

Anger surged through me, fierce and protective. I would do anything for that child. Anything.

I slowed my breathing. Unclenched my jaw. The best thing I could do for Kitty was to try and help Beth, to support her. Maybe Beth needed mothering herself.

'Some children can be... they can be a focus for all sorts of feelings. I think that she's like a little lightning conductor for strong emotions.'

'Hmm.'

'I think you'll find that when she starts to speak again, things will become a lot easier.'

Beth raised an eyebrow and gave an ironic little laugh.

'And I'm here to support you – both of you,' I went on gently. 'In whatever way you need. *Use* me.'

As if she didn't already. I was doing practically everything around this house.

She opened her mouth as if she was about to say something. I wasn't sure if she was about to confide in me about her marriage, or to tell me it would be a great help if I could weed the garden, or give the toilets a good going over.

'I miss my mum,' she said. 'I miss talking to her.'

I felt myself soften. 'What happened to your mum?'

She bit her lip, in a way that reminded me of Kitty. For the first time I could see the resemblance between them. Then she shrugged. 'She committed suicide.'

'Oh no. I'm so sorry.' Sadness welled inside me. Sadness for Beth. For myself. Suddenly I wanted to make a connection with her. Something genuine that went beyond admiring her cake decorations and providing updates on how many pieces of broccoli Kitty had eaten with dinner. 'My father had mental health problems. He... died in a horrible accident.'

Beth looked at me in horror. She hadn't expected that to come out of Mary Poppins' mouth.

'Don't worry, it wasn't in this house,' I said quickly.

Oh God. Oh God.

'I mean, of course it wasn't in *this* house,' I added with a nervous laugh. 'I mean... it didn't happen at home.'

I'd clung to that over the years. Laurel Bank had remained safe, untouched, in a bright circle of happy memories. Like a magic house in a fairytale where nothing bad could happen.

'I could make it like that again. I could make it like that for Kitty.

The longing must have shown in my face. Beth looked at me strangely.

'Anyway... it was a long time ago,' I said, as if I was finishing off a bedtime story, closing the book shut. 'Now. Can I make you a hot milk to take upstairs?'

18

JULIET

Collecott Hall

'Oh, she's a right whinger, that one,' said Nanny Brown, under her breath. 'Aren't you? A moaning Minnie today, aren't you, Monte? A Moaning Monte.' She laughed, in a tired sort of way.

Who would call their baby girl 'Montefiore'? Honestly, it was hard to fathom. There was no good way to shorten it either. The child looked up at me, thumb in her mouth, eyes the colour of treacle. Her auburn hair had been pulled into short bunches, pulling the thin strands taut across her scalp.

I sat down beside her on the mat. 'Do you want to play with the farm?'

But she looked down and squirmed on her bottom, whimpering softly. Monte was nearly three years old but she never spoke, never joined in with the other children. I didn't know why, but Nanny Brown had once muttered, under her breath, that she was 'retarded'.

'Shall I change her?'

'Changed her 'alf hour ago,' said Nanny Brown, who was sniffy about the fact that Monte wasn't toilet trained yet.

'Maybe she's hungry, then.'

'Hungry she may be, pet, but she can wait till snack time like everyone else. Carrot sticks and raisins. Parents' instructions not to overfeed her.'

'Come on, sweetheart. Shall we do sticklebricks, then?'

She inched across the mat, wincing.

'I'll change her,' I said more decisively.

Nanny Brown merely shrugged.

I took Monte into the room where we changed nappies and popped her up on the changing surface with a 'there you go'. When I took down her trousers a smell rose up – sickly, overripe, like rotting black bananas. I bent one of her legs gently to the side. In the creases of her groin and her bottom the skin was red raw and shiny.

'Ohhhhh,' I breathed. 'Ouchy ouchy. Let's get this sorted.' I dampened some cotton wool in warm water and she screamed at first as I tried to clean her.

'Shh... it's okay, my love. I know it hurts but it will help you.'

I was about to apply the nappy cream when I realised that what she needed most on her sore skin was air. Perhaps I could ask Nanny Brown if she could go without a nappy for a bit... but she probably wouldn't allow it.

Monte was rubbing her eyes now, poor love. I carried her through to the sleep room, with its blackout blinds and its sleep mats on the floor. She always had trouble with her naps. Her parents' instructions were to leave her to cry and then abandon the nap attempt if she hadn't fallen asleep in ten minutes. Ten minutes! That could feel like lifetime if you didn't know when it was going to end.

I walked over the cold, plastic-coated mats, and laid Monte down on the squashy sofa in the corner, wrapping a soft pink blanket loosely around her bare legs and bottom. Then I lay down beside her, curling my body around her.

I sang *Edelweiss* to her softly until her sobs subsided and her eyelids began to droop. Finally, her breathing slowed and she relaxed her body against mine as though it was a relief to give herself up to sleep.

That's when my own sobbing started. Great, silent sobs that tore through my body.

How had nobody noticed her poor red skin? Her parents could afford thousands to send their child to this exclusive nursery and yet couldn't take two minutes to really look at her?

I rocked her, and shushed her, and cried some more, and that's how Nanny Brown found us when she came in looking for us at snack time.

'WHAT WERE YOU THINKING?' Mr Redwood asked when I was summoned to his office.

He leaned forward, like he was genuinely curious about the answer. I caught the faint whiff of his breath, and I was reminded of the fact that it had been kedgeree for lunch.

I lifted my wrist to my face, and carefully inhaled the yellow scent of Elizabeth Arden's *Sunflowers* – Mum had given me one of her old bottles with a bit still left in it. I didn't want to breathe in any air that had passed through Mr Redwood's lungs.

'Is there something you'd like to talk to me about? Any

issues that have arisen at school or at home that I should know about?'

I just sat there and shook my head, feeling tongue-tied and stupid.

'Marjorie Parker says that your care of the children has sometimes been... erratic. That you're too emotional with them. You haven't enough of an awareness of boundaries.' He sighed heavily. 'I've got a report from your careers adviser here on my desk. In all conscience I can't recommend you as somebody who is suited to working with children. Not at the current time.'

'What?' I whispered.

'We have a duty of care – the *highest possible* duty – towards the very youngest children in our care. When you were caring for those children you were doing so as a representative of the school. We had placed you in a *position of trust*. You crossed boundaries and you were not in control of yourself. You were sobbing all over that child.'

'Monte,' I whispered. 'Her name is Montefiore. And I was... letting her air. She had bad nappy rash. Very bad. Her parents should have noticed it.'

'We have to think about whether you volunteering at the nursery is a good use of your time,' said Mr Redwood. 'And whether it is of benefit to the staff and children, or indeed the school, given these issues that have arisen. And in the meantime I want you to have a re-think about your career choices.'

'I want to apply for a Bachelor of Education at Durham. That's my first choice.'

He drummed his middle three fingers on the desk. 'At this stage you need to be keeping your options open. What are your subjects again?' He picked up my file. 'You could do something general. Business administration, perhaps?'

'But I only want to work with children,' I said. 'It's all I want to do.'

It came out sounding far less forceful than it had in my head. There seemed to be no space in this airless room for any opinions other than his.

He gave a mild smile. 'We are not always the best judge of where our own strengths lie. A business degree, a good general grounding, would leave your options open and could be a springboard to many careers. Perhaps with a little more maturity you could revisit the idea of working with children.'

I felt faint, feeble, like my heart had sunk down to my shoes and was barely able to pump the blood around my body. He was probably right. But still, I was the only one who could stop Monte crying when she was upset, who could make her hiccup, and curl into me, and close her eyes.

'Please give me one more chance at the nursery,' I managed. 'I'll be different. I'll remember the boundaries and everything, I promise.'

Mr Redwood sat looking at me, considering.

'I've known you for a long time, Joolz. So I have the benefit of a slightly different perspective from others here at Collecott Hall. I reckon you're a decent kid who's got off on the wrong foot, since coming here. But your manner is – well, I have to say, it goes against you.'

'What?'

'You seem to have a tendency towards negativity. You need to think about how that comes across to others.'

I tried to remember how I'd thought about myself before coming here, the comments on my school reports from Boxley Wood. Shy. Hardworking. Imaginative. Gentle. Kind.

It was all dissolving away.

I slid my fingers under the cuff of my shirt to feel for the pigskin scabs. The newest one felt tight and sore, barely holding together the seam of bright red blood underneath.

'I'll change. I promise.'

I'd be anything he wanted me to be. As long as he'd let me go back to the nursery. I had to keep an eye on Monte.

He looked at me again, for another long time. I had a sudden memory of creeping down to the kitchen at Laurel Bank, late one night, needing a change of nightie. Mr Redwood – 'the Lord', as I thought of him then – had been sitting at the kitchen table with my parents, whose heads were bent low over some papers he was showing them. He saw me in the doorway and lifted his finger to his lips in a 'shhhh' gesture. I melted away back into the darkness of the hall, back to my room.

Now, he nodded, as though he was the one person in the world who understood, and who could save me. 'I'll speak to Marjorie Parker,' he said with a wink – or was it a twitch of his eye? It was hard to be sure. 'Leave it with me.'

19

JULIET

Sunday afternoons had become my 'day off'. To begin with, Beth and I had agreed I'd have every Saturday and Sunday off. The first few weekends I'd headed out of the house early on the Saturday morning and driven into Sudbury to look at the market, or to Bury St Edmunds for shopping or the cinema. I'd taken long walks by the Stour, trying to find beauty in the long horizons and endless stretches of stubbly fields. I'd looked around several ancient churches and visited a country house with famous gardens, sitting alone in the tea room with a leaking teapot and a piece of dry cake. Once I'd gone to Dedham Vale to retrace the river walk that I used to do with Mum and Dad, only to find that I couldn't remember where it started off.

But soon I'd run out of nostalgic pilgrimages. They made my heart ache, made me want to be back at home, close to Kitty. I'd offered to keep an eye on her one Saturday while Beth went out to deliver a wedding cake, and then again the next Saturday when Beth wanted to take part in a badminton tournament.

I feared it would come across as over-eager if I offered to mind Kitty on Sundays too. So today, I'd simply stayed in my room, listening to music on my headphones and reading *Rebecca* for the zillionth time. I came out at around four to go downstairs and get a drink, only to find Kitty, curled up on her side outside my bedroom door, next to a completed jigsaw of a bluebell wood.

'How long have you been there, Kitten?' I'd asked. She got to her feet, a hopeful expression on her face.

'Oh, Juliet!' Beth was in the kitchen, flushed but otherwise immaculate in her velour tracksuit, a turquoise one with a 'B' spelt on the back in rhinestones. She poured herself a gin and tonic. 'Can we have a word?'

I glanced at the kitchen worktop... had she noticed? Earlier that day I'd moved the ceramic chicken egg holder I'd bought from a dark corner shelf above the microwave – where Beth had put it – to a nicer place, at the end of the worktop. That's where Mum had used to keep hers, within easy reach of the hob.

'Kitty and I have had a wonderful idea,' she went on.

'Oh?'

'Well, we couldn't have a birthday party for Kitty over the summer holidays, since nobody was around... in fact, we haven't done one before, have we, Kits? She's never been keen. She's always been a bit too shy. But I suggested to her that we'd do something this term when school went back. I've been meaning to organise it for ages, it's just been so hectic. Anyway, I've spoken to the manager at Seekings, and we're going to have a party there – swimming followed by a party tea in the garden room!'

Kitty had this expression on her face... bashful but hopeful. As if she couldn't quite imagine having her own birthday party, with friends turning up just for her, but desperately wanted to believe it might happen.

'That's great!' I said.

'Isn't it? They've only just re-opened the pool after a big refurbishment – it's been a building site all summer. Frank was on the members' committee last year, so he actually had some input on the plans.'

It didn't surprise me. Every time Frank was mentioned it was because of his great work on some committee, or trustee board.

'He's an Influencer,' explained Beth. 'High on the Dominance spectrum, too, but he's an off-the-scale Influencer.'

I winced. I didn't want to hear about Frank being on the Dominance spectrum.

'It's going to be wonderful. There's a lovely jacuzzi, and heated stone beds. The only thing is, they've said we'll need three adults in the pool. Tasha has agreed to help out, with Charlie if necessary. Will you be okay to do that too? I would do it myself, only I'll need to oversee the tea party, get the cake organised and so on.'

'I – I can't swim,' I said.

Beth's bright expression didn't change. 'Oh, don't worry about that. As long as you're in the pool, even if you're just standing. In fact there's an adjustable floor to the pool. I'll ask them to bring it up so nobody's out of their depth.'

'No, you see... I have a fear of the water.' My throat was tight, barely letting the words escape.

'Oh.' Beth pushed her lips forward into a pout. A starburst of fine lines appeared around her mouth. 'That's a problem.'

'Could one of the other parents help out? I could ask

around? Or maybe I could organise the party tea while you
go in the pool?'

Beth stared at me, her mouth fallen open slightly. I had a
sudden image of her, with her expensive highlighted hair in
rats' tails and her mascara smudged under her eyes,
welcoming the guests in to the plush lobby of the country
club. Maybe not.

'Don't worry about it,' she said, waving her hands in a
rapid, dismissive gesture. 'It's all sounding a bit complicated.
The manager said we would have to confirm today to guarantee the date.' She left a silence, in which I was probably
supposed to jump in and say I'd changed my mind. Then she
sighed. 'I'll ring her and say we'll have to let the slot go.'

I looked around for Kitty.

She'd crept under the table and was weeping silently.

'What if... what if you book it, and we could ask some of
the other parents at school, but I could be the fallback.' I was
forming a plan to pay one of the Seekings staff to do it, even if
it came out of my own pocket.

Beth raised her eyebrows at her gin and tonic. 'I suppose
that's a possibility. But I think Kitty was particularly hoping
that you'd be part of her special day.'

I frowned. How would Beth even *know* that?

As if she'd read my mind, she pulled a piece of paper
from her pocket. It was a drawing of stick people flailing
around in a heavily-crayoned blue square that must have
been a swimming pool. There was a grey lump with eyes in
the corner that might have been a hippopotamus. And a
heading at the top written Kitty's wobbly writing: 'Swimming
party with Juliet.'

Oh Jesus.

I closed my eyes for a moment, picturing Kitty's face

when she saw the scars on my arms and legs, which would be revealed in full glory under the bright pool lights once my camouflage make-up had been washed off. Would she be horrified? Curious? Scared?

Then there would be the look on Charlie's face. His sympathy. Tasha's. The conversation they might have on the way home... *Did you see her arms? And the tops of her legs! Poor thing... is there nothing they can do about that these days?* And Cammie's voice piping up in the back seat: *What happened to her? What, you mean she did that to herself? But why, Mummy? Why?*

And what about Beth herself? Would she decide I wasn't a suitable person to look after Kitty? I remembered my mother, catching sight of some of my cuts when we were living in Edinburgh, when I'd finished sixth form college and was starting to apply for nannying jobs. She'd come into my room without knocking, when I was drying off after having a bath. Horrified, she'd implored me to stop and had warned me that it might make potential employers think I was 'unstable'. She'd paid for some counselling – a course of six sessions, at a reduced price for those with limited means – with money she'd been saving from her job in Marks and Spencer. So I'd stopped, out of guilt as much as anything else. Although sometimes, I wondered if I'd simply found other ways to hurt myself.

But attitudes were different now, weren't they? More enlightened? It was clear that the scars were old, and Beth wouldn't be in the pool anyway. And this was for Kitty. Somehow she'd summoned up the courage to have a party, to step forward and be the centre of attention – and wasn't that, in some small way, something to do with me?

The truth was, nobody would care about my scars.

Nobody except me. This racing heart, this churning stomach, it was nothing but vanity. And what did it matter anyway what Charlie thought of me? What difference did it make whether he looked at me and wished he could take me to bed, or winced in sympathy and congratulated himself on ending up with Tasha?

'Book it,' I said to Beth. 'Of course I'll help out.'

She beamed and reached for her mobile phone. Underneath the table, I felt small arms embrace my lower leg.

20

JULIET

Collecott Hall

The children were unsettled on the day of the nursery inspection. It was windy outside, gusts rattling the windows, childish voices rising higher and higher as if they'd been whipped up with the same restless energy.

'I'm Pam,' said the inspector in whispery tones. Her pale face was soft and creased, greying hair swirled up on top of her head. 'Just pretend I'm not here.' She sat down on one of the tiny yellow chairs, next to where Monte and I were waiting. My job that morning – I'd been told – was to look after Monte and try to get her to join in.

Nanny Pratt corralled all the children to sit around her in a semi circle. We were going to sing some songs in French.

'Come along, Nanny Juliet and Monte,' said Nanny Pratt. 'Get in the circle.'

Monte climbed onto my knee and wedged herself between my left arm and my body, pressing herself up against me as though she'd like to climb right inside my body and disappear.

Nanny Pratt picked up a tambourine and jingled a short intro. 'Right, children! Everybody together, now!'

'Au Clair de la lun-UH!

Mon ami Pierr-OT!'

Monte looked up at me fearfully, her thumb stuck in her mouth and a snail trail of drool on her chin. I understood what she was trying to communicate – how could she sing if she couldn't even speak?

'Want to do the farm puzzle?' I whispered.

She nodded quickly.

'Come on then.'

I put my hands around her middle to pop her off me but she cried out.

'What's wrong?'

'Au clair de la lun-UH...'

Once again I went to lift Monte off my knee and this time she cried out, slid off me and curled herself into a tight ball on the mat.

Her top rode up, to reveal the first two or three nubbly bumps of her spine, and...

I drew in a breath. Those were bruises; exotic blooms flowering black and purple and green across the pale skin.

I edged her top up a little further. Christ, they were all the way up her back.

To my left, Inspector Pam's chair scraped against the floor as she stood up.

'What happened to you, baby?' I leaned over Monte, curved my body around hers, protecting her from Pam's stare.

Nanny Pratt abandoned *Claire de Lune* and came over.

'What's happening here?'

Monte, who never said anything at all, sat up, opened her mouth and said, 'Nanny hit me.'

And all the eyes in the room – the children's, Nanny Pratt's, Pam's, everyone's except Monte's, who'd curled herself back into a ball on the carpet – came to rest on *me*.

~

CHARLIE

IT WAS strange because he'd been thinking about her – just letting her be there quietly at the back of his mind, to keep him going through the muddy slog of rugby practice. And suddenly she was standing in front of him, in the middle of the path in the half-dark.

'I – I –' It sounded like she couldn't catch her breath.

He turned to Baz, Johnny and Twig, who were red-faced from the stinging rain, and covered in dirt just like him. 'You go on ahead. See you at prep.'

They walked on towards the boarding house, with its glowing windows and promise of dinner – the board had said it was lasagne tonight.

'What's the matter?' he said to Juliet. 'What's happened?'

'Everyone thinks I hurt Monte.'

He took her up to the roof space over Mr Redwood's office. She lay face down on the crash mat and cried, her dark blonde hair tumbled all around her, as she told him the story. He lay on his side next to her, filled with some kind of longing that he didn't understand.

He'd fancied girls before. But this... seeing her hurting and not being able to stop it. It was like homesickness. Something pulling on his insides.

'It's okay,' he said uselessly. 'Don't cry.'

'The thing is, it might have been me who hurt her. When I was talking to Nanny Parker afterwards, I suddenly remembered something that happened yesterday. Monte was about to jump off the high bit of the climbing frame – she'd been trying to do it all week, the monkey – and I grabbed her around the waist, quite hard. I wasn't trying to hurt her, I was trying to stop her falling. But because I hadn't remembered it straight away, it looked like I was lying about it, or making it up. When I told Nanny Parker, she looked really angry. She said there's going to be... an investigation. I'm not to go back to the nursery, and I have to go and see Redwood tomorrow.'

'Just wait and see,' said Charlie. 'It might just blow over.'

'I won't be allowed to work with children again,' she went on, dissolving into tears again. 'Even before this happened, Mr Redwood said I would be better suited to administration because of my tendency towards negativity.'

Charlie smothered a smile as he pictured rows of administrators at identical desks, stapling things together and radiating negativity.

But Juliet... she looked terrified. As if someone had told her she wouldn't be allowed to breathe oxygen again.

'It's not up to him,' Charlie spat out. 'Listen, you should call your parents and tell them what's going on.'

Surely Lynne and Graeme Hazelwood would be able to do something. Mr Redwood was an old family friend, wasn't he?

Juliet wanted him to come with her to phone home. They sat side by side on the tiny wooden bench in the half-darkness of the phone cupboard, her hip squashed against his, the fabric of her skirt stretched tight over her thighs. He wondered if she could sense the blood pumping through his body.

'D-Daddy?' she said.

Charlie could hear Graeme at the other end of the line. 'Hello, Piglet.'

He'd forgotten that Juliet's parents used to call her 'Piglet'. They'd always said it affectionately, their voices full of delight. But tonight Graeme spoke in a flat monotone that made it sound different, in a way that made Charlie wince.

'Hello. Is Mum there?'

'She's visiting Marjorie at the hospital, then going straight on to the sewing group.'

Juliet took a deep breath. 'Something's happened.'

'What's happened?'

Charlie felt a tiny movement in Juliet's leg, pressed against his. He realised that she was shaking. 'One of the little girls that I look after at the nursery. Do you remember Monte, the one I told you about? There was that bother a few weeks ago because... well. Anyway, now she's got b-bruises. I'm under investigation. They think it was me.'

There was a long silence. Then: 'Oh, Juliet.'

It was impossible to tell the emotion behind the voice. It could have been compassion or empathy. It could have been disappointment. Anxiety. Even a dull kind of anger.

Juliet shifted beside him and he could smell the damp, salty scent coming off her skin.

'So...' she said, twisting the phone cord between her fingers.

Seconds passed. Charlie started to wonder if the line had been cut off.

'It's Mr Redwood that's doing the investigation. He's speaking to witnesses and things. I was wondering if...' She looked at Charlie and he nodded in encouragement. 'I was wondering if you and Mum could maybe speak to him and try and explain things... explain that I wouldn't have done that? He thinks I'm not suited to work with children, but it's what I want to do for my... career.' Her voice tightened into a squeak.

'I see,' said Graeme eventually. 'Well. If you phone again at around ten your mother will be back. She's probably better placed to...'

As if he was delegating some dull job at the bank.

Juliet nodded, slowly at first and then faster. He could see the glint of a tear, shooting down her cheek.

'Okay,' she said. 'I'll try and phone at ten.'

Except that she wouldn't. She couldn't. They all had to be in their dorms by nine forty-five.

21

JULIET

Kitty had just come out of the bath, wrapped from the waist down in a trailing pink towel.

'You look like a mermaid,' I said. 'You look just like your mermaid dolly.' Except she didn't, of course. Kitty, with the baby pudge of her six-year-old body, and her birds-nest hair, was a thousand times more beautiful than any mermaid.

'And do you know what mermaids love doing? Brushing their hair.' I held up the brush and wiggled it. Kitty shook her head. 'How about we have a bit of a treat night, since Mummy has gone out?'

Thursday night was hot yoga at Seekings.

I didn't think Beth should have gone – she'd had a bad throat for a few days. I'd found her cursing at the computer earlier, trying to order antibiotics online.

'You should go to the doctors, Beth,' I'd said in a strict voice.

'I don't have time!'

'You need to make time for self-care,' I fussed.

She loved that. Her eyes widened and grew moist.

'Why don't you get yourself off to bed and I'll bring you up a lemon and honey drink and a hot water bottle? And I'll phone the doctors for you first thing in the morning, get you an appointment.'

'No,' she said. 'Thank you, but it's all right. I need to go out tonight. I'll see how I feel in the morning.'

So now it was just me and Kitty.

'If you get ready nicely, and put your pyjamas on and let me brush your hair, we can watch a bit of TV before bed?'

Kitty nodded, and turned and stood with her back to me, signalling that I could begin the hair brushing.

'We'll have to see what's on,' I said, spraying on little squirts of strawberry-scented tangle-tamer. 'Maybe... *Thomas the Tank Engine*?'

Kitty shook her head vigorously.

'Oh no, it's... what is it you like again? *Bob the Builder*?'

More head shaking.

'We certainly wouldn't want to watch something too grown up, like... *Police Interceptors*, would we?'

She jiggled up and down, turning her face towards me, so the brush caught in her hair with a tearing sound.

It was her absolute favourite programme. Beth had told me about it with a tinkly laugh, explaining how Kitty had happened to turn it on one evening when Beth had been icing cakes in the kitchen. And now they couldn't get her off it.

She'd watch it, wide-eyed, as police officers chased cars the wrong way down motorways, and discovered cannabis wrapped in little twists of silver foil in glove compartments.

Once, they'd found a little old lady wandering along the M6 in her nightie and Kitty had watched transfixed, her mouth fallen open and her biscuit held half way to her mouth.

'We might even watch two episodes if you're good. Hold on now, this is a big tangle.'

Kitty began to walk off, out of the bathroom. I followed, the brush still caught in the tangle.

'Hold on just a minute there, missy.'

She stopped walking and stood, shifting her weight from one foot to the other. I pulled the brush through her hair more quickly, but she caught sight of her mermaid doll on the edge of her bed and started walking over there, me still working away with the brush. She lifted her arms to pick up the doll, letting her towel drop from her waist and pool to the floor, and then she proceeded to walk over to the dolls' wardrobe and select a small satiny dressing gown, and special mermaid pyjamas that could accommodate a long tail.

We settled under a fleecy blanket in the living room – Kitty, the mermaid and I.

'Hello-oh? Do you wanna play?' said the mermaid, just as the opening music started.

Kitty shook her head.

'No thank you, Mermaid,' I said. 'We're watching this just now. Maybe later.'

Soon we were caught up in the action – hurtling along a road in Wakefield in an unmarked police car, chasing a hooded man through a field and cuffing his squirming hands behind his back when he stumbled and fell into a ditch.

'Driving without insurance,' I said, shaking my head.

'La la la, la-la la la la,' sang the doll. 'You could be a mermaid like me.'

Kitty took bite from her chocolate digestive and carefully placed it on the arm of the sofa. I could hear her crunching it as the man was asked to blow into a breathalyser machine.

'Over the limit too,' I tutted.

Still gazing intently at the screen, Kitty opened her mouth and said, 'I want to be a police when I grow up.'

One...two...three breaths.

She'd offered me her words almost casually. A handful of precious jewels.

I reached onto the coffee table and took a biscuit from the packet. 'Do you?'

Kitty bit her lip, and lifted the mermaid to her chest.

'That's cool,' I said, through a mouthful of biscuit.

I thought of Kitty, standing at a roadside trying to question a dangerous driver, unable to speak a word. My heart twisted.

'It's not something I ever thought of doing for a career,' I said thoughtfully. 'I don't know why, though. It looks very interesting. You get to drive very fast. Is that why you want to do it?'

She shrugged.

'I know, shall we get your notebook and you can write down why?'

Kitty wrinkled her nose.

I thought of the old lady in her nightie, the way Kitty had held her breath until she was safe in the police station being given a cup of hot sweet tea.

'Or is it because you want to help people?'

She nodded.

I thought of her thirteen 999 calls. What kind of help Kitty had been looking for?

'Kitty,' I said. 'Why did you call 999 all those times? I just wondered if it was something I could help with? You can talk to me, if you want to. Nothing bad will happen, I promise.'

I'd gone too far. She slipped onto the floor between the sofa and the coffee table, pulling the blanket over her.

I pretended that I was being sucked down there too, legs first and then my body. 'Help! It's a sea monster! It's getting me!'

Kitty's head emerged from the blanket. She grabbed my arm.

'We have to get to that island over there,' I said, pointing to the sofa on the other side of the room. 'We'll have to use these stepping stones.'

The coffee table had a space for magazines and newspapers underneath and I pulled some out, skimming them across the carpet. I vaguely hoped that Beth wouldn't return from hot yoga at that moment, to see me throwing things around her living room.

Kitty stepped gingerly onto a *Homes and Gardens* magazine and balanced there on one leg.

'Here!' I picked up a *Radio Times* and then an old *National Geographic* – the cover showed a woman in tribal costume with a decorated lip plate, distorting her lower lip into a disc the size of a saucer.

The room seemed to lurch.

Memories, pushing up to the surface.

The past, opening up like a huge crack you could fall into.

I was small again. Hiding behind the sofa when I was supposed to be in bed.

I could hear a low male voice: 'See this? That's what they used to hold her mouth open.'

My mother, gasping.

The low voice again: 'I'm sorry, Lynne. Perhaps I shouldn't have shown you this. But this stuff *goes on*. It's real.'

A hairy male hand appeared, placing the folder on to the floor next to the sofa, tipping it slightly so that photos spilled out onto the carpet.

I knelt forward to look, and then wished I hadn't.

There was a medical photograph of the inside of a woman's mouth – the black-red stump of her tongue where it had been cut out.

A photograph of a metal clamp.

Warmth trickled down my thighs.

Then I could hear my mother... crying? She never cried. She was always happy.

'But why?' she said.

'This was a punishment for informing on her neighbour, who was part of the trafficking gang. The gang leader – well, this is his trademark, I'm afraid. He's known as "The Tongue Tier", because he ties their tongues with razor wire before he cuts them off.'

'Good *God!*' Her voice was faint now. I wanted to fly into her arms.

But the male voice went on, soothing now. 'It's okay, Lynne. The charity took her in – she's staying at the new unit. They're teaching her sign language.'

After they'd gone I stayed hunched down behind the sofa, my wet nightie clinging to my skin, both hands clapped over my mouth.

And then I was back in the here and now, with Kitty by my side. She was tucking her blanket around me, patting it and smoothing it over me with outstretched hands.

'Thank you, darling.'

She chewed on her bottom lip, drawing it into her mouth. And she nodded carefully, her eyes cast down, never meeting mine.

22

BETH

Beth couldn't believe that she was doing this while Frank was *downstairs*. It was madness. It made her feel slightly sick when she thought about it. But he'd arrived back in Vevey a day early – something to do with flights – and it had been too late to rearrange the video call. She planned to simply close the laptop lid if she heard his footsteps on the stairs, and say she'd been watching a film. It wasn't as though she was going behind his back, exactly, just that it would be too difficult to explain everything. If she was going to stay in touch with her dad after this, she'd tell Frank about it then. Certainly she would. But no need to at the moment, when it might not go anywhere anyway.

The Social Work hadn't had any information on file about her father, and Ange was long gone. But they'd given her the name of a tracing agency. It had taken time, but now, over a year later, she'd been put in touch with him.

In his email, he'd explained that he wanted to talk to her in person, that there were some things he needed to explain that were better said face to face. But Beth had said it wouldn't be possible, because she was living out of the country for a while.

The video call had been his suggestion. She'd never used it before, and had had to set up her own email address (she couldn't use the one she shared with Frank, obviously) in order to create a log in.

But there must have been some mistake. This wizened old man appearing on the screen now wasn't her dad. He was propped up in a high-backed chair – one of those padded vinyl ones they had in care homes and hospitals – with thin plastic tubes fed into his nostrils.

'Hello, love.' His voice was just a rasp, not the strong, joyful voice that had sung Chuck Berry in the living room.

She couldn't say a word.

'Sorry about all this,' he said. 'Didn't want to tell you in an email. Truth is, I'm on my way out.'

Beth frowned. On his way out where? Why had he arranged a video call for a time when he had to go out?

'A few months, maybe a year at a stretch. That's what they're saying. It's the lungs. Well, the brain too but mainly the lungs. It's the fluid, what's causing the problem at the moment. Infections and whatnot.'

Shut up, she wanted to say. Shut up. I don't want to hear about this. I want you to explain why you left me.

She dug her nails into the palms of her hands, and waited. Downstairs, she heard Kitty shout out – in French – that she'd done a poo, and Rosa's rushed footsteps across the tiles to the bathroom.

Frank's study door didn't open – she didn't think so, anyway. Bottom wiping wasn't really his thing.

'I know I've not been the best dad.' Now he had the nerve to sniff a little, as though the thought upset him. 'It was the

Social's fault. Nobody told me that your mum had passed away. I swear. A clerical error, they called it. There I was, thinking you was with your mum, and you was in foster homes and care and all that malarkey. Jeez, Bethie...'

There it was – her heart. Soaring in her chest, wanting to believe.

'But I want to do right by you now.'

She opened her mouth to tell him about Kitty. To tell him that he had a little granddaughter who had blue-grey eyes that made her think of the seaside at Whitby, and a laugh that reminded her of her mum, before everything had gone wrong.

'The thing is, I came into a bit of money, love. Well, a lot, actually. One of the old dears – one of the regulars on the *Ocean Glory* – she left everything to me. Mrs Favoreaux, her name was. Sweet lady. The husband had been in oil, I think.'

Beth imagined the dead husband, floating in a chip pan like Viv's, with crusty bits of Ruskoline drifting across the bottom.

'I want to do right by you,' he repeated again, nodding to himself with a self-satisfied expression.

'If you send me your address, love, I'll make sure it's all done official. The will, I mean. I'm leaving, well, a very decent amount to you, Bethie, and the remainder to Tommy Gregson. He's got to have his legs off – diabetes, love – and his wife's only upped and left him.'

He said it apologetically, as though Beth would be upset with him for not leaving the whole lot to her, or would give any kind of a fuck about this Tommy Gregson and his rotting legs.

He started to cough – a low, rumbly cough. She could hear the material in his lungs. His face grew purple as it went on, and he held up a hand to indicate that it would be over in a minute.

One minute passed. Two.

Downstairs, she heard Frank's study door open – that familiar click and creak that sent a pulse of adrenaline through her body. Maybe he was going into the kitchen for a beer. His footsteps were hesitant, seemed to stop half way across the hall.

She couldn't help remembering what had happened when he'd found her messaging an old friend from school last Christmas. Afterwards, they'd promised each other they'd never talk about it again – they'd never even think about it. But now she ran her mind over it gently, like a bruise.

She reached for the laptop lid and held her hand there, just in case. A dark shape swooped across the screen and made her jump, but it was just a nurse's back, blocking her father from view for a moment as she leaned over him. Then he reappeared again, still coughing.

'Bye,' he wheezed. 'Bye.'

She snapped the laptop shut. It was unbelievable, she decided, as her heart rate returned to normal. He hadn't asked her a single question about herself. This was all about him. Chuck Berry, *Ocean Glory*, the oil widow, his decomposing lungs. It had only ever been about him.

In an automatic movement, her hand drew open the bedside drawer, and pulled out the bottle of little white pills. She swallowed two – it had been a stressful day, after all – and waited for the silence of the room to envelop her, to slide over her like cool white sheets in a freshly made bed.

23

JULIET

I was climbing the stairs to bed when I heard a noise coming from Kitty's room. A babbling noise. At first I thought it was her story CD – she must have put it on again. But was a child's voice. Kitty's voice.

And somebody else was talking too.

Holding my breath, I pushed the handle of her door down and opened it slowly, just a fraction.

The room was lit softly in the glow from the toadstool nightlight. Kitty was sitting upright in her bed, holding her mermaid doll in front of her. She'd placed stones – sparkly ones from her collection – in a circle around the doll.

The mermaid's voice was a grating whine: 'Do you wanna play with me?'

Kitty pulled the doll to her chest and curled her body around it tenderly. 'You know I love you. But why do you keep asking if I want to play with you? You know I can't do that because I have to be in bed. Her will come and tell me off if I get out of bed. Do you want to hear about my day, though?'

The doll said nothing. Kitty sighed and gave it a little shake. 'Come *on*.'

'Do you wanna brush my hair?' said the doll.

'No,' said Kitty shortly. 'You listen to my day.' She took a deep breath. 'Well. Mrs Robson gave us a maths test. That was mean because it was meant to be choosing time. But I got all of mine right – well, I only got one wrong. Or two. Are you pleased with me? Yes? Yes, me too. I got the best in the class.'

Kitty sighed.

'There's this game. It's called truth or dare I fink. If you say dare you get a rude question like, have you ever farted at school? If you say truth you get a nice question like, have fairies ever visited your house? You've probably heard of it.'

She looked at the doll, expectantly.

'Well, we could play it if you like. Here's my question, and it's a truth. So you *have* to tell the truth.' She bent low and whispered something into the doll's ear.

Seconds passed. A minute. Kitty sighed, turned onto her side and pulled the covers up to her chin. Stones slid off the duvet onto the carpet with a gentle clatter but she ignored them.

24

LYNNE

Dearest Juliet,

I woke up in the middle of the night, last week, with an idea for your birthday. I'd been having a dream that you'd just got home from nursery and we were having lunch in the garden, on a rug underneath the old monkey puzzle tree. It was chicken soup, I think. And rolls with cheese. You *adored* that tree. Daddy once told you he'd seen a monkey climbing in the branches, and you and Charlie spent the rest of that afternoon lying on your backs and staring up at the branches, making little monkey noises to coax them out. Poor old Gypsy tried to join in too – scampering around and barking as if there was really something up there!

So I'm enclosing a packet of monkey puzzle tree seeds! I just ordered them from Amazon, and I don't really know if they will grow. So, as a backup, I'm also enclosing a voucher for the garden centre, as they sell them in pots, darling. You can grow them inside and then plant them out later, when they're big enough. I know you're not exactly the green-fingered type, but honestly, Juliet, give it a chance because I think you might really take to gardening. It's so lovely to watch things grow. A little bit of sun. A little bit of rain. And time. That's all it takes.

Sending you all my love, darling. I hope you have a nice birthday.

Mum xxxxxx

25

JULIET

'So it's weird,' I said to Charlie. 'She can speak when she's on her own. Well, with that horrible doll.'

We were sitting on a low wooden bench in the school hall waiting for the Autumn Celebration Assembly to begin (the school didn't 'do' Halloween), as the chatter of parents rose higher and the music teacher played cheerful bouncy music on the piano.

I was slightly hot and out of breath, having rushed to the garden centre on the way to school to get a couple of flower pots and some compost.

Beth would be delighted that I was doing some gardening with Kitty – it was one of the things on the 'Play and Learning Plan' that I'd written up soon after arriving. Whether she'd want the garden at Laurel Bank turned into a jungle of monkey puzzle trees was less certain. But Kitty loved the idea. She'd already looked out three soft toy monkeys (and a tiny Sylvanian monkey) to help with the planting.

As I'd paid at the checkout and rushed back to the car, I'd realised something. I felt happy. I hadn't noticed it at first, because it was a quiet happiness, hidden under everyday things. But sometimes it would bubble up, like when Kitty had shot upstairs and dived under her bed to rummage for another monkey she'd just remembered about. Or when I folded her soft pyjamas to put under her pillow. Or the other day when I was at the shops and saw the exact type of red apple that she most liked, and found myself grabbing flour and oats to make a crumble.

I seemed to be making a difference to Kitty. I enjoyed working out ways to communicate with her, feeling my way through conversations using instinct, finding ways to show that I was listening to her, even when she couldn't speak. And my weeks were punctuated with these little bright spots, where I got to say hello to Charlie. He collected Cameron from school every Thursday, and he did morning drop-off most days, although he was usually in a hurry, rushing to get into the surgery before patients began to queue in the waiting room.

Today, each of the children had to hold up a picture and say what they loved about autumn. Kitty had carefully gathered some squashed leaves from the playground and glued them onto a piece of card. She was going to hold up the picture and Cameron was going to say her words for her: 'Fallen leaves make a good shelter for animals, even brown ones.'

'Brown leaves or brown animals?' I'd prompted Kitty last night, while she was writing her sentence out for Cameron at the kitchen table, but she just shrugged.

'Hmm. It's nice of you to mention brown leaves or animals. I suppose they sometimes get left out if they are just brown. I bet *most* people will just be talking about golden and red leaves.'

Kitty nodded, indicating that I was back on track now.

'Or fancy, *colourful* animals like... parrots.'

Kitty snorted.

'Yes,' I went on. 'Autumn parrots. People are always going on about them. Hey, you... are you laughing at me?' I gave Kitty a little tickle under her ribs and she squealed and dropped down under the table.

'I suppose it makes sense, though,' said Charlie now, as we waited for the class to file in to the hall. 'I mean, if it's selective mutism then it's an anxiety disorder, rather than an actual problem with speech or forming words.'

He reached forward to pick up his programme, which had fallen on the floor by my left shoe.

The scent of him. It was only just there, at the catching point of each breath. It stirred my heart with half-remembered things. Grass stains on white socks. A faded pink velvet chair by a fire. A scene of winter fields seen from a train.

'What are you thinking?' he said.

I smiled. This was a question Charlie always used to ask when we were little. He'd pause in the middle of whatever we were doing and ask me, an urgent expression on his face. It was like ordinary talking wasn't enough and he wanted to climb right inside my head.

'I just wish I could help her more. Sometimes I catch her just... just sitting staring at the wall. It's like she's switched herself off.'

'I think cognitive behavioural therapy might be one option. That would help her with the underlying anxiety. But she needs to see a specialist. They'll know what the best treatment is.'

'What's promethazine?' I asked.

He frowned. 'It's an antihistamine. It's sometimes prescribed for sleep issues.'

'There was a bottle of it in the medicine cabinet, prescribed for Kitty.'

'Does she have allergies?'

'Not that I know of.'

He shrugged, suddenly looking uncomfortable. 'Maybe you should check with Beth.'

'She might think I was sticking my nose in.'

'But surely it's your job to think about Kitty's wellbeing? To know about any health issues? Maybe you should sit down with her and go over all this stuff.'

I sighed. 'I'll have to pick my moment. Beth's hardly ever there – she's away overnight tonight again. Some wedding fayre thing. Trying to convince poor sods to buy her cakes at £600 a pop.'

Charlie's eyebrows shot up. 'Jeez.'

And as for Kitty's dad, well I still haven't even met him. He's still away "in the field". I'm starting to wonder if he even exists... I mean, have you ever seen him?'

Charlie frowned. 'I don't think so, actually.'

'And another thing...' I paused. Did it sound silly to mention this? 'The house is filled with photos of Kitty and Beth. But none of him. Maybe he's left them.'

Charlie shrugged. 'Maybe he's pig-ugly.'

Piglet ugly.

I pulled the sleeves of my cardigan down over my wrists. 'When's this going to start? It's ten past already.'

Charlie turned his face to mine and sat silent for a moment, before saying quietly, 'And how about you? How are you doing?'

'I'm fine. I'm good.'

Apart from having to fight an overpowering urge to shift a few inches along the bench, to close that aching space between us and rest my head against his shoulder.

'I've been worried about you. You've had so much to cope with and anybody would –'

'Please, Charlie. Just leave it.'

I could feel it ebbing away – my fragile new happiness.

'Okay,' he said reluctantly. 'But remember I'm here. I'm here if you want to talk about it.'

'Thank you. I really appreciate it.'

'What happened with your husband?' he blurted out, as though he'd been wondering for ages and just had to ask me.

'Eddie?' I looked down at my hands, gave a rueful laugh. 'Well, he found someone else. But it was over, really, long before that. It was the infertility treatment, I suppose. It was very tough. It put too much strain on our relationship. That's why it didn't work.'

He wasn't you. He just wasn't you.

'I guess it must be really hard.' He frowned. 'Tasha got pregnant with Cammie pretty much straight away. I just can't imagine the disappointment of –'

'He said I was too negative. I had a negative attitude. I was dragging him down.' Why was there a wobble in my voice? It wasn't as if I cared what Eddie thought. Not any more.

Charlie exhaled slowly and shook his head as if he couldn't trust himself to say what he was thinking.

'Listen,' I said on impulse. 'Do you and Cameron want to come over after school? The children can play. I'll get big brownie points if I can tell Beth that Kitty's had a playdate.'

～

CHARLIE

IT FELT strange being back at Laurel Bank again.

And even stranger watching Juliet making him a coffee in her mother's old kitchen, setting it down in front of him.

'It's like stepping back in time. They've hardly changed anything.' He looked around, taking in the layout of the kitchen. 'Even... doesn't this tablecloth look just like the one your mum had? I remember you once drawing round one of the poppies in pencil – and when you were caught you tried to blame me!'

He remembered her dark blue eyes widening: 'It was Charlie's idea!'

Now Juliet's gaze dropped, and she brushed her fingers across the patterned vinyl. 'I bought this, actually. Kitty and I saw it at the market in Sudbury.'

'Very *Great British Bake Off*. What did Beth say?'

She cast him a mischievous smile from beneath her lashes. 'How could she refuse a present from Kitty?'

Cameron and Kitty came into the kitchen. Cameron was crawling backwards dragging a Cinderella-style coach, a long-suffering look on his face. Kitty was pushing a doll's suitcase along with her foot, three Barbies clutched in each fist.

'Ha!' said Charlie, turning to Juliet. 'Do you remember Edward?'

She looked confused.

'Edward the Barbie with the long blonde hair and the orange flares? You used to force me to play Edward while you played all the girl Barbies.'

A faraway look came over her face.

'I'd forgotten.'

CHARLIE HAD WANTED to play hide and seek like usual. But Juliet had shaken her head.

'Nope. Barbies.'

'No, Juliet... please.'

'I have a man Barbie,' she said in a wheedling voice.

'I can't see any men,' Charlie said, when she'd emptied a pink Minnie Mouse suitcase onto her bedroom floor – five million Barbies and their silly clothes and shoes.

'Here. See, he is a man,' she said, picking it up and holding it in front of him.

It had long, white-ish hair and was wearing orange flares but nothing on the top half. It clearly had... um, boobs.

'He's Edward. You take him.' She shoved him at Charlie, and started arranging the other Barbies in a circle. Then she went over to her cupboard and pulled a big Barbie hairdressing salon out, making Snakes and Ladders and a Jungle Book jigsaw come clattering down, spilling bits everywhere. She swept the bits aside with her foot and dragged the hairdressing salon over.

'Edward works at the salon. He's going to cut Isabella's hair.' She went over to her desk and got out some scissors. They were proper sharp metal ones.

'Juliet... I don't think you should.'

'Don't worry.' She looked at him and then whispered, cupping her hand around her mouth. 'He doesn't really want to cut her hair.'

'Doesn't he?'

'No. He wants to make her commit ADULTERY!' And she grabbed Edward, tore off his flares and thrashed him about on top of Isabella.

'What's adultery?' Charlie asked.

'It's this,' Juliet said calmly, thrashing Edward even harder. 'Haven't you heard of the ten commandments?'

'Poor Isabella. Let's rescue her.' He picked up another Barbie and used it to push Edward away. Juliet frowned at him and put Edward right back again.

Then she grabbed another Barbie from the suitcase, one that had a dark cloak and its face had been scribbled on with marker pen so it had big pointy eyebrows and a beard.

'This is the Tongue Tier. He'll get them!'

The Tongue Tier swooped down like a great black bird and smashed into the game. Barbies were flying everywhere like a big Barbie earthquake.

'What are you up to, folks?'

Charlie jumped in fright. It was Lynne Hazelwood, peering around the door with a weird look on her face.

'Nothing.' Juliet said, stuffing Edward back in the suitcase.

'Playing Barbies?'

'Mmm-hmm.' Juliet's face was bright and closed.

'I hope you're playing nice games, Piglet.'

'Mmm-hmm,' went Juliet again.

Charlie nodded, and kept nodding until Lynne Hazelwood said the next thing: 'I've made raspberry buns if you'd like some.'

He stared back at the dolls as they left the room: Isabella lay flat on the floor with her spider-lashed eyes staring at the ceiling. Edward's bare pink legs poked upwards out of the clothes in the suitcase, like he'd dived in there to hide.

ALL THE BARBIES were stuffed into the princess coach now, and it was being pulled by Kitty. Cameron followed her, still crawling, through the door into the utility room, then Charlie heard the coach bumping down the steps into the back garden.

'So you don't remember Edward, the sex pest Barbie?'

She shrugged off the question. 'Vaguely. I must have been watching too much *Dallas* or *Dynasty* or something.'

Charlie frowned. The Hazelwoods had been very strict about television. Their set had stood in a mahogany cabinet in the living room, with heavy doors that were only opened up by Lynne when there was something suitable on – like *Blue Peter*. Even *All Creatures Great and Small* had been considered 'too adult'.

'Too much church, more like. You used to recite bits from the Bible to me about adultery. You used a funny deep voice and said you were pretending to be the Lord.'

A flush rose up her neck, suffusing her skin with pink.

'It's cool how Kitty seems to decide what she and Cammie should play – and she gets him to do what she wants! Just like you used to,' he added.

In fact, he strongly suspected that Juliet could still get him to do whatever she wanted to.

She smiled.

'The speech thing doesn't seem to be an issue between them,' he said.

'I've decided I'm not going to tell Beth that I heard Kitty talking.' Juliet looked at him, her chin slightly raised, as if she was expecting him to be shocked.

'Why not?'

'I had some counselling, once. Ages ago. The therapist asked me one day – what did I think was the purpose of my... well, my behaviour.'

Her self-harm. That's what she meant. Charlie nodded.

'She said that somewhere deep down, it would have a

very logical purpose. Well, Kitty's mutism must be serving a purpose. In her own mind, anyway. If she believes she needs it, then who am I to interfere?'

'What kind of purpose would it have?'

As soon as he said it, he knew. He watched Juliet's lips move, saying the words that were already in his mind.

'It's keeping her safe.'

26

JULIET

Later that night, when I was going up to bed, I heard voices coming from Kitty's room again.

I pushed the door open, just an inch or two. Kitty was sitting up in her bed, a small figure in the crumple of white bedlinen, the ends of her hair damp after her bath.

'I did my Autumn Assembly today.' Her voice was only just audible. 'I held up the sign and Cameron did my words. My words were this...' She took a deep breath. 'Okay, listen, they were this: "Fallen leaves make a good shelter for animals, even brown ones". What do you fink? Is that –'

'La la la, la-la la la,' cut in the doll.

Kitty sighed and sank back onto her pillows.

'When you come back, can you get me some new bed covers? Sara has ones with dogs on them.'

She sat bolt upright again and regarded the doll with wide, warning eyes. 'Remember how the zoo people visited our school yesterday? Well, a snake went into Sara's cup.'

'My, you look pretty today,' said the doll.

'Thank you,' said Kitty absently. 'Sara said she won't be drinking milk any more. She said I can have hers, but I don't want that snake cup either.'

She held the doll up to her face, but it merely stared ahead with plastic eyes.

'Oh Mummy, I wish you would speak. I get so lonely sometimes. Kitty so lonely,' she added, in a baby voice.

Mummy?

That was it. Beth might not be here to give Kitty the attention she needed, but I was. Very slowly and quietly, I pushed the door open and stepped into the room.

'Hello, Mermaid,' I began. 'Has Kitty told you about the new jigsaws we found at the charity shop in Sudbury?' I sat down on the chair by her bed, just on the very edge.

Kitty kept her eyes on the doll. Swallowed twice and opened her mouth. 'We got some new jigsaws at the charity shop. One was of two tortoises, and one was of Widzer Castle. The tortoise one was difficult because it all looked the same.'

'You could be a mermaid like me!' suggested the doll brightly.

'No fanks. There was also one of some squirrels. We nearly didn't get it because there was a notice on it saying there were two pieces missing. But we're going to make the extra pieces out of cardboard.'

We sat in silence for a few moments. Kitty shook the doll and regarded it expectantly. Then she buried her face against it and spoke in a voice that was so quiet I could barely hear it: 'Sometimes I can't get to sleep.'

'Oh dear,' I said, pretending to talk to the mermaid too. 'That can't be nice for Kitty. I wonder why she can't get to sleep.'

'If I go to sleep, I might disappear.' Her eyes were like saucers in the dim light.

'You won't disappear,' I said, in a voice that was warm but certain. 'I promise. You've gone to sleep every night of your life so far, haven't you? And I can see you just perfectly.'

And hear you. I can hear you now.

'Yes I can definitely see you. You're right...there.' I pressed the end of her nose.

She let her eyes rest on mine in a rare moment of eye contact. Then she reached out her hand, and solemnly pressed my nose back.

'Are you lonely because Mummy is away?' I asked.

Kitty nodded, and her eyes filled with tears.

'She'll be back soon,' I said. 'Tomorrow morning.'

Kitty's shoulders drooped and she shook her head. Then she turned to the mermaid again. 'I wish I could just go driftly off to sleep, like I used to before.'

I reached for my phone and did a search. 'So tell me, Mermaid. Have you ever listened to the Shipping Forecast?'

'You're the BEST!' cried the mermaid.

'It's very nice. It tells you the weather all around the coast of Great Britain. You can imagine little seaside villages, and lighthouses, and boats out in the sea. Boats sailing driftly about in the sea,' I added.

'Boats with little lights on?' Kitty asked the mermaid.

'Definitely with lights on,' I said. 'Shall we have a listen?'

She settled down on her pillows as the radio announcer began to read.

Viking: Cyclonic 4 becoming southerly or southwesterly 5 to 7. Slight or moderate become moderate or rough, wintry showers, then rain later. Good, occasionally poor.

Kitty's eyes closed and she gave a sigh.

North Utsire: West or southwest 4 or 5 increasing 5 to 7, perhaps gale 8 later.

A stormy night.

Her breathing began to soften.

'I'll keep you safe,' I whispered.

I MUST HAVE FALLEN ASLEEP TOO, because I was woken by the National Anthem, playing tinnily from my phone – the end of broadcasting on Radio 4 for the night.

And suddenly my mother was standing before me in my mind's eye. So clear that I could have reached out and touched her. She was wearing her best dress – the one with the swishy skirt the colour of peacock feathers – but had a smudge of flour on her cheek. She'd been busy in the kitchen all day getting ready for our party to celebrate the wedding of Prince Andrew to Sarah Ferguson. She'd made chicken vol-au-vents (I'd helped heat up cream of chicken soup to add to the filling), and summer pudding with thick cream. And she'd come to tell me to wash my face and get ready.

I remembered how I'd run up to her and flung my arms around her, caught up in a sudden rush of joy. She'd swung me round – so fast that one of my black patent ballet slippers flew off and knocked my clock off the bookcase.

But this was Kitty's room now. Kitty's bookcase and her clock, showing five past one. My room was upstairs. The Forget-Me-Not Room.

I stumbled my way into the bathroom and snapped on the light, still rubbing my eyes, and then –

'Jesus! Jesus Christ...'

It was the mermaid doll. Floating face down in the bath, in six inches deep of water, her hair moving gently like strands of red seaweed.

It was then that I became aware that Kitty was standing behind me.

'Kitty... it's okay, sweetheart. Juliet just got a fright.' I smiled, and rolled my eyes. 'What's the silly mermaid doll doing in the *bathroom*?!'

Kitty frowned. Her bottom lip disappeared inside her mouth. She turned as if to make her way back to her bedroom.

'Hang on there a minute, Kitty.'

I pulled the doll out of the water.

'Did you put her here, Kitty?' I asked lightly. 'Were you trying to make her swim?'

She rubbed her eyes sleepily and shook her head. A creeping feeling came over me. Had someone come into the house – into Kitty's *room* – while Kitty and I slept there?

I wrapped my arms around myself, trying to hold in my shakes.

Should I phone the police? I thought of Kitty's 999 calls over the last few months, and wondered how the police would react to my calling them about a doll that moved by itself.

'Now, I think Mermaid is a little bit cold and tired. I think you should make a little bed for her.' I pulled a fluffy white towel off the heated towel rail and handed it to Kitty. 'You stay here, okay, and make a bed for her? I'll fetch a little pillow for her. I'll be back in a minute.'

Kitty nodded and began to arrange the towel on the floor,

the tip of her tongue protruding from her lips as she concentrated.

I slipped out of the room, closing the bathroom door behind me, and locking it quietly from the outside. Standing in the hallway, I listened for any sign of life in the house.

The light from Kitty's bedroom cast shadows through the banisters of the galleried landing, making dark columns on the carpet. A low, ticking noise came from the clock in the hallway below.

I knocked on Beth's bedroom door – just in case she'd come back unexpectedly – and checked inside when there was no reply.

I went down the stairs, my feet making almost no noise on the thick carpet.

The front door was locked, with the chain secured – I'd checked it when I went upstairs earlier that evening. I made my way through the hall and the kitchen into the utility room. The back door that led to the garden, and the side door that opened onto the front patio were both locked. But there was an internal door into the garage itself. It was never used, and there were wellies lined up in front of it, but I pulled down on the handle and the door opened.

Manoeuvring past the wellies, I stepped inside and pulled on the cord to turn on the light.

The air smelt stale, like a room that had been shut up for a long time in hot weather. Beth never put her car in here – it was too narrow for her big white Range Rover.

I stepped forward, feeling grit beneath my socked feet. Something brushed my shoulder and I leapt back. But it was just the light cord, swinging back and forward.

Was that a rustle?

I held my breath and listened.

Yes, there it was again, clearer this time. The noise came from the back, near the chest freezer that stood against the wall. It sounded like someone stepping on a plastic bag.

I grabbed a garden rake in shaking hands.

'Who – who's there?' My voice sounded high like a child's.

Was someone hiding there at the back?

Every instinct was telling me to run back up the stairs to Kitty. To make sure she was safe.

But I forced myself to inch forwards. The garage was completely silent now, except for my ragged breathing and the faint hum of the freezer.

The stale smell was worse back here... sweet and over-ripe. Had the freezer stopped working? Was it full of meat that had gone off?

Next to the freezer was a pile of semi-flattened cardboard boxes. Was that where the rustle had come from? I nudged them to the side with the rake.

I screamed, dropped the rake, sprang back.

It was a dead mouse putrefying in a little pool of juice, little black specks moving over it.

Oh Jesus...

My own skin began to crawl, alive with the imagined sensation of insect legs. I looked around me, and saw a plastic bag – a thick 'bag for life' – that was caught in the space between the freezer and the wall. Checking it for dead things first, I stuck my hand inside it to form a glove. I could pick up the mouse corpse and stick it in the wheelie bin outside. That stench was repulsive.

But then a tiny shape shot across the floor, just inches from my foot, disappearing into a dark space between the cardboard boxes.

My insides heaved. No. I couldn't do this. Beth would

have to sort it out when she was back tomorrow. I might be going for 'indispensible' but I had my limits. And I had to get back to Kitty.

An old receipt fluttered out of the carrier bag as I drew my hand out. I picked it up and the items listed caught my eye.

Extra thick bleach – three bottles.

Dettol floor cleaner – two bottles.

Three rolls of heavy-duty bin bags.

A litre of milk.

All purchased at the 24-hour Tesco in Ipswich. Paid for in cash. At 23.58 on the seventh of July last year.

I knew that date – it was the prescription date on Kitty's promethazine tablets.

The day my baby had been due.

I'd spent that night on Cassie's couch – I hadn't been able to face going back home to Eddie, who hadn't even clocked the significance of the date.

But this didn't make any sense. Why would Beth have gone out so late at night? And all the way to Ipswich – an hour's round trip. Or was it Frank, Kitty's dad? Had someone been violently sick, to require such a mammoth clean-up operation? Even so... three bottles of bleach?

I opened up the bag. Right at the bottom there was another receipt.

It was for something called 'Gorilla Tape' – two rolls.

Purchased at 00.05 on the eighth of July.

Seven minutes later.

I pictured Beth walking to her car, realising she'd forgotten something and going back into the shop.

An image forced itself into my mind. Hands, taping Kitty's mouth shut.

I shoved the receipts deep into the pocket of my dressing gown and went back into the house, locking the garage door behind me.

But at the foot of the stairs, I froze.

The five house-shaped picture frames on the staircase wall – the ones that had shown mini photographs of Kitty inside the 'windows' – they'd been turned around so that they were hanging facing the wall, displaying only the fibre-board backings. Like blank eyes in a dead face.

I ran up the stairs, slipping on the top step and falling to my hands and knees.

'Kitty! Kitty? Are you okay?'

I unlocked the bathroom door from the outside. Kitty was still kneeling on the bathmat, tugging a comb through the mermaid's hair.

'Did you turn the pictures round? The ones on the stairs?'

She didn't look up.

Maybe they'd been like that all day and I hadn't noticed?

'Let's get you back to bed, sweetie.' I ushered her out of the room, picking up the mermaid doll and wrapping it in the towel.

HALF AN HOUR LATER, two police officers – a man and a woman – were sitting in the kitchen, drinking tea. I was still in my dressing gown. I'd seen, too late, in the hall mirror that my hair was wild, standing out in wisps around my head.

'So,' said PC Walters, who looked about twenty-two, with her clean-scrubbed face and neat French pleat. 'We've had a good look around the house, and we can't see anything unto-ward. No evidence of a break-in. You showed us that the pictures on the stairs were the wrong way round. But tell me again about the doll?'

'I woke up and found it floating in the bath,' I said. 'Someone had been in the house and run a bath, and put the doll in it.'

'Someone?' said the policewoman. 'But it's possible Kitty could have moved the pictures, or the doll?'

'I suppose so, but it seems very out of character.'

Did it? Did it really? I thought of how Kitty moved silently about the house, her secret conversations with the mermaid when she didn't think anyone was listening. The empty look that came into her eyes as if she were somewhere else entirely.

The officer nodded slowly. 'And your employer...' She glanced at her notebook. 'Beth Seigler. She's away for the night, you said? Have you tried calling her?'

'I... no. I didn't want to worry her in the middle of the night.'

'And is there a Mr Seigler?'

'Yes. But I haven't met him yet. He's been away on business. At least that's what Beth says.'

PC Walters gave me a questioning look.

'I found these.' I pushed the scrumpled receipts from the 24-hour Tesco across the table.

She picked them up. 'And these are...?'

'Look at the time on them – it was midnight. What was Beth doing buying all those cleaning materials in the middle of the night? And tape?'

PC Walters cleared her throat and passed the receipts to her colleague, who studied them and put them back on the table. 'I'm not clear what you're suggesting here?'

'I have no idea. I'm just showing you what I found.'

She frowned. 'Seems like a spring cleaning spree to me. My mother-in-law's always hoovering in the middle of the night. She has insomnia. She drives my father-in-law mad.'

'There's something wrong in this house,' I said. 'Kitty – she doesn't speak at all. Not even to anyone in her family. That's not typical with selective mutism. I'm worried she may have been through some kind of trauma.'

'But – just to be clear – this is purely conjecture on your part?'

I nodded.

'And you've no reason to believe that Kitty has been harmed? She hasn't said anything to that effect?'

I shook my head.

'You haven't seen any physical injuries?'

'No, nothing like that. But she called 999 thirteen times.'

The officers looked at each other.

'Again, just to be clear, what was the reason for your call this evening? Because you thought there was an intruder in the house? Or because you wanted to discuss concerns about Kitty's welfare?'

This was all going wrong. If the police told Beth that I'd raised concerns about Kitty then I'd be out on my ear. I imagined them coming to the door, asking questions about the bleach and the rolls of tape. Beth's eyes widening in disbelief.

I made a bargain with myself. I'd play this down for the moment. But I'd be all over this from now on – I'd go straight to the police if I got the slightest whiff of anything untoward.

'I was worried about intruders,' I said. 'I'm sorry. It's really late. I think I'm a bit disorientated, after waking up in the middle of the night. On reflection, I think perhaps I've panicked and overreacted.'

'Okie dokie,' said PC Walters, her voice warmer now. 'You

did the right thing, if you were worried. Better safe than sorry, eh?'

'I've wasted your time.'

'Not at all. Last week I had an emergency call-out to someone who'd run out of loo-roll.'

The officers exchanged an amused look – perhaps they thought I belonged in that category.

27

CHARLIE

Collecott Hall

The dining room was almost full – and noisy, as it always seemed to be when it was raining. It had been savoury salmon bake today, one of the worst lunches, so everybody was hanging around in case there would be seconds of pudding. Charlie was just about to go and put his tray up on the rack when Juliet came in, shoes tapping on the polished floor, making a beeline straight for him. A few of the others, still lingering at the tables, glanced up at her and looked away. There seemed to be a consensus among most of the year group, now, that nobody talked to her. Even the music crowd and the God Squad avoided her now, turning away with meaningful looks and whispers. Although he had heard the secretary of the Scripture Union society offering to pray for her.

She pulled back a chair and sat down next to him. At first he didn't really get what she was saying. Something about Mr Redwood, and Monte, and the police. Her forehead was red and blotchy from crying and she kept snatching breaths, which made her difficult to understand.

He wanted to put his hand on her back, and tell her to breathe slowly.

Tissues! He should offer her a tissue. He pulled one out of his pocket, unfolded and refolded it, to see if that made it look any less creased (it didn't) and gave it to her.

She blew her nose loudly.

When they'd been younger, she'd always been the fearless one, and him the uncertain one.

He only had a few clear memories of her, from that time. One was of her talking to him in the churchyard at St Mary's-in-the-Wood after a particularly boring Sunday school session. They must have been about five.

She'd hopped up onto a gravestone, one of the flat, slab-like ones.

'This is Dorothy Collins,' she'd said solemnly. 'And Albert Collins, and their six children. They all died from eating broccoli soup.'

Charlie had looked at the words carved on the stone. It had said something about God's beloved children, taken too soon, and a list of dates.

'It doesn't say anything about soup.' It had felt important to challenge her, or the whole world would just turn and spin exactly the way she said it.

She'd stood there on the gravestone, with her stripy t-shirt and her red shorts and the laces on her trainers undone. She'd stood looking at Charlie with her eyes big and her chin pointy, like she was frightened of everything in the world and nothing.

Charlie had taken a quick look around, to see if there were any adults watching, and he'd climbed onto the gravestone too. He stood right in front of her and leaned forward, very slowly, until his forehead was touching hers. She leaned forward too and he could feel the weight of her, pressing through her head into his. And the heat coming off her sunburnt nose.

'Juliet,' he said now, shaking his head to dispel the memory, and the rush of inexplicable feelings that came with it. 'What's wrong? Why are you crying?'

'Mr –'

'Mr –'

'It's okay,' said Charlie. 'Mr…?'

'Redwood –' she gasped. 'He called me to his office. He said that a witness has come forward. They saw me push Monte – really hard – against the bookcase in the Rainbow Room last week. They said it was because she spilled her drink and I lost my temper.'

She looked at him with pleading eyes. 'I *didn't.*'

'I know,' he said. It wasn't a question of *deciding* whether or not he believed her. He just did, and there it was.

'And they said – this person – that they'd seen me yanking the children around before. Like, when I'm changing their nappies or getting their coats on.'

'Bollocks,' he said. He'd seen her once, not long ago on his way to rugby, playing with the children in the playground. She'd been crouched in front of a little boy, putting on a winter hat and fastening the ear flaps under his chin. He'd thought about her hands, how small and soft they were and how gently they moved. She twisted them in her lap now, folding and re-folding the tissue as he had done. An angry red scratch was just visible, under the shadow of her cuff.

Jesus Christ.

The only person Juliet had ever hurt was herself.

'Mr Redwood is wrong. This so-called witness is talking crap.'

'But what if it's a member of staff, Charlie? It'll be her word against mine. Mr Redwood thinks that the police might have to become involved. He said it was –'

She drew in another shuddering gasp.

'Assault.'

Charlie felt a crushing sensation in his chest, such was his longing to pull her into his arms and keep her safe.

She leaned forward and put her head in her hands. He could see the nubs of her spine, under the thin white cotton of her blouse, the strained movement of her shoulder blades as she fought to keep her sobs in. The thin lines of her bra straps.

'So he didn't say who this witness is?' It was incredible, how his voice could stay almost normal, while all this was heaving inside him.

She shook her head. A strand of her hair fell forward onto the table, landing perilously close to a blob of creamy salmon sauce. He lifted it with a quivering finger and tucked it behind her ear, almost touching her – almost.

She lifted her head.

'Sauce,' he said, matter-of-factly, pointing to the blob.

'And there's something even worse,' she said. 'They've been looking at the nursery records, the accident book and the daily logs and so on, and they've got questions about seven other children – seven, Charlie!'

'What do you mean, questions?'

'Questions for me. They think these children might have been... assaulted too. By me.'

'No.'

'Mr Redwood said that I'm to stay away from the nursery.

And I'm not to talk to anyone about it in case the press get
hold of it. Oh Charlie... do you remember those child abuse
scandals on the news? The big enquiries and investigations? I
might end up in prison. I might –'

'Stop, Juliet. You're letting your mind run away with you.'
It was something Dad sometimes said to him.

He'd said it when he'd found Charlie crying in his room,
when his mother was first in hospital having tests, and
Charlie had asked if she was going to die.

Juliet shook her head, as if she could hardly believe what
was happening. 'Mr Redwood said he was speaking to
Monte's parents this evening. They're coming in at seven.
He'll get an idea then if they want to press charges.'

'Okay,' he said finally, putting his hands flat on the table.
'It'll be in his study, yeah? I'll go to the roof space and listen
in. I'll find out what's going on. Don't worry. I'll meet you in
the TV room at eighty-thirty.'

AT FIRST, Charlie didn't think anybody was coming. He
pulled the air vent cover to the side so he could see into
Redwood's office more easily, but seven o'clock came and
went. He lay back on the old crash mat, thinking about Juliet,
how she'd be sitting in the library doing her homework.
Once, a few weeks ago, she'd kicked off her shoes and
stretched her legs out under the table, her small, black-
socked feet resting on the chair next to his. He'd been
completely unable to concentrate on his history essay – all he
wanted to do was pull her feet onto his lap, and hold them
there.

Then, at around twenty past seven, Charlie heard the door to the study open.

'Can I see her?' It was a high female voice, spiked with anxiety.

He peered through the air vent. It was hard to see much, but he could tell one thing for sure – that wasn't Monte's mother. It was Lynne Hazelwood – Juliet's mother – in a long grey woollen coat with her wavy hair pinned back, a bit like that woman in *Brief Encounter*.

'Let's have a chat first,' said Mr Redwood with a slow nod.

They sat down on either side of his desk.

'Lynne.' He rubbed his beard, as though he was choosing his words carefully. 'I gave a brief outline on the phone of what's been going on. But the truth is, I've been having some concerns about Juliet for a while now.'

'What concerns?'

'She spends almost all of her time on her own. The other students have effectively ostracized her.'

'But she's... she's such a sweet girl. Why would they do that?'

'Juliet's demeanour is... I don't quite know how to put this. A bit negative? A bit desperate, even? Off-putting, anyway. Two of the other students came to me complaining that she was following them around, and seemed to have attached herself to them.'

'Who?' Lynne's voice was furious. 'Who said that?'

'Now, I like Juliet. I like her a lot. She's a great kid. But something seems to have happened recently. She seems to have changed. And the incident with Montefiore Sinclair – well in some ways I do wonder if it's a cry for help.'

'I don't believe for a *second* that –' began Lynne.

Mr Redwood lifted his hands in a defensive gesture. 'I'd love to share that certainty, Lynnie. I really would.'

Lynnie?

'But a witness has come forward, as I mentioned on the phone. Now, I spoke to Monte's parents this evening, just before you arrived. I think... I *think* I've managed to smooth things over there. I've explained that Juliet is going through a bit of a hard time at the moment. I've assured them that she won't be working at the nursery again, or coming into contact with any of our youngest children.'

'So are they going to...?'

'I'm hoping that the police won't be involved.'

Lynne dropped her head into her hands and a muffled sob escaped.

None of this made sense. None of it. Charlie had been up in the roof space since tea finished, and Mr Redwood had been sitting at his desk doing paperwork all evening.

'May I speak frankly?' he said.

Lynne looked up, her eyes red and her hair all frazzled now at the front. She nodded.

'I do wonder whether this is all linked to what's been going on at home.' He paused for a few seconds. 'How's Graeme's depression?'

Lynne tensed visibly. 'Nobody's used the term "depression", as such. But he's been prescribed some antidepressants. He took it hard when Gypsy died. He blamed himself for leaving those slug pellets in the shed.'

Redwood shrugged, as if to indicate that a real man would have taken such a thing in his stride.

'Oh God, I'm such a... a bitch. That's what I am.' The word sounded wrong, coming out of her mouth. Harsh and ugly.

'You haven't done *anything* wrong.'

'I haven't done anything wrong? By thinking about you? By talking to you on the phone about... about... well, talking in *that way*. That highly inappropriate *way*.'

Sweet Jesus.

Charlie thought of Juliet in the library, frowning over her homework, oblivious to the horror now unfolding in front of him. How the hell was he going to tell her about this? How the hell was he *not* going to tell her?

'You stopped the phone calls, though, didn't you? You tried to do the right thing. You tried to ignore your needs. It's just that... oh, Lynne, I don't think either of us can stop this.'

He stood up and moved round to the other side of the desk, crouched in front of her. 'I don't think that's within our power.'

Carefully, like a predator approaching its prey, Mr Redwood snaked his arm around Lynne's shoulders. Charlie saw her tense, but she didn't move away.

'We've been fighting this for years, Lynne. At some point you'll need to face up to the fact that... Well, I love Graeme to bits. You know that. We've been friends since school, haven't we? All three of us have. And I've been happy to be your friend, Lynnie. It's been one of the greatest privileges in my life. But I can't go on watching you destroy yourself. You don't love him, not in the way that a woman should love a man. He can't give you what you need. And you're destroying *him*, Lynnie, by pretending that he can. By pretending to be a happy family when you aren't. No anti-depressants in the world can fix that. And now... well, they say that the problems in a family come out in the behaviour of the children. Now it's Juliet who's suffering, poor girl.'

Lynne looked up at him, tears streaming down her face. 'I

hate you, Frank. You know that? I hate you...' Her voice softened. 'I hate you.'

'I know, my love. I know. You've been fighting so hard.' He
pulled her against him and they held each other for a few
moments, rocking back and forth. Then he pulled her onto
the floor, so that she landed on her back with a great thud,
him hovering over her. He reached for the top button of her
blouse. She arched her head back, exposing the white of her
throat, and she groaned.

'We can make this right,' said Mr Redwood, leaning
forward to kiss her throat. 'I've needed you every day, Lynne.
Every day for ten years. Every day since the last time. No,
every *hour*... your beautiful skin... the scent of you... the way
you move...'

But Lynne sat up. Folded her arms over her chest where
her blouse gaped open.

'No. I can't go back to Graeme, if I do this with you. I
cannot open the front door and walk in, and put my bag
down, and hang my coat up, and... and kiss him as if nothing
has happened. It would *break* me. It would break me into a
million pieces.'

'It'll break you if you *don't*. If you go on ignoring what you
need. Maybe not now, but in another year. Ten years. Or it
could be twenty or thirty. How long do you think it'll be until
he dies? Can you wait that long, Lynnie?'

'You're saying things you don't mean now,' said Lynne,
standing up and buttoning her blouse. She had her Sunday
school voice on now. The voice she used to use when she told
Juliet and him that they'd eaten enough sweets, or had left
their bikes out in the rain again.

'Hang on. Hang on. I'm sorry, that was out of order. But
listen, let's talk again tomorrow.'

'I'm driving back down tonight.'

'You can't, Lynne. You've only just got here. And you need to see Juliet. I'll call Juliet in tomorrow morning, and we can talk, all three of us, and try and get things sorted out. Things will seem better, I promise. We can get through this, Lynne. We've been part of each other's lives for decades, and that's not going to change. Whether we're lovers, or friends, or something in between, I'll always be here for you.'

'I can't stay. Do you think I can face her after this? I have to get back. I will telephone Juliet and talk things over with her tomorrow.'

Charlie had pins and needles in his leg. He shifted slightly to the left but misjudged it so that one knee slipped off the crash mat and the weight of his body fell on to the floor with a thud.

Shit.

'What's that?' he heard Lynne saying. 'Is someone up there?'

'You wait here.'

Charlie scrambled across the roof space, out of the little door, and ran down the fire escape stairs, his trainers slapping against the steps. Behind him, at the top of the stairs, he heard a door open, and footsteps.

He swung round the last turn of the stairs and burst through the fire door into the cold of the night air. He ran. He ran to Juliet, towards what he thought had been beginning between them, knowing all the while that he could never outrun what he'd just seen.

He found her watching *Animal Hospital* in the dark, pulling at the ends of her sleeves, running her fingers underneath. He thought of the lines of red scars and his own skin smarted in sympathy.

'Monte's parents didn't come,' he said, sliding into the seat next to her. 'He met with, well, with your Mum.'

'Mum? Mum's here?' She sat up straight in her seat.

'He said he's trying to smooth things over with Monte's parents.'

Juliet nodded distractedly. 'Where is she?'

'I think she was going straight home, Juliet. She said she had to get back.'

'Without seeing me?' Her face flooded with disbelief. 'Why?'

'I don't know.' His jaw tightened with the lie.

'I have to see her,' she said quietly. 'I need to get away from here.'

'I know. You could go tomorrow. I've got a train timetable upstairs.' But it was a way of getting out of the room, as much as anything.

For the first time in his life, he needed to get away from her.

28

BETH

The next time Beth video called her father, a nurse answered. Stan – *Dad* – was wearing an oxygen mask, lying back against pillows. He lifted the mask away from his face to speak, begging her to visit him in the hospital in Luton before it was too late. With five and a half million pounds riding on it, anyone would agree it was a trip worth making.

Frank's eyes went cold and flat when she began the conversation that night, her voice rising high and childlike with feigned surprise. She lied and told him that a private investigator had just turned up at the door that morning, completely out of the blue. Her father had hired him to find her as a matter of urgency. No expense spared, given the circumstances. No stone left unturned.

When she mentioned the sum of money involved, the cold look went out of his eyes and he laughed like a little boy, sitting down on one of the kitchen chairs with a flump.

So they made the trip back to England, and Frank said

they could stay at Laurel Bank, a property he owned in Suffolk, which she'd never even heard about. It wasn't that far from Luton. They could stay for a week or so, make the required visits to Stan.

But Stan lingered, and a week turned into a month. Two months. At the end of each visit, he'd stretch the oxygen mask away from his face and whisper, 'Please come again, love,' his eyes bleary with tears.

And then one day they took a different route back from the hospital and they passed it – an old coach house set back in a cobbled yard, hanging baskets spilling with pink and yellow flowers. Up for sale. A sign that said something about planning permission.

It sparked a memory in Beth – of a visit to a grand old stately home somewhere in the countryside, she had no idea where. Sitting at a wooden table under a big sunshade, eating warm scones, with her mother beside her, her father opposite. Then a sudden flash downpour. Water trickling down the mossy stone steps of the terrace, rivulets running into the lily pond. Running back to the car laughing with their coats over their heads.

'Look,' Beth said, touching Frank's knee to get his attention. 'That place would make an amazing café.'

'A café,' Kitty repeated softly from the back seat.

Beth turned around. 'Yes, Kitty! Good girl! A café!' As though Kitty was two, rather than nearly five.

Kitty stretched out her feet and pressed them into the back of Beth's seat. Beth thought that meant she was happy. And she'd seemed fine with the hospital visit, sitting on a chair by Stan's bed with her feet tucked under her. She'd even tried to present him with a stone she'd picked up in the little

Japanese 'garden of contemplation' they'd walked through on the way in.

She hadn't been sure about taking Kitty to the hospital, the first time, but Frank said it was important, that it would 'seal the deal'. And it wasn't as though they could leave her with a neighbour or something – Beth hadn't talked to a single soul since they'd been staying at Laurel Bank. Except the Polish girl who put through her groceries at the Spar, that time she'd nipped out for baking powder when it hadn't arrived with the shopping delivery. And the man who'd come to fix the boiler, who'd arrived early when Frank was out. He'd accepted a cup of tea and they'd talked about *Strictly Come Dancing*.

Frank would be annoyed that she'd spoken to anyone at all – he'd told her to pretend she couldn't speak English. He said he'd heard 'noises' that Rick was still looking for them. The name change would only protect them up to a point.

But surely Rick wouldn't think to look for her here, in the depths of the Suffolk countryside? They had to stop running eventually.

'If we moved here, we could get some help with Kitty's speech,' said Beth, keeping her voice light, like a child's. The tiny private nursery at the top of the hill at Vevey had raised concerns, saying that Kitty didn't talk when she was there. Even at home, her words were few and far between, and most of them spoken in French to Rosa the help. But Frank kept brushing it off whenever Beth mentioned it. He said that Kitty just got a bit tongue-tied in social situations, and that he'd been the same as a child.

When they got back to Laurel Bank, Frank sat down in the kitchen and leaned back with a smile, linking his hands behind his head.

'How would you like to move back to England, poppet? And open that café you've always talked about?'

As though it had been his idea all along.

She squealed in delight and flung her arms around him, happy to play the part of 'poppet', so that he could play the part of big hero, and they could both get what they wanted.

29

CHARLIE

Collecott Hall

Charlie was revising in the library the next afternoon when Mrs McCredie, the headmistress, came in.

'Where's Juliet Hazelwood?'

Oh Christ. He looked at his watch. She'd be at the station now. Her train was at half past three.

McCredie's head swiveled as she scanned the room, in a way that made Charlie think of one of Ridley Scott's aliens, trying to sniff out Ripley in the dark air ducts of the space-ship. Then her gaze came to rest on him.

'Charlie. Where's Juliet?'

'I'm not sure.' Well, he wasn't. She might be climbing the steep steps up to the station, or she might be in the café buying a hot chocolate for the journey.

'She wasn't feeling very great,' he added, which was also true. His heart squeezed a little. He should have insisted on going with her, instead of watching her from the common room window, trudging down the hill with a big rucksack on her back. A dark shape getting smaller and smaller.

'I need to speak to Juliet as a matter of urgency.' McCredie was using her deep, man-like voice, the one that she'd used when Archie Bowles had set fire to the cricket scoring hut last summer.

His stomach swooped. 'What's happened?'

But McCredie just gave him a sniffy look and left the room. He felt in his pocket for some change and went to the payphone.

The last thing he wanted to do was speak to Lynne. Or Graeme, for that matter. But he had to do this. For Juliet's sake. He had to find out what was going on.

A tremulous voice answered the phone. 'Yes?'

It wasn't Lynne, or Graeme. The back of his neck prickled.

'Is Lynne there? It's Charlie, one of Juliet's friends.'

A long silence. Then: 'Have you... *heard*?'

'I know they're trying to find Juliet. To tell her something.'

'Are you at the school?' Charlie heard a muffled noise as the woman covered the phone with her hand. 'Lynne. It's a boy from the school. Charlie something. Okay, dear, here you go.'

Afterwards, Charlie would wish he could somehow forget the noises that came through the phone then. Choking breaths, gasped in like she was drowning. Syllables that could have been the beginnings of words, but which dissolved into thin wails.

'Lynne?' he said. 'What's happened?'

'Graeme.'

'I –'

'Graeme... Graeme... Graeme.'

She said the words like she was pleading with Graeme himself.

The other woman took the phone again. 'It's Anne Bramwell here. A friend of the family.'

He could hear Lynne, still saying 'Graeme' in the background. As though it was the only word left.

'What's happened?' said Charlie again.

'I'm sorry, dear. Graeme's passed away. It was a car accident. Please, we would be very grateful if you could find Juliet. Someone's going to have to tell her. Lynne wanted to come up to the school herself but I don't think she'll manage that. Oh dear, I don't know what to do. Mrs McCredie said she would break the news, but –'

'I'll find her,' said Charlie.

He arrived at the station at twenty-nine minutes past, gulping in great breaths – he'd never pedalled so fast in his life. He abandoned his bike at the bottom of the steps up to the station, only vaguely registering a hope that it would be there when he got back.

Juliet was sitting on a bench on the freezing platform, hugging her rucksack to her chest.

He walked towards her, grit crunching beneath the soles of his shoes – it was forecast to snow this evening. Three rising chimes heralded an announcement for the London train. Juliet's train.

Now that he was here, he didn't know what to do, what to say.

But it must have shown in his face. She stood up when she saw him, the rucksack falling to the ground in front of her.

'What's happened?'

He stood there before her, and just shook his head when the words wouldn't come.

Her face was thin and white, pinched with cold.

'Is it Mum… or Daddy?'

'It's Graeme,' he said. 'It's your Daddy. Oh Juliet.'

Her knees buckled and she dropped in front of him. He knelt down on the cold, gritty stone and held on to her.

Oh God, how he'd longed to touch her. For months. And now it was like this.

'Come back to school, Juliet. They'll tell you what's going to happen. I think your mother may be coming up to get you.'

Her body slipped to the side and he pulled her against him, her head against his pounding chest, and he rocked her, and rocked her, and rocked her.

IT ENDED up being a week before Lynne came. Every day there was a different plan: Juliet was going to get the train down. Lynne was going to come… as soon as she was well enough. Then Mrs Bramwell was going to come and drive Juliet home on Monday. Or Tuesday, actually, as soon as the funeral arrangements had been made. It had been a heart attack at the wheel, they thought. There might have to be a post-mortem. And then there was a heavy snowfall down the east coast that stopped the trains running and brought the traffic to a standstill on the A1, and a woman died after being stuck in her car all night.

Juliet went along with school as normal – but not as normal. She sat hunched over in lessons, like she was trying to protect herself from pain. She barely said a word, and after one or two mumbling attempts at sympathy by some of the kinder girls, everyone left her alone in her bright white spot-light of grief. She wouldn't look Charlie in the eye, but she would sit by him, in the darkness of the TV room in the evenings, and he brought her hot chocolate and went through the Radio Times to find the animal programmes he knew she liked – or had liked once, before *this* – not knowing what else he could possibly do.

Then Lynne appeared in the school reception area, one day after lunch break, perched on the edge of a chair with red-rimmed eyes, her hair wet with rain.

'Charlie!' she said.

He tried to keep his face neutral, but it was no good. The secret – Lynne's fucking secret – seemed to billow into the air between them, thick and black and suffocating.

'Charlie?' She stood up and took a step towards him.

He knew he should say something. He should say that he was sorry for her loss. But his jaw was clenched shut. All he could do was shake his head, and back away like a cornered animal.

Lynne's eyes widened, and she put a grey-gloved hand up to her face.

He waited at the window at the top of the main staircase, heart jumping in his chest, until he saw them leave. Juliet struggled down the front steps with her trunk and rucksack while Lynne hurried on ahead through the rain to bring the car round.

She stopped for a moment – his girl, his Juliet – and cast a look behind her. Perhaps she was wondering why he hadn't come to say goodbye. How could he, when his face would give him away? He watched the car winding down the drive, disappearing between the dark shapes of the dripping trees.

30

JULIET

I couldn't help it, could I? The way that my heart lifted when I saw Charlie, dashing through the rain towards the gates of Boxley Wood Primary.

Running between the drops.

It was something Dad used to say. For a moment it felt like he was there beside me, his eyes twinkling at me over the top of his glasses.

Good heavens, it's Charlie-boy. Your partner in crime.

'What's up?' said Charlie. He was still out of breath, wiping the rain from his face. 'Has something happened?'

'I'm okay. But what about you? You're all wet.'

He was wearing a North Face jacket over a slightly creased work suit, and he'd been running his hand through his hair the wrong way, like he always did when he was stressed, so that it was sticking up at the side.

He gave me a 'cut the bullshit' look. 'Juliet....'

I wanted to rest my head against his chest. To hear the sleeves of his jacket rustle as his arms closed around me.

Annabel looked over, one eyebrow slightly raised, but her

two Labradors strained on the lead, pulling her away in the direction of another dog. 'Jasper! Oscar! Sit!'

'Something happened,' I said. 'We had a bit of a disturbed night.'

He glanced over at Annabel. 'Why don't you come over to mine? We can have a chat and the kids can play. I don't think we'll get any complaints from them.'

He looked up and nodded at Cameron and Kitty, who were making their way across the playground towards us. Kitty had looped her scarf around Cameron's waist and he was pulling her forward, slow and steady like a shire horse.

The rain lifted and the sun came out. Kitty and Cameron went to play outside as soon as we arrived. I'd noticed how they didn't seem to need words to communicate – they just trotted from the car, side by side, straight through the side gate into the garden. Charlie made some tea, pouring it into chunky Emma Bridgewater mugs. He didn't seem to notice that he'd given me one with pink hearts that said 'Mummy.'

'So what happened?' He was sitting on the sofa, leaning forward with his hands clasped in a V.

I explained about falling asleep in Kitty's room, about the mermaid doll drowned in the bath. The receipts. I told him about the police officers coming over.

'So either Kitty did it – which is kind of terrifying, actually – or I did it. Maybe I sleepwalked or something.'

'Have you ever sleepwalked before?'

'No, I don't think so. Is that even possible? I mean, can people just start sleepwalking for no reason?'

'Well.' Charlie sighed. 'The obvious questions would be… whether you'd taken any new medications or anything? Whether you'd had alcohol or caffeine before bed. That sort of thing.'

I shook my head.

'Whether you've been under unusual stress lately?' His voice was gentle but matter-of-fact. He was quiet for a moment, leaving a space for me to respond.

'It's not hard looking after Kitty. It's one of the easiest jobs I've had.'

Apart from the fear of losing her. The fear that sometimes stopped me in my tracks, in the middle of what I was doing, that crumpled my insides like I was made of paper. It was the flip side of this... this new happiness, or whatever it was. It had happened in the supermarket last week when I was looking at yoghurts for Kitty, and an old lady had touched me on the arm and asked if I was all right.

And what was this about, really? Had some part of me wanted to kill Kitty's 'mummy', as she called the mermaid doll? Had some twisted, rage-filled part of me wanted to take her place?

I looked down at the mummy mug – such a beautiful thing with its cherry-pink hearts against a cream background – and a lump swelled in my throat.

'Sleepwalking usually occurs in the first few hours after falling asleep,' said Charlie. 'When you're in deep sleep. Or if you've been disturbed when you're in deep sleep – by a noise or something.'

'It was. In the first few hours of being asleep, I mean.'

'Well, there you go. I don't think it's anything to worry about.'

'But... drowning a doll?'

Charlie sat there, his full attention on me.

'What if I'm going mad?'

He shook his head. 'You're not going mad. Not even remotely. I promise.'

'What if I sleepwalk again when Beth's there? Or what if she finds out what I said to the police about... the receipts and everything? Being worried about Kitty?'

He shrugged. 'Maybe your instincts are right about Kitty.'

'Do you think it was her, drowning the doll and everything? Turning the pictures the wrong way round? Do you think it was a cry for help?'

He frowned. 'It doesn't seem to fit, somehow. It sounds more like... I don't know. A joke. A prank. Someone who finds themselves funny.'

I stood up. Looked around the sitting room. At the smiling family photographs adorning the walls (well, Tasha and Charlie were smiling, and Cameron was frowning in most of them), and Cameron's sprawling Lego town, taking up all of the space around the bay window.

A family home. The kind of home I would never have.

The crumpling feeling again. I sank down on the sofa, my face in my hands.

'Juliet.'

I felt the sofa cushion shift as he sat down beside me. A feeling of warmth down that side of my body.

'I've been debating with myself as to whether to tell you this or not.'

'What?'

'I could really get into some serious trouble for discussing this. So please – *please* – keep this under your hat. But the waiting list for kids' speech therapy is only around three months at the moment. One of the other GPs was commenting on it today because it's so unusual. I think they've expanded their team or something.'

I frowned. 'Are you sure?'

He nodded. 'There's something odd about it.'

Almost as if Beth wanted Kitty to stay silent. I looked at Charlie and could see the same thought, moving across his face like a shadow.

Then there was the sound of a car door slamming outside. I sat up quickly. Guiltily.

Charlie swallowed. 'Anyway. Sounds like Tasha's home'.

31

CHARLIE

'You seem to be getting on very well with *Juliet*,' said Tasha with a hint of a smile, dumping her handbag on the table by the door. She tossed her keys into the little seashell tray where they landed with a loud clink, making the tray scoot across the polished wood. He winced – Cameron had made that for their Christmas present last year, and it had already fallen off the table once. He'd had to help Cammie glue on the broken bits of shell, and he'd moped around the house for the rest of the day looking like someone had died.

Why did she have to go around with that enormous bunch of keys, anyway? It made her look like a prison warden. She'd talked him through them all once – two keys for the front door of the Old Coach House, one for the door out onto the terrace, four separate ones for the doors here, including the garage and the shed. I mean, who carried a shed key around with them all day?

There was also a key for the door to the maid's rooms upstairs where he, Charlie, lived. Or at least, where he slept, climbing the stairs obediently every night, as if he had to be locked in there for his own good, like a werewolf. Not that they ever did lock it, though. Because that might upset Cameron, Tasha had explained with a look that suggested that should have been obvious.

Sometimes it felt like his whole life was a series of complicated doors, and a bewildering bunch of pointless keys that never seemed to fit.

Which may have been a bit Freudian. But at the moment he was too tired to work it out.

'Cammie and Kitty wanted to come back and play in the garden.' He hated the defensive note that had crept into his voice. It made him feel small, and petty. He wished he could just say, 'Yes, I enjoy spending time with Juliet. It makes me happier than I've felt in years.'

'Did you go to Tesco's on the way home?' she asked, in a bright, knowing voice, as though she was asking him if he'd done his homework and tidied his room, but suspected he had not.

'There are those chicken pies in the freezer,' he said. 'I can do mash, if you like?'

'Okay then,' she sighed. 'I'm absolutely bushed. A coach load of National Trust biddies came in.'

'Same here,' he said quietly. 'I mean, I'm bushed.' Not that a coach load of National Trust biddies had come into his surgery. Although they might as well have done. He had almost no memory of the twenty-five patients he'd seen that morning. Or the handful of home visits he'd completed before picking up Cammie from school. Maybe he was losing his short-term memory. He rubbed his temples, wishing the tight band round his eyes would go away.

Tasha went to the garage freezer to fetch the chicken pies

and Charlie began to run water into the sink to peel the potatoes. He stared out of the window, his gaze drawn to the two copper beech trees that stood side by side at the far end of the garden. 'Mature trees!' Tasha had said gleefully, when they'd first looked around the house. But to him they looked like a pair of tired old lungs, their capillaries spread out against the winter sky.

She came back in, clunking the pies down on the work surface and switching on the oven. 'Charlie?' A slightly sheepish look had come over her face. 'Can we try and get Cammie off to bed in good time tonight?'

'Sure.'

He didn't ask why. He didn't have to. Tash wanted to make sure that he, Charlie, could be dismissed to his quarters as soon as possible. It was Thursday, after all – date night.

Date night for Tasha and Shami.

IN HIS MIND, Charlie divided his married life into 'before Cyprus' and 'after Cyprus'.

And bloody Cyprus hadn't even been his idea in the first place. He had said it would be too hot in July, and he'd been proven right, though he'd managed to restrain himself from pointing this out to Tasha.

With Cameron being only two and a half, lying around by the pool at the hotel wasn't an option. More was the pity.

There'd be loads of other things to do, Tasha had said.

Roman ruins, she'd said, widening her eyes at Cameron as though she was offering Disneyland.

That day, the guidebook had brought them along a winding coastal road to a ruined Roman town with an ancient amphitheatre which Tasha had insisted would be 'stunning', and well worth the long drive from their hotel.

Cameron had been fretting since they'd left the car park. There'd been no toilets, Charlie had noted with dismay. Cammie hadn't long been potty trained and couldn't hang on very long. Tasha had brushed his concerns aside – she had spare trousers for him in the rucksack. So they'd set off, and now Cammie was crying and pulling off his sunhat every time Tasha tried to squish it back onto his head, and rubbing his eyes with his fists. A warm wind whipped the dust off the ground and into their eyes as they pressed on up the hill.

In part of the ruins that had once been a grand Roman villa, Charlie recognised the names of the rooms from his old Latin textbook.

Quintus est in triclinium

Caecilius est in horto

'Did you do Caecilius and Quintus and all that lot, at school?' he asked Tasha, for the sake of making conversation.

'Did I do *what*?' She wrinkled her nose, as though he'd asked her if she'd shagged her way through the rugby team or something. She seemed to have a knack of misinterpreting things he said, in a way that cast him as a buffoon, shooting off inappropriate comments. He sometimes wondered if she did it on purpose.

Juliet had used to test him on Latin declensions in the sun-warmed study rooms at the top of Collecott Hall. He'd make mistakes on purpose so that she would stop and correct him, reading the words out in her clear, quiet voice.

He was used to Juliet popping into his head at odd moments – he'd mentally say hello to her before going on with his day. Sometimes it felt to him like their minds were still in touching distance even after all these years. Or maybe,

since he'd known her from before he could remember, she'd
laid down pathways in his brain that caused his nerves to
vibrate sometimes with the sense of her. For no reason. Like
the pain from a phantom limb.

'You see?' said Tasha, out of breath, when they reached
the brow of the hill and the ruined amphitheatre opened out
below them, carved into the rock of the hillside, overlooking
the sparkling sea.

Charlie nodded grudgingly. Cameron threw back his
head and wailed.

'Will you be okay with Cammie for a bit? I want to get
some decent photos.' Without waiting for an answer, Tasha
trotted off down the crumbling stone steps, carrying the new
camera she'd given him yesterday for his birthday – he hadn't
even used it himself yet. Charlie found a shady spot next to a
flowering bush that had sprouted from the rock. He
wondered how the flowers managed to survive, so fresh and
pink, in this blistering heat.

'You okay there, buddy?' he asked Cameron, who was
now flopped against Charlie's shoulder, exhausted. His t-shirt
was stuck to his back and strands of hair were plastered to his
forehead with sun cream. 'That's it. You have a bit of a sleep.'

He felt Cameron relax against him and his breathing
soften.

Beside him on the stone step, Tasha's phone vibrated and
a notification came up.

Afterwards, he thought a lot about that moment. Why
had he looked at the phone? Was he being nosy, or was it just
a reflex? What if he hadn't looked at it – would he never have
found out? Would that have been a good thing or a bad?

It was a message from Keeley, a friend of Tasha's whom
they'd met at the NCT classes they'd attended when

expecting Cameron. Her husband, Simon, had his own busi-ness making retro things like knitted toilet roll covers. Every time they met up he'd moan about how tough it was for small businesses like his to succeed. Well, yes.

'I can't stop thinking about you.'

And that was it. Six words that shot a bullet through the back of his world.

He picked up the phone. He knew Tasha's password, because she used the same password for everything – her birthday, backwards.

Keeley and Tasha had texted each other forty-nine times since breakfast that morning. He thought back to the drive here, with Tasha continually tapping at her phone 'to check the directions'.

He scrolled up through the messages, to the first one of the day.

Keeley: Did you have sex?

Tasha: Oh babe. I'm so sorry. It was his birthday. We did talk about this, yeah? I promise I did not enjoy it one bit. I just tuned out, like I was at the gynaecologist or something.

The gynaecologist?! Charlie thought of his solemn thrust-ings into Tasha, as she lay on the bed with her legs apart, and shook his head to dispel the image.

Tasha: Are you ok, hun?

Keeley: Not sure what to think tbh.

Tasha: You know we always do it on his birthday. It didn't
mean anything. Anyway, that'll do him for another
year now.

Keeley: I guess. What about your anniversary?

Tasha: I'll pretend I'm asleep or too drunk or something.

Their anniversary was another *eight months* away.

Had Tasha decided that this... this three-way set-up, in
which he, Charlie, held all the allure of a medical procedure,
was their new normal? The future – those eight months and
beyond – stretched in front of him like a desert, devoid of sex.
Of closeness. Not that there'd been any of that for a long
time, but now... now it made sense.

Keeley: I'm not sure I can sleep with you again. I can't
stand to think of his hands on your body. His thing in you.

Tasha: You said that last year, babe. We'll get through
this. I promise.

Anger. That was what he felt. Surely.

He felt it surge for a moment and then sputter away. It
was like turning the ignition in a tired old car that refused to
start.

'Daddy,' murmured Cameron, stirring against his
shoulder.

'I'm here, my love.' He put down the phone and pulled
Cameron closer, one hand stretched over his back and the
other cupping the back of his head.

He looked down at Tasha, still busy with the camera at

the bottom of the amphitheatre, so familiar with her long blonde pleat threaded through the gap at the back of her baseball cap. Then he lifted his eyes and rested them on the deep blue of the Mediterranean, stretching to the horizon and the hazy sky beyond.

Charlie had once got a book out of the school library about the Greek myths – he'd guiltily discovered it in his dad's house a few years ago. It had told of Theseus, sailing back from Crete after slaying the Minotaur, so caught up in himself that he forgot to change the sails from black to white. And his father, watching from the cliffs as the black shape came over the horizon, and plunging to his death in sorrow.

Perhaps he could send the book in with Cameron, next time he had library period.

Sorrow.

It was over. Their little family was over.

Charlie buried his face against Cameron's silky hair, and squeezed his eyes shut.

They might as well have been out there in the ocean, tossed about in the waves and sucked under by unseen currents.

They would drown in this.

Just like Dad and him, after Mum died. He couldn't remember much about the immediate aftermath, or the funeral, although he had a vague impression of relatives' hushed voices, and the sickly stink of flowers, rotting in vases around the house because Charlie didn't know if he should throw them away. His clearest memory of that time was making soft boiled eggs and buttering white toast, because it was all Dad could stomach for the first few months. And a rainy afternoon spent up in his room with his calculator, and a pile of bills. He'd worked through her cheque book, the stubs filled in meticulously in her small, rounded hand-writing.

Charlie's violin teacher – £40

Butcher (Easter beef joint) – £15

School trip to Jorvik Viking Centre – £8

He'd curled himself into a silent ball on the floor, his knuckles stuffed into his mouth, thinking that he would die with the pain.

He couldn't let Cameron drown.

'I'll sort this out,' he promised. 'I'll keep you safe.'

32

LYNNE

Dearest Juliet,

How are you? I hope you are very, very we darling. What's been happening here? Well I' been doing some clearing out. Cupboards and whatnot. I been a bit of a chore, but I found a pile of my old *Scho Friend* annuals, and I've enclosed one here for you. It mig give you a bit of a giggle. *The Silent Three* on page thirty – c you remember them? You made me sew that outfit for yc with the black cape and hood. I thought you looked adorab in it, with your big eyes peeping out.

I don't know if I have told you enough how much I lo you. How much I delight in you, darling. You light up n world.

The Robinsons came over yesterday and took me for walk along the river at the Braids. I was in that wretch chair, but we managed twenty minutes or so. It made n think of our summer walks at Dedham Vale, and that wic bend in the river where we used to have our picnic Remember how we used to take our shoes off and roll up ol trousers, and paddle in the water? And our skin looked golden under the water – your little feet, and my bigger ones. I used to worry about you, darling, not having any brothers or sisters. I don't know if I was enough fun for you. At least you had Charlie, though. I think he came with us sometimes, didn't he? On our picnics? I'm sure I remember him there, at least once. Audrey sent him with prawn sandwiches that were a bit iffy by the time we sat down to eat.

And Daddy would always carry the picnic basket. That ridiculously heavy wicker one that had plates and cups inside with little yellow ducks on them. But he never complained because he knew how much you liked it. And you always wanted the sandwiches wrapped in greaseproof paper, because it was like the Famous Five.

It's sad, in a way, how all the photos are of you and me. He's always the one taking the photos. But the one that I've enclosed sort of has him in it – see the shadow falling across the ground? That's him. That's Daddy.

I'm going to sign off for now, love. I'm a bit tired after today. But I've got an apple charlotte for pudding – Sue Robinson brought it. So I'm looking forward to that.

Night night xxxx

33

JULIET

The changing rooms in Seekings we unrecognizable from how they'd been in n parents' golf club days. Gone was the moul grouting and stagnant smell – it was all soothing, crean marble and under-floor heating.

We were very early. Beth had wanted to decorate tl garden room and set up all the food well in advance.

I'd explained to Kitty last night about my scars, while sl was brushing her teeth, carefully working her toothbru round the gaps.

'When we go swimming tomorrow,' I'd said, 'you'll s that I have lots of old scars on my arms and legs. They lo like little lines. I don't want you to be scared, okay? They' nothing to worry about and they don't hurt any more.'

I'd pulled back my sleeve and she leaned in to look, the glanced up. Was she was asking me how I'd got them? Wi Kitty, I'd learned to feel for the conversational thread, sense it in her face and body language.

'When I was younger – a teenager – I used to hurt myself. On purpose.'

She frowned.

'I was very unhappy about myself,' I explained. 'And hurting myself was my way of dealing with it. I should have spoken to my mum, or a –'

But then I stopped. I was talking to a child who couldn't speak to anybody about anything.

'Well, I was trying to cope with things all on my own.'

She nodded slowly, her pupils widening.

Now, in the changing room, she was trembling as I helped her to take off her clothes. I wondered for a moment if she had picked up on my own emotions – because I was shaking too, at the thought of walking out there in my swimming costume, in front of all the mums. In front of Charlie.

But then I remembered that Kitty was just as scared of being seen as I was. For her, this birthday party was an act of bravery.

'Do you know something, Kitty?' I said, as she pulled her swimming costume on. 'I'm so proud of you.'

She looked down, folding her leggings, smaller and smaller.

'Come on,' I said. My plan was to try and get into the pool, safely under the water, before any of the other guests arrived.

But it wasn't to be. An aqua-aerobics class was just finishing and we had to wait by the pool on the sun-lounger seats. I sat uncomfortably in my plain black swimming costume, ordered online last week – I hadn't been swimming in twenty years. I crossed my legs. Uncrossed them. Perched on the edge of the sunlounger. Lay back as though I was relaxed, and I didn't hate my pale, scarred, pig-skinned body.

And – *Christ* – I should have done something with my bikini line.

Charlie, Tasha and Cameron arrived early too, just as the aqua-aerobics ladies were climbing out of the pool.

'Hello.' I stood up, steering Kitty round in front of me 'Did you manage to find it okay?'

Stupid question. They would hardly be standing here they hadn't, would they? And it was less than a mile from their house. But they'd have to keep looking at my face, as long as I was talking.

'Oh yes,' said Charlie, kind as always. 'The directions on the invitation were very clear. And there's plenty of parking so that's great.'

'Great.' I could hear the shake in my voice.

And I could feel Tasha's eyes on me, as I leaned forward to welcome Cameron, and suggested to Kitty that she show him where to get into the pool.

'How are you doing?' Tasha said later, once everyone had arrived and we were safely in the water.

It was a beautifully open question, but I could see the look in her eyes – something between curiosity and concern. For a moment, I had the urge to confide in her. To tell her how it felt to be covered in ugly scars. To be the only person here who couldn't have children, who didn't have a family of their own. And how it felt to love Charlie. How much it had hurt to come alive again, like a dead tree splitting into blossom.

'Oh, good thanks. Today has been a little hectic!'

I watched as her husband reached for a beach ball and tossed it back and forth across the pool with Robin and Tyler, Mimi's twins. They were the troublemakers in the class and Charlie was making valiant efforts to keep them occupied.

struck me that I hadn't seen him in swimming trunks since we were little kids ourselves. His adult body was new to me – the constellation of freckles on his right shoulder, the thickening of muscle in his upper arms. The soft tracing of hair across his chest. I longed to place my head there and close my eyes.

'Are you okay, lovely?'

I nodded. 'So did you go to the PTA meeting last night?'

Tasha brightened, and began to tell me about the fundraiser for the musical instrument fund, and the mother who had complained that the play kitchen in the recreation room was 'perpetuating gender stereotypes'.

'Not if the boys play in it too,' I said.

'Exactly,' said Tasha, and went on to tell me about Cameron's attempts to make a gingerbread railway station, after being inspired by *The Great British Bake-Off*.

I smiled vaguely, my mind racing with thoughts about what I would do with the recreation room if I was in charge. But then there was a commotion from the other side of the pool. Kitty was holding her face, the beach ball bobbing on the surface of the water beside her. Cameron was shouting, in a reedy, high-pitched voice: 'Stop it, we don't like it!'

'Retards!' shouted Tyler, and Robin tipped his head back in a delighted cackle.

'Mong!' Tyler stuck his tongue out and wiggled it around.

Charlie strode through the water towards them.

Suddenly Kitty was beside me. She wrapped her arms and legs around me like a monkey, burying her wet face into the crook of my neck.

Jesus.

I'd held Kitty before, when she'd had one of her tantrums, or when she'd got upset. But she'd never come to

me like this, needing the comfort of my arms, bursting n
heart like a little heat-seeking missile.

Her body was slippery, almost weightless in the water.
thought of the babies I'd never held, skin against my skin.

Tasha was staring at me, slightly open-mouthed.

Charlie came over. 'Are you okay, Kitty? Do you want n
to take a look at your face?'

'Kitten?'

But despite our gentle promptings, she couldn't respond
cupped the back of her head, wet like a seal.

Cammie approached in an earnest doggy paddle, his ey
wide and urgent.

'Robin threw the ball at Kitty's face on purpose! I sa
him! He said that Kitty should get out of the pool –' l
gasped in a breath ' – because she might wee-wee it becau
she's a... retard?' He frowned, looking to Tasha for confirm
tion of the word. 'And Mummy, yesterday at break they to
Kitty that she couldn't stay at our school and that she'll ha
to leave at the end of term. She'll have to go to a speci
school in Bury St Edmunds where they all wear big nappies

I felt Kitty shiver in my arms.

'Is that true, Mummy?' whispered Cameron, pushing
clump of wet hair away from his eyes.

'No,' said Tasha. 'That's nonsense. Very ignorant. Po
Kitty. I'll speak to his mum afterwards.'

I glanced at the clock. There was only five minutes un
we were supposed to get the children out. 'Do you want to ξ
and get changed, Kitty? We can check that Mum's got all tl
food out?'

She nodded.

We swam to the side of the pool. I let Kitty climb up fir
her hands squeaking as they gripped the steel ladder. Then

followed, water cascading from my cheap black swimming costume as I hauled my body up.

I became aware of a shadow blocking the light. A dark pillar of a person, standing there with Kitty.

'Well, well, well. If it isn't Mistress Kitten.'

It was a man – around sixty, perhaps? – his dark hair shot through with wiry grey, and a tanned face with a hint of looseness beneath the jaw.

He wore dark jeans with a pale blue shirt tucked in at the waist, sleeves dragged up to the elbows to reveal hairy forearms. His feet were bare, as per the poolside rules.

Inexplicably, I thought of Jesus.

Kumbaya, m'lord, kumbaya.

Except that his beard was missing. And then he turned to look at Charlie, who'd climbed out of the pool and was standing beside me. I saw him in a half-profile, the slow, wolfish widening of his smile.

Oh Christ.

Mr Redwood.

It was Mr Redwood from Collecott Hall.

What was he doing here? Here by the side of a swimming pool at Boxley Wood?

I felt water trickling down my body, over the tracks of my scars, pooling on the tiles beneath me as if I'd wet myself.

Charlie stepped in closer and placed his hand on the back of my arm.

'It's okay,' he murmured.

The man in front of us beamed and threw his arms out, indicating that Kitty should jump into them.

'Daddy's home!'

Kitty went as still as a board and allowed herself to be hugged. My body stiffened in sympathy, until I heard Char-

lie's voice behind me, seeming to come from a long w
away.

'I'm Charlie. Good to meet you. My son, Cameron,
friends with Kitty. And my wife, Tasha, works with Beth
the Old Coach House.'

'Ah – you're the GP?' said Frank, taking his hand. 'I
heard about you.'

'I'm Juliet Monklands,' I muttered. 'Kitty's nanny.'

He smiled again. I saw that his lower front teeth we
narrow, with spaces between them that I'd never notice
before – they must have eroded with age. He held out a har
to shake mine. My fingers were soft and wrinkly from bei
in the water and I recoiled at the sensation of his skin.

It made me think of drowned corpses. A shudder to
through me. I felt Charlie's grip tighten.

'What am I thinking?' said Mr Redwood. 'You folks ̧
and get changed, you're freezing to death.'

WHEN I EMERGED from the changing rooms, Mr Redwood
Frank – was holding court in the Garden Room, with a grou
of school mums gathered around him. They'd pulled sever
chairs together so they could all sit around the same lo
table.

Beth sat next to him, her cheeks aglow, pushing ba
strands of hair that had fallen down from her artfully mes
chignon.

I could barely hear the conversation for the though
racing through my head.

Mr Redwood wasn't just a teacher at Collecott Hall – he'd be
a friend of my parents.

He knew Laurel Bank was my childhood home.

He'd know I'd lied to Beth.

They'd tell me to leave and I'd never see Kitty again.

Where was Kitty? She'd been beside me a minute ago. I looked around and saw that she'd left the Garden Room. She was out in the lobby, sitting quietly on the first turn of the stairs, her arms held tightly around her knees.

Maybe, just maybe, with my shorter hair and my married surname...

'So have you been away doing things with your charity?' Tasha was saying. Cameron was perched on her knee, frowning and picking nigella seeds off a sausage roll.

Annabel was there too, sitting next to Mimi, who was studiously ignoring her twins as they wreaked havoc around the room.

'I've been helping to set up a new women's centre in Somalia,' said Frank. 'They do amazing work. STI and HIV testing. Gynae checks.'

He waved two fingers around. I looked away quickly.

'Amazing work,' echoed Annabel. 'Wow. Just, wow.'

I stood up, intending to go and check on Kitty, but Beth motioned towards the platters on the table that held mini sausages, grapes and tortilla chips, indicating to me that I should hand them around. For a moment I was eight years old again, handing round crisps and nuts at my parents' cheese and wine evenings.

'It's terribly sad,' Frank went on. 'Many of the women who've undergone childbirth without medical supervision have a condition called fistula, where the back passage –'

'Mini sausage, Charlie?' said Beth, grabbing the platter from my hands and thrusting it towards him.

Charlie took a sausage and sat there, holding it. He

seemed unsure of whether, as a medical professional, he w:
supposed to comment on the fistula situation.

'We had a run-in with some Somali pirates on the w:
back,' said Frank quietly, looking down to stir his tea a1
raising an eyebrow.

Cameron looked up, his eyes glowing. He slipped c
Tasha's knee and moved closer to his dad.

'Gosh!' said Annabel.

'Yeah. We'd just set sail from Mogadishu, setting tl
safest course that we could across the Gulf of Aden. Did1
want to risk the airport, you see, as there was talk of anoth
siege. We had a gunman riding with us. But they shot him
the back of the head.' He looked at me and I winced
sympathy, imagining splattered brains and blood on tl
deck. 'They're feral, these people. Feral. They kept us capti
in the hold of their boat for three days. The conditions we
appalling. Forty degree heat. Pissing in a bucket.'

'Frank,' said Beth, inclining her head towards tl
children.

'How did you get away?' I asked.

Frank sat back on his chair. Bellowed with laughter, wi
pure pleasure.

Cameron's eyes clouded over, his face confused. It w:
one of Frank's jokes. I couldn't believe I'd been sucked i
even for a moment.

'They do have problems with pirates in Somalia thoug
don't they?' said Charlie. I loved him for trying to save fa
for Cameron. And for me.

Frank shrugged. 'So I've heard, Charlie, my man. So I'\
heard. Ah... you'll have to forgive me for making light
things. The women's centre has serious problems. It's nev
really been accepted within the community. The intentic

was to expand it, but it looks like we might have to close it down. It's hard to explain the reality of it, you know. What it's like. On the ground.' He shook his head slowly, indicating that we, with our sheltered lives, could never understand.

I looked across at Charlie. He didn't know what to say either. Beth sat, looking at her hands, her expression closed. It was like Frank took up all the space in the room, his personality ballooning out so there was no space left to breathe.

When he finally broke the silence, his voice was quiet and thoughtful. 'Charlie, you'll have to help me out.'

Charlie looked up, expectant and polite, as if an elderly relative had just asked him to fetch his glasses, or to close the window to stop the draught.

'Charlie McGrath, you see. *Charlie McGrath*... it sounds familiar. And your face, too. The longer I've been sitting here, the more I feel that we've met before. Come on. Tell me where.'

Charlie glanced at me. I felt like a mouse, backing into a corner, pawed by a cat. Sweat prickled on my back.

'I wondered that too,' Charlie said, eventually. 'You look a lot like a teacher I used to know, but his name was Frank Redwood.'

'Aha!' Frank's breath gusted across the table. 'That's it. Collecott Hall, yes? You were in my moral studies group. Of course.'

My heart hammered as I waited for him to turn his attention to me, for him to twig who I was.

It was Annabel who rescued me. 'You changed your name?' she asked.

'We... *rebranded* ourselves when we moved to Switzerland.

Sometimes in life it's necessary to make a new start.' He sh
a glance at Beth.

'My ex...' began Beth, and then bit her lip.

Tasha closed her eyes and nodded. She volunteered for
domestic violence helpline every Tuesday.

'It wasn't just Beth's stuff, to be honest,' said Frank with
sigh. 'I let the charity get on top of me. I needed to get awa
To be someone else for a while. Mental health... it's n
something we talk about often enough. But we should.'

There was a moment of silence in the group – a sense of
barrier having been crossed. A sense that a real intimacy ha
emerged through the conversation, quite different from t
usual chat around the school gates.

Frank's gaze lingered on me for a moment and my pul
ticked up again. But then he yawned. 'I'm bushed. Have
slept in thirty-six hours. I think I'll go home and get my hea
down.'

Beth opened her mouth and closed it again.

'We should get going too,' said Annabel, pulling her eno
mous handbag onto her lap.

'Don't go,' said Beth. 'We've still got the cake and t
piñata to do.'

He raised his hand as he got up. 'Bye, all. And goodby
Mistress Kitten. Bring me home a piece of cake.' He wink
in the direction of the floor by my feet.

I swung round and realised that Kitty, who had been
the stairs a few moments ago, was lying on her tumn
behind my chair, holding tightly on to one of its legs,
though the room was a ship in a storm, and she might l
tossed away at any moment.

34

CHARLIE

Charlie stood with Juliet in the middle of the Garden Room surveying the debris: streamers, balloons, paper plates with squashed fragments of birthday cake. Bowls containing leftover cucumber sticks and cubes of sweaty cheese. Shards of tortilla chips underfoot. Charlie felt something on the bottom of his shoe, and lifted it to find a squashed grape. He wiped it off with a *Frozen* napkin.

Beth had left quickly after the party bags had been handed out, saying Kitty was exhausted and needed to be taken home, and would Juliet be a total star and 'do the last little bit of tidying up'.

'Charlie will help,' Tasha had cut in. 'Won't you, love?'

He'd opened and closed his mouth. He'd been about to offer anyway.

'It won't take long,' he said to Juliet now. But she just stood there, looking straight ahead out of the window, towards the patio area and the golf course beyond. Rain had begun falling softly, pattering on the sloping glass roof.

'Do you think he recognised me?' she said eventually.

He paused. 'I don't think so.'

'Hmm.'

He didn't know what to say. If Frank had recognised Juli there was nothing that they could do about it now. And wh would that mean for Juliet? For Kitty?

For him? He tried to imagine Boxley Wood without Juli in it, and felt a hollowness behind his ribs.

'What if I go back and they tell me to go upstairs and pa my bags, there and then?'

'You would just have to tell the truth – explain to the that you didn't want to talk about your family, and the tin when you lived at Laurel Bank, because it's... well, i personal. And it's a bit raw, particularly at the moment.'

'What the hell is he doing in my parents' house?'

'Well, you won't know that unless you ask him.'

She gave no indication of having heard him.

He shook open a black bin bag, and began to work h way along the table, sweeping the rubbish into it.

When he looked up, Juliet was standing by the windo holding a bunch of flowers. Tasha had brought them for Be – they'd stopped at the garden centre on the way here. Ar Beth had left them there on the windowsill, perhaps becau she didn't care about them, or perhaps because she thoug Juliet would bring them back to Laurel Bank, along with of Kitty's presents.

'Yellow roses,' said Juliet. 'Mum's favourite.'

She tipped her head forward to inhale their scent, and swathe of hair slipped from behind her ear and fell over h face.

He recalled a long ago summer's day, kneeling with her

the daisy-studded grass at Laurel Bank, lifting a buttercup to each of their chins in turn to see if it would make their skin glow yellow.

He'd told her that her chin hadn't gone yellow and so she couldn't like butter. She frowned and instructed him to wait until the sun came out from behind a cloud and check again.

He could remember kneeling there in front of her, the buttercup quivering on its stem, Juliet's breath warm against the inside of his wrist. Then the sun came out, and the under-curve of her chin was bathed in a soft buttery light, like she'd been lit up from within.

'Yes,' confirmed Charlie, and Juliet's face broke into a gappy-toothed smile. She fell back onto the grass, flinging her arms and legs out so that she was a star, lying there amongst the daisies. He lay down quietly beside her and they'd watched the wisps of cloud floating across the sky.

Who would have thought they would end up here, in this room, just two miles from Laurel Bank, so many years later? Him with a bin bag and grapes squashed on the bottom of his shoes. Juliet, holding someone else's bunch of roses, holding in all the things she couldn't say.

'They're her absolute favourite,' she repeated.

'Juliet,' he said softly, putting down the bin bag.

She turned to him, her eyes full and pleading. But this time she didn't push him away or change the subject.

'I'm so sorry about your mum,' he said.

A single tear swelled on her lower eyelid and shot down the side of her face. He reached into his pocket for a crumpled tissue, and pressed the wetness away. The tissue came away with a creamy tinge where her make-up had come off.

'She's gone,' Juliet whispered.

'I know, baby, I know,' he said, the endearment escapir before he could stop it.

'She died.' Her hands went up to her face. She stood the for a moment, so rigid and so alone that he couldn't stand He longed to reach out and draw her towards him, to sett her against the contours of his body.

'I know,' he said.

'She tried to do it so gently,' went on Juliet, her voir muffled against her hands. 'To die, I mean. If she was in pai she hid it. And if she was scared, I never saw it. There were r tears, no upsets. She was only ever worried about me, ar what would happen to me. She wanted to stay until I'd g pregnant. She wanted that so much.'

He couldn't say anything. It was surging through him this need to hold her.

'She was on her own. At the end. When it... happened.'

'But she was in hospital?'

'Yes. She was very weak. Things were starting to sh down, and the nurses had said it would only be a few day She told me to go out, have a break, have a look round tl shops or something. I went to the shops and tried on all the maternity jeans. And then I went home and... Eddie w there, waiting for me. To tell me he wanted to split up.'

The bastard, thought Charlie. The utter bastard.

'He said that he couldn't go through it with me, l couldn't pretend to be my rock. Couldn't sit on the front ro with me, at the funeral. Not when all he could think abo was when it would be okay to leave me. It makes sense, if yo think about it?' She looked up at him.

He shrugged.

'And he didn't want to go through with the IVF, obvious We were waiting for news about whether any of the embryc were viable. The truth is, deep down, he didn't *want* them to be.'

'Spineless twat.'

'And then the nurse phoned. Her name was Carmelita – don't you think that's a pretty name? She was phoning to tell me that Mum had gone. It happened very quickly, she said. She'd been in to top up her morphine and move her pillows, and make sure she was as comfortable as possible. Then she looked in about ten minutes later, and Mum seemed to be semi-conscious. She was moving her lips like she was talking to someone. The nurse said she thought she'd heard her say "Juliet". She tried to phone me, but I never heard it ring. It must have been when I was in the shop.'

'It's okay,' said Charlie.

'But she was on her *own*.'

'Maybe she needed to be on her own.' Charlie thought back to when Tasha had been in labour with Cameron, and the midwife had suggested he pop along to the cafeteria to get a coffee. And sure enough, it had all started happening when he was gone. He'd only just got back in time. Afterwards, the midwife had told him that sometimes, labouring mothers needed to be on their own so that they could 'let go.' Maybe it was the same for death as it was for birth.

'The nurse said that people often... seem like they're talking to people. At the end.'

He nodded. 'I've seen that. I did a stint in a hospice when I was training.'

'Is that like, you know, a near death experience?'

'I'm not sure. There's some science behind it I think – something to do with the neurons shutting down. Endorphins or oxygen deprivation or something. I read something

once which said that the brain creates hallucinations
shield itself from the reality of death.'

As soon as he said it, he wished he hadn't. Who was he
explain away such mysteries with talk about science an
neurochemicals? Once he'd gone to a call-out for a ninet
five-year-old man whose last wish had been to die at hom
Charlie had just sat quietly by the bed while the man chatte
to his father, who'd died forty years ago and who seemed
be sitting just to the left of Charlie. He'd even asked his fath
if he should bring a smart jacket.

Then he thought of his own father, dressed in a neat shi
and tie and pressed trousers, every day in the nursing hom
What would he make of all this? Of Charlie being here li
this with Juliet, while his wife and son waited for him
home? Dad adored Tasha, strangely even more so in th
confusion of his dementia – she reminded him of Charli
mother.

'Shhh, it's okay,' he said now to Juliet. Or maybe he w
saying it to himself.

'The nurse said that she seemed peaceful. There was r
struggle or anything, she just stopped breathing. She just
stopped.'

Juliet looked up at Charlie, as though he might be able
explain the impossible.

He nodded dumbly.

'And she was on her own,' she said again, like it was stu
in a loop in her head.

'What about you?' he said. 'Did you have anyone there f
you?'

'It was a strange time,' she said. 'I had to pack up all m
stuff from Eddie's flat, and I took it to Mum's flat – I had

stay there, because I didn't have anywhere to go. I just took to her bed. I stayed there for days.'

Charlie's heart turned over at the thought of it. She'd lost her mother, her husband, and the family she'd hoped to have. Her past and her future, wiped out in one afternoon.

'Mum had already pre-arranged the funeral, and she'd packed up most of her stuff. It was all sorted into cardboard boxes for the charity shop. She didn't want me to have the job of going through her things, not when I was going through the IVF and everything.'

Charlie could imagine Lynne sorting things into boxes, labelling them with her neat handwriting and fastening them with tape. Making the final payment to the funeral directors. Tidying herself away.

'So there were just boxes, piled up everywhere. It looked just like it had when we first moved there, after leaving Boxley Wood. After Dad died.'

Charlie tried to remember, to get it straight in his head.

'I thought you went to live with your Granny after your dad died. When I tried to get in touch...'

He thought of the phone calls he'd made to Laurel Bank after Graeme had died and Juliet had left Collecott Hall, of Lynne saying in a strange, blank voice that she'd pass on his messages.

She shook her head. 'I stayed with Granny to begin with, just for a few months while Mum sorted things out in Boxley Wood. But once Mum moved up, she wanted to be independent. She got a job in Marks and Spencer. After all those years of being a housewife, of being looked after. But she never complained. She said she liked it. She said she liked having a uniform so she didn't have to decide what to wear every day.'

'She was a brave lady.' Why could he only say suc useless things?

'She kept working as long as she could, even throug chemo and everything. But the drugs stopped working, ar they told her that she had, well, maybe six months to a ye: left. She wrote me letters, and bought little presents ar things. Things to arrive after she'd gone. She arranged it wit her solicitors, the ones who're dealing with her will.'

'She must have loved you very much,' he said.

Juliet nodded.

'Does it help, getting the letters?'

'Yes. It's like she's not quite gone. It's just enough to kee me going, you know? And I write back, sometimes.' Sl looked up at him. 'It sounds stupid, doesn't it?'

'Not at all.'

'It's funny. I can tell her things I never would have whe she was actually here.'

'When someone dies,' Charlie began awkwardly, doesn't mean your relationship with them ends.' He thoug of his mother, how he'd imagine sitting with her in the café Dedham Vale, on long nights when he couldn't sleep. Son nights he'd focused so hard that he could hear the clink her cup and saucer. The soft sound as she sipped her tea.

'But I don't know how many more letters there are goir to be. Her handwriting... it's getting all faint and shaky. I dor know if they'll tell me, when it's the last one. Or if I'll just l waiting for another one and it won't ever come.'

Charlie nodded. He understood. The end of the lette would be like losing her, all over again.

'Sometimes it feels like she's building up to somethin Something important she wants to say.'

Charlie thought of all that he would have to tell her, and for a moment it made him exhausted.

But then it all fell away and there was only him and Juliet, as if someone had stuck a pin through time and space, fixing them in this moment. His arms closed around her, pulling her to him. Encircling her grief, and his grief, like the shore around a fathomless sea.

35

JULIET

L aurel Bank was in darkness when I got back fro Seekings and pulled up in the driveway, my mir still buzzing with what had just happened – h; Charlie really held me like that? Had I dreamed it?

Frank had said he was going to bed, but where were Be and Kitty? I turned my key in the lock and shushed the do over the mat. The house seemed to be waiting, buzzing wi silence. I clicked on the table lamp in the hall and made n way towards the kitchen. The door was closed and I opened slowly to a cheering, whooping sound.

What?

Beth and Frank were standing there, Frank beaming ar holding a bottle of champagne and an envelope.

What was in there? My P45?

Beth whooped again and pulled the string of a par popper. Coloured streamers fell limply across the kitche table.

'Er...' I began.

'We thought we would have a little celebration in your honour,' said Frank. 'Just a little thank you for all you've done with Kitty.'

Where *was* Kitty? I looked round the room and saw that she was sitting on the floor in the utility room, peering round the door into the kitchen, the monkey jigsaw partly completed on the tiles in front of her.

I held out my hand and she scampered over, burying her head against my skirt.

'You're very welcome. There's no need to –'

'Beth has been telling me about all the progress you've made. A birthday party for Kitty would have been inconceivable last year. And yet I hear that this swimming party was actually Kitty's own idea?'

I looked at Beth, remembering Kitty's swimming pool drawing. 'I think it was, yes.'

'And Kitty's on the Pupil Committee at school?'

'Er... yes. She's come up with some ideas that have proved quite popular.'

'Amazing. Just amazing.'

'Kitty's good at having ideas.' I tried to keep my voice neutral. Just because Kitty couldn't speak, it didn't mean she was stupid.

'And the Old Coach House is going from strength to strength,' Beth chipped in. 'It's been invaluable having the time to really *focus* on it. I really don't know what we would do without you, Juliet.'

'The last time I came home from a trip, I found Beth in tears in the bathroom and Kitty rocking back and forward in the cupboard under the stairs!' He said it as if it was a joke. My heart clenched.

'And this time, it couldn't be more different. You'
nothing short of a miracle, Juliet Monklands.' He shook h
head in wonder.

'So we got you this,' said Beth, taking the envelope ar
thrusting it towards me with wide eyes. 'Think of it as
bonus.'

It was a voucher for £250, for the beauty spa at Seeking
with 'THANKS A MILLION!' scrawled into the space for
message.

'Wow.'

'You treat yourself,' went on Beth. 'Have a massage or
facial, whatever you like. They have an amazing aestheticia
who comes in on Mondays and Wednesdays. She does tl
usual Botox and fillers, but also specialized stuff – laser ther
pies and all sorts. They can work wonders.' She wrinkled h
nose and brushed her hand back and forth quickly along h
forearm.

My scars. She meant my scars.

'Go in and have a consultation, anyway. See what th
say.'

'Thank you.' I forced my face into a grateful smile. 'Tha
incredibly generous.'

'Fantastic,' enthused Frank, joining in again now that tl
'ladies' matters' were out of the way. 'Shall we?' He lifted tl
champagne bottle and eased the cork out with a po
Bubbles foamed over the rim, and Beth slid the champagi
glasses across the table. I pulled a carton of apple juice out
the fridge and poured some for Kitty.

'To homecomings,' said Frank, flicking a glance at me.

'Homecomings!' said Beth.

'Er... cheers.'

I lifted my glass to Kitty's.

'Clink,' she said, in a tiny voice.

Beth's hands flew to her face. Frank bellowed with laughter.

'That's my girl, Kitty. That's my girl.'

36

CHARLIE

Edinburgh, three months ago

The smell hit him the second he stepped throug the door. The air even *looked* green. Could brocco take a gaseous form if you boiled it hard and loi enough? He remembered a diagram from one of his GCS textbooks – the cilia in the nasal passages, green wavy lines indicate the odour wafting past. He hoped it didn't cling his clothes. On the other hand, maybe it would guarant him a table to himself on the train back home later.

Ward 10 – a sign indicated that it was up the stairs. I walked past the antiseptic gel dispenser on the way to tl nurses' station, his trainers squeaking on the plastic floc Then he stopped, guiltily, and turned around and squirt some onto his hands, rubbing vigorously.

'I'm looking for Lynne Hazelwood,' he said to the nurse.

She nodded. 'She's in room four – first on the left. I thii she may be sleeping but you're fine to look in.'

The curtains were drawn round her bed to form a cubicl

with just a narrow opening at the front. It felt too intimate to go in. He stood there and cleared his throat softly.

'Charlie.' Her voice was weak, as though she only had little puffs of breath left that couldn't quite propel her words into the space between them.

'Mrs Hazelwood.' He drew the curtain back a little, making it rattle on the metal rail.

The bed was inclined at the pillow end so that she was propped semi-upright. He could see the shape of her legs under the cellular blanket, bent out at the knees, froglike.

There was a plastic seat next to the bed but it had various things on it – a tin of shortbread, two puzzle books and a women's magazine.

Five steps to your beach-beautiful body!

Ashley Jarrod's celebration cakes

It seemed cruel to him that somebody had brought her this magazine, full of articles directing the reader towards a better future. A slimmer body. A more stylish home. The perfect summer barbecue that would bring your whole family together. And Lynne had no future. Not beyond the walls of this broccoli-smelling ward.

'Thank you for coming, Charlie,' she said. 'You can move those things. Just put them on the...' She motioned towards the cupboard on wheels that stood by the bed. 'Yes, that's right.'

'I'm sorry to have dragged you here on such a lovely sunny day, Charlie. I'm sure you have lots of other things you'd rather be doing.'

'That's okay,' he murmured. 'It's no problem.' He tried not to focus on how much time he had before he'd have to leg it to the taxi rank and get himself back to Waverley Station. He was on the three o'clock train. Lynne didn't seem to know

that he lived in Suffolk now, and it had seemed churlish
remind her when she'd sent him a message on LinkedIn la
week, asking to him to come to see her about somethii
important. A Macmillan nurse had helped her to find him.

'I told Juliet to go shopping, do something nice f
herself. She needed to get out of this place for a while. Ta
her mind off things. She's waiting to hear about this IVF.'

The long sentence seemed to have tired her out. She l;
silent for a few moments.

'I'm taking a liberty, Charlie, I know that. In burdenii
you with this. The thing is, you're the only person I can tell.'

'It's not a burden, Mrs Hazelwood. What can I do to helf
Why did he feel like he was seven years old again? In sho
trousers with knobbly, grass-stained knees.

She lay for a few minutes. 'Charlie, darling, perhaps yc
could buzz for the nurse. I think I might need a top-up.'

The buzzer lay just a few centimetres out of the reach
her left hand. He reached over and pressed it, and moved tl
control nearer to her.

'I went about things all wrong, after Graeme died. I kno
that now.'

Charlie shifted in his chair, his feet itching to stand hi
up and get him out of this place and into the breezy Edi
burgh sunshine.

She sighed, a weak little whistle of a sound, which ga\
way to a fit of coughing. Uncertainly, Charlie lifted a plast
cup of water from the bedside table, and held it up near h
face. The pale green striped drinking straw flipped to tl
wrong side and hung limply.

He looked around for a nurse, but the coughing subside
and her breathing grew steady again.

'Graeme's car accident.' She closed her eyes in a slo

blink. Her eyes moved under her closed eyelids as if she was seeing something.

Charlie began to feel a little sick. The bacon roll that he'd eaten on the train seemed to sit like a rock in his stomach.

'I know you saw us, Charlie. You saw Frank and me, at Collecott Hall, when he called me up to discuss that business with the child at the nursery. I don't know how, but you did. It was written all over your face.'

Charlie nodded. 'You rushed off home afterwards. Juliet didn't understand why you hadn't come to see her.'

'You know why though, don't you, Charlie?'

'You couldn't face her.'

'I just wanted to get back home,' Lynne said in a rush of breath. 'To sort things out with Graeme. But when I was driving down the motorway, getting closer to home, I knew I couldn't face going back. I couldn't look him in the eye until I'd sorted my head out. Then one of my migraines started. I knew I'd be useless for driving that night so I booked into a Travel Inn by the motorway, to take some painkillers and sleep it off. I called Graeme to say I wouldn't be back until the next day. He sounded so disappointed, Charlie.' She looked at him, deep furrows in the grey skin of her brow. 'It made me think that maybe he knew. Maybe he knew about Frank and me. But I told myself that he was just a bit lonely. I'd left him a stew to heat up, and I'd peeled some potatoes and left them in the pan to boil. But he never liked to eat on his own.'

'It was nice of you to leave him dinner,' he said, uselessly.

'I reminded him,' she went on, 'that the Bramwells were coming to dinner the next day, and that I was going to make Beef Wellington, which was his favourite, and that I was going to try profiteroles again – with the Delia recipe this time. And then said I was sorry. I said, "I'm so sorry, my

darling," and I thought he might make fun of me, because
must have sounded so earnest. But he just said, "That's oka
my love. It's all okay."'

Once again he leaned in with the water cup and the lin
straw. 'Would you like...?'

He put it back on the cabinet again. Why had his bedsic
manner – which he'd spent years perfecting – complete
deserted him now, when he most needed it?

'I couldn't sleep that night. The migraine wore off after I
taken the painkillers and had a lie-down, but I was stuc
there in that hotel room with nowhere to hide, just left the
with what I'd done. I don't mean to sound sorry for myse
not in light of what Graeme was going through... oh I ju
can't bear it, Charlie. I can't *bear* it.'

Awkwardly, he reached for her hand. She gripped
tightly, the skin stretched white over her knuckles.

'Shh,' he said. 'You're okay.' Although of course, sh
wasn't at all. Her body was giving up on her. About to let h
fall.

'So I sat at the little desk, there in the hotel room, and
wrote a letter to Graeme. I had to get it all out – the tru
about Frank. And about how I wanted to make a new sta
with our marriage. Then I lay down on the bed for anoth
hour or two, listening to the traffic going past on the moto
way, and watching the sky go from black to grey. I got in tl
car and I drove the rest of the way home.'

Charlie shifted in his seat. He wanted to run, run as far
he could out of this ward. But he had to let her tell him.

'But it was too late. There was a police car waiting for n
at Laurel Bank. They took me inside and sat me down on tl
sofa. The policewoman leaned in close, and put her hand c
my arm. She told me there'd been an accident. Graeme ha

crashed his car. Into that big beech tree, the one on that blind corner just past the church. She didn't say straight away that he was dead. She waited for me to ask that. I remember wondering if that was part of their training – to break the news in stages.

'She asked if there was anybody she could call for me, and I remember thinking that I'd have to phone the Bramwells and cancel, and how they'd be awfully put out because I'd had to cancel the last time, when Graeme had had the flu.

'And then I asked her, very politely, to excuse me, and I went out of the room. I went round the whole house, Charlie. And I've never told anybody this. I went round ever so quietly, so she wouldn't hear. Checking in each room. Even in the cupboard under the stairs. In case they'd made a mistake. In case he was still there.'

She turned to look at Charlie, to really look him in the eye, where before her gaze had been drifting as though she were seeing somewhere far away. 'Please forgive me, Charlie, for telling you this next part. In some ways it's a story that should never be told, that doesn't bear the telling. And that's why – that's *why*, Charlie – I didn't tell Juliet. I meant to, but I just couldn't find the words.'

'You can tell me.'

'The rest of that day I can hardly remember. Anne Bramwell came round. The doctor came too and gave me something to calm me down. But Frank phoned me later that day – officially in a school capacity, to discuss how to handle things with Juliet. But he said there was something he needed to tell me. He said he'd called the house the night before, because he wanted to check I'd got home okay, and he got Graeme. He said they'd 'had words', and that Graeme had

accused him of having an affair with me. Frank denied it
course, and said that it could be the new antidepressants th
were messing up his head, and he should talk to the doct
But that made things worse, because Graeme saw that
'proof positive' that we were having affair – because I'd to
Frank about the antidepressants, which was a private matt
between me and him. He said Graeme's voice changed the
and all the anger went out of it. He just sounded calm, ar
dull, like he was in a long meeting at the bank. Then he sa
very quietly, 'That's it, then. I'm done. I can't keep going aft
this. Please tell Lynne I'm sorry.' Then he hung up the phon
Frank said he'd been debating whether to tell me or not. H
said he blamed himself, because he hadn't raised the alarm.

'But that doesn't mean –'

'When I phoned him from the Travel Inn to say I would
be home that night he'd sounded so... *disappointed*. Like I
didn't want to have to wait another few hours to see me. B
he... he did *that* so that he would never see me again!'

'It wasn't his fault,' he said. 'Or yours. If he did... do that
it was because he wasn't well.'

'I lied to Juliet,' she went on. 'Or at least I didn't tell he
There was an inquest, you see, because the police couldn't l
sure what caused the accident. They asked a lot of questio
about Graeme's state of mind and his depression, and I ha
to tell them what Frank had said about the phone call. So
sent Juliet off to stay with my mother, in Edinburgh, so th
she wasn't there when the inquest was held, and she would
hear the rumours going around the village.'

Charlie felt hollow, right down to the pit of his stomac
This was going to destroy Juliet. He had a sudden image
her, drawing a card for Graeme's birthday – she'd drawn
man playing golf beside an enormous birthday cake. He sa

the pink tip of her tongue, protruding as she concentrated, her soft hands reaching for a felt-tip pen and then another. He'd quietly questioned the size of the cake, saying that it appeared to be taller than Graeme himself, but Juliet had just frowned and ignored him.

Lynne lay there, eyes closed. He began to wonder if she'd lapsed out of consciousness. He reached over towards the buzzer again.

'Inquest... gave an open verdict. Not enough evidence for... suicide.' She shifted her head on the pillow, her forehead creasing into a deeper frown. Was it the pain? Or was it the pain of saying that last word, puffing it out into the stale air of the ward?

She craned her neck back as though she was gripped with a spasm of pain. Or praying to heaven, pleading with that blank-faced God they'd sung to every Sunday morning at St Mary's-in-the-Wood. 'I just wish... I *wish* I could go back and change it.'

Charlie pressed the buzzer again. Where was the nurse?

'I need to understand why you're telling me this, Lynne.'

'Because you already know about me and Frank. You know that I'm not the person everyone thinks I am. You're closer to the truth than anyone else.'

'Do you want me to *tell* Juliet?'

'Oh Charlie, I don't know. I don't know what's best. I've run out of time.'

He saw then that Lynne didn't want him to *do* anything with what she'd told him. She just wanted him to hold it. To hold it for her so she could let go.

'I understand,' he said. 'It's okay. You can leave this with me.'

'And Charlie, there's something else. I need you to forgive

me. You phoned a few times, after Graeme died. When Juli
was staying with my mother in Edinburgh. And I nev
passed on the messages. I wanted her to have a new life
didn't want anyone from Boxley Wood contacting her,
from that school. You knew about... about me and Frank
couldn't let that... contaminate things... couldn't let th
follow us to Edinburgh.'

The room seemed to spin around him. All he could s
was Juliet. Juliet in pain and grieving after her father's deat
Juliet thinking that he hadn't bothered to contact her. T
little crack in his heart widened like a faultline, making h
breath feel tight in his chest, making his eyes smart.

His response, when it came, was an expression straig
from his own father's mouth, recalled from moments
childhood stress – the time he fell off his bike and dislocate
his shoulder, the time he was sick all down his front befo
the school carol service. 'Oh, Lordy.'

'I thought I could protect her from... from knowing abo
me and Frank, the whole wretched business... from knowi
that Graeme hadn't wanted to live. From knowing that he le
us. I thought I could push all that away, far away from h
But all I did was push her away from me.'

'I'm sure that's not true.' he said.

'I've written down her number for you.' She looked ov
at the bedside table, where a page from her crossword boo
had been torn out, and a number pencilled in the margin
spidery writing.

He nodded and folded the paper carefully, putting in in
his jacket pocket.

She looked like a child now, her eyes wide and dark, tl
only living things in her white waxen face. She was pleadi
with him. 'Make it go away.'

He stood up, his plastic seat screeching across the floor, and he leaned across and held her awkwardly, one hand on each of her shoulders, there as she lay on the bed, wracked with sobs that came harder and harder until it seemed like her body would break.

'Make it go away, Charlie.'

'Shhhhh,' he said.

'Make it go away.'

He couldn't make it go away. Any of it.

Her body grew soft. Gently, he let go her, sat back in his seat.

'This marriage... Eddie... the IVF... it's all...' she frowned again, and clenched her jaw. And then, something that sounded like: 'Go and get her, Charlie.'

'What?' He leaned closer in again. 'You want me to bring her here?'

'You. She needs you. You were... the other part of her.'

He bit his lip, suddenly uneasy. It wasn't the right time to tell her that he was married, that he had to look after Tasha and Cameron now. That he couldn't be the other part of Juliet. Not any more.

But he shushed Lynne, like he shushed Cameron when he woke from his bad dreams in the darkest hours of the night, his body shaking and slick with sweat.

'You just sleep, Lynne. You don't need to do anything now. You just relax and have a nice sleep.'

'The other part of her puzzle.'

'A nice sleep,' he repeated, whispering now because his voice seemed to have disappeared, caught tight in his throat.

'My Juliet,' said Lynne, so weak now that he could barely hear her. 'My monkey puzzle.'

37

JULIET

A day passed. Two... three. I was beginning to hoｐ I'd got away with it.

Then, on Tuesday morning, Frank cornerｅ me as I was taking the clean laundry basket upstairs, ｍ cheek pressed against a pile of Kitty's socks on the top, tryiｒ to stop them falling. He popped his head out from his stuｄ door.

'Have you got five minutes for a chat, Joolz?'

I froze.

Breathe, Juliet.

With a smile, he indicated that I should go into tｌ kitchen. I did so, and stood there obediently, holding tｌ washing basket until he took it from me and set it down ｃ the floor.

'Please sit.'

The lower tier of a wedding cake stood proudly on decorating stand in the middle of the kitchen table. Beth hａ been working on it that morning, before heading out to tｌ Old Coach House to help Tasha with the mid-morning ruｓ

I'd watched her apply white icing over its top and sides, as smooth and pristine as a new fall of snow.

From nowhere, a memory had come – of a walk across the Common on one long ago winter's afternoon, swinging between my parents' arms, the low sun casting three long shadows on the snow in front of us. The crazy patterns of Gypsy's paw prints as he wheeled around us.

'It's lovely,' I'd told Beth. 'How do you get it so perfect?'

'You just have to slow down and take your time. It's as good as meditation,' she'd said with a smile, straightening up and rubbing her neck. And she did look genuinely relaxed for once, her cheeks flushed and her eyes bright.

Frank glanced at the cake now as he pulled his chair out and sat down.

'Beth's got quite a talent,' I said with a nervous little laugh.

He looked at me blankly, as if he hadn't heard me.

'It's quite –' I began again.

'I expect you've been wondering if I've recognised you.'

His brow creased in concern, a look I remembered from his Head of Pastoral Care days.

'I suppose I thought you must have your reasons for pretending to be someone else. But it seems rather futile to dance around it like this. So please enlighten me. What in the Lord's name is this all about?'

My practically perfect persona wouldn't come. I was Joolz, the awkward social outcast again. The girl who cut her thick white pig skin in the dorm washroom.

'Lynne passed away recently, didn't she?' said Frank. 'I was sorry to hear about that. Has that got something to do with you coming here?'

There was no point trying to hold in the truth now. It was coming, hot and fast, like the urge to vomit.

'I had just buried her ashes at St-Mary's-in-the-Woo
That day, when I first came here and met Kitty in tl
garden.'

'I'm sorry,' Frank said in a low voice. 'Please accept n
condolences, Juliet.'

Silence fell as he watched me and I tried to process tl
unthinkable, yet again.

Mum. Ashes.

'I cared deeply for your mother.'

That, I knew to be true.

For a mad moment, I wanted to ask him to tell me eve
single thing he remembered about her, starting at the begi
ning, when he'd known my parents from school. I wanted
hear about school dances and hockey matches and end
term prizes. About my parents' wedding day. I wanted
know what exact words they'd used when they'd told hi
they were expecting me. And what he and Dad had talke
about, those times when he came to stay and they drar
whisky and stayed up late into the night. He knew bits
Mum's story, and Dad's – the lost pieces that might make it a
make sense. He could make them spark into life again, lil
the fragments of a broken mirror.

'It's what she wanted,' I said eventually. 'To be in the san
place as Dad, at St Mary's-in-the-Wood. We had a tir
service, just the vicar and me.'

I'd been surprised to find that the vicar was only abo
the same age as me, a thin woman with wispy brown ha
that kept whipping about in the wind, and funky, red-fram
spectacles. She'd held on to me while I attempted to read o
Christina Rosetti's *Remember*. And afterwards, when I w.
thanking her at the door of the church, she'd taken both n
hands and looked me in the eye, her voice slow and clear lil

she was imparting crucial information: 'Don't worry. Every-thing is going to be all right.'

'After the ceremony, I just stopped by to have a look at the house. To remember, you know, happier times. And Kitty came out into the garden and – well, then the police arrived. I helped Beth to smooth things over with the police and she invited me in for a cup of coffee.'

Frank closed his eyes and nodded.

I thought of Charlie's words, and his suggestion that I simply tell the truth.

'I guess I was feeling so... so raw, about Mum, that I didn't want to go into it. I didn't want to explain. It was easier to be someone else. And then it got too late. Too late to tell.' I sounded like a child, appealing to an adult not to be angry.

'Okay. Lets see what we can salvage from this.' He glanced at the cake again – once, twice, as if it bothered him – and shifted his chair slightly, so he was facing away from it. He steepled his hands and frowned more deeply as he considered.

'Well, I've said this before, of course, but it seems to me that you're good for Kitty. Beth says she seems happier, and she's interacting more at school.'

'She is. She really is.'

'But what you've done – it's a breach of trust, Juliet.' He tutted and screwed up his face in annoyance. 'And trust is key to these arrangements, isn't it? When someone's looking after your child? And I think it might undermine Beth's trust if she were to find out that you have, well, a *history*.' He threw out his hands. 'I'm torn here, Joolz. Help me out.'

I looked at him, trying to fathom him. He did look torn – but in the way an actor on stage might look torn, working every gesture and facial expression for maximum effect.

I floundered around for my own lines. 'If... if you give n
another chance...'

'Kitty clearly adores you,' he cut in. 'And all credit to yo
you've clearly managed to make a career out of childcare.'

He shrugged, seeming to indicate he would never ha'
thought it possible. I thought back to that time in his office
Collecott Hall when he'd said I wasn't suited to working wi
children, and that was before I was suspected of assaulting
abusing – children at the nursery. Eight of them, includii
poor Monty. My skin felt tender at the memory of tho
bruises on her back.

'I'm good at it.' It came out as a croak.

'But Beth would let you go in a heartbeat if she thoug
you hadn't been honest. So... to keep you on – which I thii
is best for Kitty – I have to be less than honest myself. Wi
my own wife.'

He held my gaze too long. 'I have to take *your* dishones
and make it *mine*.'

I looked down, and saw that there was a small oily ma
on my top, a perfectly round shape just near my left nippl
How had that got there? Maybe when we'd made pancak
this morning, melted butter flying all over the place as Kit
plopped ladles of batter into the skillet. I crossed my arn
wishing I had a cardigan I could pull round me.

'I could have pretended I didn't recognise you, of course
he went on. 'But then there'd be that tension between u
wouldn't there? Not knowing who knew what?'

'But why... why are *you* here?' I managed to whisper. '
my parents' house?'

He gave a heavy sigh. 'Sadly, your father left your moth
in a great deal of financial difficulty. Lynne was in no state
deal with it – that task fell to me. Graham had named me a

the executor of his will, and we'd always had an understanding that I would make sure Lynne was taken care of if
the worst were to happen. He was like a brother to me, you
see. But I just couldn't make the numbers add up. There was
no way of paying off the debts without using the equity in the
house. Lynne and I, we agreed we would transfer the house
into my name, on the basis that I would work some financial
magic and settle the debts. It was a way of allowing Lynne to
continue living here, without worrying about bailiffs
knocking at the door.'

'Debts? What debts?'

He nodded slowly. 'Your parents were involved in a... a
venture. A charitable venture. It went wrong. There were huge
liabilities.'

That did ring some vague bells... I racked my brains to try
and remember. But transferring the house to Frank? That
didn't make any sense. I stared at him, feeling like a dim-
witted sixth-former in his moral studies class.

'But why did she move to Edinburgh, if the plan was for
her to stay here in the house?'

I saw his jaw tighten and release. He blinked slowly. 'I
personally think it was the wrong decision. But she wanted a
clean break.'

'When I came here, I didn't know that Kitty's father would
be... would be *you*.'

As if it would have been fine to lie to someone else, as
long as it wasn't him.

'Evidently not,' he said.

'I'm sorry.' But rage bubbled up inside me, even as I
said it.

It's you who should be sorry. You.

'So. I'm glad we've had this little chat.' He got up.

'But... what are you going to do about –'

'If something ain't broke...' He gave an exaggerated shru

It was only when I was upstairs again, opening up tl
airing cupboard, that I realised I'd forgotten the washin
basket. I made my way back down to the kitchen and scoope
it up from the floor, along with a few stray socks that ha
fallen out. But as I stood up, I saw something was differer
The wedding cake still stood on the table on its revolvir
plastic stand, but there now was a hole in the white expan
of the icing, showing through to the sticky darkness of tl
fruit cake beneath. Someone had stuck a finger into it, rig
up to the knuckle.

38

LYNNE

Dear Juliet,
Oh, I was feeling a bit fed up today. Everyone goes on about how 'positive' I am all the time, and such an 'inspiration', but I'm not always like that on the inside. Sometimes I get tired of trying to be those things just so that other people will feel better about the fact that I'm dying.

Your visit really cheered me up though, and I want to make sure you know that. I hope that I didn't upset you. When I mentioned my funeral, and those two hymns I'd like, your face went all closed off, and you looked away.

I wish that we could talk about these things more easily, because they're the things on my mind now. What you have to understand is that you have a future, Juliet. You can think about what you're going to do next summer, or whether you'll move house once you have your baby (because you will, darling, you WILL). But I don't have a future, so my thoughts are smaller. Things like hoping it'll be sunny tomorrow so I'll get to sit out in the garden with my morning cup of tea. Or

going through the Radio Times and highlighting tl
programmes I want to watch over the next few days. And n
thoughts are bigger, too. So big that they scare me. Life ar
death and what it all means.

But what I wanted to say, really, was that I went upstairs
bed early, because I was just in one of those moods whe
nothing was right, and there didn't seem any point
anything. Not when there is really only the end to loc
forward to. And quite possibly a pretty miserable one at tha
I get scared when I think about it. I know that there might l
pain beyond what I can imagine. I'm scared of losing n
mind, with it. Of losing myself, at the end. I suppose that pa
will be over with quickly, though. That's what I'm tellir
myself. Sometimes I have to comfort myself, like a child. I sa
'You're safe, you're safe.' Because that's one thing I've learne
through this whole wretched business – if you can stop fla
ping around and just kind of *lean* on yourself, there's a plac
inside you where you'll always be safe.

Now. I'm not telling you all this to upset you, sweethea
but because I want to be REAL with you – and so that you
understand what happened next. Because when I lay down
my bed, quite exhausted by all of these thoughts, and wi
trying to be brave – well, I'd left the window open, and
blackbird was singing in the garden. Oh, Juliet, the sound
it. Like liquid silver, spilling through the darkness.

They always make me think of Daddy. And you.

There was this one afternoon, when you were about nin
and it was just before my birthday. I'd mentioned
lunchtime that I thought that a family of blackbirds mu
have nested in the garden, and how the sound of the
singing made me feel so happy. While I did the dishes, yc
and Daddy had a whispered conversation up in your rooi

And then Daddy fixed a long extension lead on to your cassette recorder, and set up the stepladder under the big chestnut tree in the back garden. You told me that you were 'helping Daddy with the garden,' and you winked at one another as you went out the back door (except you'd never managed to get the hang of winking, so you blinked instead). Then Daddy stood there holding the stepladder while you kneeled on the top, holding the cassette recorder up as near to the branches as you could get. Daddy told me afterwards how it had taken ages, because every time a van went past on the road, or Gypsy barked, or a neighbour started up with the lawnmower, you insisted on starting all over again. You got quite frustrated, until Daddy told you that I might like the noises of an ordinary Sunday afternoon, and that it would be more 'authentic'.

You drew a little cover which you slotted in to the plastic box, with a picture of a mummy and daddy blackbird, and a baby, with orange beaks. The paper was only thin – I could still the 'Dixons' logo underneath. But it was the most beautiful present I've ever received. I've still got it in my drawer, darling, even though I don't have a cassette player any more.

And that's what the blackbird made me think of, tonight. The sight of you, reaching up, up to the sky with your little cassette recorder. And Daddy, standing so patiently at the bottom of the stepladder, keeping you safe.

I'm off to sleep now, darling. Hope you sleep tight too, wherever you are.

Mum xxxxxxxxx

39

JULIET

If Frank or Beth had walked past and seen me the1 sitting on the floor outside Kitty's room at just aft. midnight, I wouldn't have known what to tell them. didn't want to lie awake, alone, in the stifling silence of tl Forget-Me-Not Room. Mum's letter had hit me hard, earli that day... that surge of joy at hearing from her, then tl emptiness, stretching on afterwards.

Kitty had been lost in her own world all day. She had1 done her homework earlier, pretending that she could1 hear my repeated requests to get her folder and pencil ca out of her schoolbag. And she'd ignored the made-fror scratch lasagne I served up for dinner, nibbling only on tl bread that I set out on the table.

Then she'd disappeared upstairs to play with her Sylvania1 while I did my next job – washing the dishes and prepari1 another sitting of dinner for Beth and Frank. Somehow, in tl last couple of weeks since Frank's return, my job descripti seemed to have expanded to include being a private chef. It w even more important, now, to be indispensible. I'd felt a rush of relief when Frank crowed in delight over the lasagne and the bottle of Chianti I'd set out on the table to go with it.

Now they'd gone upstairs to bed and the house was dark, apart from the glow of the table lamp in the hall downstairs, and a yellow sliver of light coming from Kitty's just-open door.

Finally, I heard what I'd been waiting for – Kitty's voice. She was talking to her mermaid again. I held my breath and listened.

'She was cross because I didn't eat my dinner. My tummy was funny.'

'Awesome!' said the mermaid. 'You're super cool!'

There was a long silence. I began to wonder if Kitty had fallen asleep, or if she'd sensed my presence outside her door.

'Do you wanna play?' asked the mermaid eventually.

'Not just now, Mummy.'

Mummy? It was one thing for Kitty to pretend the doll was her mother when Beth was away for the weekend. But now Beth was right there in the next room.

'I was thinking. When you get back, will my nanny stay here too with us?'

Silence. The mermaid clearly didn't have an answer to that. A prickly, uneasy feeling came over me. It was almost as if...

'It's been better since she came.'

Oh Kitty.

'Tyler was mean to me today. He said that I have to give him two pounds or he'll tell Mrs Robson that I hit him.'

'La la la, la-la la la.'

'But I don't have two pounds. I only have one pound ar
eight pence.'

I heard her open her bedside drawer. There was a gent
clinking noise as she pulled out her piggy bank and emptie
it out.

'My tummy is all wriggly.'

Oh, my little love. She'd been too anxious to eat at dinn
time.

'What should I do?' she said softly.

And then came a tinny American whine: 'The Tongu
Tier will get your tongue!'

What?

I sprang up and pushed Kitty's door open. She was sittir
up in bed, both hands clamped over her mouth.

The Tongue Tier... what the hell?

'Has your mermaid doll gone funny?' I asked.

She nodded, pulling up the back of the mermaid's dres
looking for the off switch.

'La la la la,' said the doll.

'Give it here, Kitty. Hmm... I think the switch must l
broken. I could probably take out the batteries if you like? C
would you like me to take her to my room for tonight?'

Kitty swung her legs out of bed, and the contents of h
piggy bank spilled from her duvet onto the floor.

With shaking fingers, I picked up a handful of coins,
tiny silver key, and a heart-shaped wooden button, and fe
them into the slot on the pig's back.

Kitty crouched down next to me and leant in close. Sl
took a breath and held it; released it, so it shivered against n
ear. Finally, she whispered: 'Her has done this before.'

'What do you mean?'

She led me down the stairs, her legs pale little stal

beneath her *Frozen* nightdress. The doll dangled from her left hand. She held it in a way that reminded me of Mum, when she'd disposed of the dead mice she sometimes found in the garage.

'Where are we going, Kitten?'

She reached into the kitchen drawer and pulled out the back door key.

'You want to go outside? Well, okay. Just for a minute. Here... put your trainers on. And be careful on the steps.'

The night smelled of rain, and fresh, damp earth. A breeze shifted through the tops of the trees, setting the leaves rustling.

Was there someone out there?

It was impossible to tell. An arc of light fell on the grass from the open back door behind us, but beyond that was darkness. The sky was black, with an icy glitter of stars.

Kitty led me forward, off the paving and on to the grass. We advanced slowly past the black monster-shapes of the yew bushes, and the monkey puzzle tree, its uppermost branches spiky against the sky. I could hear my breathing, the clicking sound in my ears as I swallowed.

'Kitty, where are we going?'

Why had I let her lead me out here? What would Beth and Frank think, if they heard something and looked out of the window? I glanced behind me, half expecting to see lights snapping on all over the house.

But she didn't stop until we'd reached the very bottom of the garden, where the ground became muddy, squishing under our feet.

'Oh Kitty, we're going to get all muddy.'

She reached up on her tiptoes, and tossed the doll over the top of the wooden fence.

'Well. Nice job. I don't think she'll be saying any mo
silly things, will she?' I kept my voice bright, reassuring.

I took Kitty back to bed, and she settled under the cove
without a fuss. I put on her lantern to help her get off
sleep.

But I lay awake. Had the doll really said that? Had
misheard? Or was it just one of its set phrases? Wasn't the
something in the *Little Mermaid* story – the original version
about tongues? She'd given up her voice, hadn't she? She
given it up to the witch.

~

*WHO WOULD BE RINGING the doorbell in the middle of the nigh
And why is nobody answering it?*

*I make my way down the stairs. When I pull the door ope
it's you.*

*'You came back! Mummy, you came back!' I throw my arr
around you and hold on tighter and tighter. I cry and cry until
feel like my heart will crack inside me.*

*'You can sleep in the Forget-Me-Not Room with me,' I sa
'Come along. We'll get you settled in.'*

*You look like you need to get to bed right now. You look like ω
the energy is draining out of your body, second by second, like tω
twist of water down a plughole. Like the last time I saw you in tω
hospital.*

*You put down your bag by the bed, and as you pass by me I s
that one side of your face has fallen away. I shouldn't be able to s
inside your head, into the dark space of your skull.*

*'I'll get you an aspirin.' I rummage in the bedside drawer
find one, and when I look up again, you've gone. The bed's empty.*

All night long I hear it. The turning of the door handle to the Forget-Me-Not Room, the rattle of the latch against the frame. Whenever I get up to open it, there's nobody there, just the dark hallway.

I WOKE with what felt like a crash, an impact through my entire body. I lay there, heart pounding, pain shooting through every nerve.

A dream. It was a dream.

Calm down, Juliet. Breathe.

Notice five things you can see.

I stared up towards the ceiling, watching swirling patterns begin to form as my eyes tried to make sense of the blackness. I wondered what it would be like to be dead.

That probably wasn't the sort of thing you were supposed to think about during mindfulness. I reached over to turn on the bedside lamp, and that's when I saw it.

The mermaid doll, her pink face streaked with mud. She was lying on the other pillow, her smiling eyes fixed on the ceiling.

I scrambled out of the bed, but my legs were so weak with the fright that they wouldn't hold me. Down on the floor, I tried to breathe evenly, to tell myself that everything was okay. But I caught sight of myself in the wardrobe mirror, a dark shape crouching on the floor like an animal, a monster hiding behind my own bed, and a fresh wave of horror swept through me.

Had I done this? In my sleep? Had I lost my mind?

Or had Kitty done it? Had she changed her mind and brought the doll back inside? I forced myself to get up and

find a plastic bag. Shakily, I wrapped the mermaid in it, ar
shoved it to the back of my wardrobe.

Then I lay awake thinking, as the night inched towar(
morning.

I'd come back to Laurel Bank thinking it was a safe have
a place where I could recreate, for Kitty, the nostalg
comforts of my own childhood. But I'd been wrong. Tl
walls of this house had seen too much. They were soaked i
sadness. It was seeping out of them.

I tried to imagine Mum – the real Mum – to dispel tl
grey, rattling creature in my dream.

It'll be morning soon and things will look different, she said.

What should I do? I asked her.

But she was gone – nothing but silence, ringing in n
ears.

I just couldn't believe that Kitty had gone out into tl
garden by herself, opened up the gate in the fence ar
fetched the mermaid doll.

Her has done this before.

That's what Kitty had said. Had she meant that tl
mermaid had said strange things before?

It's been much better since she came.

Kitty had used 'she' when talking about me. Not 'her'.

Then I thought of the huge meltdown she'd had when I
pointed out the difference between 'she' and 'her', when we
been working on her Weekend News.

And I sat upright in bed, my heart pounding.

In her bedroom, Kitty was still fast asleep, her duvet pull(
up under her chin, the curves of her face soft in the glow fro
the toadstool light. On the top shelf of her wardrobe there w.
a Tesco bag stuffed with exercise books and paintings fro

school. I'd noticed it before, wondering why nobody had bothered to sort through it, wondering what Beth would say if I were to stick some of the art work up on the fridge, or even frame it and hang it on the walls, as Harry's parents had used to do. I lifted the bag quietly and took it back to my room.

It wasn't long before I found what I was looking for – a yellow exercise book that contained last year's Weekend News.

At the beginning, the 'news' was mainly in the form of pictures, labelled with one or two words in huge wobbly handwriting. But by the summer term, Kitty had been able to write short paragraphs. One Monday last April, Kitty had written:

'Wun day my mummy went awey and she dident come bak. I pleyed Silvaliens and ait sereyel on my own and then Her came in the house wiv Daddy. I had a nise weekend.'

The teacher had crossed out 'Her' and written in 'She' above, but hadn't corrected the spelling mistakes. She'd added a stamp that said 'Nice work!'

I read Kitty's words out loud, slowly, ignoring the spelling and reading phonetically. I wanted to make sure she was saying what I thought she was.

The next entry described how Kitty had gone shopping with Daddy in Sudbury and he had bought a new Sylvanian Hotel for her bedroom. She'd drawn a Sylvanian badger on the page opposite.

But a few pages later Kitty had written:

'Wun day my mummy got swopped. Wun day she was their and then she was gonne. She is a mermaid now. She spiks to me and I spik bak. Her came insted and daddy pritens Her is mummy. I had a nise weekend.'

The teacher had written, 'What an imagination!' and ha amended 'Her' to 'she' in both places.

A trickle of cold went down my back. Kitty knew how use the word 'she' perfectly well. 'Her' wasn't a pronoun. was a name.

Kitty had been talking all along. It was just that noboc had been listening.

40

CHARLIE

He tried to talk to her after dinner, while Cameron was watching television in the other room – Tasha allowed him one hour of screen time per day, and timed it with an enormous sand-filled hourglass she had ordered on Amazon.

'Tash. Can we talk, please?'

She removed her washing-up gloves, hung them on the little peg by the sink, and wiped her hands on a tea towel. 'What's up?'

He stood there, tongue-tied, as she waited for him to respond. He'd been building up to this all day, nerves fizzing in his stomach as he'd typed prescriptions, handed out tissues to the lonely, and listened earnestly to descriptions of people's bowel movements. But the words he had to say were too big, too dangerous. It didn't seem right to let them loose in this neat, bright kitchen. He looked around and saw it as if from outside, looking in... Cammie's best drawings, and his latest swimming certificate, stuck on the fridge. His giraffe height chart on the wall by the door. The collection of wonky

earthenware jugs that Tasha had made at an evening cla
last year, crowded onto a shelf above the sink. A faded Pet
Rabbit cup, soapy and draining on the rack, soon to be fill
with Cammie's bedtime milk.

What, of all this, would survive?

'I'm not sure that this is working for me any more.' I
could hear something like a whine in his voice – he sound
like an entitled teenager on some reality TV show.

Tasha's eyes flicked up to the ceiling, in something th
wasn't quite an eye-roll. More a 'God give me strengt
moment.

'Is this to do with Juliet?'

It was how she spoke to Cameron when he had a flip-ou
What's this really about? It's not really about sausages, is it?

'No. Juliet and I aren't... But – I mean, what if I did wa
to, well, to have another relationship? At some point. Ho
would that even work?'

'Well, that would be *your* responsibility.'

Like he'd asked her if he could get a hamster
something.

'You'd have to ensure it didn't impact on Cameron.'

That word – 'impact'. Tasha thought that her relationsh
with Shami didn't 'impact' on Cameron at all, because I
thought they were just friends. But Charlie wondered som
times about the impact of the things they never said.

'We've worked hard on this, Charlie,' she said. 'Too ha
to let it all fall apart now. Remember, we made a commitme
to each other?'

He did remember. Standing in a draughty church ar
making vows, once upon a time in some other life that r
longer felt like his.

'We put Cameron at the centre of this,' she went on. 'Ar

we agreed after... after Cyprus... that everything we did, from that point onwards, would be about him.'

From this day forward...

'Our North Star,' said Charlie. They'd had a long, tearful talk that went on all through the night on the balcony of their hotel room, as crickets chirped in the gardens below. He'd gazed up at the night sky, at the dark stretching endless in all directions, and tried to find something to say – something to grasp on to – that would make sense.

'Exactly.' Tash's voice was softer now. She put down the tea towel, her rings clinking gently on the worktop.

Charlie let himself imagine – just for a moment – being with Juliet. Bringing her back here and having to take her up to the maid's quarters, pretending she was just a friend while Cameron was put to bed in his bedroom just below, asking questions of Tasha about why Juliet was here, and where was Kitty, and why couldn't they all play together?

He imagined the look on his face when they told him. When they explained that Mummy and Daddy didn't love each other any more – not in that way. But that it was okay, because they both still loved him.

And his face when he realised that this idyllic family life, which they'd kept on life support for him, was only a fairy-tale. Something much beloved but only real for children, like Santa or the tooth fairy.

He pressed the heels of his hands into his aching eye sockets.

Tasha patted his shoulder in a rare moment of physical contact.

'I know it's not easy,' she said. 'I don't have all the answers either. But we keep on keeping on, don't we?'

'But Tash –'

He couldn't stand it – another circular conversatic where they ended up in exactly the same place as they ha begun. He was meeting Juliet tomorrow, just before pick-u time. She'd texted to say there was something she needed discuss with him, without the kids around. What if... it was wild thought, but what if she was going to say somethi about how she felt? Because she could feel this too. He kne she could. How could he even begin that conversatic when... what did he have to offer her, really? An invitation the upstairs flat, where all his things still stood around removal boxes. Date night one night a week – not on a Thur day, obviously. A life of secrecy, where she could only ever l a 'friend'.

'Oh God, sorry Charlie, I must ring Mum back,' sa Tasha, picking up her phone from the worktop. 'She's bee on her own all day. The carer was off sick again.'

The tone of her voice conveyed that the conversation ha ended. Tasha was a grown-up with grown-up things to de with. She walked out of the room, pressing numbers into h phone, turning her back on him and his despair, so th could keep on keeping on.

41

JULIET

I had to wait two days to get what I needed – a free run of the house. Finally, on Wednesday, Frank took the early train to Leeds for a charity board meeting. Beth went off to the Old Coach House, saying she wouldn't be back until late as she had to bake two hundred wedding cupcakes.

And Kitty was at school. She'd seemed no different than usual after the mermaid incident. I hadn't told her that it had appeared on my pillow. If Beth or Frank had done it as some kind of odd prank, then there was no reason for Kitty to know. If she'd done it herself, well, I needed more time to figure out how to deal with that. In the meantime, the mermaid still lay wrapped in a plastic bag at the bottom of my wardrobe, gouges in its back where I'd tried to force off the cover to the battery compartment with a screwdriver.

It spoke occasionally, asking if I wanted to play, or telling me I looked pretty. Last night, just as I was falling asleep, I thought it had asked if I wanted to die. So I piled spare blankets on top of it. Then a couple of pillows. And then towels from the airing cupboard.

There were lots of things that weren't normal about th house. But one was that there were no papers lying around none at all. I thought of my Mum's flat in Edinburgh, the wa it had been before she'd packed it all away into boxes – bar statements and old letters, spilling out of drawers. A shii birthday gift bag full of old letters, cards and photograpl which lived under the pink velvet chair in her bedroom. Tl pinboard on the kitchen wall sprouting receipts, invitatioi and appointment letters. The passport, birth certificate ar ancient National Insurance card that she'd kept in a met box in the cupboard under the sink in the bathroom, 'In ca of identity robbers, darling.'

The locked filing cabinet in Frank's study – that's whe my sights were set today.

Buzzing from the effects of two strong cups of coffee, went through the whole house looking for the key, includir searching through Beth and Frank's bedside drawers ar dresser with shaking fingers. I even tried to open the lo with one of Kitty's kirby grips, following instructions I four on YouTube. After the third failed attempt I remembered tl little silver key in Kitty's piggy bank.

It was possible she'd seen it and taken it for one of h games. Or to keep it safe. Maybe she'd even wanted me find it.

Breathless from running up and down the stairs, wiggled the key in the lock, and – I could hardly believe it the top drawer slid open. There was a row of cardboard slin containing utility bills, council tax letters, and mobile phoi contracts. In the next drawer down was a folder containii extended warranties for the dishwasher, oven and fridge, ar documentation from the letting agency that had let oi Laurel Bank while the Seiglers had been abroad, including lengthy exchange of emails about a leaking boiler. There was an envelope containing Frank and Beth's wills, drawn up by a solicitor in Bury St Edmunds, and a number of letters from a firm of solicitors who'd been the executors for Beth's father's will. I skimmed through them, telling myself I'd come back to them later.

The bottom drawer seemed to be devoted to health matters. I opened an envelope containing an appointment letter for Beth from a *clinique psychiatrique* in Geneva, and a follow-up letter which I tried to read but my schoolgirl French wasn't up to it.

There was an invoice for £6,540 for dental work carried out six years ago, with the words 'paid' scrawled across it.

Right at the back was a cardboard file marked 'Kitty', with height and weight charts, a vaccination record. And, in an envelope postmarked last summer, a letter from a psychiatrist at a private hospital in Bury St Edmunds, addressed to a GP at the local practice.

PATIENT REFERRED:
CATRIONA ("KITTY") SEIGLER

ISSUES:
1. Symptoms suggestive of selective or progressive mutism
2. Symptoms suggestive of Capgras syndrome

CURRENT MEDICATION:
Nil.

RECOMMENDATION:
1. Cranial MRI organised.

2. Further psychiatric assessment to confirm diagnosis.

MEDICAL HISTORY:

Kitty sustained a head injury while playing at home in July this year and was treated for concussion at West Suffolk Hospital. No other significant medical problems.

FAMILY HISTORY:

Kitty's mother, Beth, was referred to me some five years ago when she was suffering from PTSD symptoms following violent attacks by her ex-husband. At this time she had remarried and was pregnant with Kitty, and I subsequently saw her when Kitty was around a month old, as Beth felt she may have been suffering from post-natal depression. The Seiglers moved to Switzerland shortly afterwards so I did not see Beth again, however she tells me that her symptoms gradually settled over time.

Kitty's maternal grandfather died of lung cancer in July this year. Her maternal grandmother committed suicide at the age of thirty-one, following a struggle with mental health issues and substance addiction. Kitty's father is in good health. Both paternal grandparents died in accidents some years ago.

FOLLOW-UP:

Many thanks for referring this five-year-old girl. She has two sets of symptoms running in parallel. There is a possibility that these symptoms are all linked but there is equally a possibility that they are not.

When I saw Kitty, her affect was somewhat tense, but alert. She avoided eye contact with me but nodded and shook her head in response to my questions and appeared to understand what I was saying.

I took a history of Kitty's symptoms from her parents, who are firstly concerned that Kitty may be displaying signs of selective mutism.

The family recently moved back from Switzerland to the UK to be near Kitty's grandfather who was terminally ill and has since died. Prior to this Kitty attended a small private nursery in Switzerland where the staff reported that Kitty did not speak to peers or staff, and that she avoided eye contact. Kitty's parents sought advice from you as their GP on their return to the UK, and I understand you have organised a referral to a speech and language therapist. Kitty has now started school at Boxley Wood and staff have reported that she is completely non-verbal.

In recent months, Kitty's mutism has become progressive, affecting her at home as well as in 'outside' social situations, to the point where she will not talk to her parents, and communicates only through nodding and shaking her head, or writing in a notebook. However, as her writing skills are very limited given her young age, this has not proved an effective means of communication for Kitty.

Selective (or progressive) mutism is generally recognised as a type of anxiety disorder. Treatment is typically arranged through a speech and language therapist and may include cognitive behavioural therapy, and other techniques such as stimulus fading and desensitisation therapy.

However, in this case Kitty's mutism needs to be considered in light of her other symptoms, and it may be that there are more complex aspects to her condition that need to be considered. Firstly, it may be significant that the worsening in Kitty's mutism symptoms followed the head injury she sustained in an accident at home, for which she was treated at the Accident and Emergency Department at West Suffolk Hospital.

Another symptom manifested itself around this time, which was that Kitty became increasingly agitated around her mother, and wrote a message to one of her teachers saying that Beth was not her real mother and that she had been 'swapped'. She has also communicated this belief to her father on a few occasions, through nodding and shaking her head in response to his questions. The Seiglers sought advice, and the possibility has been raised that she might have Capgras syndrome. I can understand where this diagnostic thinking has come from and I agree it is a possibility. Capgras syndrome is a distressing psychological condition which is also known as 'imposter syndrome'. People who experience the syndrome will have an irrational belief that someone they know has been replaced by an imposter who looks identical. We most commonly see Capgras syndrome in older patients with Alzheimer's disease or other types of dementia, or in cases of schizophrenia, in particular paranoid hallucinatory schizophrenia. However, it has also been associated with brain injury, in particular where there are lesions to the area of the brain that process facial recognition, and this is a possibility that concerns me, given the head injury that Kitty sustained a few months ago.

Capgras syndrome is not well understood, but research indicates that people who suffer from this condition may have an impaired neural pathway between the visual face recognition area in the right temporal lobe of the brain and the area of the brain that provides the emotional response to that face. So, while they can recognise the individual, they have a compelling sense that there is 'something wrong' with that person, as they do not experience the feeling of warm familiarity that one normally associates with seeing a loved one.

Given that language delay and withdrawal from family members and peers may, in very rare cases, be symptoms that are indicative of early onset childhood schizophrenia, we also need to be cognisant of the possibility that Kitty may be suffering from delusions associated with this type of condition.

As a first step I have organised a cranial MRI scan to rule out or confirm the presence of brain lesions, and recommend that a full psychological evaluation be carried out over the next few months. I will see Kitty again with the result of the MRI scan and discuss with her parents at that point how to take matters forward. If brain lesions can be ruled out, then combined treatment of an antipsychotic medication plus an SSRI may lead to a good clinical outcome with a remission of the psychotic symptoms.

Many thanks for the referral.

Yours sincerely

James Watt MRCPsych
Consultant Psychiatrist

42

JULIET

Charlie and I met, half an hour before pick-up, in a grubby little café just around the corner from the school. The air was thick with frying bacon and the tang of coffee grounds – the smell was already starting to cling to my coat and my hair.

First I told him about the latest mermaid incident, and about Kitty's Weekend News.

Charlie looked confused. 'Hang on a minute. The mermaid doll said *what*?'

I sighed. 'I might have heard wrong. It was very late at night and I was tired.'

'You used to go on about the Tongue Tier when you were little. Remember the Barbie you had with the dark cloak? Maybe you did imagine it. Or someone might have been messing around with it, I suppose.'

'I just can't think why, though. Unless someone wanted to frighten Kitty.'

'It all sounds a bit...' Charlie's voice trailed off. He looked at me, the way my mother used to look at me when I wasn't

feeling well, and she was deciding whether to take n
temperature or put me to bed with Calpol.

No, Charlie. Please believe me.

'Why don't you bring me the mermaid? I'll get it open ar
take a look at it. It's probably... *Frank*.' Charlie said the nan
as though it tasted bad in his mouth. 'He must have put it (
your pillow as a sick joke. I can't see Kitty going into tl
garden in the dead of night to get it. Why would she eve
think of doing that?'

'Maybe.' Frank did like his 'jokes'. He loved to lead peop
up the garden path and then make them feel stupid. Could
have been a prank aimed at *me*... rather than Kitty? Was I
waiting for me to raise my concerns, only so he could bello
with laughter? Was he seeing how far he could push n
before I cracked, and then he would sadly have no choice b
to reveal my 'history' to Beth?

'I mean, what we've got to remember is that they are
normal people, are they? And there must be somethir
pretty screwed up in that family if Kitty has been writing
her Weekend News that Beth isn't really her mother. You'
got to wonder what's triggered that.'

'Well that's the other thing – I found this.' I thrust n
phone at him. 'It's a letter from a psychiatrist about Kitty.
found it in Frank's filing cabinet. Can you read it?'

'You *found* it?' he said with a raised eyebrow.

I'd photographed sections of the letter. Charlie had
enlarge the photos as far as they'd go and read through tl
text in each one, squinting his eyes to see the small print.

I tried to swallow down the lump in my throat, to keep tl
wobble out of my voice. 'It says she might have... schiz
phrenia.'

Still reading, Charlie shook his head. 'Schizophrenia

extremely rare in children. I think it's practically unheard of in children of Kitty's age. It's not my area, but I think it would be too early to diagnose something like that, even if there were psychotic symptoms.'

'The letter says she was going to have an MRI,' I said. 'I have two questions. Firstly, why hasn't all this been followed up?'

'Maybe it has,' he said softly, reaching the end of the letter and scrolling back to the first photograph to read it again.

'Well there's no sign of any of these *antipsychotic medications*, is there? She hasn't so much as seen the GP in the time I've been here, let alone a psychiatrist.'

Charlie shrugged, his face confused. 'Maybe the scan showed that she did have a brain injury, and they decided there was no treatment other than to just wait and see.'

'How can...' I was going to ask him how I could find out. The possibility hung between us, unspoken. I knew that Charlie could look Kitty up on the computer system at the surgery.

'I think the only way to check would be to ask Beth, or Frank,' he said. 'I can't look into this for you, Juliet. I'm sorry, but I just can't. Every time someone accesses a patient's record it leaves a footprint – they can check who was logged in, and if there's no legitimate need to access the record then it's a disciplinary offence. A sackable offence. A get-struck-off-the-register type offence.'

'What if I brought Kitty in to see you? *In loco parentis*?'

'If I knew you were going against Beth's wishes, then I couldn't see her. It would be unethical.'

His voice changed and his face closed over. I felt a flash of anger, even though I knew it wasn't fair. Was I the only one

who wanted to help Kitty? Charlie would rather protect h
nice safe job and his nice safe family.

I shook my head and tried to banish the awful thoughts.

'I'll see what I can find out about Capgras syndrome,' l
said. 'But this might not be a "condition" at all. It might ju
be a childhood thing. A developmental thing. When Ta:
and I were in Tesco a few weeks ago, we saw a little girl wh
was having a God-awful tantrum. She was trying to wrenc
the trolley away from her mother and towards a display
toys, and she was shouting, "You're not my mummy!" Tl
poor woman looked mortified. Tash went over and offered
help.'

I could just imagine Tasha intervening in that situatio
She would put a sympathetic hand on the woman's arm, ar
say something like, 'You're doing an amazing job.'

'But the letter said it might be schizophrenia,'
whispered.

'No,' he said, reaching a hand across the table so that h
fingers almost touched mine. 'I'm sure that's not it.'

I thought of the wild tantrums, the biting and screamin
The way Kitty seemed caught up in her own world most
the time. The conversations she had with the mermaid doll.

Drowning it in the bath.

The history of mental illness in the family.

Of suicide.

I stretched my hand out and grasped his fingers.

At that moment Annabel walked past outside tl
window, a ship in full sail in her long winter coat, her do
trotting behind her. She caught my eye and then her ga.
flicked to Charlie before she looked away, her lips presse
into a thin line.

'Oh no!'

'Just ignore her,' said Charlie. 'We're doing nothing wrong.'

Which only made me think of the wrong things we *could* be doing. I imagined Charlie leaning forward, taking my face in his hands... I felt a flush rise up my neck.

'If Kitty had a significant head injury,' he went on. 'Then that could cause all sorts of problems.'

'But the head injury... what happened? I mean, could they have hurt her? Maybe they hurt her and she's reacted against them. If she does have this Capgras syndrome, why didn't Beth just say? Why keep it from me?'

Charlie shrugged uncomfortably. 'Maybe she was embarrassed. Or maybe she feels bad about the accident when Kitty got her head injury, and doesn't want to talk about it. Who knows.'

'If Kitty does have this syndrome, if she does think that Beth has been... swapped... then it must be absolutely terrifying.'

'And horrible for Beth. You can see why she might not want to talk about it. I know that when dementia patients have these sorts of delusions, the advice these days is to go along with it.'

'What do you mean?'

'So, in this case, Beth might say to Kitty, "I know I'm not Beth, and that must be very upsetting for you. But Beth has sent me to look after you. We both love you very much."'

I shuddered, to think of this Almost-Beth, trying to win Kitty's confidence.

'Maybe I should talk to Beth. Get it all out in the open. Tell her that I know. We could research some strategies to help. That way, it might make things easier for Kitty, and Beth might be more likely to keep me on.'

'But you'd also have to explain how you found the letter.

'And that I was snooping around in their filing cabinets, groaned.

I imagined Frank with his sorrowful Jesus-eyes, telling n that this latest 'breach of trust' was the last straw. That would have to pack my bags and leave.

I thought of the long drive back up to Edinburg opening up Mum's old flat. Making up the bed with co blankets. Would it be like before, lying there with tl curtains closed, one day merging into the next? Would the be anything left in the world to make me get up?

'Pick-up time,' said Charlie, looking at his watch.

'I'm trapped,' I said, suddenly comprehending the situ tion I was in. 'I can't move forward – with Kitty, I mean. I ca *do* anything. And I can't move back, either.'

I couldn't un-love her.

'I think you have to tread very carefully,' said Charli 'Until we understand what we're dealing with here.'

We.

'Please be careful,' he said, almost in a whisper. 'Pleas Juliet.'

And I saw in his eyes that it wasn't just me who w trapped.

'It'll be okay,' I said, in the voice I used for Kitty when sl was scared. 'It'll be okay.'

43

BETH

I t struck Beth, as she moved quietly across the landing, that she sometimes felt like a ghost in her own home. She'd taken to wearing long cotton nightdresses, like a girl from some Victorian drama. She'd ordered them online, since Frank was still insisting on all this 'lie low' nonsense. As if Rick would be waiting for her in the lingerie department of Debenhams, brandishing an iron.

She pressed her fingers to her jaw, imagining the steel implants that the dentist had screwed into the bone to hold the new teeth. She'd caught sight of one of them – a wicked flash of metal – as she lay in the dentist's chair and thought she might faint.

Downstairs, she slid quickly past the hall mirror, not wanting to see the dark shadows in her face or her sunken eyes. She knew she wasn't looking well. But she couldn't go to the doctor – they'd just tell her to stop taking the pills.

Tonight she'd taken one instead of two before bed, but that was probably the reason why it was half past one and she hadn't yet fallen asleep. She told herself that if a cup of warm milk didn't help, then she'd take another in half a hour.

How was she supposed to control her nerves witho them? That's what nobody seemed to have any answers t *Méditation* – that's what the annoying doctor in Vevey ha kept going on about. She was trying to do it every evenin but it was hopeless with Kitty around. Last night, she'd la on her bed and focused on her breathing for ten minute when she'd heard a thumping sound from Kitty's rooi When she'd gone through, she'd found that Kitty ha climbed up the shelves that were built into one side of h wardrobe, scaling them like a monkey, trying to reach son dolly that Beth had tried to hide on the top – a hideoi mermaid thing. She had grabbed Kitty round the waist ar pulled her down, arms and legs flailing. The mermaid ha fallen down too and bounced onto the carpet. Beth ha seized it and wrenched its plastic head off.

'You could have brought the whole wardrobe down c top of you! You could have killed yourself! Jesus Christ!'

She cringed now to think of it. How did other mothe manage? How did they cope with the responsibility, this nee to be constantly vigilant, never off duty? She'd never realise quite how much Rosa had done for her, while she'd doze her days away in that tall shuttered house in Vevey.

Milk, though. Warm milk. The quicker she drank it, tl quicker she could allow herself another pill.

Passing the study door, she realised that she could he Frank's voice. Was he on the phone, at this time of night? Sl stopped right outside, and held her breath to listen.

'Madam wants me to buy her a café.' He spoke in a ironic, long-suffering way, like she was a spoilt child who asked him for a pony.

Christ, he had a nerve. Beth was going to buy the café with the money she'd inherit from Stan. She'd thought it all out, researched recipes, even made a business plan.

'Yeah,' he said, 'But then I thought, well why not? A nice little cash business. What do you think? Yeah, Len can do all that, that's no problem. This could really work for us.'

A cash business? That usually meant something dodgy, didn't it? And who the hell was 'us'?

'Accounts? God, no. I'd do all that side of things. Remember, this is a woman who doesn't have a GCSE to her name!'

That was wrong. Beth had got a B in home economics and a C in French. What a pig he could be sometimes.

'I mean, the cancer thing was just small potatoes. We could do so much more if I'm back here full time.'

What cancer thing? For a horrible moment she thought maybe Frank had somehow given Stan the cancer, so they could get his money after he died. That wasn't possible, was it? No. You couldn't give someone cancer. She massaged her temples. Her head was so fuzzy sometimes. No. Frank was involved in a charity that raised money for teenagers with cancer. Maybe that was what he meant. But an image came to her mind of her father, his lungs sprouting with cancerous potatoes. Hadn't that happened once? She'd seen it on the news. A man had been told he had cancer but it turned out to be a potato plant that had taken root in his lungs. She'd seen that, hadn't she? Or was it a pea plant? Beth twisted her fingers anxiously as she tried to remember. Cancer, cancer, cancer... it was one of those words that started to sound strange if you said it too much.

The person at the other end was clearly going on at length. Beth couldn't hear the voice but she suspected, from the way Frank was reacting, that it was a woman. In fact, she

was pretty sure she knew exactly who it was. He kept inte
jecting warmly, with 'Mm-hmm,' and 'Yeah, sure,' and the
he gave a bellowing laugh.

'We're filming a piece for the website at the oncolo
centre – the relaxation room that we funded. Coloured ligh
and lavender and all that malarkey. It's right next to th
chemo ward. I could arrange another... *photoshoot*... for you
page.'

That cow at the other end of the phone was speakin
again, the voice growing higher pitched and squeaky.

'Fair enough. Well, think about it,' he said.

Then his voice changed, became deeper and playful. '(
course I'm remembering. As business partners, yes
naturally.'

Beth didn't want to hear any more. She decided she
creep back up the stairs to bed, and not bother with the mill

But then came the most almighty crash that shook th
floor where Beth was standing. It had come from upstair
From the direction of Kitty's room – oh God, oh God.

Beth ran, almost tripping over her nightdress. She hear
Frank swearing, the noise of the study door cracking on i
hinges as it was flung open... his footsteps behind her. Sh
fell forward on the stairs, scampering up them on her han
and knees, a scared white animal with a wolf snapping at h
heels. On reaching the landing she tried to run but her leg
had gone to jelly. She sank to the soft-carpeted floor, h
nightdress billowing around her.

44

CHARLIE

C harlie had burned the dinner. He'd been reading articles about schizophrenia in children while trying to grill sausages at the same time. Tasha had tipped the whole lot in the bin – burned sausages were carcinogenic, she said – and they'd had cheese and cucumber wraps instead. Cammie had wept uncontrollably, and tears were still glistening on his cheeks when Tasha rushed him out of the door to go to a family yoga class (taught by Shami – there was a shock).

He did the dishes, and then retreated upstairs and texted Juliet with a link to a mental health charity for children – they were open twenty-four hours and she could phone the helpline and talk to a trained adviser.

She replied a few minutes later: *Thanks. Maybe in a bit. Dealing with a minor flood here (another mermaid in bath incident).*

His heart leapt. His fingers trembled as he typed a reply: *Can I help? I could be with you in five minutes.*

SHE LOOKED close to tears when she dragged open the fro
door and ushered him into the hallway at Laurel Bank. The
were wet patches on her jeans and her sleeves were pulled ι
to the elbows.

'What happened?'

'It's that bloody doll again. When we got back fro
school, Kitty went upstairs to play and I made her son
cheese on toast and soup for an early tea.'

He nodded.

'But when I went upstairs to get her... well, come ar
see.'

She led the way up the stairs. The carpet was sog¦
underfoot, water dripping down the paintwork between tl
balustrades of the galleried landing. A bucket stood outsiᴄ
the bathroom, with a mop leaning against the wall.

Charlie surveyed the sodden carpet. 'It'll dry out. Tℎ
house insurance will probably supply a dehumidifier.'

'The internet says that the carpet will need replacing.'

'Why?'

'Because it might get infected with black mould. It's ve
dangerous.' She pulled her phone out of her pocket. 'Look
"Symptoms of black mould exposure include fatigu
headaches, confusion, seizures, tremors, coughin
pulmonary decay, bleeding of the lungs and death."'

Charlie took the phone. 'You do realise this is from
website for a professional carpet-drying company?'

'Beth and Frank are going to be furious. I shouldn't ha·
left her unsupervised.'

'You were making Kitty's tea. You can't be in two places
once.'

Juliet shook her head and went to knock softly on one of the closed doors on the landing.

'Kitty? Can I come in?'

She'd curled herself into a ball on the floor behind her bed, her face hidden, feet poking out behind.

'Kitty? Charlie's come over.' Then: 'I'm sorry I shouted at you.'

The ball on the floor didn't move.

'She's been like that for ages. What do you think I should do?' she asked Charlie in a whisper, as she closed the door.

He was at a loss. All he could think of was the time Cammie had found a sick hedgehog in the garden. They'd put it in a cardboard box with a hot water bottle wrapped in a towel and a bowl of cat food. Cammie had hovered over it, asking it if it was all right, in a clear, loud voice like you might use with someone who didn't speak English. He had wanted to sleep in the shed with it, in case it woke up and needed something in the night.

He spoke in his authoritative GP's voice. 'Have you got any food she could have? A hot water bottle?'

Juliet nodded, and they went downstairs to the kitchen.

'So what happened?' he asked as they waited for the kettle to boil.

'She must have gone looking through my room and found the mermaid in my wardrobe. She tried to drown it again.'

'Huh?'

'I found it in the bath, with the taps on. It was just floating there face down – its hair had got caught in the overflow and the water was coming over the top of the bath.'

She looked down. 'I shouted at her, Charlie.'

'I'm pretty sure I would have shouted at Cameron if he'd flooded the house.'

She still looked distraught. 'Maybe it's karma,' he went (
in a mock-serious voice. 'Didn't you once cause a flood wi
Edward-The-Sex-Pest Barbie?'

'That was a fire,' she said forlornly. 'I tried to dry him o
in the microwave.'

'There you go then,' he said, reassuringly, as thoug
murdering dolls was perfectly normal childhood behaviour.

'His face melted a bit,' she went on. 'He looked horribl
Mum made me throw him away.'

'That must have been a relief for the other Barbies.'

He thought for a moment that she might smile. But sl
shook her head again.

'She'd been through my room looking for that doll. Tha
what's bothering me. It's *sneaky*. And she's denying it w
her.'

'Are you completely sure it *was* her?' he asked. 'I mean,
could have been another one of Frank's... jokes.'

Juliet picked up a plate of congealed cheese-and-toa
wrinkled her nose at it, and tipped it into the bin. 'Frank's
Leeds. Beth's working late at the café. I can hardly blame it (
them. I should have been watching Kitty. It must have bee
her the other night, too. She must have fetched the merma
from the garden, put it on my pillow, and gone looking for
when I didn't give it back to her. Her issues – I think they ;
very deep, Charlie. For the first time, I feel out of my dep
with her. Completely out of my depth.'

Juliet handed him a hot water bottle with a knitted pol
bear cover, and he filled it from the kettle while she rippe
open a pack of Jammy Dodgers and put three on a plate. The
he watched as she cut an apple into slices, the deft movemen
of her fingers, the steel flash of the knife. His heart beat a litt.

faster as he followed her up the stairs, and he had the oddest notion that they were children again, smuggling illicit snacks up to Juliet's room, to be eaten in a blanket tent by torchlight.

She placed them on the floor next to Kitty. Then she took a pink blanket from the end of Kitty's bed and draped it over the hump of her back with a little stroke.

Just as they were leaving the room, Kitty rolled on to her back and held her arms out. Her eyes were shut and her face was crumpled and flushed.

Juliet flew over and scooped her into her arms.

Charlie crouched down beside them. 'Kitty, do you want to help me with an important job?'

Kitty's face remained buried against Juliet's shoulder, but she nodded.

'If you can show me where you keep the towels then we can lay some down on the wet carpet and walk over them to help soak up the water.'

Juliet released Kitty. 'They're in the airing cupboard, just outside the Forget-Me-Not... I mean, outside my room.'

'Come along then, Miss Kitty,' said Charlie.

Upstairs, he knelt down on the floor as Kitty pulled towels off the wooden shelves and piled them into his arms.

'Hey, steady on,' he said as she stood on tiptoe to reach more.

He was aware of Juliet's tread on the stairs, of her walking around the back of him, opening the door of the Forget-Me-Not Room.

'I'm going to change out of these jeans – won't be a sec.'

He turned to look at her, silhouetted in the doorway, pressing her outstretched hands down the wet denim.

'Charlie... Charlie, are you all right?'

He tried to say he was, but instead he made a stran
sound in his throat.

For a second he'd thought – some very old, deep-dov
part of himself had thought – that it wasn't Juliet standii
there at all.

He'd thought it was Lynne.

HE KNEW *they shouldn't have run away from Sunday school. B *
*the teacher had told them about the miracle of the loaves and fish *
*and Juliet wanted to play a game of it. When they had to pr *
*afterwards, Juliet put her hands together and her head down, b *
*then turned it to the side so she was looking at him through h *
*eyelashes. He knew what she was thinking, just like he always di *

*They slipped away through the side door and ran through t *
*churchyard and the bluebell wood to Juliet's house. She got a cha *
*and climbed up on the kitchen worktop to open the cupboard a *
she pulled out a loaf of Allinson's bread.

*'We'll have to find some fishes,' she said, tearing crusts off h *
*slice and offering them to Charlie. He took them doubtfull *
wondering whether she expected him to do a miracle with them.

'We could play dog hide and seek,' he suggested.

*'I'll be the dog,' she said quickly, as if they'd been talking abo *
dogs all along. 'You be the owner.'

*She hid in the airing cupboard, right up on the top floor, whe *
*the roof sloped and it was hotter than the rest of the house. She d *
*a quiet little woof, so Charlie could find her. He knew she didn't li *
hiding in the dark for too long.

*Charlie got into the airing cupboard next to her. She hand *
*him a crust that was warm and soggy from her hand, and *
pushed it under a pile of yellow towels.

'What are you thinking?' he asked.

'There's a thumping noise,' she said. 'I was thinking about that.'

She was right – there was a thumping noise coming from somewhere. And a little cry like someone had hurt themselves.

'Maybe it's another dog,' she said. Her eyes were big and dark and her breath smelled sweet and bready. 'A big one with big teeth.'

They crawled out of the cupboard, woofing quietly. The thumping was coming from the room that they called the Forget-Me-Not Room. Juliet had said that was in case they forgot about it, being on the top floor.

Juliet pushed the door open, still on her hands and knees.

Lynne Hazelwood was lying on the bed and a man was kneeling over her, pushing her so that it made the end of the bed thump against the wall.

Charlie pulled Juliet back from the door. He thought they should probably go back in the airing cupboard.

'Who's that?' he whispered.

'Oh, it's the Lord,' she said. 'His name's Frank.'

On the bed, they stopped moving suddenly. Then Lynne Hazelwood slid round and stood up, smoothing her skirt down over her legs and knees. It was a green skirt with red cherries on it, quite thick, as though she'd made it from felt out of the Sunday school arts and crafts box. She was standing in the doorway now, blocking it like she didn't want them to see in the room.

'Juliet! And Charlie.' Her smile looked like a clown's smile. Drawn on.

'Why is Frank thumping you on that bed?' asked Juliet.

She laughed. And then stopped and went quiet for a while. And laughed again.

'Frank is a trained fizzy therapist. He was helping me with my back, darling. You know it's been so sore.'

She screwed up her face and reached round to rub her ba
with one hand.

The man stood up too. His belt was undone and his trouse
were sliding off a bit like he hadn't bothered to get dressed proper
'Good work. Keep doing those exercises I showed you,' he said
Lynne Hazelwood.

Juliet turned to Charlie. 'Okay, you be the dog now.'

Charlie stayed for lunch. The Lord man stayed too – Graer
Hazelwood was back from church by then and they needed to ha
a meeting about something.

After lunch, which was roast beef, Lynne Hazelwood got o
the fruit bowl.

Lord Frank took an apple and Charlie saw Juliet frow
because the apples were from her tree. She stared right at him a
he took a sharp knife from the board and began to peel it, all in o
long strand.

Lynne Hazelwood and Graeme and Lord Frank were talki
about how they might raise some money for orphans in Ind
Graeme was offering him to stay in their house when they h
meetings about it.

Juliet's chin was sticking out now, her mouth tight shut.

Lynne went into the garage to find some more wine, and call
Graeme in to help reach it. Lord Frank put his finger to his lips a
made a 'shh' sign. Then he took the apple knife and, looking Jul
straight in the eye, he dragged the sharp point of it across the tip
his tongue. Little blobs of red sprang up.

Juliet breathed in quickly. 'Mummy,' she said.

Lynne Hazelwood came back in, going on about doing
fundraiser, and getting people to give things for the tombola. A ca
sale.

Then the Lord picked up the apple and started peeling it agai
Juliet scrunched up her hands, tight, so tight, under the tab

When they went upstairs to play afterwards Charlie saw that her
nails had made funny marks on her palms like little thin moons.

'*Look what you've done,*' *he said.*

But she scrunched her nails in again. And again. Like she
wanted it to hurt.

'YOU LOOK like you've seen a ghost,' said Juliet.

Kitty had draped a large bath sheet over her back and was
on all fours, nudging his arm with her head.

'Come on, Kitty-Doggy,' said Juliet. 'Let's take the towels
down and see what we can do about the carpet.'

Suddenly he was overwhelmed with a longing to tell her
everything. All of it. He wanted to ask her if she remembered
too. To ask her how she could stand to live here in the same
house as Frank.

To ask her if she felt it too, this thing between them.

She stood there, smiling at him, a little confused, her
hands on her hips. Her sleeves were pulled up to the elbows,
revealing the patterns of little white scars. He wanted to pull
her close to him, to wrap himself around her so she would
never be hurt again.

How the hell had it happened – that he was the one who
would have to hurt her?

Downstairs, a key turned in the front door.

'Hello-ooo! Anyone in?'

It was Frank. There was silence for a few moments, and
then the slow tread of his feet on the stairs.

'Oh dear, oh dear, oh *dear*.'

He looked amused when Charlie followed Juliet down
onto the lower landing.

'You *have* been busy.'

'I'm really sorry,' said Juliet. 'We had an issue with tl
bath.'

Frank stood there rubbing his jaw slowly, looking aroun
Charlie could see Juliet biting her lip like a child about to g
into trouble, needing Frank's assurance that it was all a
right.

Frank's eyes were alight with some sort of emotion – ⸢
was that the right word? He had the look of a cat that ha
cornered a mouse.

He nodded. Once. Twice. 'I'll dig out the details of tl
insurance company. If you wouldn't mind giving them a ca
in the morning, Juliet? Will you have time to do that? I kno
you've got your hands full with Kitty.'

She nodded briskly, her eyes filling with tears of relief.

Charlie couldn't stand to watch it. Every muscle in h
body had tightened. He felt it firing down every nerve – tl
impulse to get Juliet away. To get her far, far away from th
house.

D ear Juliet,
Now this letter is a bit awkward, because it talks about things we have never talked about.

I just want you to know that the trouble we had with money, when Daddy died, was NOT HIS FAULT.

I don't want you to feel let down, or that Daddy didn't look after us properly. All Daddy ever did was try to look after us. That was what he was *all about*, darling.

When you were little, about five or six, we got involved with a charity, and Daddy was a trustee for the charity, along with Frank Redwood. It was a charity which had been set up to build and run a school in India for children who'd been orphaned – do you remember, I did several fundraisers at Church? The bring-and-buy sales, and the garden party over at Belton Hall? I made that enormous pavlova. Frank, your father and I were trustees, and so was the Vicar of St-Mary's-in-the-Wood, in Boxley Wood, and the treasurer from the high school across at Langley Park. The meetings were in St Mary's Church hall, four times a year – Lady Day,

Midsummer Day, Michaelmas, and the week before Chris
mas, when we had mince pies and sherry.

Well, at one point the charity got into difficulties. The
had been extremely heavy rain in that part of India, whic
made all the ground turn to mud, and one of the walls of tl
school collapsed. Daddy arranged a loan for the charity, ar
made us guarantors, which means that if the charity couldr
pay back the loan, we would have to step in. Apparently
was the only way of getting the loan, and in fact it was n
who convinced Daddy to do it. A little seven-year-old bc
had lost both of his legs in the accident, and part of tl
money was to get him the medical treatment he needed, ar
pay for a wheelchair and so on.

There were problems. The charity couldn't pay back tl
loan. There was another accident at the school, and this tin
a teacher died. It turned out that the building hadn't bec
constructed properly. There was legal action against the cha
ity, and we needed more loans to pay the legal fees, and, oh
won't bore you with all the details, darling, but over the ne
few years we ended up in a lot of debt.

Daddy was devastated about it all, darling. He felt that,
a bank manager, he was the last person who should have g
into that situation. It undermined his whole sense of who l
was. But it was *my* fault – I insisted that we guarantee tho
loans, because I couldn't stop thinking about that poor bc
and his legs. Frank showed us a photo of him, lying on
rickety bed with dirty sheets, with bloodied bandages on tl
stumps of his legs, and this look on his face. He had nobocl
in the world. Nobody.

I often wonder what happened to him. The charity had
close down all its operations in the end. Frank and I tried
find out the boy's details so that we could send him mone

direct. But it proved impossible. All I knew was that his name was Jayesh. Not much to go on in a country of over a billion people. He was just lost, out there, somewhere in India. Little Jayesh.

And if I'm honest, I felt that your Dad was lost too, after that. I couldn't find him any more. I felt invisible, like a ghost in my own house.

The doctor suggested a change of scenery for Daddy, so I took him away on a little road trip up to Skye. We stayed at a farmhouse B&B where we used to go on holiday before we had you. They did good breakfasts – proper sausages and freshly laid eggs. And there was a little shingle beach nearby where we used to sit out at night, watching the stars, and the light rippling on the water, and talking – really talking. I suppose we were just a young couple in love, at that point where everything about the other person seems magical, and you just want to know every thought that comes into their head. But not that last time. He said he didn't want to sit out, that there were too many midges. I said that was fine, and I found something for us to watch on the little television in our room – a nice comedy to cheer us up, and a cup of tea. Except the comedy wasn't really funny. And the tea tasted funny with UHT milk. I don't think I even drank mine.

People didn't understand about depression then, not the way they do now. I wish we had talked more. I wish I had known that you have to let sadness in, not push it away.

I wish I had kept looking until I found him.

Sorry for the rather grim letter, Juliet. I never felt it was something that I could discuss with you, as a child. But if I don't tell you now, you'll never know.

Lots of love,

Mum xxxxxx

Dear Juliet,

Further to your recent email, please
note that the enclosed is the final
letter that your mother instructed us
to forward on to you.

Anna will be in touch regarding
outstanding matters re your mother's
estate. However, in the meantime please
do not hesitate to contact us if we can
be of any further assistance.

Kind regards,

Angela Browne,
Senior Associate

46

JULIET

Beth and Frank weren't going to Kitty's nativity play. I'd thought I'd misheard Beth when she first told me, but no – she had a wedding fayre up in Harrogate, and Frank had gone with her. They were going to stay in a little boutique hotel where they'd 'honeymooned'. Beth had fluttered a look at me, hinting at what she and Frank might get up to.

No wonder Kitty had this Capgras syndrome or whatever it was. If Beth was my mother I'd be in denial too.

I arrived at the church early, taking a seat in the second row from the front. I'd told Kitty that her parents had instructed me to take lots of photos, although that wasn't true.

The pews began to fill up. Someone's grandparents had taken the two seats to the left of me, leaving a space big enough for three between me and the aisle.

Mimi and her husband walked past, scanning the pews for spaces. 'Gawd, it's busy,' she was muttering. 'I told you we should have left earlier.'

I budged up a little. 'There's room here... Mimi?'

She caught my eye then looked away quickly. 'Come o
Robert.' She took her husband's arm and they walked ba
up the aisle.

Then Annabel, who'd been helping with the costum
backstage, walked past carrying a roll of gold card and a se
otape dispenser.

I smiled and motioned to the spaces next to me.

She gave a crooked, 'You must be joking' smile, ar
continued past.

Perhaps she had to put the card and sellotape away. Th
must be it.

Or were these seats supposed to be reserved for the teac
ers, perhaps? Had someone forgotten to put a sign on them?

But the seats stayed empty, even though a couple
people were now standing at the back. Nerves prickled in n
stomach. Was I imagining this? Or had the scandalous nev
spread through the *whole* school, in the two days sin
Annabel had seen Charlie and me holding hands at tl
coffee shop?

I turned and scanned the rows behind me. There w
Charlie a few rows back, arms crossed and staring up into tl
shadowy spaces of the vaulted ceiling. Tasha was beside hir
chatting and laughing with Shami, the yoga teacher. She w
sitting in the row in front of them, wrapped in a soft bla
shawl studded with sequins.

If the gossip had reached Tasha, she didn't seem to l
bothered by it.

With just moments to go until the show was due to start
was saved by another grandmother. She sat down to my rig
and even said a polite hello, sending a puff of sherry-scent
breath in my direction.

The lights went down, and a thin voice piped up:

Once in Royal David's City
Stood a lowly cattle shed

The children filed in holding LED candles. Slowly they took their places, kneeling around the edges of the stable scene.

Kitty was solemn in her white woolly lamb costume, with black socks on all four hands and feet and her nose blackened with face-paint.

The nativity story was told from the point of view of the grumpy donkey, who was ninety-six in human years, and just wanted to retire.

All I want is a field somewhere
With apples to eat, and lots of fresh air
And a stable at night, with a warm bed of straw
Is that too much to ask? Ee-aw, ee-aw?

When the tinsel-crowned angels appeared on the starlit hillside and told the shepherds the news about the newborn king, Kitty stayed stonily silent while the other sheep baa-ed loudly and scampered around, and one of the shepherds fainted in shock.

But later, once everyone was gathered around the crib, her expression changed to one of intense focus. When the donkey said, 'Well I suppose I *could* stay on a bit longer. If you *really* want me to,' Kitty joined in the answering chorus of baas, moos and yeses, giving a single, soft little bleat that probably only I would have noticed.

Afterwards, I stood up and clapped and cheered as if it had been a concert at the Royal Albert Hall and Kitty had been the soloist.

She caught my eye, stifling a shy smile, and joined the queue of children filing out. They moved slowly, because the

headmistress was standing at the back handing out swee
from a tin of Quality Street. It was a tradition that had bee
going since my own nativity plays at St Mary's.

Once, when I was about seven, I'd been given the part
Balthazar. I'd cried silent tears in bed because my teach
clearly thought I looked like a man, big and unfeminin
while the other girls in my class were shimmering angels
cute little lambs. As for Mary – the smug Susan Reese, with
football tucked under the waistband of her stretchy bl
dress – my dark heart had twisted with jealousy and I had
even been able to *look* at her for weeks. Once in the church
remained silent through *Silent Night* and *Away in a Mang*
uncomfortable in my cardboard crown and my stuck-c
beard. But then, walking back to my place after presentii
the Tiny-Tears Jesus with his myrrh, I caught my mother
eye, sitting in the front row in her peacock-coloured skirt, h
hair shining in the candlelight. She placed her hand on h
heart. And I was Juliet again.

The parents were filing out now, voices rising higher ov
the sound of the organ.

Adorable, wasn't it?

What are you doing for Christmas?

Oh, Meribel again? Perfect.

The church was nearly empty.

I sat there, in almost exactly the same place as my moth
had sat all those years ago, and I realised that it wasn't just n
– the Juliet I was now – who'd lost her.

It was that uncertain seven-year-old who'd playe
Balthazar.

It was the eight-year-old who'd swung round in her mot
er's arms on the day of the royal wedding, feeling that h
heart would burst with love.

It was the nine-year-old who'd spent all day up a stepladder, trying to record birdsong onto a Dixons cassette to make the best birthday present ever.

The sixteen-year-old who'd phoned home from boarding school each night, trying to hide the wobble in her voice.

They had all lost her too.

And it wasn't just the elderly invalid, lying weak in the hospital bed, who'd gone. It was the rosy-cheeked woman with her eyes shining, wiping floury hands on her apron as she answered the phone. It was the young mother with glossy hair and a swishy, peacock-coloured skirt.

The loss went back, as far as I could remember. It went forward, to the parts of my life still to come, in which she wouldn't be there.

A great ragged tear, all the way through my life from beginning to end. All the way through me.

I tipped forward, burying my face in my hands.

Then I heard a shuffling noise as someone sat down on the pew next to me. A hymn book falling on to the ground.

'*Christ.*'

Charlie.

'You should go,' I said. 'Tasha will be waiting for you.'

'Tasha's fine,' he said.

'I think people have been talking about us.'

He huffed out a half-sigh, half-laugh. 'Do I look like I care?'

'Tasha might.'

'She's fine,' he repeated. 'She's gone with Shami to have mulled wine in the hall. What's up?'

'Mum's last letter arrived this morning.' My voice sounded like someone had their hands around my throat. 'I just couldn't believe it... it was a *nothing* letter. Just about

some charity in India, and the financial problems she ar
Dad got into. I thought the last letter would be... I dor
know... about how much she loved me, or something.
thought there would be an ending – a point to the letters. B
it was like reading a story that just... stopped. Right in tl
middle. Just like her life. It's so brutal, Charlie. So mea
ingless.'

'Her story is finished... I mean, her life story.' He pause
and sighed, as though he couldn't find the words he w.
looking for. Then he spoke again, his words slow and delibe
ate. 'But the story of *her life in you* is not.'

'I don't understand what that means.'

'I'm sorry,' he said, shifting uncomfortably. 'Listen, Juli
there's something –'

'Are you coming, Charlie?' It was Tasha, walking up tl
aisle towards us. 'Shami wants to ask you about her eczem
It's got really bad.'

'What, since I last spoke to her two minutes ago?'

'You go,' I whispered.

'Sorry...' he said again and shuffled out of the pew
follow Tasha to the church hall.

BACK IN THE kitchen at Laurel Bank, I gave Kitty a quick tea
sausages and beans, and an apple cut into pieces on a plat
with raspberries dotted in between.

'You were great in the play,' I told her, stealing a raspber
'I thought it was fantastic. The best nativity play I've ev
seen.'

It was true. I'd sat through dozens of them in my years
nannying and had never really 'got it' until I heard Kitty's b

– something gentle and hopeful and brave, held up against all that was wrong in the world.

She smiled without looking up, pretending to be fully focused on her apple pieces.

'And you're going to the pantomime tomorrow, aren't you, with your class? At Bury St Edmunds?'

Her face went blank. She shook her head. She'd had the same reaction every time I'd mentioned it, over the last few weeks.

I remembered being scared of the pantomime myself, at that age. The scheming villains, wicked stepmothers and ugly sisters. The shrieks and shouts of 'he's behind you!'

'It's *Hansel and Gretel*, isn't it?'

She shrugged, as though she was telling me it didn't make any difference what it was because she wouldn't be going.

Up in her bedroom, later on, she winced as I pulled her top over her head.

I gasped. 'What happened?'

She had two big areas of bruising on her back, angry red fading into purple.

Kitty pouted and pulled her tights up so the waistband was chest high, taut over the s-curve of her tummy and bottom.

'Oh Kitty, let me see it. That looks sore. Did that happen at school?' Surely she hadn't done it here? 'Were you doing gymnastics? Did you fall off the bench again?'

She shook her head.

'Let's get you in the bath. I'll put some bath salts in, okay? Maybe that'll be nice and soothing for you.'

She covered her ears as she ran through the hallway – she was scared of the big bulk of the dehumidifier with its metal

grilles, humming in the corner. The insurance company ha
sent it round earlier that day.

She pulled off the tights and climbed into the bat
swirling the bath salts around until the water was pale pink.

'It smells of fairies,' I observed, and Kitty nodded.

'You know, I think I'm going to call Charlie and ask wh
to do about your bruises.'

He was round in half an hour, standing there in tl
doorway in his trousers and jacket, looking a bit disheveled
though he'd had to throw his clothes on again to come ot
Looking so much like *home,* somehow, that it took all tl
strength out of my legs.

'Hey,' he said, stepping forward. His hands hovered by n
elbows. 'What's this? It's okay. Don't cry.'

'She's black and blue. I don't know how this could hav
happened.'

'Don't panic. She's probably just taken a tumble at schoc
Or maybe it happened at the church. I saw some of the kic
jumping on and off the stone steps.'

Kitty was sitting cross-legged on her bed, taping Sellotaʃ
over the mermaid's mouth.

'Hey, Kitty,' said Charlie. 'Juliet says you've got son
bruises? If you like, I could have a look and check you'
okay?'

She nodded and shifted round to face the wall so that
could lift the back of her pyjama top. Charlie's eyebrows sh
up. He breathed out slowly through pursed lips. 'Can yc
take a deep breath in for me? And another. How does th
feel?'

Her shoulders moved incrementally – a shrug.

'I'm just going to touch your back very gently, Kitty. I'll t
not to hurt you.' He leaned forward, frowning, and presse

around the bruised area. I guessed he was worried about broken ribs.

'Hmm, I think you'll live, young lady,' said Charlie. 'It looks worse than it is. Have you got any frozen peas?'

Kitty looked over her shoulder and frowned.

'I'm hungry,' said Charlie rubbing his tummy. 'Only kidding. Did you know that cold things like ice packs or frozen peas are good to bring down swelling and stop things hurting?'

'Ooooh,' I said. 'We've got some ice lollies. Would they do?'

Kitty smiled.

'And paracetamol or ibuprofen before bed, and every four hours tomorrow.'

His voice was warm and practical. His calm manner suggested that ibuprofen and frozen peas would fix this. The churning in my stomach told me that wasn't true.

47

CHARLIE

Juliet made tea for him after she'd settled Kitty in bed, moving around the kitchen with shaking hand 'Are you sure you have time?' she fretted, almo splashing milk on the mermaid doll who was lyir there on the counter top. Juliet had said she'd 'look after he for tonight, and Kitty had nodded and handed her over.

'Don't you need to get back to Tasha?'

He shook his head. 'Cammie's in bed, and...' He was abo to say that Shami was there tonight because it was a Thursd night. He'd seen her yoga mat rolled up by the front door he'd slipped out. He'd been seized by a sudden urge to sab tage it in some way... by sprinkling itching powder on perhaps? Or spilling some brightly-coloured sugary drink it, like Red Bull or Irn Bru – not that there was anything li that in the house. Oat milk wouldn't have quite the same effe

They'd be pleased when they realised he'd gone out. I pictured Tasha opening a bottle of wine and putting on Divo' at low volume through the mid-price Bluetooth speak he'd got her for her birthday. (Shami had given her a slim, second-hand volume of Rilke poems with notes scribbled in the margins.)

'Have you got a screwdriver?' he asked. 'I could have a look at that doll while I'm here.' If he had something to do with his hands maybe it would stop this feeling of the blood boiling under his skin. At least it would be something he could *do*. Something that might help Kitty, the poor little mite. And Juliet.

'Yes, I'll get it. I've already tried to get it open though – the screws won't budge.' She looked at him, appraisingly. 'Charlie, are you okay?'

'Am I doing the Skeletor face?'

She nodded, giving a little half-smile.

He rubbed his cheeks and sighed. 'It's just so....'

'I know. What do you think I should do? I'll have to tell Beth and Frank about the bruises. What if they think...'

He wanted to cut in and say how ridiculous that was – that it would be obvious to anyone that Juliet was incapable of harming a child.

But this was Frank they were talking about.

'Monte,' he said, because someone had to say it. 'The little girl at the Collecott Hall nursery. That's what I keep thinking about.'

She nodded. 'It's like history repeating itself. I just get this horrible feeling that everyone's going to blame *me*. Just like they did back then.'

He put his head in his hands, just for a second.

Come on, Charlie. Think like a scientist.

It's what his mother used to say to him when he got upset, or complained something was too hard.

'What would you normally do in this situation – if a chi
you were looking after had bruises?'

'I would tell the parents, of course, and try to work o
what had happened. But it's different here because of Frank
need to tread really carefully. If he thinks I'm stepping out
line, well, he could tell Beth about me... about me growing u
here, and all that. But he could also bring up what happene
with Monte – how I was under suspicion. Remember, he sa
I shouldn't work with children. Oh, Charlie... he could go
the Care Commission and get me investigated. He could g
onto one of those nanny websites and put up bad reviev
about me. He knows he could kill my career, my nannyin
stone dead.'

'One malicious review can't –'

'It can, Charlie. It can.' She shook her head slowly, ar
her hand flew up to swipe away a tear. 'I've seen it happen.'

'So are you suggesting that Frank – or Beth – hurt Kitty
a kind of threat against you?'

'I don't know. I can't put my finger on it. It just feels like
it feels like –'

'A manoeuvre.'

She nodded. 'A move in a game.'

The kitchen fell silent, other than the sound of the dis
washer swishing.

'And there's the psychiatrist's letter,' said Juli
'Remember it talked about Kitty being hurt before – in a
'accident'.'

'The head injury? Yes. That did occur to me too.'

Her dark blue eyes grew even darker, and he saw that h
fists were clenched in her lap. 'I just keep getting this feelin
Charlie. That I should take her and run. Get her away fro
here, as far as possible.'

He shook his head. 'That won't help anything, my –'

My love.

Just when he thought he was in control of himself... it would come. It always came. Like a huge wave crashing in. Spilling across the shore.

He put his head in his hands and closed his eyes. 'Let's think this through logically. I mean, the whole thing with Monte was off, somehow. Frank never even met with Monte's parents. He told your Mum he had, but he hadn't.'

'He also said there was a witness – someone who saw me hurt Monte. I mean, who was that?'

She sat there, twisting a lock of hair around her pinkie, tighter and tighter until there were red marks on the skin. He wanted to reach for her hand and hold it in his own. He wanted to smooth the marks away. Rub them out.

'Well, there clearly wasn't any witness, because you didn't hurt Monte. Or the seven other children who were supposedly hurt. I mean, don't you think that if eight children had been harmed, the police would have been involved? Don't you think they would have wanted to speak to you if there was any chance they thought you were responsible?'

'I wasn't there – I'd left Collecott Hall.'

'So what? You think the police wouldn't have come to Boxley Wood, or Edinburgh?'

'But my Dad...'

'You think the police just drop their enquiries if the suspect suffers a bereavement? Do you think they put a big stamp on the file saying, "Don't bother"?'

She sighed. 'It sounds silly, when you put it like that.'

'It really, really does,' he said.

'I've been terrified, all this time, that it would catch up

with me. That people would find out what happened ba‹
then.'

'I think it was worked up to be something it wasn't. Frai
was trying to frighten you, for some reason. He was a di‹
then and he's a dick now.'

'I never thanked you,' she said quietly. 'For helping m
when nobody else at that place believed me – or would eve
talk to me. For trying to find out what was going on.'

Charlie shook his head. 'No need to thank me.'

'That time I came to find you, in the lunch hall. The w;
you looked at me... I don't know what it was.'

He remembered the emotions churning inside him ;
he'd sat watching her, bent in pain over the empty plates; tl
instinct to protect her, so powerful that it made his han‹
shake.

'Sometimes I've wondered –' she began.

'I was in love with you.' The words were out there befo
he could calculate what they might mean. 'Hopelessly ;
love.'

Even that was a half-truth. The past tense made it a ha
truth.

The look on her face...

'And I'm sorry,' he went on, because it was all going
come out now. 'I'm sorry that I didn't come with you to tl
station, when you ran away from school to go home. Wh‹
you needed to speak to your mum. I'm sorry that I was;
there for you after your dad –'

'Shh. It's all in the past now.'

'It's not that I didn't want to be. It was... complicated.' I
pressed the heels of his hands to his eyes. Lynne's secret w;
burrowing through his brain like some parasite that he cou
never get out of him.

'Sometimes,' she said, 'I imagine us. Together. In another lifetime.'

He didn't trust himself to speak.

'If I had another chance,' she went on. 'Another life. I would come and find you, and tell you. Before it was too late.'

'Tell me what?'

'It's too late to say it, Charlie. You have a life with Tasha and Cameron. You can't unravel all that. I'm sorry I said anything. I shouldn't have. We had our chance, and we didn't take it.'

But you don't know why I didn't take it. Why I couldn't take it.

She was sitting forward in her chair, chin in her hands. The kitchen lights were catching the creamy skin of her shoulder, the curve of her cheek, making her appear lit up from within.

He thought of how it might feel. To take her up to the Forget-Me-Not Room and lay her down on the bed. The way she would press her body against him, lifting her throat to his mouth, her hips towards his.

Then he thought of Lynne's red-rimmed eyes, watching him in the entrance hall at Collecott Hall when she came to take Juliet home. And the faltering letters he'd written to Juliet, in the weeks that followed, but never sent. How desperately he had wanted to smash away the secret that held them as far apart as the hundreds of miles stretching between them. Except that it would hurt her too much.

Now, so many years later, he found that it was time. Time to reach for her hand, and wrap it in his, to say what he had to. She looked down at his fingers, interlaced with hers, as though she didn't quite understand what they were doing there.

'We need to talk, Juliet. We need to talk about what

happened at Collecott Hall. About that night when I went
listen in to Frank's meeting with your mum.'

It felt terrible. He wanted to pull her tight into his che
to protect her from the violence of the words he had to say.

'It seems like they were having... I don't know. A *thing*.'

Her body stiffened. 'What kind of thing? Do you mean ɛ
affair?'

He nodded. 'I think they'd had a fling – years ago. Ar
your mum had ended it, but they'd got into a habit, while yc
were at Collecott Hall, of talking on the phone. He was tryir
to get her to leave your Dad, and she was... well, she wɛ
torn.'

There was a long pause. 'And you couldn't face me, aft
you found out,' she said finally. 'Is that why things went deɛ
between us?'

Something about her voice made him think of Camero
He'd described just yesterday how a snail had 'went dea
after a bad boy had thrown it across the playground.

'They were never dead on my part, Juliet.' He took
breath, tried to steady his voice. 'Never. I was churning insid
all mixed up with, well, how I felt about you, and trying
protect you. I was trying to protect you by not telling yc
about it.'

'You didn't feel real.'

'No. I know. I tried to be there for you, but somethir
felt... well, rotten. About the whole business with your dad.'

She nodded slowly, and withdrew her hand from his. Sl
looked at each of her fingernails in turn.

'And then, Juliet, your Mum contacted me out of the blu
Just before she died.'

Her head shot up.

'I went to see her in hospital. I'm sorry I didn't tell you. I didn't know how to. When you were talking this afternoon about how the letters just stopped... I think that's why she called me in to see her. Because she hadn't told you everything.'

She paused for a moment, and then gave a short, bitter laugh.

'She wanted to tell you about my dad. How they thought it might have been suicide. The open verdict.'

Jesus Christ.

'You mean... you knew?'

'How could I not know? Boxley Wood is a small town. She thought that sending me off to Granny in Edinburgh would stop me finding out. Or maybe that's not fair. Maybe she did intend to tell me, when she thought the time was right. I could see this look on her face sometimes, like she was thinking about telling me. Sometimes she'd even open her mouth, and then close it again.'

'And do you know...' he swallowed hard. 'Do you know the details?'

Juliet sighed, and covered her face with her hands. 'Looking back, it's obvious he'd been depressed for a while. Mum used to talk about his 'back trouble', and how it had kept him in bed for the day, or had stopped him going in to work. But there was clearly more to it. And there were money troubles – to do with a charity or something. After Dad died, Mum transferred the house to Frank's name so he could sort out all the debts. That makes sense now – if they were *together*. If they'd been planning to live here as a couple.'

She was frowning, her face contorted, like she was struggling to get her head around it. 'Poor Dad,' she whispered.

'I know,' he said, helplessly.

'Was this why they thought Dad killed himself? Becau of the affair?'

'Your Mum mentioned something about a phone ca between Frank and your Dad. He said he knew about tl affair. This was just before the accident.'

Her chin trembled, her face stiffening as she tried control it. 'I always thought that he'd killed himself becau of *me*.'

'Because of you? Oh no, Juliet, no...'

'Yes. Because of how I'd turned out.' She looked down her feet, pushing her lips into a pout. 'Because of the troub with me and Monte. I thought maybe that was the last stra when they'd spent all that money sending me to Collecc Hall.'

'No,' he said again. 'God, no, Juliet. Of course it was your fault.'

He thought of the time he'd sat with her in the phoi cupboard at Collecott Hall, and Graeme's strange, flat, 'O Juliet', when she told him about the trouble with Monte. Tl unbearable silence that followed. All Juliet had heard w disappointment. But Charlie recognised now, all these yea later, the emotion in Graeme's voice – that deep, achii sadness of a parent when their child is hurting and they cai help. But nobody had known how to talk to each other in th family.

Was it enough? Had he told her enough, to bring dow the barrier between them?

Yes. Surely he had. He tried to smile. Tried to loosen tl tension in his throat.

But he couldn't. The sad secrets in that house seemed

choke him, as insidious as the black mould spores that Juliet feared.

'There's something else I need to tell you,' he blurted out. 'I need to tell you about the time we ran away from Sunday school when you were five, and I was six. I need to tell you about what we saw.'

48

JULIET

It wasn't that I remembered what Charlie w describing, exactly. But it felt familiar. Like when yc start watching a film and realise you must have seen before because you already know how it will end. The sto just seemed to fit. It seemed to fit the exact shape of son sadness deep inside me.

I sat for a long time, as everything about my childhoo about Laurel Bank and its secrets, fell into place.

'It's okay.' Charlie's hand was firm on my shoulder as n body began to shake. 'It's just the shock. Just let it pass.'

One long-ago hot summer's day there had been an ear tremor here – an unusually big one for this part of the worl I'd screamed from the back garden, crouching low on a fours as water sloshed over the sides of my paddling poc Mum had coming running, then, her arms outstretched, pile of clean laundry dropped on the back door steps. But sl couldn't come running for this.

I was losing her. I was losing her all over again. She was

who I'd thought she was. She was a blank face behind a mask. She was –

My body buckled, folded in half.

Charlie came and knelt on the floor by me. He stroked my back while I cried. I could smell the heat of his skin, and the scent of his cologne, faint and woody at the end of the long day. I wanted to settle into his arms. To let this love surround me. Because surely that was what it was.

But then I thought of Kitty upstairs in her bed... of Cameron, in the house on the other side of the orchard, sleeping safe under his Superman duvet. I thought of my mother, smoothing her skirts in the doorway to the Forget-Me-Not Room. My Dad, his face obliterated by the shards of glass from the windscreen.

I pulled away from him, sat back in the chair.

'Juliet? Are you okay?'`

'I'm really tired.' My voice didn't even sound like mine. It was wooden, dead.

'All right... God. I'm sorry.' He stood up, picked up his jacket, waited for me to say something. But there was too much to say. Too much to know where to start.

'I'll get going then. If you want me to?'

I nodded.

'What about Kitty? The bruises?'

'I suppose I'll have to tell Beth and Frank about it when they get back. What else can I do?'

'You could report it, I guess. To Social Services. If you thought they were hurting her. That would be the nuclear option.'

'And then what? If they believe me, she ends up in foster care, at the mercy of the system. If they don't, Frank and Beth get rid of me anyway.'

All paths seemed set to wind up in the same place. M
without Kitty. Me without Charlie.

On the way to the front door, he turned around sudden
'Me and Tasha... it's not what it seems.'

'It never is.' I slipped past him and opened the front doc
'It never is.'

I LAY awake for hours after Charlie had gone, staring up
the ceiling in the Forget-Me-Not Room, trying to get my hea
around it all.

My mother hadn't been who I thought she was. She
kept herself hidden. Hidden behind bright smiles and ginge
bread and church fetes.

Frank had spread all the way through her – all the wa
through our family – like a bruise through a perfect apple.

And then there was me, caught in the middle, complete
misunderstanding it all.

Dad didn't kill himself because of me. Finding out abo
Frank and Mum had been the last straw for him, after yea
of struggling with depression.

The guilt that I'd carried with me, so grey and heavy a
those years, suddenly ignited into rage.

Frank had destroyed my family.

Now I would destroy his.

I would find something. Some evidence to prove ho
rotten he was. To prove he and Beth weren't fit to be parents

And I had to act now. If they saw Kitty's bruises tomorro
and sent me packing, then I'd never set foot in this hou
again.

Light-headed with adrenaline, I went through the filir

cabinet again, and all the drawers in Frank's desk. I looked through the kitchen drawers and all the boxes in the garage.

At two o'clock I started on the wardrobe in their bedroom. I found three different vibrators and a pair of handcuffs. There was a tube of haemorrhoid cream shoved into its cardboard box, the instruction leaflet poking out as though someone had tried to fold it up again and then not bothered.

And then, hidden right at the back, a Victoria biscuits box.

Sitting cross-legged on the thick cream carpet, I went through the contents. I found Beth's birth certificate. A crumpled red rosette and a souvenir programme for the Royal Ballet. A collection of faded postcards signed 'Dad.' A couple of grainy photos with names and dates written on the back in a childish hand: 'Mum and Dad – Cornwall, 1984'. 'Viv and me – summer 1986.' A hospital bracelet with 'Baby Seigler' written on it in faded biro, next to Kitty's date of birth.

Then more photographs – a series of Frank holding Kitty as a newborn. Kitty as a baby in a sunny garden, kicking on a rug. One of the three of them, in a boat on Lake Geneva, the jagged shape of the Evian hills behind. One of Kitty as a toddler in Frank's arms, standing in front of a swimming pool, pink Bougainvillea blooming along the dazzling white wall of the house. Another one with Kitty and Frank in a similar pose, but with Beth standing proudly alongside, sunglasses pushed up onto the top of her head.

She looked so smug and self-satisfied. I had a sudden, creeping sense that the photos had been hidden there for me to find. I glanced behind me, half expecting to see a laughing Frank standing in the doorway.

Joke!

But there was something not right about the photo. I

looked closer, screwing up my eyes. Checking again ar
again until I was sure. In the picture, Beth's mole was on tl
wrong side of her face.

Which meant...

Which meant somebody had photoshopped this pho
They'd edited it to add in Beth, but they'd accidental
reversed her image.

I sat perfectly still on the floor for a moment.

I was right. I was right.

With shaking hands, I picked up the photos that had bo
Beth and young Kitty in them and looked at them carefully.
they'd been edited, then they'd been done well. In each or
Beth was standing separately from Kitty and Frank, just
figure against the wall, so that it would have been relative
easy to do.

But what about the photos downstairs? The triptych
black and white images of Beth and Kitty as a baby above tl
fireplace?

Quietly, I went downstairs and snapped on the light. Tl
three framed photos were beautiful, perfectly structure
with soft, velvety lighting. They had clearly been done in
studio. How could Beth and Frank have photoshopped thes

The baby's dark blue eyes gazed out from behind tl
scratched glass. When I'd first seen the photographs, I'd on
just met Kitty. I didn't know her then. I hadn't learned l
heart, as a mother would, each freckle, the shape of her ea
or the sweetness of her chin. I hadn't studied the way her li
were formed, the little rosebud pinch at the top. Or tl
almond-shaped sweep of her eyelids. Now I saw what I had
seen before.

The baby wasn't Kitty.

There was a shuffling noise behind me. I turned to s

Kitty standing in the doorway, looking like a little ghost in her nightie. She was watching me, one hand on the door handle, neither in the room nor out of it.

She frowned when she saw my face, the tears that were spilling down my cheeks.

'The photos in this house,' I said. 'They're all messed up.'

Her eyes widened. She nodded urgently.

'Is that why you scratched them? And turned the ones on the stairs back to front?'

Her body sagged in relief. Someone had finally got it.

I took her upstairs and tucked her into bed. She watched me closely as I turned off the big light, switched on the toadstool nightlight and smoothed her covers. I leant over and hugged her, kissing the top of her head.

'I know,' I whispered. 'I know about Mummy.'

Her body stiffened. She took a breath in and didn't let it out.

'Shhh,' I said. 'We'll sort it out. We'll sort it all out. But now, it's time to sleep.'

49

BETH

Beth pulled a carrot out of the bag and got to wo⟩ peeling again. If she finished making this damn⟨ cake maybe she'd feel better. More like the domest goddess she never quite managed to be.

She'd be the first to admit, this evening hadn't been h finest hour. In fact, let's face it – it had been a disaster. Kit had barely slept in the week since her wardrobe h⟨ collapsed in the middle of the night. After that nightmari⟨ dash up the stairs, they'd found her cowering in the corner her room, terrified. They still didn't know whether she attempted to climb up it again, or whether it had collapsed its own accord as she slept.

Beth had been terrified that Frank would be angry – th he would blame her somehow for the wardrobe collapsin or be angry at her for being downstairs in the middle of tl night, where she couldn't hear Kitty – but he had been kin He'd tucked Beth into bed, his forehead creased in concer and he said he'd get her some more pills – he could see ho bad her nerves were. He could see she couldn't manage without them just now. But he made her promise to try and wean herself off them once this bad patch had passed.

As for Kitty's insomnia, Beth had tried everything. She'd administered warm milk and warm baths before bed. She'd let Kitty watch soothing programmes in bed on her iPad, and let her sleep with the lights on. She'd even ordered a new mermaid doll online, to replace the one whose head she'd ripped off – it was a fancy, high-tech thing that could be programmed to talk back when you spoke to it and she'd told Kitty that the mermaid's special job was to keep her company in the night. Because Mummy couldn't be there all the time, could she? Mummy had to sleep.

None of it had worked. Against Frank's wishes, Beth had taken Kitty to the doctors that morning. They'd let her see the duty doctor even though they weren't registered with the practice yet, but they'd had to wait until the end of surgery, and the waiting room had gradually emptied of all the pensioners and snotty-nosed toddlers. The doctor had talked in patronising tones about bedtime routines and sodding warm milk until Beth had started to cry, and then he'd reluctantly agreed to prescribe a mild antihistamine, just for a few days to get Kitty's sleep routine back on track. Then they'd queued for twenty minutes at the pharmacy to get the medicine, but when they'd got home Kitty had point black refused to let Beth administer it, covering her mouth with her hands.

'He said take it at *night*.'

'You haven't slept for five days,' Beth had said through gritted teeth.

But Kitty had just shaken her head.

Then Beth had said, 'How dare you behave like this when

your grandpa's in a coma?' and she'd burst into angry tea
Which had surprised her, because until that moment sl
hadn't realised that she didn't want Stan to die. Money or i
money. She'd sat by his bedside yesterday and willed him
wake up. Just to wake up, even if he never could explain wl
he'd left her. She wanted to look into his eyes again, ar
decide once and for all if it was love she could see there,
just some kind of nostalgic regret.

Kitty had burst into tears too, and Beth had taken a fe
deep breaths and used her 'nice mummy' voice to sugge
that they start the day again, as a cosy 'pyjama day' this tim
watching CBeebies beneath fleecy blankets and drinking h
chocolate. Beth had allowed herself an extra tablet
lunchtime, and she'd dozed on the sofa for a couple of hou
But by evening, boredom had set in and curdled Kitty's moo

'This has been the boring-est day *ever*,' she'd announce
as Beth had begun clearing up the dishes after a boring tea
fishfingers (again).

'I'm sorry, Kitty, but you were tired, weren't you? I thii
it's time for an early night.'

Kitty's voice had risen in a high-pitched wail. 'You sa
we'd do *baking*!'

Oh, for God's sake. She'd thought Kitty had forgotte
about the baking. She'd done a quick mental calculation –
would be quicker to mix up the ingredients for a cake than
weather a full-scale tantrum. There had been no butter in tl
fridge so she'd decided it would have to be carrot cake agai
She had pulled a bag of carrots out of the fridge and begu
peeling them and chopping their ends off, asking Kitty
weigh out the sultanas. Kitty had huffed when she wasi
allowed to do the cutting – she had wanted to hold the 'to
sharp-knife'.

Then she had insisted on being the one to measure out the sunflower oil, holding the bottle in wobbly hands.

'I can DO it, Mummy,' she had whined, her face flushed and pouting.

The bottle had lurched and oil had flowed down the outside of the measuring jug. Beth had moved forward instinctively. 'Here, let me help.'

Kitty had snatched the bottle away from Beth, managing to hold it upright, but sending the jug over the edge of the table and skittering onto the floor. It had bounced, once, twice, three times, sending a dribbly path of oil over the tiles.

And Beth had growled. She had actually growled. It was awful to think of it now.

'I TOLD you. That I. Would help you.'

Kitty's face had crumpled with hurt and betrayal.

'Go 'way!' she'd shouted, fat globes of tears swelling on her lower lashes.

'I'm not going away,' Beth had snapped back. 'I've got to clear up this bloody mess. YOU go away.' She had known she was behaving like a child but in that moment she couldn't help it. She'd thought of the packet of pills upstairs in her bedside drawer, the cool white smoothness that would flood through her head later. She'd been trying to wait until Kitty had gone to bed, but this day had been going on *forever*. Doctor's visits. Comas. And now oil on the floor.

'No YOU go 'way. You're the meanest mummy in the world! I wish I could have another mummy, nicer than you.' And she'd run out of the room sobbing.

Beth had followed her upstairs, counting to ten and taking deep breaths and willing 'nice mummy' to take over.

Nice Mummy had managed to calm Kitty down, administer the promethazine and get her bathed and off to bed.

And Nice Mummy would finish making this cake, and tl
smell of it baking would drift through the house so that Kit
could breathe it in as she slept and know that she was sa
and loved. And in the morning she'd wake up feeling we
again and they would both have a slice of carrot cake fc
breakfast. It was probably healthier than cereal, with tl
carrots and sultanas and whatnot.

Beth was peeling the final carrot when she heard tl
sound of Frank's car in the drive, and then the front do
being unlocked. She kept peeling. She didn't want him to se
her tears. But then she heard the clop of heels on the kitche
tiles behind her.

Oh for God's sake, not *her*. Standing there in her pos
coat and a slash of red lipstick. Tonight of all nights
really?

'What do you want?' demanded Beth.

The woman pushed her mouth into a pout, revealing tl
paler pink of her inner lips. Beth thought it looked like
dog's bottom.

'I'm just here for a little chat, babe.'

Frank appeared behind her in the doorway.

Beth felt quite exhausted. Why couldn't the pair of the
just go away and leave her alone? She was in the middle
baking a carrot cake. The smell of it was going to drift up
Kitty as she slept. It was important. More important tha
having some sort of soap opera showdown about Frank an
where he may or may not have put his cock.

'I'm busy.'

'It's about the café,' said Frank. 'It's great news. Barba
has agreed to come in as a business partner.'

Business partner, business partner... Frank couldn't eve
mention the woman's name without saying 'business pai

ner'. As if that made her whiter than white. But Beth had seen the looks that passed between them.

'She can do the business side of things – the payroll, the accounts, the VAT.' Frank raised his eyebrows, as if the mere mention of VAT would send Beth into a fit of the vapours. But he was wrong. She'd been reading up on the internet about how to do it all.

'That's kind of her,' said Beth. 'But I've got it covered.'

'That way, you can concentrate on the fun stuff – the baking and so on.'

Beth felt like a child, being told that her idea was lovely, but the grown-ups were taking over now.

'I'm doing this for *you*,' said Frank. 'I don't want you being under too much pressure. Remember how you were after Rick? I couldn't bear to see you go back to square one again.'

How long, Beth wondered. How long would she have to feel grateful to him? How long would she have to see that look on his face – as if he was her Lord and Saviour?

Her hands were shaking as she turned to the sink and took up the knife again. Damn it. She thought of the tablets, the unwinding feeling that would start as soon as she popped them out of the blister pack. Not long now.

'Beth, come on. Please talk it through with Barbara. She's got the experience – she ran 'A Piece of Cake' practically singlehandedly.'

That was one of Frank's charities – a café staffed by people who'd had mental breakdowns. It had closed down last year, which was hardly the greatest advert for Barbara's abilities.

'I'm buying the café with *my* money, Frank.' Well, it would be her money soon, after Stan was gone.

Suddenly her heart felt empty. Hollow and empty.

'I'll do this,' said Barbara. 'But there are a few things y[
need to understand, babe.'

'Barbara,' came Frank's voice in a warning tone.

Beth turned around, and opened her mouth to tell Dog
Bottom that she wasn't anybody's babe, and especially n
hers.

But the oil on the floor...

In the moment that her foot went from under her – th
oh-so-slow moment arcing outside of normal time and ba[
again – she cursed herself for not cleaning it up.

Some faulty instinct made her grip the knife hard, but t[
impact forced it through her fingers as she landed. The bla[
twisted, slicing through the heel of her right hand, ar
lodged itself deep into the soft underside of her wrist. She
sharpened all the knives just a few days ago, after unpacki[
the last of the kitchen stuff from the boxes, thinking that th
was the sort of thing a domestic goddess would do. She
stood there like a bloody fool and sharpened the knife th
was going to kill her.

She pulled herself upright, and reached out her oth[
hand to cover the gash. Blood spurted through her finge[
pulsed beneath her palm when she pressed it down hard. [
warm. She remembered one time when she'd wet herself [
the playground, the gush of warm down her legs. Viv h[
driven to school with spare pants and a skirt, sweeping h[
into a fierce hug as she'd sat there crying in the school nurs[
office.

'Call a bloody ambulance,' said the woman to Frank no[

Frank screwed up his nose as though he was weighi[
things up. He sat down on one of the kitchen chairs, scrapi[
it across the tiles. 'Too late for that, I think.'

There was no Viv to help Beth now. She had to stop t[

bleeding somehow. She needed to use something as a bandage. She tried to unbutton her shirt with her left hand, but her fingers were too shaky to get them undone.

'Help me!'

There was a tea towel, hanging from the oven door... could she crawl over there? But even if she had something to use as a bandage she'd never be able to get it tight enough with one hand.

Frank picked up the tea towel and came over and kneeled by her side. Thank God.

But he wrapped the tea towel around his own fingers, before taking hold of the knife and twisting it deeper into the wound.

'Sorry, Bethie.' His knees cracked as he straightened up and went back to his chair. 'Just try to relax. It'll be over soon.'

Didn't they say that your whole life flashed before your eyes, just before you died? But it wasn't the life she'd *had* that was filling her senses, burning brighter than the kitchen which was fading into black now. She was seeing the life she hadn't quite managed to have – the one she'd stored up for the future. She'd wanted to catch the train to Whitby with Kitty, eating fish and chips on the promenade with the wind whipping their hair around their faces. And Buckingham Palace – Kitty had wanted to see the guards with the tall furry hats. And they'd planned to visit every single stately home in England until they found the very one where Beth and her parents had eaten warm scones, and been caught in the summer downpour – Stan had managed to say that he thought it was somewhere in Yorkshire, but couldn't be sure. Then there was the Old Coach House, her café... she'd get herself off the pills and make something of herself finally. Kitty was going to come in there after school and eat iced

buns, swinging her feet from the bar stool, her socks wri
kled down around her ankles. And who would take Kitty
the new doctors to ask about speech therapy? She'd made a
appointment at the surgery when they'd been there th
morning, and put it in the calendar, but would Frank eve
notice it there?

It wasn't supposed to be this way. She was supposed
have more time.

The disappointment was crushing. It was like going c
holiday and having to turn round and go home again as soc
as the plane had touched down. Like going to your ow
wedding and the groom not turning up.

She tried to make her lips form words, but they wouldi
work properly... all that came out were weird howlii
sounds. Frank just sat there with his legs stretched in front c
him, crossed at the ankles, looking at his watch.

The woman stood with her hands on her hips, her fa
twisted in an expression of disgust, as though Beth was
squashed spider or a dead mouse. 'How long is this going
take?' she said. 'Do you even know?' As though it we
Frank's fault that Beth was taking so long to die.

It occurred to Beth that she'd never have got away wi
talking to him like that. Maybe he'd met his match in he
Maybe it was what he needed.

She couldn't summon up the energy to be angry.
seemed to her that she'd ghosted away her life, only ev
living half-heartedly. These two were simply allowing
to end.

But then she thought of Kitty, sleeping upstairs in h
bed. Waking up tomorrow with no carrot cake for breakfa
How disappointed she'd be.

Anger blazed up inside, searing through her lungs, her brain, stripping her clean.

Look after her.

She had to pray with her mind, as her lips wouldn't work. She didn't even know who she was praying to, except this bright nuclear ball raging inside her.

Look after her. Look after

I t was just before dawn when she came to me, climbir
into my bed and clinging on, as though she w.
expecting me to get up from the bed and leave her.

'Hey, little monkey.' Half asleep, I forgot that she wasi
mine. I cupped my hand around the back of her head ar
pulled her close, breathing the salty, sleepy scent of her skin

'Dooliet?'

My heart stopped. Just melted away in my chest. M
name had never, ever sounded so beautiful. A few momen
passed before I could speak.

'Yes, my love.'

'My mummy went away.'

One, two, three breaths.

'I'm listening. Thank you for telling me.'

'It was because of me.' Her eyes were squeezed tight shu

'Why do you think that?'

'We went to the doctor that day, to get some special slee
medicine.'

I remembered the promethazine in the bathroom cabine

Charlie had said it was sometimes prescribed for sleep problems.

'And Mummy was cross after because I wouldn't take my medicine, even though we had to queue for ages at the chemist. And she kept crying because Grandpa was in a comber machine.'

'You have a Grandpa?' I asked, stroking her hair.

'And we couldn't go to the hospital to see him because I took too long at the doctors. And then we made carrot cake but I spilled oil. I said that I wished I had a different mummy. And then the next morning, she was gone.'

'What do you mean, she was gone?'

She pulled on my arms, pushed her head against my collarbone, like she was trying to break the boundaries of skin and bone and climb inside me.

'I woke up the next morning, and there was nobody here. I came downstairs and I waited. But they didn't come.'

She mumbled the words into the fabric of my pyjamas. I could feel the damp warmth of her breath.

'You were on your own in the house?'

'Yes.'

'With nobody to look after you?'

She nodded. 'I found cereal in the cupboard and I ate some of that, and I climbed up on a chair so I could get a drink of water. There was no carrot cake. I think she must have taken that with her. I played with my Sylvaliens all day but I couldn't get the TV on. And then when it got dark I went to bed.'

'Where was Daddy?'

'Gone too, but when I woke up the next morning, I came down to the kitchen and Daddy was here eating bacon and eggs. With Her.'

'Is 'Her' the lady that lives here now?'

She nodded vigorously, her hair mussing against me. asked Daddy where Mummy was, and he just pretended th Her had been here all along.'

'Oh no. Oh no.'

'I thought maybe Daddy didn't know it was a differe mummy.' She lifted her face and looked at me, full of dou and confusion. 'Because it was *me* that asked for a differe mummy.'

'It wasn't because of anything you said. I *promise* you th Kitty. I promise.'

Her silence had made complete sense, I realised now. T only possible response to a life, a home, a family, that h become a lie.

'Did you try to tell anybody what had happened? Anyo at school or anything?'

As soon as I'd said them, I wished I could take the wor back. She'd tried so hard, with her 999 calls, and h Weekend News.

'I didn't go to school then. Mummy said that I was goir to get some special lessons so my words would work proper before I started school. But I didn't have any lessons.'

'No – but you've managed to get your words to work all l yourself,' I said.

'Yes. Mummy will be so pleased when she gets back.'

We lay in silence for a while. I stroked her silky ha feeling her breathing soften and sync with mine.

'Kitty?'

I felt her head move as she lifted her chin to look at me.

'Did you see any special doctors about you not speakin or about you thinking your mummy had been swapped?'

She looked confused. Shook her head.

The letter from the psychiatrist. Frank had faked it, paid for it, whatever. But he had also planted it. He'd intended for me to find it. That's why the key to the filing cabinet had conveniently appeared.

'How did you get the bruises on your back?'

'Daddy kicked me.'

I kept stroking, trying to keep breathing, to stop my heart bursting out of my chest. 'What happened?'

'It was a bit like when Her kicked me when I was under the table.'

'Oh... when you were hiding under there doing jigsaws? That was an accident, wasn't it?'

'Yes. It was like that, but I wasn't under the table.'

'Where were you?'

'Lying on the floor in the living room. I was watching my tablet.'

'Oh... were you on the rug?' Kitty liked to curl up in front of the electric fire like a cat.

'Yes. Daddy walked past there and kicked me. Five or maybe seven times.'

'Oh. I see.' I tried to keep my voice even. 'Well I won't let anybody kick you again.'

Staring at the ceiling, feeling her body rise and fall with my breath, I thought about what I should do. As far as I could see there were two options, neither of them good. One was to sit on this and say nothing. I could stay here with Kitty and look after her – perhaps even for years – until the Seiglers terminated our arrangement. I could collude in the lies that had silenced Kitty in order to buy more time with her, and protect her as best I could. Then when the time came, I'd have to leave her to continue her life with Frank and Beth. If Kitty ever remembered the night when she'd clung to me and

whispered her terrible truth into my shoulder, she mig]
wonder if it had ever actually happened. Or if maybe, lil
everyone else, I simply hadn't heard her.

But Frank had *kicked* her.

The only other option was to break the whole thing apa
to tell what I knew and let the police and social services so
it all out. Perhaps I could offer myself to social services ;
some kind of continuity of care for Kitty, but I didn't eve
have a house, a job, anything without the Seiglers. The mo
likely outcome was a foster home for her. Or worse still, Be
and Frank might talk their way out of it. There would l
insufficient evidence to prove anything. There'd be psych
atric evaluations for Kitty, and disgrace for me for makii
wild accusations about a family. I'd never get another job
nannying. Not that that would matter much, if I never sa
Kitty again. Nothing would.

Kitty stirred beside me. 'I don't want you to go,' she sai
her little voice clear in the silence of the room. 'Will yc
promise to stay forever?'

And then I saw how this love, this love I'd let happen, w
going to break not only my heart, but hers.

Now it was my words that wouldn't work. Instead I sai
to her. I sang all the songs my mother had sung to me, c
dark nights when I wasn't feeling well, or when I couldn't g
to sleep. *Edelweiss. The White Cliffs of Dover. Somewhere ov
the Rainbow.*

Songs of longing and hopefulness. Songs about home.

51

JULIET

I called Charlie the next morning. Kitty had gone into the garden to put our toast crusts on the bird table.

I'd decided to keep her off school. Relief had flooded her face when I told her she wouldn't have to endure *Hansel and Gretel.*

I told him about my decision to go to the police.

'Are you sure about this?' Charlie's voice was full of concern. 'It's possible the bruises were an accident. Or that Kitty's angry with her dad and, well...'

I shook my head. 'She would never do that.'

'Think about it, though. If she really thinks Frank has done all this, well, she *must* be angry. And we don't really know what this is all about, do we, this thing about old Beth and new Beth? And Kitty... well, she's got issues, hasn't she? Severe anxiety for one thing. We don't really know what her reality is like, inside her head.'

'But either these things have happened as she said, and she needs to be taken out of this situation. Completely. Or

they haven't, and she's got problems – *serious* problem
Charlie – and they are just blind to it. She needs psycholo
ical help that they aren't giving her. Either way, things can't ⅋
on as they are. Don't you see?'

'I do see. But at least if you're there you can watch out fⲓ
her, and give her some of the help she needs. You could st⸱
until, well, either things get worse, or they ask you to leaᵥ
Then you could go to the police, or social services.'

'But they would wonder why I didn't report it at the tim
as soon as I knew. As soon as I first saw her bruises. If th
happens, it'll look like I've just got a grudge against Fraⲓ
and Beth for sacking me. It wouldn't ring true.'

'I'm just worried about you, Juliet.' He said it in a smⲁ
voice. 'This is all very unpredictable. I don't want you to g
hurt.'

It was too late for that. Far too late.

'Why not think about it for a bit? Wait till after Christmⲓ
at least? You said you were going to go away for Christmⲁ
didn't you?'

'Only because I don't have a choice. The Seiglers made
clear that my services won't be required.'

I'd been planning to go back to Edinburgh, to speⲓ
Christmas in Mum's flat and get it ready to go on the mark
in the New Year. Cassie had invited me over for Boxing Dⲁ
which was sweet of her. But I couldn't leave Kitty alone wiⲓ
Frank and Beth for a whole ten days.

On the other hand... I thought of Kitty, shipped off ⸱
some foster family and having to spend Christmas wiⲓ
strangers.

'Would she be taken away immediately, if they thoug
she was at risk?'

Charlie sighed. 'I don't know. From what I've seen, it takes a lot – a *lot*, Juliet – for social services to remove a child from the parents. Do you want me to have a word with Sandra? She's one of the social workers I've dealt with through work. She's very sensible.'

I could feel the temptation... to think about things... to talk to people... to let the crisis blow over. Anything so long as I could stay.

'But Charlie, I need to think about Kitty. She's six years old. If I do this now, they might get her out of there and into a new family that can love her properly, and help her. She can have a chance at a proper childhood.'

Even if it's without me.

'Okay,' he said. 'I understand.'

'I'm going to do it tomorrow,' I said. 'When Kitty's at school. I'll go into the police station in town and I'll ask to speak to someone senior. I'll just tell them everything I know, and they'll know what to do. Do you think they'll try to interview Kitty? Or would social workers do that?' I gave a shuddering sigh, at the thought of it – Kitty sitting silently, twisting her hands.

'I'll do it,' he blurted out. 'If I speak to the police, then you can pretend you didn't know anything about it. Then Frank and Beth might keep you on... if, you know, they don't get charged. If things stay the same.'

I thought about it for a minute. 'It wouldn't work. Kitty told *me*, not you. Your statement wouldn't match up with what she says, if they ever get her to talk to them.'

'I could say I was suspicious about them... that as a GP I'm concerned about them not getting help with Kitty's speech. That I've noticed bruises on her. That might be

enough for them to at least interview them, and it wou
keep you out of it.'

'I think it's got to be me, Charlie.'

'I'll come with you, then. I'll back up your story.'

I thought of walking up the steps to the police static
with Charlie beside me. 'Would you really do that?'

'Of course I will,' he said. 'I'll arrange for cover at th
surgery.'

It was just over twenty-four hours away. I couldn't begin
imagine what tomorrow held. But today I was going to have
day with Kitty.

I GAVE Kitty ten pounds for her purse, and took her to tl
Christmas market in Sudbury. She bought a soft felt robin f
the tree – she'd decided she wanted that instead of an angel
and a snow globe that she wanted to give to Cameron. V
went into the tiny bookshop on the cobbled street that l
down from the market place, with its mullioned sho
window and the bell that rang when you opened the doc
We each chose a present for the other, coming out of tl
shop with mysterious smiles, our purchases wrapped car
fully in brown paper bags.

On the way back I took her to the café next to St Mary
in-the-Wood for a hot chocolate and a muffin. It was ju
warm enough to sit outside on the terrace, wrapped up in ou
coats, and we sat looking over the woods and the churchyar
There was a group of older women chatting at a nearby tab
– their weekly knitting group had just finished, over at tl
church hall. They were talking about the blankets that they

just been packaging up to send away to orphaned children in Syria.

I watched Kitty take her mug in both hands and sip carefully from it.

Then she tipped her chair back to look at the clouds. I wondered if she was seeing shapes in them.

'Look, I think I can see an elephant on a motorcycle,' I said. 'Oh, and a hairdrier.'

My Dad used to play this game with me. He used to see all sorts – the Black & Decker drill he'd lost last week, or Granny's old toothbrush.

Kitty's lips twitched, and she screwed up her eyes and looked harder, pointing her toes against the paving so that her chair tipped further back. I put my hand on the back of the chair, making sure she couldn't fall.

And I took all of those moments and I secured them in my heart. So that one day I could look back, and I could think, I had a child. I had a child for a little while. For one perfect day.

She hadn't spoken today, but she kept looking at me when she thought I wasn't watching.

'Thank you for talking to me last night,' I said. 'It was very good that you told me those things. I haven't forgotten them. We both know them now.'

She looked up at me, made a little sound of acknowledgement.

'Did you know that if someone loves you – really loves you – it makes a little glow inside? Right here.' I placed my hand on my chest.

Kitty copied me and placed her hand on her own chest.

'Can you feel it, all warm inside you? Sometimes it helps if you rub it a little bit.'

She rubbed her chest and turned to look at me, her ey
all lit up.

'And if you're ever sad or lonely, and that person is
there, the glow will still be there. If you stop and check, y
can always feel it. However far away they are. However mu
you miss them. The glow will be there.'

She nodded slowly. Then she turned to me, her ey
solemn, and said, 'Can I have another muffin?'

The glow broke over both of us then, like the sun comi
out from behind a cloud. She laughed and threw back h
head so I could see her mouthful of gappy little white teeth.

From the next table, one of the ladies looked over fond
She probably thought that Kitty was my daughter. She did
know about the black bruises down her back, the unspea
able secrets she'd kept locked inside.

I would speak them for her. Whatever the cost.

I pulled Kitty towards me, and I mumbled into the top
her head. 'Just for the avoidance of doubt... do you kno
what that means, Kitty? It means, just in case you don't kno
I love you.'

She placed her hand on her chest and I copied her.
asked the waitress for another muffin for Kitty and we s
there for a while, listening to a blackbird singing in th
woods by the churchyard.

'Are there dead people there?' Kitty nodded towards th
gravestones on the other side of the stone wall.

'Their bodies are buried there,' I confirmed. 'Or the
ashes, sometimes. My parents' ashes are here.'

Her eyes widened.

I looked at my watch. Beth and Frank were due ba
soon.

'We can go over and have a look if you like?'

She nodded.

I steered Kitty back through the café, between the crowded tables and chairs, out onto the pavement and through the squeaky iron gate into the churchyard.

My mother's name had been carved onto the headstone now, underneath my father's.

Lynne Hazelwood
Beloved wife and mother

I wanted to demand that she explain herself. To ask her what she ever saw in Frank. Why Dad hadn't been enough.

I would never be able to ask her now. Never.

I wished I had asked her why she was sad, that day when I saw her crying in the empty church. Or when I saw the crumpled look that appeared on her face sometimes, when she hugged Daddy goodbye in the mornings, or kissed the top of his head while he dozed with the Sunday papers. I wished I had told her that I'd heard the rumours about his death.

I wrenched a tangle of twigs and grass away from the front of the headstone, feeling the soil catching underneath my fingernails.

'It's a bit messy isn't it?' I said to Kitty. 'I'll just tidy it up a bit.'

I took a tissue out of my coat pocket and carefully rubbed away a smear of mud from underneath my mother's name.

Just as she had cleaned my face when I was very small. A tissue from her pocket and a dab of spit. I remembered screwing up my face, my arms pushing her away in protest.

Now all I wanted to do was throw my arms around this block of cold stone.

I took Kitty's hand, felt her soft fingers close around mine.

We went home the back way through the woods, the trees

bare and stark against the December sky. I pointed out
robin, watching us from a low branch, a clump of pale toa
stools on a blackened tree stump, and showed her tl
patches of dark, tangled undergrowth where the bluebel
used to grow in spring.

52

JULIET

Frank was waiting for me in the kitchen the next morning, when I got back to Laurel Bank after dropping Kitty at school for the last day of term.

'Sit down, Juliet, please.'

I was back at Collecott Hall again, being summoned to his office to answer for some misdemeanor.

It all made sense now, those meetings with him back then, the way he'd seemed to take a special interest in me, and the problems that had befallen me. They were all opportunities for him, grist to his mill. I imagined his sympathetic gaze fixed on my mother, his offers to help. His hands on her, his lips on her face and her neck.

'The truth is, Beth and I have decided this isn't working out.'

My heart thumped. My throat closed. It was happening.

'When I was away working a lot,' Frank went on, 'it made sense for Beth to have another adult in the house, so she could concentrate on the business and so on, but I think she was a bit ahead of herself in asking you to stay, to be a live-in nanny. I'm going to be working mainly from home over tl next few months, and I'll need the house to myself during tl day.'

'But...' I racked my brains. I couldn't force them to let n stay in their house if they didn't want me to. 'I'll live out. I get a flat nearby. I'm happy to do that. I can still do Kitty school pick-ups.' I'd rearrange my entire life so I could s her, even if it was just for half an hour a day.

'I'm sorry, but no.'

'What about you just use me on an ad hoc basis? If I st in the village, I'd be on hand for babysitting as and when y need me.' I was stumbling over my words. 'If Beth busy, ge busy, at the Old Coach House, or you have, you have to ; abroad again or something.'

The bargaining stage. I'd read about it in one of tl leaflets they'd given me after Mum had died. It was one of tl first stages of grief.

Frank just looked at me. This was the end. It was cle from his face.

I was losing my girl.

For the last twenty-four hours I'd been trying to prepa myself for this, but it was unimaginable. It was pain ar emptiness at the same time, as though my insides were beir scooped out, a little deeper with every second that passe with the realization that came, again and again, that this w real.

I thought of my plan to go to the police station ar wondered if I'd ever have had the guts to go through with Charlie had known, he'd known that it would be too hard that had been the hesitation in his voice yesterday. It wou have been like cutting off my own arm.

'In fact, Beth and I need to ask you to stay away from Kitty completely.'

'W-why?'

'Kitty has bruises on her body. Beth noticed them last night. I'm not...' He paused, considering his choice of words. 'I'm not *accusing* you. It's more like... something between a sensible precaution and a gut instinct.'

'But Kitty said –' I shut my mouth. Kitty had trusted me with her words. I needed to be very sure about what I decided to do with them. 'I would *never* hurt her. Never.'

'We'll pay you a month's wages in lieu of notice,' he said, getting up.

'I need to see her.' It came out as a splutter, a gasp for air before drowning.

He winced, and gave a sigh. 'You see, Juliet, this is what I mean. Your attachment to Kitty has an *unhealthy* quality about it. This is what's bothering us. Kitty is a very vulnerable little girl with a complex set of psychological issues. We cannot risk you making things worse for her. Feeding her delusions.'

Was he talking about Capgras syndrome?

'Our approach with Kitty is to keep things very simple, very low key. No emotional dramas.'

For a moment I wondered whether this was the advice they'd got from the psychiatrist.

But the mole, said a small voice in my head.

The mole on the wrong side of her face.

It was like trying to wind a clock the wrong way. To remind myself that Kitty didn't have Capgras syndrome. She had never seen a psychiatrist. The Seiglers had been lying all along.

'I'd be grateful if you'd go upstairs and pack your things

now. If you go without making a fuss, I'll agree to provide
basic reference.'

'But she'll wonder where I've gone. Why I didn't s[a]
goodbye.'

'When Beth brings Kitty home from school, we're goi[ng]
to tell her that you've accepted another position. That you'[ve]
gone back to the last family you worked for.'

I shook my head. 'She won't believe you. She knows tha[t I]
wouldn't leave so suddenly, and certainly not without sayi[ng]
goodbye.'

Frank smiled. 'We'll tell her that you're going to drop [by]
this evening to say goodbye – that you're going to explai[n.]
And that you've got a little present for her.'

I seized on his words without processing what t[he]
crooked smile meant. 'What time?'

'You misunderstand, Juliet. There is no time. Because y[ou]
won't be coming.'

No. I thought of Kitty's disbelief when she came ba[ck]
from school to find me gone. I thought of her listening for t[he]
doorbell, watching at the window as it got dark outsi[de]
waiting for me to come and somehow make things all rig[ht]
to explain the inexplicable. The look on her face when sh[e]
realised that I wasn't coming. That I'd let her down. That I[']
left her. What if she thought it was because of what she[']
said? Because she'd broken her silence and spoken to m[e,]
pressing her face into my shoulder in the dark? I saw her [in]
my mind's eye, her mouth drawn into a tight line as if it h[ad]
been stitched shut.

'Let me come. Please. I'll say whatever you want – that I'[m]
going back to Harry's family. Whatever. Just let me s[ay]
goodbye.'

'You need to leave now.'

Stunned, I took myself up to the Forget-Me-Not Room. They had collected my bits and pieces from around the house and placed them in a pile on my bed – my toothbrush and toothpaste, a box of tea I'd kept in the kitchen. A heart-shaped pin cushion that Kitty had made for me at school.

I'd never see her again.

I gripped the edge of the bed, my body bent over with the pain. But Kitty's voice sounded in my head.

I wouldn't take my medicine.

I rushed to the bathroom, opened the bathroom cabinet. And there it was – the bottle of promethazine. Prescribed on the seventh of July last year.

That was the day when Kitty's mum disappeared. I knew the date, if not the how and why.

I wrapped it in a plastic bag and shoved it at the bottom of my suitcase, not putting it past Frank to search my bags on the way out.

'James Watt, the psychiatrist,' I managed to say, as Frank showed me out of the front door. 'Did you pay him? Or did you just forge the letter yourself?'

'Get yourself some help, Juliet,' he said softly.

He closed the door and I stood there on the front path, where I had stood the first day I met Kitty, when she had showed me all her stones.

I thought of her face when she realised I wasn't coming back.

I thought of my parents, their ashes in the churchyard.

I would destroy Frank. I would destroy him.

～

'RIGHT, MRS MONKLANDS.' The police officer tossed a th
cardboard file on the desk, scraped back his chair and s
down. 'Sorry to keep you waiting. I understand that yo
wanted to speak to us about some concerns.'

'I explained to the officer at the desk. I need to talk to yo
about the Seigler family – Frank and Beth Seigler and the
daughter... well, Frank's daughter, Kitty. I've been workin
there as Kitty's nanny.'

'I'm glad you've come in for a chat, as it happens. You'
saved me a trip. You see, we spoke to Mr and Mrs Seigl
yesterday.'

'You... what?' My heart lifted. Were the police on to the
already?

Hadn't Beth and Frank been in Harrogate yesterday?

'Now, I'm just going to pop on the audio recorder. It's ou
policy to record all interviews that we conduct here at th
station – that okay with you?'

I nodded uneasily. Why was it that I was starting to fe
like a suspect here?

'Perhaps you could tell me about what's happened in you
own words, Mrs Monklands.'

It was a relief to offload it all. I told him about my susp
cions over the last few weeks, Kitty's Weekend News and ho
she'd opened up and spoken to me to tell me what ha
happened to her. I described her bruises, and got out m
phone to show him my photographs of the James Watt lette
and the photo of Beth with the mole on the wrong side of h
face. I produced the promethazine in its plastic bag, realisin
as I did so that it was no evidence at all.

'And another thing – she won't go to the doctors – or th
dentist. I think she's paranoid they'd access the real Beth
records and they'd realise it's not her.'

The policeman sat back in his chair and sighed.

'So, Mrs Monklands, I'll fill you in with a bit of background. When my colleague and I spoke to the Seiglers yesterday, they explained they were planning to speak to you today, to terminate your employment as their nanny. They said they were concerned about how Kitty may have sustained her bruises, and also, they were very troubled that you seemed to have developed this notion about them. That Mrs Seigler is not who she says she is. That she's not Kitty's mother. Well, Mrs Seigler was happy to show us her passport so that we could satisfy ourselves as to her identity. They also showed us photographs, going back several years to their time living in Switzerland, showing all of the family together.'

'That's fake,' I cut in. 'The photos are photoshopped, and the passport... I don't know how they did that. But I'm sure there are ways if you have the money... I mean, can't you get that sort of thing on the dark web?'

'Mr Seigler also gave me these.' He drew some papers out of the file and pushed them towards me. 'They appear to be letters written from you to your mother – who I understand died some months ago. I'm sorry. They're very personal, I know.'

My letters. It was like he'd emptied my heart across the desk. I picked up the top one and read through it.

'The mermaid doll – it's creepy. Sometimes it looks at me with its blank eyes and I swear there's something inside there. Kind of like... a presence. And last night it spoke – I'm sure it did. It said something about the Tongue Tier. For a horrible moment I wondered if Kitty was somehow controlling it, or speaking through it, but I think I've probably just seen too many horror films. There are so many about dolls, aren't there? Creepy, possessed dolls. The

*most likely explanation is that it's me who's going crazy. Char.
thinks I should talk to someone about everything that's happene
About Dad. About you. And the way things ended with Eddie. Po
traumatic stress, that was what he said. It can affect you in c
kinds of ways. He said it's far more common than people reali:
and that talking therapy can help. But I don't know what I cou
possibly say that would make any difference.'*

I put my head in my hands.

'There *is* something weird about that doll.' I wished
could take it back, as soon as the words had left my mouth.

'Now, Mrs Monklands. In our view – and I explained th
to Mr Seigler yesterday – this is more of a mental heal
matter than a police matter. I can put you in touch with son
organisations that can help. We've got some leaflets at tl
front desk. Given that Kitty has a bit of bruising, we're goii
to make a referral to social services, just to keep ourselv.
right. They'll send someone around to see the Seiglers ar
assess whether they think there's any risk to Kitty, or wheth
any additional support is needed. They might also want
speak to you, to try and establish how the bruises we
sustained. But – and I'm sure I don't need to spell this out
you need to respect the Seiglers' wishes and stay away fro
them, and from Kitty. Otherwise this might turn into
harassment matter and we'll be having a very different chat.

'Have you even checked out Frank's record? His record :
Frank Redwood, I mean? Don't you think it's suspicious th
he's changed his name?'

DC Brunston's face was kind. He spoke gently. 'I c.
assure you that we've been able to verify everything that tl
Seiglers told us. You don't need to worry about Kitty. Tl
child protection team will check everything out. My advice
you is to take on board what this friend of yours has said – g

some support for yourself. PTSD can be a bugger of a thing. I've known colleagues who've been floored by it. Mr Seigler mentioned that your dad had committed suicide.'

I gasped.

'Never underestimate the effect that can have on those left behind, Mrs Monklands.'

53

JULIET

Charlie was waiting for me in the reception are leaning forward in his chair, his hands clasped front of him.

He took one look at me and stood up. 'Don't worry. I speak to them. Make a statement, or...'

I shook my head and nodded to the doorway to sign that we should leave.

'Juliet,' he said, when were sitting in the car. 'Juli please. Tell me what happened.'

'They think I'm crazy. Frank and Beth told the police was mentally unbalanced. Suffering from PTSD. They ob ously came across all... *concerned* about me to the police, b at the same time insinuating that I hurt Kitty – that I gave h those bruises. They showed the police their ID, apparent and they don't see any grounds to take it further. I mean, I' no expert, right, but isn't it possible to fake these things? turned to Charlie with questioning eyes.

'I don't know. They'd have the real Beth's birth certifica and all that stuff, so they could apply for a new passport guess. They might have talked someone into countersigning the photo.'

Beth had probably asked one of the mums from school – Suzy Barnes, perhaps, who was a part-time solicitor at the local estate agent and was always hanging around the coffee shop. I could just picture Beth saying 'Oh, I know you haven't known me *quite* as long as it says on the silly form, but *would* you? We have to get the application off today for our holiday in the Maldives. Oh, you're an angel.'

I closed my eyes and shuddered. 'They'd also found – well, stolen – some letters I'd written to Mum, and they showed them to the police, too. The letters were a bit... you know... a bit of an outpouring.' I rubbed my hand across my eyes. 'They weren't meant to be read.'

He thumped his fists down on the steering wheel. 'For fuck's sake. The *bastards*.'

'I've lost her, Charlie. I'm not allowed to see Kitty again.' My voice disappeared into a choke. 'Not ever. And if I try, they'll take action against me for harassment... I'll get a restraining order against me or something.'

He stared straight ahead through the windscreen, moving his teeth over his lower lip like he was thinking about something.

'If they let Kitty stay friends with Cameron – and I know they probably won't – will you keep an eye on her? Even if you only just catch sight of her in the playground, or at pick-up? Will you email me sometimes to let me know how she's getting on?'

Maybe I could ask him to order an extra copy of the class photo and send it to me. Or he could email video clips from the summer concerts... next year's nativity play. The occasional glimpse of her, changing, growing up, becoming a

young woman I would never know. That would have to l
enough.

Because I wouldn't be here. I couldn't stay at Boxley Woc
any more. I'd have to go back to Edinburgh, and try to fir
some threads of my old life to pick up. Try to carry c
somehow.

Which meant I was losing not only Kitty, but Charli
And that was right – I couldn't stay here, getting in the way
him and Tasha. I turned to look at him, and tried to impri
him on my memory, as I had with Kitty yesterday. The way I
held his body, lifting his chin as he always did when he w:
thinking deeply. The stubble of his beard and the way
glinted gold in a certain light. The kind lines around his ey
when he smiled. The scar on his chin from the time wh
we'd raced our bikes home from school and he'd fallen hea
first into the ditch.

Then he turned to me. I thought he was going to give n
a speech about letting go. Moving on. But his eyes were full
light and purpose.

'Screw that. How about we find more evidence?'

'We?'

He nodded. 'Yes. We. You're not in this alone, Juliet. We
do this together.'

It felt as though I'd been holding my breath. For yea:
Without even realising it. And now someone was telling n
that it was safe to let it go. Except that I couldn't.

'But Charlie, there can't be a "we". Not when there's
Tasha.'

He reached across and took my cold hand in his tv
warm ones. He leaned forward and held it to his lips f
several moments, his forehead pinched as though somethir
was hurting him.

Then he looked up, looked me straight in the eye. 'There's something I need to explain to you about me and Tasha. It's a bit of a long story.'

'SO YOU AND Tasha don't live together? You live in the maid's flat upstairs, and she lives downstairs?'

He nodded. 'Yup. That's why we chose the house in the first place. We made an agreement that we would keep things as normal as possible for Cameron. He knows that our... arrangements... are a bit different from other people's and that I sleep upstairs, but we've told him that Mummy and Daddy still love each other – because we do, in a way – and that we'll be a family no matter what.'

I thought of the confused look on Cammie's face. How he seemed to hold so much inside himself.

'Tasha and I talked it all through at the time. We went away for a weekend and we talked, and we even wrote a load of stuff down. She called it a renewal of our... our commitment.'

I'd thought he was going to say 'vows'. I imagined the two of them, away for the weekend in some nice hotel with a swimming pool. A mini-break to end a marriage.

'The way she saw it, our relationship was changing into something different, but it was still a relationship. We agreed that we wouldn't openly see other people. Not while Cammie's still young.' He looked down, clearing his throat. 'Cammie thinks Tasha and Shami are best friends. Not... you know. Lovers.'

'And this is for how long? Until Cammie's grown up and left home?'

Charlie looked away.

'I'm sorry. I didn't mean to sound...'

He held his hands up in a defensive gesture. 'Who knov
how you're supposed to work this shit out. We're just doir
the best we can. For Cammie.'

'And what about what's best for you? And Tasha, at tl
end of the day? Look, Charlie, you know this – I grew up in
house where it was all perfect on the surface, and noboo
talked about what was really going on underneath.
destroyed my dad, and my mum, pretty much. And, well...
thought of the mess of scars underneath my clothes. 'It wasi
brilliant for me, either.'

'It was working out okay.' He looked at me, his eyes full
longing. 'Until you came along. But now... I can't think abou
anything except how I want to be with you. I wake u
thinking about you. I fall asleep every night, thinking abo
you.' His voiced dropped so it was barely more than a whi
per. 'It's like I carry you with me. Wherever I go.'

My heart leapt in my chest. But then I pulled away, looke
out of the window.

'How can you want me? How can you want me when I'
nothing? I'm nothing but a washed-up old nanny wh
couldn't have kids of her own and got too close to –'

'That's bollocks,' he cut in. 'Sorry, Juliet, but it is. You g
close to Kitty because she needed you. Because at some lev
you saw that, and you have a beautiful and open hea
Which is one of the reasons why I love you. Not that there a
reasons, really. Or rather, there is only one reason. And tha
because you are you.'

Love...? Had he really said that? But then I realised that
wasn't surprised. I had known. How could I not know wh
was in his heart, when he was the other half of me?

'Please don't leave Boxley Wood,' he said simply.

'I've got nowhere to go.'

'Stay with me in the flat,' he said. 'I'll tell Tasha and Cameron the truth – that you had to leave the Seiglers and you have nowhere to stay.'

'What if it messes things up between you and Tasha? What if she says the arrangement isn't working any more – you won't be able to live with Cameron anymore. You'll only see him every second weekend.'

A look of pain flashed across his face.

'Things are already messed up between me and Tash. I've barely been able to talk to her these past few months. I know it's not fair but I'm so fricking angry with her. For making me play this part. This part of somebody who doesn't need warmth, or physical connection, or love. Who doesn't need... you.'

Physical connection. He looked so right... so much like home. His hands, strong and warm and holding mine. His pulse, jumping in the hollow of his neck, just above the collar of his polo shirt. His lips, pressed together with emotion, so that a tiny dimple formed on his chin.

We drove to his flat and he led me to his room. Just a bed, a wardrobe, and a few bits and pieces lying around. Boxes piled at the side of the room.

He pulled my t-shirt up and over my head. I stood there, my head rushing and dizzy, like I was falling off a high, high place.

I kept my eyes tight shut, imagining what he'd be seeing. White scars, like threads across my arms. In little clusters across my stomach as though thin white worms had got under my skin and burrowed there.

His hands moved lightly over my arms, down to my stom-

ach. Then they stopped on either side of my waist. 'Show me
he said.

Slowly, I pulled off my jeans. The tops of my thighs we
an even worse mess. The skin was bumpy, deformed fro
one particularly deep cut. The skin looked old – like old lac
skin. I remembered myself in my black swimming costum
the pity in everyone's eyes. My legs began to shake.

'Look at me, Juliet.' His voice was low. 'Look at me.'

There was nowhere to hide. His hands were on my shou
ders and his blue eyes were staring into mine, perfect
steady.

'Everyone has got hurts,' he said. 'I see it every day. I
what I do. Some people carry them deep inside so nobo
can see. Some people they carry them in their faces, in tl
way they move or hold themselves. Yours are written on
your skin in little silver lines. You are beautiful to me, in eve
way.'

My instinct was to look away, not to believe it. But l
lifted a hand to my face, holding the curve of my cheek.

'You're safe,' he said. 'You're safe with me.'

CHARLIE

HE WAS LOST IN HER. Totally lost. In the silky warmth of h
skin against his, and the shape of her body moving und
him, in the way she lifted her hips to close those achir
spaces between them. All the years of longing for her, ar
missing her, and needing her, converged into one slo
endless push into her.

He was where he was supposed to be – moving in he

mind and body and something that went beyond even that. He felt waves building in her, wave upon wave until she tipped over the edge, and he wrapped his arms tight around her as she arched back and cried out. In the act of holding her, holding her through it, he gave himself up to her. Emptied himself into her. Again and again and again.

He fell on to the bed, broken open, finished. And then he reached for her, pulling her against him because even a few seconds apart felt too long. He lay there feeling the air move in and out of his lungs, feeling her heartbeat against his own chest. Everything, and nothing, had changed.

Juliet was the end of him, and the beginning and everything in between.

54

JULIET

I'd never understood what people meant when the talked about their 'other half'. Not until that afternoo lying quietly in Charlie's arms as the December afte noon faded outside. I was still Juliet, and he was still Charli but together we were something more than the sum of bo of us. Something mysterious, intertwined. For a moment, felt it as a presence, as clear as if someone else was in tl room.

We slept for a while, warm in the tangle of sheel protected from the rest of the world.

But I woke to the sound of the church tower clock strikir from across the fields. It was three o'clock. At Boxley Wo(Primary, the bell would be ringing for the end of school, ar parents would be gathering at the school gate for the la time this year, asking each other what they'd be doing ov the holidays.

I wondered if I'd be able to feel it – the moment whe they told Kitty I'd left her. Her world turning upside dow into confusion and loss – yet more loss.

'Shh,' whispered Charlie into my hair. 'Don't think about it. It's only temporary. We're going to fix this.'

By ten o'clock we were on our third bottle of wine. Plates of cheese and biscuits and empty crisp packets lay strewn on the floor beside us. Tasha had phoned to remind Charlie that she was taking Cameron to an end-of-term pizza night at Mimi's. Most of the children in the class were going, in fact, although Kitty hadn't been invited.

Mimi had told Annabel (who had told Tasha who had told Charlie) that it was because the party was going to be very 'interactive' and she didn't want Kitty to feel 'uncomfortable'.

'It's just bizarre. I can't see how they could possibly get away with something like that.'

'I thought you said Kitty wouldn't have wanted to go anyway,' said Charlie, looking confused.

I pushed him gently on the arm. 'I'm talking about Frank again. How he could have passed off "Her" as Kitty's mother.' We'd been back and forwards over it all, talking about it all night.

He nodded and frowned, making an effort to focus. 'Could it be because they had just moved to the area, and nobody had really met Beth yet?'

'And why *did* they move, at that point? I get that Frank owned the house, that it was standing empty – which is odd in itself, if you ask me. But what triggered the move?'

'I don't know.'

I racked my brains. 'The psychiatrist's letter had said something about them moving back when...'

'But the psychiatrist's letter was a fake.'

'Oh, bloody hell. I keep forgetting. What's *wrong* with me?'

Charlie rubbed his eyes with both hands, catching h
hair so that it stuck up on one side. 'Tell me again what Kit
told you.'

'She didn't say very much. She said that she'd been to tl
doctor's to get the medicine, and that they couldn't go to s(
Grandpa in the hospital because she was ill.'

'But there's never been any mention of a Grandpa, h
there?'

'Well, I guess he died. She said he was on a comb
machine. I'd been imagining an old man with a giant com'
over, but I think she must have meant –'

'A coma?' Charlie sat up straight and put his wine gla
down with a clunk. 'So! Maybe they moved back becau
Grandpa was dying. Was he rich? Could that be it? Were th(
after his money?'

'Maybe he left money to Beth, to Kitty's mother. Mayl
Fake Beth – "Her" – stepped in to play the part, so she ar
Frank could keep the money. How could they possibly thir
they'd get away with it, though?'

Charlie shrugged. 'Because if they were new round he1
nobody would know Beth wasn't Beth. Except Kitty, of cours
But they were counting on her not being able to tell anyone.

I shuddered. 'They were making use of her disability.'

Charlie sat up straight again. 'Have you got a1
photographs of Beth? I mean "Her".'

'Only the mole-on-the-wrong-side-of-her-face one. It's (
my phone.'

'That'll do. Forward it to me. We can try a reverse ima;
search.'

Charlie fiddled around with a search engine, and th(
downloaded an app. 'This one's supposed to use face recogr
tion technology. We'll give it a go.'

Pages of images came up, showing people who looked nothing like Her. We looked closely at all of them.

On the third page of hits, there was a picture of a woman with no hair, sitting in a reclining chair attached to a drip, giving a weak-looking thumbs up. I nearly scrolled past it, but Charlie put a hand on my arm.

'That looks a bit like her – look at the mole.'

We visited the page, but a message came up saying that the page no longer existed.

Charlie picked up his laptop from the table and started tapping away.

'What are you doing?'

'Seeing if I can access an older version of the page, before it was taken down. There's a website that lets you do that.' He bit his lip, tapping harder in impatience.

I jiggled in my seat.

'There we go – it's a crowdfunding website.'

Help Barbara Wilson fight for her life! For the past two years Barbara has been battling a very rare form of leukaemia. Doctors have said there are no further treatment options in the UK, and Barbara is facing the likelihood that she may never see her five-year-old daughter grow up. Her only hope is to travel for specialist treatment in the US. This comes with a hefty price tag and Barbara and her family need to raise £350k.

'Cancer treatment?' I frowned at the screen. The page was from eighteen months ago.

He opened a new window and searched for 'Barbara Wilson leukaemia'.

'Here's some kind of support site for people with

leukaemia. She seems to be mentioned in a thread about
new form of treatment. A miracle cure.'

I leaned forward to look.

Rainbow Sue: What about that new treatment in the US?
Someone from my sister's church is crowdfunding to go
over there. It's supposed to be a magic bullet treatment.

Darcy42: Do u mean Barbara Wilson?

Rainbow Sue: Why?

Darcy42: Leukaemia my arse.

Rainbow Sue: Huh???

Darcy42: I'm sorry to tell you, lovely, but that's a scam.
Police on to it and everything. If there was a magic bullet
treatment we'd all know about it. #falsehope #so cruel

Then there was a message from the moderators sayii
that the thread had been closed for comments.

'We can take this to the police.' My face felt hot wii
excitement.

'I think we need to do a bit more digging. It might n
even be her. All those other images came up, of loads
people who weren't her. It's not exactly conclusive.'

'Still – they can look up this Barbara person, can't they?
the police were on to the cancer scam then they'll ha
records of her. Fingerprints. Mug shots.'

I went back to the crowdfunding website and clicke
through the pages.

'There's an email address for her! barbara.e.wilson@xmail.com.'

'I'm not sure that helps us very much, though.'

My mind was racing. Pulling all the pieces of the jigsaw together.

'I've seen... wait.' I pictured myself finding a yellow Post-it note on the bottom of my shoe, that day at the Old Coach House. I'd shoved it in the pocket of... what had I been wearing? My Scottish rugby hoodie. I ran into the room where my case still lay unopened on the floor. Rummaged through it until I found the hoodie. The Post-it note was still there, crumpled up in the pocket.

BEW1975xmpw

'Barbara E. Wilson 1975 – that's the year of her birth probably – X-Mail Pass Word.'

I grabbed the laptop and went onto the x-mail home page, typed in the email address and the password with trembling fingers.

'Shit! It says my sign-in attempt has been blocked. It says that since I'm signing in from an unknown device, I need to verify my identity.'

Charlie, looking over my shoulder, scanned down the possibilities. 'You can ask to receive a text, or a call... although that would go to her mobile, no doubt. Or you can verify from another email address.'

I slumped back on the sofa. 'It's the right password, though. If I could only get on to it, I could find out... well, who knows what.'

Charlie sat, pondering. 'You might even be able to find out where they went that night. The seventh of July last year. Through her location history.'

'We need to take this to the police. Now.'

He reached out and stroked my arm. 'Nothing is going happen between now and the morning. If we rock up at tl police station now, clearly having had one too many glass. of wine, waving around a Post-it note...'

I was desperate to go. I was thinking about Kitty, sitting the window at Laurel Bank, waiting for me. Wondering why hadn't come to say goodbye and give her a present.

'You're right. The police already think I'm mad.'

'And there might be nothing in the account that incrim nates her at all. If there was, she's probably deleted anyway.'

I shook my head. 'It's hopeless.'

'But Juliet, if we can find this stuff in, what, half an hou the police will be able to turn something up. I'm sure of There's hope. That's the main thing.'

'I suppose.'

'We should get to bed.'

'I won't be able to get to sleep.'

'Well, then you can just close your eyes and rest.'

It was what my mother used to say to me, when I couldi sleep.

'I'll be right here with you. And we'll sort it all o tomorrow.'

55

JULIET

At four in the morning I woke suddenly, and sat up straight in bed. It was as if my brain had figured it all out while I slept in Charlie's arms.

If my sign-in attempt had been blocked, Beth – *Barbara* – would receive an email alert about it. She'd know it was me and she'd go into her account and delete everything.

But it was possible that she wouldn't see the email till the morning. What I had to do – it was clear now – was sign in using a device that *was* recognised. A device which she'd used before to sign into her account.

I was thinking of the computer I'd seen in the office at the Old Coach House. And Tasha, with her big bunch of jailer's keys, sitting in the seashell bowl on the dresser downstairs. And the door between this flat and Tasha's part of the house which always remained unlocked.

'I'm sorry, Charlie,' I whispered, tracing my fingers down the side of his face. In my minds eye, I saw Tasha's face when she realised what I'd done. How she would blame Charlie for

bringing an unsuitable person into their house. I got up, ar
pulled on some clothes.

∾

IT WAS ALMOST TOO EASY. The eight-digit alarm code w
written on the key tag, in very faint pencil, as if that wou
stop people knowing what it was.

Barbara's computer fired up easily when I entered tl
password from the sheet in her desk drawer. Her e-mε
account let me in this time.

The only recent emails were from Windylea Care Hon
in Great Yarmouth. They seemed to be talking abo
someone called Margaret, and changes in fee rates. But fir
things first – I went into the 'locations' tab, and then into 'hi
tory', and looked up the seventh of July last year.

She'd been up near Durham. Why on earth? Th
couldn't be right... the location was just near Collecott Hall.

If Frank and Barbara had killed Kitty's real mother th
night, and wrapped the body in plastic sheeting – though
still sounded ridiculous – why would they have driven all tl
way to Collecott Hall?

With shaking hands I took my own phone ar
photographed the screen, showing the location history, tl
position on the map.

And now I had to get out of there. I began to shut dov
the computer. It whirred and the screen went black.

Then came the soft creak of the door.

∾

'OH, JOOLZ,' said Frank in a soft voice. 'Did you think I wouldn't find you? We've been waiting up tonight, waiting for Barbara's email to ping with another security alert.'

'Get away from me. I know what you've done.' I stood up and backed away. 'You killed Kitty's mother. You killed Beth.'

'Dammit, I'm not a *killer*. Don't you see that?'

'The police will be able to prove it.'

Frank shook his head. 'You've got this all wrong. Beth slipped in the kitchen and sliced through her wrist with a paring knife. It was a tragic accident.'

His face was open. There was no guilt there at all.

'Why didn't you go to the police then?'

'It would have looked... unfortunate. I mean, they say it's always the husband, don't they? And then there was the money to consider. A life-changing amount. That money was for Kitty's future.'

'So this was, what... good parenting? To mess with Kitty's head and try and make her believe some other woman was her mother... just for the sake of money?'

'If you'd known Beth, you'd have known that she was barely a mother at all to Kitty. She was off her face on prescription drugs most of the time.' He spoke as though I were a particularly stupid child, who hadn't understood some important adult matter. 'And Kitty was so young. We knew that after a few months of having a proper mother, in Barbara, she would barely remember Beth.'

'Rubbish.' My voice came out braver than I felt.

'My mother left when I was four years old, Juliet. I can hardly remember her, and what I do remember comes from looking at photos, and what my brother told me... memories of memories. They're not even real. I feel nothing when I think of her. Nothing.'

'So you thought that if you got rid of the photos of Bet and never, ever spoke about her, she would cease to exist.'

He shrugged. 'We thought it would minimize the effect (Kitty. As I say, Beth wasn't much to write home about.'

'You *married* her.'

'I changed her life. Do you know she was homeless whe she met me? She'd been passed around from pillar to post ɑ through her childhood and when she came to me, most her teeth had been knocked out by her ex? The first thing did was sort out dental treatment for her. Nobody ever looke after her properly until me.'

I thought of how she must have looked at him to beg with – her knight in shining armour. Like a Sleeping Beau might look at her prince.

It happened in a split second – he hooked his foot arour my ankle and pushed me hard, so that I fell forward onto tl flagstones. Then he was on top of me, his full weight on h bent knee, pressing it onto my neck. Struggling to breathe didn't even process it until it was too late. He'd tied my han behind my back. And then, with his knee crushing the sma of my back this time, he bound my ankles.

I think I passed out. The next thing I was aware of w Frank's voice coming from the kitchen. It sounded like he w on his phone.

'Get that old sleeping bag from the garage, and n training weights. It'll have to be the lake. Well, have you g any better ideas?'

The lake. He was talking about the lake at Collecott Ha The one place on the grounds where nobody ever wer where nobody was allowed to go, after that boy drowned the 1970s. I remembered how the woods around the lake we separated from the road – a narrow lane winding through tl bottom of the valley – by a crumbling stone wall. It would be easy to drive the car up there in the middle of the night, for the two of them to drag a body through the woods to the water's edge, to weigh it down with stones and slide it in. It was the perfect place.

I'd loved Collecott Hall. I'd hated it. And now it was claiming me back. I would lie there under the water, rotting away forever with Kitty's mother.

'Pills?' Frank was saying. 'Okay, well bring them. Be quick.'

He was walking towards me now. I forced my lips to move. 'Don't kill me.'

'I'm not a killer, Juliet. It's you... you're making me into one.' His voice was irritated, disgusted, like I'd forced him to clean a toilet or pick up dog shit. 'You're giving me no choice, damn you.'

'There is a choice.' Pinpricks of light were dancing in my eyes and I was losing the feeling in my hands now. 'We make a deal. I don't tell the police what I've found, and you... you take me back as a nanny. I'll make sure Kitty never gives the game away. Then... then I'll be an accessory. We'll be in it together.'

Frank came and crouched in front of me. I cringed, dreading the weight of his knee on my neck again. But he just looked at me, pityingly.

'All I want,' I said, pausing to snatch in a breath, 'is Kitty.'

'And all I want is an easy life'. The words emerged with a puff of sweet, rotten-meat breath. 'Which you seem determined to take away from me.'

Then I saw that he had a plastic bag in his hands – a large food storage bag. He was going to put it over my head and

suffocate me, so I'd be no trouble any more, and easier
dispose of in the lake.

He pulled open the bag. This was it. Kitty would nev
know what happened to me. Nor would Charlie. He wou
just think I'd left. That I'd woken up in his bed, in the hollo
next to his warm, sleeping body, and decided I would get ı
and leave and never see him again.

But suddenly Charlie was in my head, he was flooding ɩ
through me, as clear and strong as the fear. Telling me th
everything was okay. Telling me that I needed to concentra
on buying more time. That it was the only thing I needed
do right now.

You're okay.

I had a sudden image of myself with the bag over n
head, the plastic sucking in at my mouth and nose as I triɩ
to gasp in air.

No, Juliet. Breathe. Keep him talking.

I needed to find a subject that would interest him.

'Did you love my mother? Or was it just that you hatɩ
Dad?'

Frank sat down, his back against the counter, and he toɩ
a box of cigarettes from his pocket. He looked for a momeı
at the warning on the front of the packet – a picture of
person with half of their face eaten away by cancer – and shı
me a smile that was almost conspiratorial, as if this was ɑ
part of a game. Then he drew out a cigarette and lit it. I
took a deep drag that hollowed out the contours of h
cheeks, so that for a moment his face was more shadow thɑ
light.

'*They* loved *me*,' he said. 'Isn't that the point? They cou
only see the best in people. I found them... irresistible. Thɩ
were like a couple of babes, Juliet. The school in India suckɩ

them right in.' He threw his head back in a half-hearted laugh.

'There was no school?'

'Oh, there was a school. I set up the charity myself. It was connected with Collecott Hall originally – they had visions of it being a sort of sister school, and we had school fundraisers for it for a while, until the new Head decided it was a bit of a lost cause. A bit of an embarrassment. So I kept it going myself. I enjoyed my trips to India. And my little jaunts down to Boxley Wood for the meetings. Your parents were very hospitable.'

Once, when I was about eight, my mother had driven all the way to Heathrow to pick Frank up after one of his India trips. He'd stayed at our house, talking into the night with all the stories of hardship and hunger, and hope against the odds, all tanned and wiry and his eyes too bright. Dad had got his Christmas whisky out of the drinks cabinet. I remembered the clink of ice against crystal, the peaty liquid emerging from the neck of the bottle with a silky, glugging sound. And me, hovering, not wanting to go to bed, offering Frank crisps and peanuts from Mum's willow pattern serving bowls. He had scooped them up into his mouth with dirty-looking fingers, without looking at me.

'What happened to the school?'

'It closed down after a few years – but not because there was an accident. The children went off to another school run by a bigger charity. But it only took a heart-wrenching story and a few photos of some random street boy who'd lost his legs, and Graeme and Lynne signed their lives away with the various loans and guarantees. Lynne always had... an overdeveloped sense of guilt. I needed the money.' He looked up at me, as though expecting me to nod and agree. 'So that I'd be

able to give Lynne the life she deserved. Once she'd come
her senses.'

'My mother spent the rest of her life wondering wh
happened to that boy. To Jayesh.' I remembered how she
described the haunted black eyes, staring out from tl
photograph.

'What you've got to understand, Juliet, is that she w.
always trying to make things better for people. It was h
Achilles heel. She phoned me up, not long after the Indi:
school business came to a head, begging for me to help g
Charlie McGrath a bursary at Collecott Hall, telling me ho
his dad hadn't been coping since his mother had died
cancer. I sorted it all out for her. And a place for you, too.'

'What a hero.'

He shrugged. 'I needed to show her that I was stron
where your father was weak. That I could step in and f
things, where your own father couldn't. I'd assumed you'd c
well at school. But when you didn't, I made that work, too.'

'Monte,' I said. 'Tell me about Monte. The investigation.'

He shrugged and gave a ghastly, modest smile. As thou
he'd been waiting all these years to tell someone how clev
he'd been.

'The *investigation* was very short,' he said. 'Monte had
little accident at home.'

I gasped. 'An accident at home? You knew that? And y
let me think...'

'I needed you to have a little crisis,' he said with a shrug.
wanted to get your mother up to Collecott Hall.'

Concentrate. Keep him talking.

'Mum said you phoned Dad. After she'd left Collecc
Hall that night she came up to see you. The night Dad died.'

'I did,' said Frank, raising his eyebrows and nodding.

'What did you say to him?'

He exhaled loudly, puffing smoke into the air between us. 'I told him about your mother's affair with me.'

'Mum said that he told you he was going to end it... to kill himself.'

'Not... exactly.'

'What then?'

'If you want the truth, he said that he wasn't going to discuss Lynne, and what she had or hadn't done, unless she was there to answer for herself.'

That was just like Dad. The perfect gentleman.

'And then he said goodbye and put the phone down.' Frank shrugged.

'So you let Mum think that Dad killed himself because of her, and what she'd done with *you*. She died thinking that he left her. Left *us*.'

Dad had been Mum's anchor. The one she went to for comfort and shelter, the one she turned to when she needed to know that all was right with the world. She could believe it because *he* believed it. That was why his depression had hit them both so hard.

'Don't you see what you've done? She died thinking that my Dad had *given up*... that the bad in the world was stronger than the good.'

'Oh, come on, Juliet. We're not going to pretend that Graeme driving into that tree was an accident, are we?'

The way he spoke, it was like he was turning my mind upside down.

'You should have heard him on the phone.' He whistled softly, eyes cast towards the ceiling as though he was imagining it. 'He was so polite, never raised his voice. But there was such pain behind it. I've never heard anything like it.

And have you ever noticed, Juliet? There's a part inside all of us that longs for oblivion. That draws us back to th state of nothingness where we came from. Dust to dus Ashes to ashes. It's the law of the Universe, Juliet.' H looked down at me, his eyes wide with his fake-Jesu sadness. 'By the end, when he was deep in depression, you father was fighting that impulse every day. It took *every l* of his strength.'

Was it true? Had Dad given in?

I thought of the week I'd spent in my mother's bed, morn ings turning to evenings as the shadows moved slowly acro the floor. And of the day when I'd buried her ashes next Dad as the vicar held me upright. Hadn't there been tim when I was so tired of it all that I just wanted to get the end?

No, Juliet. Breathe. Keep him talking.

'Why did you tell Mum that Dad said he was going to k himself?'

Frank shrugged. 'The man had destroyed himself. On way or another – it doesn't really matter how. I helped a litt along the way of course... the financial stuff... leaving the sl pellets out for the dog.' He laughed softly and glanced at n to see my reaction. 'Oh yes – I had to wrap them in litt strips of Lynne's excellent marmalade-glazed ham, but I wolfed them down. Stupid hound.'

'Oh no...' I saw Dad's face, contorted and wet as he he Gypsy's head on his lap. The way he'd bent over him as I convulsed, his big brown eyes rolling back in his hea Blaming himself for not locking the shed door.

'That was the easy part. What I needed to do next,' Fran went on slowly, 'was destroy *the version of him that Lynne he in her head.*'

He smiled. A terrifying, dry smile. There was a noise, like the inside of his lips unsticking from his teeth.

It was so utterly wrong, so upside down. Like someone smiling at a crash on the motorway, or at the scene of an earthquake, or when the twin towers fell.

'He was dead, Joolz. Dead and gone. All I did was take control of the narrative. It's surprisingly easy to do, when people are in shock. And it's as easy as pie to spread rumours in a small town.'

'Mum was the most compassionate person I've ever known. She would've known that if he'd killed himself, it was because he was in more pain than it was possible to bear. She never judged him. I'm sure of that.'

'Maybe not consciously. She was a good Christian woman – she believed she'd forgiven him. But at a deeper level, Juliet, she was filled with rage. At the thought he had abandoned you both. Your mother had a deep need to be looked after. To be rescued.'

I thought of her signing the house over to him, trusting that he would sort out the spiralling debts. Probably thinking that it would be best to let a man – Graeme's best friend, no less – deal with that side of things. And Frank, slowly taking control, biding his time...

'How come she didn't end up with you, then? Why didn't your great plan work?'

Frank's face didn't change. He took another draw on his cigarette.

'She made the wrong decision. She didn't want to move on with her life. She preferred to live with the memory of a dead man who'd abandoned her.'

'He didn't *abandon* her.'

'He abandoned her emotionally. He wasted her life in a

loveless marriage.' He looked at me, curiously. 'Do you kno
that they almost never had sex?'

My heart leapt as I heard a car draw up outside – but the
the back door opened and in came Beth/Barbara wearing h
turquoise velour tracksuit. I could see she'd parked round tl
back in the loading area, not in the customer parking are
that was visible from the road.

'You realise you're going to have to chuck that tracksι
after this?' said Frank.

She gave Frank a look. 'I swear to God –'

'If you'd deleted that account like I told you to –'

'Like you "told me to"? God give me strength,' she sp
out. 'I got rid of the phone. I thought that would be enoug
I'm not a sodding IT expert.'

'I remember. You bloody threw it out the window on tl
AI. Could have caused a pile-up.'

She rolled her eyes and turned her attention to m
pulling her tracksuit sleeves up to her elbows to reveal h
carefully spray-tanned forearms.

'Right, Juliet. I want you to know this is nothing person;
okay?'

She said it as though she was about to tell me my hair w
a mess or that my designer handbag was a few seasons out
date.

'The problem is, once you've made a decision – like tl
one Frank and I made that night – well, you have to follo
through. You have to tidy up loose ends.'

Keep them talking, said Charlie in my head.

'What I don't understand,' I said, 'is why you didn't ju
take the money and run – go off to Brazil or something. WI
stick around?'

'Not while Mummy's in the care home,' said Barbara. 'She doesn't have long. I can't leave her.'

Out of Barbara's line of vision, Frank rolled his eyes.

'Are you after her money too?'

'She doesn't have a cent to her name,' said Barbara dramatically, like a character from a bad TV show. 'Who do you think's paying a grand a week for a care home with a sea view?'

'Well, Beth's paying for that, isn't she, really?'

'Blood is thicker than water,' said Barbara. 'That's one of the things I learned from having cancer. Some people stick around, but most don't.'

'You didn't *have* cancer!'

She shrugged. 'I thought I did, for a few weeks. Until the doctors decided it was Lyme's disease.'

'And by then it seemed too late to disappoint people,' added Frank.

Barbara gasped. 'Cheeky bastard.'

'So do all your friends think you're dead now, or...?'

'I'm having treatment in LA. It seemed best to get away, once the rumour mill started.'

She spoke as though she actually believed her own fiction.

'This way was best for everybody,' she said. 'Beth's money doesn't go to waste, just because of an unfortunate accident. I can look after Mummy. Frank and I can be a family unit for Kitty and minimise the –'

Frank gave a bitter laugh. 'Family unit! You're nothing but a liability. You're lucky to be getting a penny out of this.'

'Well, what are you going to do then, Frank?' said Barbara in silky, dangerous tones. 'Are you going to pretend to be Beth yourself?'

'Where is Kitty now?' I demanded. 'Have you left her
the house on her own again?'

Barbara shot a glance at Frank. 'She doesn't have scho
in the morning. She'll just stay in bed doing her jigsaws
whatever. She'll hardly notice we've gone. Anyway, we've g
the mermaid switched on.' She pulled her phone out of h
pocket and tapped on an app.

I could hear faint music – Kitty had turned on her fai
toadstool nightlight and pressed the button for the lullaby.

She must have woken up and put it on to help herself fa
back asleep. Had she realised she was alone in the house? M
heart felt like it would explode.

'Jesus Christ. Switch that thing off,' said Frank.

A listening device. The mermaid was a baby listenir
device. I'd heard stories about families using these to spy o
their nannies – one of my friends had even lost her jo
because she'd been heard chatting to a friend about tl
mother's latest Botox bill. I should have realised.

I thought of Frank and Barbara, listening in to Kitty
faltering words, and the conversations I'd managed to ha
with her through the doll. There I'd been, planning and plo
ting when I was only ever a pawn in a game.

I thought of them listening in, that night when Kitty anc
had taken the doll into the garden and flung it over the wall.

'Did you go and get it in from the garden, that night?'
asked. 'Did you put it on my *pillow*?'

Frank smiled. 'It's an expensive piece of kit, that.'

'It's very clever.' Barbara was scrolling through her phon
keying something in. 'We can programme in our ow
messages to reassure her.'

The mermaid's transatlantic drawl sounded through tl
phone: 'Night night, sleep tight.'

'See?' said Barbara, as if she'd just proved herself parent of the year.

The tinny voice sounded again: 'The Tongue Tier will get your tongue.'

Then came a frightened little noise that was half moan, half sob.

Oh my love.

Barbara hastily swiped the screen away and put the phone in her pocket.

Frank laughed.

'Aren't you going to put it back on?' I demanded. 'So you can at least hear her?'

'She's fine,' said Barbara. 'Now Juliet, we've got a bit of a Plan B for you to consider.'

'What?' Anything would be better than Plan A – being suffocated or drowned in the lake at Collecott Hall.

She drew a bottle of pills out of her pocket. They were Beth's, from the medicine cabinet at Laurel Bank.

'So I've brought these... and these.' She drew an envelope out of her handbag. 'They're what they use to knock Mummy out at night. And I thought that if you would agree to just take these, we can just tiptoe away and leave you here in peace. It would be of benefit to you as well as us.'

'And to Charlie,' said Frank slyly. 'He'll know what's happened to you. Suicide, plain and simple. It'll make sense – suicide often runs in the family, after all. Better than years of wondering, wouldn't you say?'

'And it would be better for Kitty,' said Barbara. 'We can explain to her that you were very unwell, and that it was such a pity that you didn't get the help you needed, but you decided that you couldn't go on. These things happen some-

times.' She said it sadly, like she was practising how she'd s:
it to Kitty.

I thought of Kitty, bewildered and silent as Barbara bro]
the news.

Of Charlie, his face distorted in pain.

Of Tasha, coming in to open up the café in a few hour
She might even bring Cameron in with her, as it was scho
holidays. I wondered which of them would notice my boc
first. Or maybe Frank would stuff my body into a cupboard :
nobody would notice it until I started to smell.

Then I thought of them never knowing what ha
happened to me – thinking I'd gone off somewhere. Aba
doned them.

What would it be like to suffocate? To drown? Takii
Beth's pills and just falling asleep would be the easier optic
– at least it would be over and done with quicker.

Don't you fricking dare, said Charlie.

'No thank you,' I said, my voice shaking. 'No thank yo'
No thank you.'

The words felt like a comfort. They sounded like me.
was going to be Juliet, right up until the end.

Frank sighed, stood up and kicked my face so that n
neck snapped back. Pain exploded through my head, red ar
hot. Something splintered and crackled in my cheek as
opened my mouth to cry out. Then warmth flooded betwee
my legs as they rolled me onto the opened-out sleeping b:
and put tape over my mouth.

Together they zipped up the sides then hauled me out
the back door, the nubs of my spine catching on the edges
each of the stone steps, and on the metal rim of the car boot

'Jesus,' spat Frank, wiping wetness off his hands. 'Zip it :
the way up.'

I remembered the time I'd fallen down some steps at Edinburgh Waverley – the humiliation at the loss of control, the desperation to get up and prove to everyone that I was okay, the weak, crumpled feel of my foot with its broken bones.

Barbara's eye caught mine as she was closing the bag over my head, and the last chink of light disappeared. There was a pause, during which I heard a car door clunk – Frank getting into the driver's seat – and she pulled the zip back, just an inch. Enough to breathe.

There was a muffled, bad-tempered debate, in which Frank seemed to be saying they should move his training weights into the back seat footwell in case I somehow tried to use them to break out of the boot. I shrank away as the boot door opened and clunked shut again.

This was it. The end.

56

KITTY

'Y ou're through to an emergency service operato
What service do you require?'

Silence.

'Hello, is anyone there, please? What's the nature of yo
emergency?'

Silence.

'If you need an emergency service but are unable
speak, please tap the handset.'

Tapping noise.

'You are being connected to the police.'

'Hello, you're through to the police control room. Wha
your emergency?'

Silence.

'What's –'

'H... h... hi... h.. hello?'

'Hello, my love. Tell me what's happening.'

'My daddy is going to hurt my Dooliet.'

'Where are you, sweetheart?'

'In my kitchen in my house.'

'Who's with you in the house?'

'Nobody.'

'Where's your daddy now?'

'Daddy phoned Her and told her to get the sleeping bag and go to the café.'

'The café?'

'Yes. Her thought I was in bed but I was under the table.'

'Stay on the phone, my love. I'm going to send a car out to your house. You and I will keep talking until they arrive. Can you tell me your name?'

Tapping noise.

'Are you still there, love?'

Tapping noise.

'Are you still there?'

57

JULIET

T *hink of five things you can see...*
Black. Black. Black. Black. Black.
I tried to breathe as calmly as I could, inhalir the car carpet smell, and the smell of mud, and somethir that might have been dog dirt – they'd both thrown the wellies in beside me. My head throbbed, intensifying in sickening pain when the car took a corner or went over bump in the road.

It would be a four-hour drive to Collecott Hall – mayl more if Frank used back roads to avoid motorway cameras Barbara had suggested. How could I get through four mo hours of this?

But it was four hours in which I'd still be alive. Four hou to think about Kitty and Charlie. To remember every detail their faces. The feeling of Charlie's hands on my body, ar the exact way his eyes lit up with everything I did. The loc on Kitty's face when her classmates first came to play at tl jigsaw bench. The sound of her voice that night she can into my bed.

Will you promise to stay forever?

I tried, Kitten. I would have done anything. Anything.

Then a wave of adrenaline swamped me. I thought of the murky lake water rushing into my lungs, filling my mouth and hitting the back of my throat. Or would they hit me over the head first? Strangle me? How much was it going to hurt?

I wanted my mother. To burrow my head into her lap.

'That part will be over with quickly,' she said, inside my head. 'You're safe. You're safe.'

I wriggled round onto my back – my hands were all pins and needles. But then the opening in the sleeping back was behind my head. Maybe my hands would just go numb eventually. Maybe they'd start to turn black after four hours. Not that it mattered much, considering they'd be waterlogged, rotting flesh by this time tomorrow.

I thought of my mother's letters. I tried to remember every single one… and the feel of each of her gifts in my hands – the soft wool of the gloves. The rattle of the monkey puzzle seeds in their envelope. The old book smell and worn pages of the *School Friend* annual.

As the minutes passed, it became harder to breathe. I worked my mouth to see if I could get the tape loose, but only succeeded in dislodging a broken tooth which slid into the space under my tongue. Blood flooded my mouth. I had nowhere to spit. I was going to vomit –

Don't panic.

It was Charlie's voice now. It was in my head and yet not in my head. I thought of what he'd said about near-death experiences, about the mind trying to comfort itself when it was close to the end.

Imagine you're lying safe in bed with my arms around you.

He reached around me and held the back of my achir head. Held the pain safe in his hand.

I closed my eyes.

One... Two... Three... That's it.

My breathing began to slow. Perhaps I could sleep for while. I could sleep here in this velvety darkness until it w; all over.

I thought I was imagining the sirens at first – they seem(to be there and then fade away. But then there was anoth. blast, loud and right behind us. I felt the car speed up, tl engine revving harder. My body rolled against the side of tl boot as we swerved tight around a bend, and then bounced : the bottom of the car scraped over one speed bump and th(another.

A car horn sounded long and hard, its wail fading into tl distance too quickly. I heard Beth and Frank's muffled voice rising in pitch. More sirens, coming from in front, behind.

Then brakes screeching. An explosion of steel and glas Blinding light and pain beyond imagining and th(blackness.

58

CHARLIE

For Charlie it seemed that this hospital room was like somewhere between worlds. Hadn't there been a place like that in one of the Narnia books? He remembered a forest full of dark pools – one might take you back to the world you'd just left, safe and sound. Another might take you to a ravaged, broken world where the sun was dying, and there was no way of getting back.

Charlie knew that, if Cyprus had divided his life into before and after, this in-between time at the hospital would do the same thing.

Sleep wasn't possible. Eating wasn't, either. He couldn't find anything on his phone to distract him, except a photo he'd taken of Kitty and Cameron at the Seekings birthday party, which had Juliet's face in the background, caught in mid-laugh. So different from the white, shadowy face on the pillow next to him.

He just had to wait. Wait to see which of those worlds he'd end up in.

He'd sat in the waiting area at A&E for five hours,

wondering what the hell was happening. They'd said h
head injury was their immediate concern – she had reduc(
consciousness but she was responding to stimulation. Th
was something. He'd repeated it to himself silently, as l
perched on the edge of the hard plastic chair... Responding
stimulation. Responding to stimulation.

At least she'd been moved to the neurosurgical unit no
She was in the best place – a platitude he'd trotted out
patients' families countless times. They'd done a CT sca
and she would be taken away for an MRI at some poir
Charlie didn't know when. The consultant had spoke
quickly, not even sitting down. He had said the CT sc{
showed some bleeding, indicating damage to the bloc
vessels. It might or might not require surgery. And there w:
the possibility of a diffuse axonal injury – the stretching ar
tearing of the nerve fibres, caused by the brain movir
rapidly back and forward in the skull when the impa
happened.

He felt sick. All his years as a doctor, including a stint
A&E when he was training, and he'd never felt squeamis'
not once.

He'd asked, in a wobbly voice, when Juliet was going
wake up. The consultant's voice had softened, and he'd sa
that it was early days. They were keeping her under sedatic
for the time being, to minimize any secondary damage to tl
brain.

Charlie nodded, his head full of a million questions th
he couldn't bring himself to ask. Could they tell from the C
scan which areas of the brain might be affected? Would it l
her short-term memory... her motor function... her visior
He tried to remember his notes from his training, tl
diagrams of the brain and central nervous system, but l

couldn't remember any of it. It was as if his own brain had been wiped clean.

The consultant gave a bland, sympathetic smile and left him.

It felt awful to be on the 'patient' side of this equation. He'd never felt so helpless. Not since...

He remembered sitting with his mother as she writhed under thin hospital covers, her eyes closed and her mouth stretched into an 'O'. He'd been too afraid to even touch her hand.

And now here he was with his Juliet. The longer he sat there, the more he longed to climb onto the bed, to lie quietly next to her, to hear her heart beating. His body ached for him to do it. Instead, he leaned over the bed, careful to avoid all the lines and tubes, and laid his cheek, very gently, on her forehead.

It came to him in a flash – a sudden memory of lying next to her in the garden at Laurel Bank, under the monkey puzzle tree.

They'd just got home from nursery – from *nursery*... they could only have been about four – and Lynne had given them both apples, to keep them going until dinner. He remembered thinking that Juliet's teeth were very sharp and white and that it was funny how she screwed up her nose when she took a bite.

'You sound very crunchy,' he'd said.

'Put your ear on top of my head.'

Charlie did what she said, because he always did. Her hair was blonde and soft and warm like sunshine under his cheek. She crunched, and he felt it and heard it through his whole head, as loud as a dinosaur crunching bones. Like it was him who was eating – or being eaten...?

Or like he was inside her head.

'Me and Mummy were making a list of the crunchie foods before you came,' she explained. 'And that's the be way to test them. We're going to do rock cakes next.'

He'd felt strange when he sat up straight again. Differer He'd never been inside another person's head before.

He sat up now, his heart racing. This wasn't right, memory like that coming from nowhere, as real as the day happened.

Was this it? Their life together flashing before his eyes?

Come on, Charlie. Think like a scientist.

But he rang for the nurse, because nothing he felt abo Juliet could be explained by science.

'Just check on her?' he asked, and she nodded in unde standing.

At tea time he nipped home to take a shower and get change of clothes. The nurses had said there wouldn't be an change, not while she was still under sedation.

Cameron came and lay down on Charlie's bed while I was drying off and getting changed. Charlie guessed that he come up so that he could talk in private. Kitty was downstai in the kitchen. Tasha had coaxed her into helping to ice Yule log.

'Is Juliet very, very hurt?'

'She hurt her head in the accident,' said Charlie. 'But th doctors are doing everything they can to make her better.'

'You're a doctor. Can you make her better? Is that wl you've been there?'

'No,' said Charlie, swallowing hard. 'I'm there as a frien So that there'll be a familiar face when she wakes up.'

Please God.

Cammie sat up on the bed and turned so that he w

facing Charlie. 'Are you in love with Juliet? Like Mummy's in love with Shami?'

His face was a mixture of confusion and intense focus. It was a look Charlie had seen before, when Cammie was struggling with a maths sum, or trying to understand why penguins have wings but can't fly.

Charlie sat for a moment, thinking. He thought of all the things that his son had needed from him over the years. The hours he'd spent rocking him to sleep as a baby. The rough and tumble 'daddy games' as a toddler. *Guess How Much I Love You?* read aloud each night for six months – the record was fourteen times in one night. Man-to-man advice on how to deal with the class troublemakers. Spelling words, repeated endlessly on the way to school on Friday mornings, when the terrifying weekly spelling quiz took place.

And now, Cameron needed the truth.

'Yes,' he said. 'That's right.'

He waited for his son's face to crumple. Or for a barrage of questions about what it all meant, how would Mummy feel about it, where they would live... and if Daddy lived somewhere else would he still get to see him every day, or only on weekends?

But Cameron just nodded, and Charlie realised that they had been his own questions, not Cameron's. The questions that had been going around in his head since long before Juliet came back.

'You can ask me anything you like, you know. We'll talk about it a lot. But I promise, Mummy and I will figure everything out and make sure you're okay. We both love you so much.'

Cameron nodded.

'Can we still go to the zoo on my birthday?'

'Yes! Of course we can.'

'Can Kitty and Juliet come?'

'Er... if you want them to?'

And if Juliet was still here, and they made it out of this.

He thought of her, being wheeled off for surgery if tl MRI results were bad. Of the nurses' kind faces as he lean(over and whispered goodbye, just in case.

He had to sit down on the bed, and pretend to be dryir his face with the towel.

'Kitty!' shouted Cameron, jumping up. 'Guess what!'

'We'd better check with...' Charlie began, but it was t(late.

He watched him fly out of the room and down the stai1 his beloved boy, his North Star, shining even here in this i1 between world.

59

JULIET

I f this was what it was like to be dead, it wasn't so bad. There was pain – pulsing and red hot, like the inside of a volcano – but it was far below me. I was drifting above, on currents of warm air.

And I could hear Charlie's voice. I couldn't understand what he was saying. It just came in snatches of a few words at a time, with darkness in between.

Perhaps I was in some nothing-place between life and death, and my dying neurons were playing back Charlie's voice, trying to make some kind of sense of the dark.

The volcano bubbled, the fire swelling up ready to blow, and I heard the noise of someone crying out. Then I realised it was me.

What was this?

I forced open my eyes and saw Charlie.

'It's okay,' he said. 'It's okay.' I didn't know who he was saying it to – me, or himself. His voice was choked with tears.

I closed my eyes again.

'You go back to sleep and rest now. You're okay. It's safe sleep. I'll be here when you wake up.'

WHEN I WOKE AGAIN, I saw Kitty's face, inches from mine, h(
eyes enormous.

Charlie was behind her, his hands squeezing her shou
ders. 'Give her some space, Kitty. Let her breathe.'

Kitty's eyes widened even further as she prepared
impart urgent information. 'TPAC,' she said.

Tactical pursuit and containment.

Why was Kitty talking about *Police Interceptors*? It was t(
confusing. Maybe I should just go back to sleep.

'You're in hospital,' explained Charlie. 'There was an ac(
dent. The police intercepted the Seiglers' car. You've got
head injury – the car flipped over and the side of the c.
caved in. You've been under sedation for a little while so do1
worry if you don't feel quite like yourself yet.'

I had dreamed about the scream of sirens. A man with a
Irish accent in green scrubs. Hairy forearms and latex glove
A blur of voices.

Bright ceiling lights above me, streaking past.

'Okay,' I managed to say. Charlie's face broke into a smile

I felt Kitty's pinkie interlink itself with mine and l
myself drift.

THE NEXT TIME I woke up, Kitty wasn't there. Charl
explained that she'd gone home with Tasha and Cameron
watch a movie and have pizza. I saw that she'd left a sm;

Sylvanian hedgehog on the cabinet by the bed. It was her way of saying she'd be back.

'Tasha knows, by the way,' he said. 'About us. I had to explain about... you know, her keys. She's being a bit tight-lipped about it all, but I have to say, she's been great with Kitty.'

'Sorry.'

'Shhh,' he said, stroking back a lock of hair from my fore-head. 'You don't need to say anything. I understand.'

'Collecott Hall – the lake there,' I said, trying to sit up and then falling back down as the volcano threatened to bubble up again.

'Just rest,' said Charlie. 'There'll be time to deal with everything later.'

'The police need to look there for Beth's body. They need to arrest Frank and Beth – where are they?'

Charlie explained to me that Barbara had survived the accident with just a few cuts and bruises, and she was in police custody. Frank had been killed.

'It was one of his training weights,' he said. 'God knows why he put them on the back seat. It would have hit him like a missile.'

'Does Kitty know?'

He nodded, took my hand. 'We're going to have to be very careful there,' he said. 'It was Kitty who called the police.'

'No...' My little girl who couldn't speak, who'd been trying to phone the police for months before I'd arrived – she'd done it. For me.

I was silent for several moments, trying to swallow down my tears. Charlie took a tissue from his pocket, reached over and wiped my cheek, very gently.

'She might blame herself,' I said.

'That's what I mean.'

'Has she been talking?'

'A little bit, yes. Nothing about Frank or Beth, or wh happened, but she's been asking if you are okay, and whe she can see you. She whispers things to Cameron, and l says them out loud. And apparently when the police arrive at Laurel Bank that night, and asked if there was any oth family they could call, she said, "Cameron McGratl mummy and daddy"'.

'Thank you,' I whispered, not strong enough to say ever thing that was contained in those two words. Thank you fe being someone she could trust, when most of the adults her life had either lied to her or ignored her. Thank you fe looking after her when I couldn't. Thank you for being her For telling Tasha about us. For breaking your life wide ope so that you could love me.

'I went straight round there. When I arrived, she w standing by the front door with a rucksack full of stones.'

Just as she had been on that very first day, the first tin I'd seen her. She'd called the police and she was all packe up and ready to leave.

'Oh God.' I closed my eyes. It was too huge, Kitty's loss. felt as if it was breaking me.

'I took her to Tasha and then I came straight to the hosp tal,' he said. 'You... you haven't been on your own.'

Somehow, in the darkness, I'd known that.

'The police want to speak to you when you're up to i Charlie said gently. 'You can tell them about Collecott Hall.'

'If she *is* there in the lake – Beth, I mean – then we'll hav to tell Kitty. We'll have to tell her that she's lost *both* of he parents. And what will happen then? They'll want to put he into foster care or something...'

'They seem happy for her to stay at ours, in the short term, anyway,' said Charlie. 'In familiar surroundings, and all that. Kitty's case worker is Sandra – the one I mentioned before? I know her from work. Don't worry, Juliet. We'll work things out together. Once you're better. All you need to do right now is rest and let nature do its thing.'

60

JULIET

W hen I was discharged from hospital, Charl[ie] took me home and installed me in the maic [ ] flat with him. Kitty shared a room wi[th] Cameron downstairs.

Tasha brought me up some turkey broth that she [ ] whizzed up in her Kenwood Chef so that I didn't have [to] chew. Awkwardly, I assured her that I was going to mal[e] other arrangements as soon as I could.

But Tasha told me to stop being ridiculous, and that al[l I] had to do right now was concentrate on getting better.

'Thank you... for Kitty's presents.' Charlie had told m[e] that Tasha had done a raid of the shops on Christmas E[ve] and come home laden with jigsaws and Sylvanian familie[s] and a pile of new clothes so that nobody would have to [go] back to Laurel Bank.

She shrugged away my thanks and went downstai[rs] saying that she had to 'get on'. But when Charlie was workir[g] the next day, she got Shami round to try some Reiki on n[e] for the pain in my neck and head, and I lay on the sofa afterwards and dozed while they chatted.

Then came the day that I'd been dreading. The police came round to tell us that the human remains found in the lake at Collecott Hall had been confirmed as Beth's, and that a charge of murder would be added to the list of charges that Barbara was already facing. Details were going to be released to the press.

Later on, Tasha brought Kitty into the living room to talk to me while she took a protesting Cameron off to the kitchen to help make dinner.

I knew Kitty sensed that something was wrong. I could see it in the little white pinches along her brow, in the stiffness of her shoulders as I sat her down on the sofa. She perched on the edge, her feet in their clumpy school shoes dangling a few inches above the carpet, her legs pale and thin above the cuffs of her white socks.

She was *too* pale – she hadn't been sleeping. She'd been waking with nightmares two or three times a night, and she was scared to go to sleep in case she disappeared while she was asleep.

I sat down next to her and smoothed my skirt, my heart jumping in my chest. How was I going to do this? What was the right way?

'There's something I need to tell you.' I tried to keep my voice calm and reassuring, but the words caught in my throat.

'Oh Kitty,' I whispered. 'It's very sad.'

Silence in the room. Just the clock ticking. She pulled her legs out straight, regarded the pattern on her socks, then lowered her feet back down again.

'Mummy,' she said in a tiny voice.

A dimple appeared in her chin in her effort to keep from wobbling.

'Yes, it's Mummy.' There was no right way to do this. N way to make it better.

'Oh, darling. Mummy's died.'

In a stiff, slow movement, she tipped sideways so that h head rested on my shoulder. A little wooden doll.

Something surged through me, some kind of strength certainty. It seemed that everything in my life – all the stru gles and dead ends and disappointments – had led me up precisely this time and place, to be there for Kitty.

I had the sudden sense of Beth – that ghost of a wom; whom I somehow knew but would never know – standing the doorway, watching us. And of my mother, sitting in tl armchair opposite, nodding at me, her eyes full of tears.

There *was* no right way to do this. Except to love her, a let my love join with Beth's love, and that of my own moth in me, carrying it all forward into this impossible space a beyond.

'I've got this,' I whispered to Beth, as I pulled Kitty clo and buried my face in her hair as she began to sob.

'I've got this,' I whispered to Mum, and in that momen understood how it was that she had never really left me.

61

JULIET

January. Raw, cold January. The time for gritting your teeth and going on.

Those first few weeks weren't easy. Kitty didn't want to be out of my sight. There were tears every day before school. She didn't understand why I had to rest so much, and Charlie had to pull her out of my bed in the evenings so I could sleep.

Whenever my exhaustion began to lift, anxiety was waiting, ready to creep in. I had nowhere to live except here in Tasha and Charlie's house. And I had no job, nor any prospect of getting one until I'd recovered completely. I couldn't even drive. And Kitty's future was still in the hands of others... there would be more social workers' visits... assessments and applications...

When I cried, Charlie would take me in his arms and whisper into my hair that everything would be okay.

Sometimes I felt sorry for Barbara – in prison with nothing to do except think about everything that had gone

wrong. And about Frank's head, rolling on the wet tarma
torn from his body by his own training weights.

She'd been sucked in by Frank, but then, hadn't we all?
thought of myself cowering before him in his study at College
Hall. Hadn't I believed in his version of me – Joolz the awkwa
black sheep – and carried it with me all my life? And hadn't n
mother fallen hopelessly for the romantic, *Brief Encoun*
version of herself that he'd reflected back to her? Barbara h;
only ever been an actor in his pantomime, a woman in dress-u

Kitty didn't want to see her.

But then, she didn't want to do anything much. Sl
wouldn't go back to Laurel Bank. She didn't want to go
school. Didn't want to eat anything except egg-in-a-cup ar
toast. Didn't want to go to bed, in case she got nightmares.

One wet Sunday afternoon, while Charlie started c
dinner, I sat Kitty down by the gas fire in the tiny upstai
sitting room, and handed her what I'd made.

'A book?' she said.

'Yes,' I said. 'About your Mummy.'

It had taken a lot of digging around, some bold pho1
calls, and an unashamedly heartrending post on Faceboc
which had been shared over a thousand times. But I'd h;
little else to do, resting for days on end in Charlie's bed.

I'd put in the photo of Beth as a child which I'd found
the Victoria's biscuit box in the Seiglers' cupboard.

I'd included words from an email from one of Betl
foster sisters – they'd lived together for a year or so befo
moving on to other families.

*'I was always sorry I lost touch with Beth. I remember h
well. She used to let me come into her bed when I had nightmar
One night she read* Five Go to Smuggler's Top *until I fell asleep*

Then a class photo that I'd managed to get hold of from Beth's old primary school. She sat there looking nervous in the front row, her ankles crossed and her hair in bunches.

On the next page there were words taken from an email from Chantelle Price, who'd been the cleaner at the bar where Beth lived with her first husband.

'Beth was a quiet one but she was a sweetheart once you got to know her. One time someone robbed my purse down the town centre, and Beth gave me forty pounds to buy a birthday present for my daughter.'

A handwritten letter from Rosa, who'd been the Seigler's home help in Vevey:

'Madame Seigler was always so kind to me. The poor little Kitty. I pray to God to send her many blessings.'

There was even an email from the dentist who'd fixed Beth's teeth.

'I do remember her. She was a brave lady. A lovely lady. She told me they did lovely French toast at the garden centre near here. I still take my mother there sometimes on Sundays.'

A note from the man who'd come to fix the boiler at Laurel Bank, just a few weeks before Beth had died.

'She liked Strictly Come Dancing. *She said she watched it with the wee girl every week and they'd dance along to it in the living room.'*

Fragments of a life. I hadn't been able to salvage much.

Kitty looked through the pages carefully. I saw her reading, mouthing the words silently.

Was it too soon? Was she going to burst into tears? Maybe it would have been kinder to just let the memories of Beth fade away.

I'd left the second half of the book blank. This had been

out of necessity at first – I didn't have enough to fill it. B
then I'd had another idea.

'I've left blank pages here. Do you know why?'

Kitty shook her head.

'Because her story isn't finished yet. It goes on forev
through you.'

She gave me a questioning look.

'So, if you find a really nice stone and you think Mumn
would have liked it, we can take a picture of it and put it
the book. Or we could make her favourite cake – what w
that?'

Kitty said in a tiny voice: 'Chocolate mousse cake.'

'We could make that on her birthday. And we could put
a picture of us eating it. Or maybe we could even vi:
Mummy's foster sister in Doncaster one day, and you cou
ask her all about what Mummy liked to do when she w
little. And when we get back we could write about that ar
stick it in the book.'

She nodded.

I thought of what Frank had said about my fathe
and how he'd set out to destroy him in Mum's mind. She
lived the rest of her life – and she'd died –believing he
killed himself because of her. It must have twisted all h
memories of him, distorted them, so that they could offer
comfort. Sometimes, on restless nights, I dreamed
receiving urgent phone calls saying that Mum was still aliv
that I had to rush to her bedside to tell her the truth abo
Dad before it was too late. In the dreams I was always stu
on a snowbound train, or on a gridlocked motorway, or tryir
to run through a maze of Edinburgh streets, but my le
simply wouldn't move fast enough. I never got there in tim
Because it was something that I could never put right.

But I could do this for Kitty.

'Don't worry, Kitty. I'll make sure that you never forget Mummy.'

She gave a deep sigh as if in relief. She curled her legs up onto the couch, pulled the throw under her chin, and laid her head on my lap. She fell asleep for six hours straight, until Charlie lifted her gently and put her into her bed where, for the first time in weeks, she finally slept a full night.

One year later

L aurel Bank, my childhood home. One day, not loɪ
after Christmas, we went back there for the la
time. The new owners would be moving in tʰ
following week and there were just one or two more things
be taken away – a couple of pictures, and the antiqu
crockery on the dresser in the dining room.

I set Kitty and Cameron to work with a roll of bubb
wrap and a tape dispenser.

'*I* want to do the wrapping!' said Cammie, when Kit
thrust the tape dispenser at him and dragged the roll ɑ
bubble wrap over to her side of the room.

'No!' cried Kitty. Thrusting out her chin, she poked ʰ
finger into one bubble with a pop, and then another. 'I let yɑ
have the last sausage at lunch because you said I could do tʰ
bubble wrap! I told you it was my favourite, and it was de
nitely my favourite first! You can cut the tape.'

For a little girl who'd barely been able to say a word, a year ago, she'd certainly found her voice.

'It's not *fair!*'

'You can swap over,' said Charlie, setting down some cardboard boxes he'd brought in from the car. 'I'll set a timer for two minutes. And you can't pop it all, or it won't work.' He rolled his eyes at me and I smiled back.

A lot could change in a year.

It had turned out the Seiglers had been up to their necks in debt at the point of Frank's death. Beth's inheritance hadn't yet been paid out – her father's estate was still being sorted out by the lawyers. The money that she would have been entitled to, had she lived, was now going to be paid to the residuary legatee in her father's will – a disabled friend who needed round-the-clock care.

But it had transpired that the document that Frank had got my mother to sign all those years ago – to transfer Laurel Bank into his name, so that he could settle all her 'debts' – hadn't been worth the paper it was printed on. It appeared that Frank had tried to register the change in title, but the solicitor had raised a number of queries, and Frank had taken fright. So at the time of his death, the house was still in my mother's name. When I'd stopped on the street to look at it, that day I'd first met Kitty, I'd been looking at my own inheritance.

Sometimes I wondered about the instinct that had stopped me walking away that day. Had I sensed, somehow, that Kitty's future and mine were inextricably linked, that I would be walking away from my own child? I could still hardly believe it was true, but Charlie and I had been approved to provide foster care for Kitty and we were going to

start the process of adopting her once we were married ne
month.

The three of us had moved in to a compact but neat ar
cosy new-build on the new estate, just one street along fro
the GP surgery, and a five-minute walk from Tasha's.

Tasha and Shami had clubbed together and raised a bus
ness loan to buy The Old Coach House. Shami was going
have a Reiki treatment room through the back, and the
would move the chairs and tables aside on Monday ar
Wednesday evenings to hold yoga sessions. They wanted
make it a 'wellness hub' for the community and their faces
up like children every time they talked about it.

I'd begun working part time in a special school ne
Sudbury, an arrangement made possible by the fact th
Tasha picked up Kitty and Cameron from school on
Monday and Wednesday, and Charlie covered Thursdays.

It hadn't all been plain sailing. When Cameron w
having a bad day, he would ask why Kitty should get to li
with his Daddy every day of the week, when he, Camero
only came twice a week. And Kitty's face would go white ar
blank, as if she was preparing to lose her family all ov
again.

And sometimes, when she felt overwhelmed, Kitty wou
stop speaking again. When that happened I would st
everything. I would sit with her watching television, or 1
quietly with her on her bed, stroking her hair, so that sl
would know that she could go back to her silent place if sl
needed to, but she would never again have to be alone there

Cammie and Kitty had given up wrapping the crocke
now, and they were playing a game with one of the cardboa
boxes, which involved periods of silence followed by volle
of ear-splitting shrieks. Leaving them to it, Charlie and I to

the stairs up to the Forget-Me-Not Room for the last time, and stood at the window looking over the tops of the bare trees to the churchyard.

It still seemed inconceivable that Mum was there, ashes beneath the ground.

I tried to bring her to mind, but all I could think of was how she'd looked when I'd said goodbye that last time. Her cheeks brushed with blusher in a shade brighter than she normally wore. Her bluebell-pattern dress and her warmest cardigan. A locket Dad had given her when they got married. And the black patent court shoes I'd handed to the under-taker in a tired-looking Sainsbury's bag for life. Mum had bought them for a wedding the previous summer and had fretted about whether the silver buckles were 'too much'. She'd been too ill to go to it in the end.

It was the shoes that undid me. My legs weakened and I gripped the windowsill.

Charlie was beside me in an instant, his arms tightening around me.

'I've got you,' he whispered into my hair. 'I've got you.'

It was something that I'd learned over the past year – grief came in waves, but Charlie was my anchor.

And I was his.

We sat down in the space where the bed had been, the carpet still fluffy there and a deeper shade of blue, and then we lay down, hands linked like snow angels in the winter light that slanted from the window.

'You know, when I came here,' I said to Charlie, 'it was because I'd been longing for this place. *Longing* for it. Just to be here again.'

Charlie nodded. 'I know. I felt that pull too – that's why we came back to Boxley Wood.'

'But now I see that it wasn't a place I was looking for.
was a time. And that can never come back.'

'Yes, I can see that. It was a time. But also a feelin
maybe?'

He was right. It was the feeling of being safe.

The kind of safe you could only feel when you were
child being held in the heart of a family.

The kind of safe that we would give to our own children.

We could hear them clumping up the stairs now.

'Dooliet?'

She marched in with Cameron in tow, holding h
mermaid doll. 'I found this in my old room,' she said.

'Oh yes...' She'd left it here on the night of the car acc
dent, and it had been here ever since. I'd come across it whe
clearing out the house a few months ago and hadn't know
what to do with it.

'Mummy isn't in this dolly any more,' she said, matter-c
factly.

'No, darling.'

I hadn't told her that the mermaid was a listening devic
and that Frank and Barbara had used it to spy on us. I had
told her about the words that they'd programmed it to say. I
debated with myself about it, wondering if I should expla
that the horrible things the doll had said were nothing to c
with Kitty's mother. I still didn't know whether Frank ar
Barbara had been trying to upset Kitty, or whether they
been gas-lighting *me*. But whichever way you looked at it, tl
horror was real.

Kitty nodded. She went out into the hall, opened tl
airing cupboard and crawled into the space under tl
wooden shelves. I heard a grunting noise as she pushed tl
doll right to the back.

'I want to leave her here for the next people,' she explained when she emerged.

'That'll be a nice surprise for them,' Charlie muttered under his breath.

'We'd better get going,' I said. It was beginning to get dark outside, and we had to stop at the shops on the way home – I'd promised Kitty we could make a cake for tea.

'Can we make ginger cake?' she said now, her eyes wide. 'With an extra spoonful of golden syrup to make it super sticky?'

'Of course,' I said, pulling her to me, my precious girl.

I'd thought that I had lost everything, that terrible day when Mum died, and Eddie left me. All the love from my childhood. The love I would have given to my own children. My past and my future.

But none of it had been lost. None of it.

I checked all the windows while Charlie put the boxes in the boot and strapped the children in to their car seats. Then he came back in to ask if I was ready to go.

The hall turned to shadows as I switched off the light.

The front door shushed over the doormat, as it had always done.

I closed it behind me, locked it carefully, and took Charlie's hand.

EPILOGUE

When Lynne woke the sun was streaming through the window, and the beech leaves we dancing a pattern of shadows on the bed cove She could hear children playing in the little play are outside. And the pain was gone. Not just pushed furth away, dulled in a morphine haze... but gone.

And there was Graeme, sitting back on the plastic cha with his legs crossed at the knee, wearing his brown cor and the old black fleece he liked to wear around the house weekends.

'How long have you been there?' she asked.

He smiled. 'Oh, long enough. I've been waiting for you wake up.'

Funny how she'd forgotten that – the way he used watch her when she was sleeping. One night on honeymoo in Skye, on one of those summer nights when it never real got dark, he'd stayed up the whole night just to watch her. S he said, anyway. It always used to fluster her, the thought him watching her with no make-up, and her hair all muss up. And now, with barely any hair at all, just fuzz like a baby bird.

'My love,' he said. 'You have never looked more beautiful.'

Was he real? She stared into his eyes, green with saffron strands around the pupils. The deep grey circle around the irises. The creases around his eyes from laughing. Such a kind face. Such kind hands, encircling hers now with warmth and pressure.

She realised how tightly she'd held him, inside her body – in the way she still reached for him unconsciously, half-waking in the grey light of dawn, or sometimes set out two mugs when she boiled the kettle. He'd been there in her head, reminding her to check her mirrors on the motorway, or badgering her to get an early night when she had a cold. Telling her to get out for a walk in the sunshine, in those first few inconceivable months after he'd gone, when it was hard to even drag her head from the pillow. She thought of the way she'd crawled into bed, on getting home after the first scan results, and had felt the mattress shift as though he'd got into bed beside her. The way she'd felt his breath on her cheek that night as she fell asleep. And how she laughed for both of them, when she saw something on the television that he would have found funny.

And now her body was loosening. Loosening its hold on her, and on the Graeme she carried inside her. So that he could simply be there.

'You didn't kill yourself.' The statement came easily. There was no need for it to be a question. Why had she tortured herself over it all these years?

He shook his head.

'But the debts... the money... they said...'

'I wouldn't have left you,' he said simply.

'The crash... everyone said....' It was like the last piece of puzzle slotting into place. Making an entirely differe picture. Why did everything seem so clear now? 'It was Fran Redwood.' She clutched Graeme's hand. 'That... that...'

'Bastard? Psycho?'

But they seemed silly words. Silly words when there w this glow in the room. This glow that had started somewhe in her chest but seemed to be all around them now.

'You knew about me and Frank, didn't you?'

He just kept stroking her hand.

'He said you drove into that tree because you wanted end it all.'

'I got in the car to drive to that bloody Travel Inn!' H voice rose in indignation. 'To make sure you were all right. try and have a proper talk and make things right between again. I couldn't bear to think of you there on your ow worrying about everything. It was my own fault for drivir too fast. You were always telling me to slow down on th bend.'

'I'm sorry, darling. I'm so, so, sorry. Please forgive me.'

He shook his head. 'There's nothing to forgive. He hoo winked both of us, my love.'

She smiled. 'Hoodwinked.'

'Yep.' The creases around his eyes, oh how she love them. How could she have forgotten?

'What a business, eh? What a business.'

She pulled herself up and he drew her into his arm holding her head tenderly against his shoulder. She breathe in the smell of him, the grey-blue scent of woodsmoke autumn, felt the bobbly texture of the fleece against he cheek.

He dropped a kiss on the top of her head. 'Shall we go, my love? Are you ready?'

She turned to look at her crossword book and pen, lying on the bedside table. Her glasses, for her eyes that had been too blurry to see the words recently. And her body, just an empty thing now, lying there in the bed.

'But what about Juliet? She'll be coming back soon. She might be finding out about her IVF today. I can't leave her. I can't leave my little girl.'

She went over to the window, to see if she could see Juliet parking her car, or making her way along the path, past the line of beech trees that bordered the hospital grounds. To see her just one more time, in her old navy jacket, shoulders hunched and chin tilted down, hurrying.

'Juliet will be all right. She'll be all right.'

This love, the leaving of it, and the never leaving it, so impossibly beautiful.

She stood back and looked at him, trying to find the words.

'I know,' he nodded.

She held out her hand, and he took it. Or at least she thought so, because it was hard to know now where she ended and he began.

And then it seemed that they were not in the ward any more, with the smell of old dinners and the clatter of the tea trolley down the corridor – but out there. Out there where the leaves whispered high up in the trees, and a blackbird sang now in the stillness of the afternoon.

A NOTE FROM LUCY

Thank you for reading *The Child In My House*! I really hope you enjoyed it. If you would like to find out what happens next, I have written a mini-sequel called *Kitty's Secret,* which I would like to offer you as a free gift and a thank you! Download your copy here:

https://BookHip.com/HZNBHGS

Reviews are so important to us authors, especially those of us who publish independently. I would be really grateful if you could spend a moment to write an honest review on Amazon (it doesn't need to be long or detailed – even a line or two would be great).

If you would like to get in touch, I would be very happy to hear from you – please email me at lucy@lucylawrie.com

ACKNOWLEDGEMENTS

First I want to thank Matt (without whom there would be a 64-year-old dog in this book). Thank you for happy after-noons playing plot Lego with A3 paper and pencils, and for your unwavering belief in me.

Thank you to Emily and Charlotte for your wild plot ideas, including helping me to decide how Frank should dispose of Beth's body to avoid detection. I am not so sure about the enormous vat of acid, but I will definitely work in a scary abandoned circus next time! And thank you to Becca for listening to all of this and not reporting us to the police!

Thank you to Jane Farquharson and Lesley McLaren, who helped me to wrestle this story into shape and bring it to life. And for your painstaking editing work on the manuscript, Jane. Writing is a perilous journey, not to be embarked upon alone, and I am so lucky to have found such wonderful friends to come along with me. Put simply, I couldn't have written this book without you.

To my agent, Joanna Swainson – thank you for your help with the manuscript and for all your support with my writing

over the last few years. Thank you also to the hugely talent(
Emma Graves for creating a cover that captured the essen(
of the book.

Thank you to Dad and Anne, and to Katy and Arlene, f(
all your belief and support. And thank you to John and G;
for welcoming me into your lovely family.

I also want to mention my friend Alethea Dawson, whc
thought of often while writing this book. You will never l
forgotten.

To my mother, who passed away just as this book w;
getting started – thank you for all the ways you've stayed wi
me. I find you every day in things that are beautiful. Your lo
is written into every page.

Printed in Great Britain
by Amazon